Better the Day

by

David O'Neil

A-Argus Books

For information:
A-Argus Better Book Publishers, LLC
9001 Ridge Hill Street
Kernersville, North Carolina 27285
www.a-argusbooks.com

ISBN: 978-0-6158625-2-1
ISBN: 0-9158625-2-7

Book Cover designed by Dubya

Printed in the United States of America

Chapter One

The irregular clink of the ammunition belt hitting the metal armor of the bridge screen made him aware that he was still alive, He stirred with a groan as he felt the stab of pain as his shoulder moved against the edge of torn metal where the shell had gone through the armor plating killing AB Turner the helmsman, instantly. Peter Murray hurt all over, but as he dragged himself to his feet he realized that apart from twinges and bruises there was no blood. Since all his limbs seemed to work nothing could be seriously wrong. He leaned against the remains of the bridge armor and looked around the shattered wreck of the MGB. Toby Parker, the baby Midshipman was hanging over the side being sick. The deck was a mess, splinters of wood and bits of glass and metal from the shattered wireless mast and bridge screen littered the deck.

The burly figure of PO Walters came up the companion way followed by PO Ifor Williams, the ERA. Seeing Murray on his feet, Walters approached and made his report.

"We've three feet of water in the bilges, sir, but the pumps are coping. Taffy here reckons the engines will start and get us home."

PO Ifor Williams drew himself up to his full height, all 5ft 7in and looked up at the burly figure of the cox'n. "I am quite capable of making my own report, Petty Officer; I'll thank you to keep your opinions on my machinery to yourself." Turning to Murray he said with dignity, "Ready to proceed when you are, sir."

Sub Lieutenant Peter Murray RNVR straightened up and nodded in acknowledgement "Carry on, Chief. Give us what you can."

He turned to the Walters, saying quietly, "Bring her about to a course nor' nor' east to start, I'll go and sort out a proper bearing for you. Start the men clearing up the mess. As he turned to go below his eye fell on the skipper, sitting on the deck, leaning back against the forward screen his hands holding his stomach, the blood leaking between them. He was covered in the shattered glass from the bridge screen. The figure stirred and Peter stooped to help the man he had thought dead.

Lieutenant Martin Tanner, RNVR, smiled wanly, bareheaded, his fair hair as always falling over his forehead "I don't think I'll be able to move for a while, you carry on Peter, get us home and we'll see what's what when we get there. Meanwhile I'm tired. I'll just rest for a while."

PO Walters looked at Peter as he rose and shook his head; feeling very old. Peter braced himself once more and went below to work out the course for base. The engines started with a shudder, settled down to a steady throb and the MGB came to life once more.

Over the chart table the lamp, still miraculously intact, cast its light on the worn chart. Peter Murray carefully drew the line showing the course for Portsmouth, he stood upright and stretched his back. His head hurt and his shoulder was sore but he reckoned he'd live. On deck he passed the new course to the helmsman and turned to the Cox'n. Petty Officer Jim Walters was a big man with a cheerful battered face and fists like hams. He was not smiling now,

"Skipper's had it sir; there was nothing we could do." He sounded sad; the body of Lieutenant Martin Tanner was shrouded in a tarp still lying on deck where he fell. The boat crew had been together now for three months, the edges had rubbed off and they had become a smooth running team under the leadership of Martin Tanner. Peter regarded himself lucky to have been posted to this boat after six months in a minesweeping trawler. Martin Tanner had been a good skipper and had taught him a lot.

"Right Cox'n, carry on clearing up. We'll move him when we get to Pompey. What's the damage?"

"We lost three killed; four wounded; one not likely to make it. Cookie is with them now, but all he can do is slap on patches and sedate them until we make it home."

"We should be there in roughly two hours. Meanwhile see if you can rustle up some food and a hot drink."

Like Peter, Walters was saddened by the loss of Martin Tanner. The dead skipper had a way of keeping control of things without fuss and bother. He had been one of those officers who was able to get obedience and respect without shouting or pushing his weight about. Luckily it seemed to have rubbed off on Peter Murray. His instant grasp of the events of the morning and immediate assumption of command without any fuss was a good omen. He shrugged thinking to himself, *we'll see, officers come and officers go; the Navy carried on regardless,* he grinned, *as long as there are POs to take the strain.*

The entry into Portsmouth harbor was a quiet business as the other craft in the harbor saw the damage caused by the returning Messerschmitt 110. The broken mast and the shattered wheelhouse were bad enough, the Bofors gun on the foredeck leaned drunkenly to one side, having taken a direct hit from the aircraft's 20mm cannon.

They moored alongside at the small-craft quay, where the MTB's and ML's were based.

Peter Murray watched the bodies being passed up to the waiting ambulances; the stretchers of the wounded carefully manoeuvred first followed by the wrapped bodies of the dead.

"Tough luck, Peter." The sound of the voice behind him made him start he hadn't heard the man approach.

He drew himself up to attention and saluted the heavily decorated figure of Captain Gerald Harper, DSO. RN. Harper was the second in command of the Coastal Forces currently based in Portsmouth. The command comprised the three flotillas of MTB/MGBs, and the flotilla of minesweepers currently occupying Portsmouth. The Captain had been recalled from retirement for the duration of hostilities and his term at Portsmouth had made things much easier for the RNVR officers who operated the majority of the boats stationed within the base.

"Sorry, Sir, I didn't see you coming. We lost the Skipper when the Messerschmitt came out of the sun. No warning, no chance!"

"Report to me when you've sorted things out here, there are new orders for us all!"

He nodded, returned Peter's salute and strode off. A stocky erect figure, shoulders back, getting on with his job as best he could.

He was popular with the flotilla. Unlike many RN officers he did not regard the RNVR officers as a bunch of dilettante ex-yachtsmen. Wherever they came from, to the Captain they were like a breath of fresh air, long needed by the peacetime navy. They risked their necks daily patrolling in all weathers; driving high speed plywood boats powered by huge engines. Fuelled by a huge quantity of high octane petrol, that would erupt at the slightest hint of a spark. The Captain was proud to be associated with these men, they knew the risks, and they undertook them day after day.

In the Captain's office one hour later Peter stood in front of the desk listening in astonishment to his new orders.

"Your promotion to Lieutenant has come through along with orders to take command of one of the new Fairmile boats, being assembled at Weymouth, you'll be part of a General Service flotilla of mixed MGB's and MTB's, your new command is, I believe, a dual purpose boat 115' overall, that can be armed with torpedoes or heavy weapons or possibly both. I am not really sure."

Captain Harper stood up and walked over to the window overlooking the dockyard. The battered shape of 419 was below him looking forlorn with her broken mast and shattered cabin and deck; the boat brought in by the young man standing the other side of the desk. He shrugged. *Why did they all seem so young? Could it be that it's me getting old?* He turned and spoke to Peter.

"You were due a command. Martin Tanner had already recommended you, and from what I've seen since I arrived here you thoroughly deserve it."He held out his hand and shook Peters. "Enjoy your leave and your new command. Good luck Peter."

Peter saluted "Thank you sir, I'll do my best." He turned and left the office, his orders in his hand.

Chapter Two

The boat rocked gently on the quiet waters of the English Channel. Just on the edge of vision the starlight illuminated the outline of the gunner strapped in his place swinging the barrels of the twin Oerlikon from side to side, searching for any sign of the small convoy they were expecting to appear.

Peter leaned against the screen and stared, letting his eyes roam over the forward horizon without concentrating on any particular section. Something he had learned when looking for things at night, it allowed his eyes to pick up odd movements. Meanwhile his thoughts drifted back to his last leave.

The little village where his family had their boatbuilding yard was located was on the Avon 400 yards upriver from Christchurch Harbor, his father was still building boats though now for the Admiralty. While he was at home he had watched the 60-foot hull of a harbor service launch being fitted with its last touches before the launching on the day he left. Already another boat was on the stocks ready to take its place.

He had enjoyed his leave though he had little time to socialise; most of the time was spent with his father working alongside him in the woodworking shed shaping the frames for the next project.

Peter enjoyed working with wood, the scent of the newly sanded frames mixing with the sharp acrid smell of the glue, a natural combination that he had known all his life.

His thoughts were interrupted as he noticed a movement on the port side to the west of their position. This was wrong the convoy was expected from the east. What he was seeing was the white bow wave of a high speed craft, and another; no two more racing towards the three waiting MGB's.

He pressed the alarm for action stations, though the men were already at their posts. The engine room telegraph was silent as he thrust the lever to slow ahead and heard the quiet rumble of the engines turning over. "Bunts, signal the leader; three bogies approaching from the east."

The leader was stationed to the west of the 806 boat commanded by Peter. Without waiting for his acknowledgement Peter turned to Sub Lieutenant King who had joined him on the bridge. "Take the fore deck Charlie, it looks like we've been rumbled by E Boats, from the look of things. Stand by for close action!"

"Aye, aye, skipper." Charlie ran onto the fore deck beside the Power turret 2 pdr Pompom the gunner already strapped in. Peter swung the boat round to parallel the course of the approaching boats before releasing the helm to the Cox'n who had rejoined him on the bridge. "All hands closed up sir," The calm voice reported over the increasing noise of the four big Packard engines.

The lazy string of lights reaching towards the MGB dropped behind into the water as the gunner on the enemy boat misjudged the increasing speed of the Fairmile. The Oerlikons started to stutter as the gunner lined up the twin barrels and commenced firing at the racing E boat nearest to them. By now the other boats of the flotilla were active and all up on the plane contributing their part to the increasing racket of gunfire lighting the night sky with flashes of tracer.

"Depth charges, shallow setting," called Peter. "Prepare to drop on my signal."

At the stern of the MGB, the torpedo gunner's mate adjusted the depth charge settings to shallow, and waited for his Captain's order. His hand clasped round the firing lever ready.

The forward Pompom was hammering away at the nearest E boat, whose fire had slackened under the battering it was receiving from the guns. The .303 machine guns mounted behind the bridge in their rotating turrets had joined the party now the E boat was in range. The course of the MGB was converging on the racing E boat narrowing the gap and her more powerful engines were allowing her to head reach gradually pulling ahead until Peter judged they were in the right position. "Depth Charges; fire, hard a starboard, Cox'n."

The boat heeled over to starboard as the wheel spun, everyone grabbed something to hang onto; two Depth Charges rolled off the racks, tumbling into the water across the path of the racing E boat, which started to turn away. The first charge exploded and Peter cringed at the closeness of the huge mound of water off their stern. The luckless E boat ran right into it, the second charge exploding immediately under the boat broke it in two, sending the bow section high in the air, the stern section dropped shattered end first into the water plunging still driven by the racing engines into the waiting depths, gone without trace of its passing.

Peter shivered as he watched the death of the E Boat. *That could have been us*, he thought. Dismissing the thought he swung round to see what was happening with the other boats.

The remaining E boats were engaged with the other five boats of the flotilla, and as Peter watched he saw one unfortunate boat, 406 the Vosper Captained by Paul Masters, the oldest boat with the newest skipper, suddenly stop dead in the water outlined by the burning fuel leaking from her punctured tanks. One second she was there, and then she was gone in a mighty flash, as her tanks exploded.

The night suddenly became very dark until the watcher's eyes recovered. One of the other E boats was burning; the third had turned and was making off to the French coast at high speed, with two MGB's in pursuit.

Peter motored over to the place where the Vosper had exploded searching for survivors, though with little hope.

As they sailed through the breakwater, the five boats, though they had been tidied up were still showing signs of the night action. Splintered bullet holes, and the leader had a shattered windscreen.

In the Depot ship Peter joined the other skippers for the debriefing. Lt Commander Roger Taylor RN. DSO sat at his desk and listened to the reports one by one. Commander Michael Hawthorne RN. CO of the Squadron; strutted impatiently through the ward room waiting for the debrief report. He was a dapper man, 5ft eight inches tall, and it was said that he wore lifts in his highly polished shoes to enhance his height. Always immaculate, his white shirt cuffs with the gold cufflinks jutted aggressively from the navy of his moleskin jacket, matching the three straight gold bands of his rank.

After rising to acknowledge his presence, the tired boat officers relaxed, winding down from the tension of the nights action. Commander Hawthorne was not popular. He made it clear that he was here on a temporary basis, until some position of importance could be found to display his talents properly. Meanwhile he had made it his mission in life to demonstrate to the amateur ex-yachtsmen under his command what a proper Naval Officer was capable of. So far he had alienated everyone in the room including his deputy, currently debriefing the remaining officers.

The flotilla leader Lieutenant Commander Bill Hamilton RNR came from the debriefing and called him Peter over.

"Drink, Peter?"

"Not just now Skipper, I'm just off to bed."

"Before you go, you had better get the deputy stripe up on your boat. Joe Longman has been beached. This last do caused his back to go and the quack has sent him off to Haslar Hospital for assessment. Doesn't think he'll be back on operations for a while, if ever poor sod, so you're now my number two for your sins. Off you go. I'll see you in the morning and we'll sort everything out then."

Dazed, Peter wandered off to his bunk, not quite ready to believe that he was now deputy flotilla leader.

1940 moved into 1941 with a party they still talk about in the quiet times between actions. Peter, now accepting and carrying his position as Deputy Leader, was preoccupied with paperwork and administration he had never dreamed about as a rookie skipper. The weather had really begun to settle down; the late May sunshine seemed as if it would be here for good, the men now appearing wearing less and less clothing where they could get away with it.

He sat back at the desk he had inherited and stretched, with luck he would be on leave in—he looked at his watch—twenty-two minutes. He was looking forward to spending a little time in London this time, Bill Longman had been mentioning that the night life was still interesting enough to make the trip worthwhile and there were several shows and clubs that were worth serious consideration. Of course the unspoken implication was that female company was also available and Peter was not quite sure how that would work out, but the idea seemed worth pursuing.

His experience of the female gender was confined to encounters at school before he was sent off to Winchester as a boarder. There—though the subject came up—was little opportunity to meet let alone get to know girls. His encounters after returning home before leaving for University had been brief cuddles and kisses behind the village hall after the local hop and the habit of having a sly pint did little to encourage the extended petting required for what had been referred to as the real thing.

He rose, grabbed his cap and left the office, striding along the hard to the accommodation quarters. He picked up his bag and stepped out into the warm sunshine, already relaxing heading for the gate and seven glorious days of, no paperwork, no call-outs in the middle of the night, no breakdowns in awkward places, and no last minute tearing off to the other side of the channel to meet a convoy.

"Lucky bugger, off on the tiles are we?" Charlie King; newly promoted to Lieutenant RNVR showed the typical disrespect of his privileged position as Peter's ex-number two, and now CO of his own boat.

"You're a cheeky young bugger who needs a lesson in manners, so watch your back, I'm only away for a week, just pray that I have a good time and you might just escape my wrath." Peter grinned as he said it. He found it difficult to get upset with Charlie King whose wise cracking humour helped keep the flotilla sane.

As he reached the outer wall a hail caused him to stop and look over to the smiling face of the officer whose head poked above the level of the quay. There was a large new ML alongside with its lines singled up. As he walked over to the edge of the quay the figure was revealed as a tall slim man wearing an old uniform shirt with the two and a half interlaced rings of an RNR officer standing on the deck of the ML, wiping his hands on a piece of cloth. He spoke again.

"Like a lift to Christchurch? I'm just off to Dover; I can drop you off on the way."

The offer came from Paul Waterstone; Lieutenant Commander RNR, former Second Mate on an Atlantic liner; currently charged with the distribution and collection of the small craft used by the Royal Navy all along the south coast.

"Rather." Peter jumped at the offer. Apart from the convenience of being dropped off at the doorstep, it would be a chance to try out the ML, one of the latest Fairmile boats, 110 foot long, brand new and without heavy armament, speed therefore over 30 knots.

Throwing his bag down to the waiting seaman standing on the foredeck, he climbed down the dock ladder and boarded the new ML.

Paul called out to the bow man and the lines were taken aboard and the boat edged away from the wall and crept out onto the fairway engines muttering quietly as they negotiated the boom into the open sea.

Peter had heard of Paul Waterstone and in fact had competed against him in some of the offshore races along the south coast before the war. Though they knew each other in passing they had not really met formally. Paul's presence at Weymouth had been in passing, delivering and collecting boats; so the two men chatted about mutual acquaintances as they cleared the dock area.

Once offshore Paul opened the throttles and the boat sank its stern the bow lifted onto the plane and with the rising song of the motors the boat settled down to the high speed run along the south coast. The crewman disappeared below muttering something about tea.

"Not bad, is she?" Paul was quietly proud of the boat's performance.

A female voice called out from below and a tousled blond head appeared with a tray of mugs of tea, steaming in the air. The boat hit a wave and the tray teetered dangerously but was expertly recovered by the blond who called for them to help themselves before the whole lot finished on the deck.

Peter raised an eyebrow at Paul, though he was known to have a healthy disrespect for authority, women were not permitted on RN craft at sea.

Paul grinned "There's no such thing as a free lunch, Peter, meet my sister Claire. Claire meet Peter Murray, hero of the RNVR, driver of fast boats and the person who will probably smuggle you ashore at Christchurch."

Peter having taken a good look at Claire Waterstone decided that if Paul had asked him to escort his sister to Paris for breakfast—Germans or not—he would have volunteered.

"How do you do?" he managed; "Please accept my condolences for being related to this poor apology for a naval officer. I would be delighted to escort you ashore at Christchurch, and I do not regard it as a task, rather as a reward."

"Can I have my hand back?" Claire said plaintively.

Peter hurriedly dropped it embarrassed; she burst out laughing closely followed by Paul and then the shamefaced Peter.

It turned out that she was a WREN Second Officer, on leave and expecting to spend the next week with her brother. Paul had been recalled before he got started on his leave, and was now due to report to Middle East command after delivery of the ML at Dover. "So you see I have now been dumped in limbo whilst my brother departs for distant parts. I shall just have to do something else with my precious leave."

Peter looked into the blue eyes that were gazing at him in mock self pity and without thinking said "I'm at a loose end this week; if you like we can find something to do together." He blushed "Um – what I mean is we could perhaps keep each other company....Oh hell!"

Paul's snort followed by a loud burst of laughter, caused Claire to turn on him swiftly, "So what's so funny, brother? At least there is one gentleman present.

Claire turned back to Peter, "You really don't need to waste your leave looking after me I will find something to do, never fear."

"If you would rather not....?" Peter's voice trailed off as Claire looked at him searchingly

"If I've understood what you are saying, I think I might like to take you up on that. Is there somewhere I could stay in Christchurch?"

Completely abashed and blushing furiously, Peter said hurriedly, "There is a local hotel, but if you don't mind roughing it we have tons of room at home. I'm sure Ma would be delighted to have another woman in the house to talk to."

After another searching look Claire said, "I think I might like that, at least I would not be among complete strangers, and since this wretch failed to tell me about his orders until today," she indicated her brother. "I have made no other arrangements I accept." She smiled.

"There, that's settled then, let's enjoy the day," said Paul, pushing the throttles right forward causing the bow to rise further as the ML reached its top speed in the comparatively calm waters of the channel. The boat logged 34 knots which was pretty good as far as it went. Without the foredeck gun or the Depth Charge load; and not even a single torpedo, the craft was light in the water. The performance was not really meaningful, but it was fun.

Peter discovered that Claire was an experienced sailor, having crewed for her brother on many occasions before the war; she had also had her own boat that was still held at Cowes, in secure storage.

As the ML rounded Durlston Head and swept into Poole Bay; sea traffic became heavier and Paul reluctantly throttled down for the final three miles to the entrance of Christchurch Harbor, creeping past Mudeford Spit festooned with barbed wire and still boasting the beach huts of peace time. Cautiously the ML nosed up the buoyed channel to Tuckton on the river Avon where she dropped her two passengers and their bags into the dinghy to be taken ashore. The Fairmile was too big for the final stretch up to the family boatyard. From the shore Peter and Claire waved at the boat until it reversed round the bend before turning, and disappeared down the channel once more.

Hoisting Claire's bag onto his shoulder and carrying his own in his hand, Peter led the way along the towpath to the Tea Gardens that were closed, then over the road bridge crossing to the other bank and walking down the short drive to Murray's yard.

Claire looked at the sprawling area of yard, the stacks of lumber and the big workshop with the covered slipway, from which the sound of hammers and the whine of the circular saw were coming. Behind the yard was the house, a big rambling building that had grown over the centuries since its beginnings in 1708. The creeper covering the side of the building was covered with blossom, the area beside and behind the house was grassed with a scatter of what looked like fruit trees stretching over an area of about an acre. Peter watched Claire as she stopped and looked, he hair glowing like a halo in the summer sun, his heart lurched.

Claire turned to him and said, "It's beautiful, what a wonderful house, I can't wait to see it!"

Picking up the bags once more Peter said "Well, what are we waiting for?" He strode off to the gate behind the yard into the garden and from there to the house. Walking straight in through the open door he called out "Anyone home?" Claire followed rather diffidently behind.

A slim, good-looking, woman with a dust of grey in her hair came into the hall carrying some sheets.

"Peter! I didn't expect you till later on." She dropped the sheets onto the big settee and put her arms round his neck and kissed him. Then seeing Claire said "Hullo you, what a pretty girl you are. I presume you're Peter's friend?"

Peter stepped in "Not exactly, Ma, this is Claire Waterstone. I've mentioned Paul her brother. Well it's complicated, I'll explain later. Just now if we have a spare bed for Claire and if it's alright, she will be staying with us for the week."

Grace Murray smiled "No problem," to Claire she said "You can have Peter's old room, he used to share with his brother, but now John is away, he can use John's room. Come along with me and we can get things sorted out while Peter puts the kettle on." With that, trailed by Claire, Peters mother swept out of the room, once more carrying the sheets.

When they came down later they found Peter sitting in the living room gazing out over the garden with a cup of tea in his hand. On the table the big teapot stood with a jug of milk, beside the cups and plates and a plate of scones with butter and jam and a bowl of cream.

"Well done Peter, I see you found everything. Come, Claire, sit down. Tea? Do try the scones; I made them this morning. The jam came from the village shop. Now tell me all." She sat back with her tea and looked at them expectantly.

"Well." Both Peter and Claire started simultaneously.

"One at a time please" Grace suggested. "Why don't you start, Claire?"

"Well, I had arranged to spend my leave with my brother Paul. I'm in the WRNS and I came down to Weymouth to join him. When I arrived he told me his leave was cancelled and he had to deliver a boat to Dover before disappearing of to distant parts, as he put it. Anyway, he was going to give me a ride—strictly against the rules—along the coast and drop me off somewhere before Dover. He remembered that Peter would be off on leave the same week and thought he could offer him a lift and get Peter to take me ashore and see me on my way. He put off leaving Weymouth until he saw Peter walking down the hard with his bag and offered him a lift to Christchurch, guessing Peter would be coming here. Peter jumped at the chance as my wily brother anticipated. Then once we were at sea I was produced and poor Peter was lumbered with the task of getting me ashore and on my way.

"Peter suggested that since I was at a loose end and so was he as well, perhaps I would like to share the week, staying here. He didn't look too dangerous so I took a chance and said yes, and here I am."

Grace nodded slowly, thinking her son was no fool. "What a wonderful idea! I am delighted. I do get fed up only having men to talk to in the house, and there are plenty of things to do in this area. Peter's sloop is still in the water, and the train service to London is pretty good even now, so if you want a day up town it's quite possible." Just then the door crashed open and a big bronzed man came in,

"Joe reckoned he saw Peter walk in with a real smashing blond. Oh hullo!" he said sheepishly to Claire then, "I see Joe was right!"

"Michael, this is Claire, a friend of Peter's. Claire, this big lummox is my husband Michael, Peter's father. Now sit down, Michael. I'll pour you some tea now you're here."

Michael sat in a big chair and waved to Peter. "Hi, son," he said, "Staying long?"

Before Peter could reply his mother interjected, "Drink your tea. I'll send Peter out in a short while but he will not be working for you this week so just make your mind up to that." With that she turned back to the others, chatting cheerfully to Claire about the rations and how difficult it was to get good shoes these days. Peter and his father slipped out unnoticed a few minutes later.

The week passed all too quickly for Peter. After that first half day spent in the yard with his father, he managed to get hold of the family car and take Claire out for the day through the Hampshire countryside away from the family and the navy. They lunched in a pub outside Ringwood and lay in the sunshine on Markway Hill in the New Forest.

Peter was uncertain about his feelings though he was happy in the company of Claire, and as they lay there he felt a shiver of excitement. It was as if something was starting, something new in his life. None of the girls he had encountered before had been as exciting as Claire. He wondered whether he was in love, was this what it was all about. He looked at Claire lying on the grass beside him.

As he watched her she turned and saw him looking. With a smile she leaned across and kissed him, "Come on, lazybones time you got up." She jumped to her feet and pulled him up. "Let's get going, we have some walking to do yet."

There was no pressure and over the next two days they sailed Peter's sloop within Christchurch harbor, and they walked and got better acquainted; both finding real pleasure in each other's company. Walking through the summer countryside suited them both and when Claire stumbled and Peter caught her hand to steady her, neither found it odd that he did not let go, and when they parted briefly at a farm gate he took her hand again without any awkwardness. Neither felt the need to say anything, they just accepted that what was happening was right.

They went to London to see a show, it was late when it finished and neither felt the need to rush back. They stayed at Claire's London flat overnight; there was only one bedroom, and since they had been comfortable in each other's company for the past few days, sharing the bed seemed the most natural thing in the world.

The rest of their leave went in a haze as far as Peter was concerned and as they parted finally at Dorchester, Peter returning to Weymouth, Claire to Plymouth, both had decided to get together wherever and whenever they could.

Chapter Three

Gibraltar was hot; the six boats of the flotilla sat on their reflections on the blue water, hardly a ripple disturbing the surface of the bay. Scattered over the expanse of water was an assortment of grey ships, the collection of cruisers, destroyers and the single battleship dwarfed the flotilla of MGB's and MTB's that had slipped in during the night and moored, awaiting orders. In the admin office of the Port Admiral, Gibraltar; Peter and Bill Hamilton sat waiting for the call to the office of Captain Fraser RN, the admiral's aide. The call finally came and as they entered and came to attention in front of the desk, he quickly asked them to seat themselves and apologised for keeping them waiting. He was pleasant and quietly spoken, another man called back from retirement for the duration of hostilities.

He began "I understand that you have been more or less in action since the beginning of the war, so I won't waste time. From here you will be going to Malta where the flotilla will be split, the MTB's will stay at Malta to join the force there interfering with Rommel's supply convoys. The MGB's will continue to Alexandria where they will be attached to the base command. I'm not too sure of the duties you'll be expected to perform; I rather think it will include Special Operations whatever that means, considerable night action, both along the North African coast and across the Med, I guess. I'll say no more on that subject. Now how will you arrange things? I asked for you both to attend as I presumed that you would split the command between you."

Both officers nodded in agreement,

"Since my boat is an MTB and Lieutenant Murray has an MGB, I'll be staying at Malta with two boats."

"Good, that's easily arranged. I'll also arrange for Lieutenant Murray to receive acting rank as Lieutenant Commander for the posting and issue orders for you both. I presume there will be no problems for you leaving Gibraltar tomorrow evening? You'll be joining a convoy as part of the escort. Put the half ring up as soon as possible, there is a Gieves in Gibraltar that will sort you out before you go."

The two friends grabbed a lift into town and used the moment for a quiet drink in the hotel almost next door to the Services outfitter's establishment.

"Well, here's to the half ring then" Bill Longman lifted his glass to Peter.

"Oh its only interim, you know that." Peter, a little embarrassed replied.

"Don't kid yourself, it will be confirmed." Bill was quite serious. "I can assure you that you have been recommended for the half ring by me and Captain Harper; it has only been a matter of time, so cheers – enjoy the fruits and the penalties of command." He clinked his glass against Peters and emptied it. "Your round, I think."

Chief Petty Officer James Meredith Walters strode down the quay to the admin office that came under the command of the CNO Gibraltar. Within the walls of this building the fate of each and every person in the RN establishment on the Rock, was decided. The Chief had been here for far too long; posted to Gibraltar from Portsmouth to this shore establishment he had been missing the boats. It was now just on one year in Gibraltar and for some time he had been seeking a way out, with little success. After all there was only so much beer to be drunk and so many ladies to thrill and after a year Jim Walters had had enough.

Having seen the Flotilla in the Harbor and identified them by their boat numbers, he was aware that his old mate CPO Ifor Williams was engineer on the Half Leader's MGB.

That was young Peter Murray's boat so now would be a good time to wangle his way back to where he belonged. Young Murray would have made a good Skipper, he kept a cool head when it all turned nasty and the Skipper, Lieutenant Martin got killed. He shivered, he still remembered that bloody 110 coming out of the sun, chewing the boat half to bits.

He swung into the admin office and stood by as the harassed-looking Lieutenant went past with a sheet of paper in his hand. "Harrington, get this to the CO of the MTB flotilla soonest. They will be sailing in three hours; they'll need to do something in a hurry." He turned to the half closed office door beside him, "Chief, have we got anyone available for immediate transfer, to step in as CPO for an MGB. Must be available now otherwise the poor bastard on board will have to wait until they get to Malta to get home, by then he may have lost his entire family."

Walters leaned forward and looked past the officer at the CPO sitting at his desk in the office. He caught his eye and nodded, straightening hurriedly as the officer turned round. "Oh sorry, Chief, I didn't see you there. What can we do for you today?"

"Just called in as I was passing, to see if my posting had come through yet, sir. CPO Hastings promised to keep an eye out for me." From within the office Chief Hastings called, "No sign yet, Jim, but if you can be ready in two hours I have a berth on one of those toy boats in the harbor. It was MGB's wasn't it?"

"Who do I report to?"

"Acting Lieutenant Commander Murray RNVR on the 806 boat; be on the quay by 1600 hours with your gear, I'll get your orders made out now so by the time you get back here they'll be ready, okay?"

"Thank you, sir." Jim spoke to the officer. "I'll be on my way then." He saluted and dashed out of the office and along the quay before anyone could change their mind.

Back at his own office he called in and saw his boss, Lieutenant Cameron, who had been wounded in the first war, and had a wooden leg. He lived in Gibraltar and ran the inter-services facilities with the help of Jim Walters and two other NCOs from the Army and the RAF.

"Sorry, sir, I've just had an emergency posting to one of the MGB's in the Harbor. I'm afraid I have to go right now."

Cameron grinned, "You jammy bastard, Jim. I don't know how you wangled that, but the best of luck," he swung round and opened the cupboard behind his desk. Producing a bottle of Scotch he passed it to the big CPO. "Thanks for everything Jim now bugger off and let me get on with the war." He shook Jim's hand and waved him out of the office.

At 1600 Jim stood on the quay watching the harbor launch approach. When it came alongside he took the lines and dropped them over the bollards and then threw his kit down to the leading hand in the boat, and climbed down. The replaced CPO with the worried face tossed the lines into the boat, and set off along the quay with his kit.

On 806 Peter Murray smiled when he recognised the burly figure in the approaching boat, and as the new CPO came aboard he acknowledged his salute and then shook hands with him. "Good to have you back, Chief."

On the foredeck the gunner nudged his loading number, "They was on the Skipper's first boat together, seems they were nearly wrecked by a Me110 in the Channel. I 'spose surviving something like that they makes you mates of some sort."

His loader looked at the new Chief in some awe, noting the breadth of his shoulders and his size decided then and there not to cross his path the wrong way.

The entire flotilla sailed that evening, joining the convoy that was passing through the straits en route to Malta. On the orders of the Convoy Commander the boats separated and stationed themselves around the convoy, covering the gaps between the eight destroyers and corvettes already in place. The Command ship was the cruiser *HMS Cardigan* in the centre of the convoy, the carrier *HMS Argus* was scheduled to join later.

The sea was quiet and silvered by the moonlight and standing on the bridge Peter enjoyed the breeze created by the speed of the boat as she took up her station beside the fast convoy.

The first three days were quiet; *HMS Argus,* the converted merchantman now a carrier by virtue of the wooden deck built onto her hull joined one day out of Gibraltar. Her aircraft were a welcome addition to the protection of the convoy. The addition of the MGB's and MTB's had filled gaps between the other escorts making the convoy less vulnerable to seaborne attack.

On the fourth night Bill Hamilton was ranging out ahead of the convoy. He stopped to listen, out of earshot of the other ships. The sound of approaching engines became apparent, several E boats from the sound of it.

He called Peter on the Radio Telephone asking him to inform the Convoy CO by light, and to assemble the MGB's and motor quietly ahead of the convoy to his position. The group ghosted out of the darkness, and with quiet instructions over the RT he placed them ready to receive the approaching boats.

One destroyer sent by the convoy commander as back up lay back behind the boats, ready to support them if they needed it. It was a fleet destroyer *HMS Kintyre* armed with four 4.7 inch guns in two twin turrets forward with two more turrets aft. As Peter watched, the turrets swung back and forth the barrels rising and settling back as the action was tested. It was a reassurance to have the warship behind them.

As an ambush it worked fine. The MTB commanded by Bill Hamilton was on the extreme left of the group, the northern side, Peter was stationed in the centre with two other boats to the south, these big boats were all armed with a fore deck guns. The MTB's had a 2 pdr Bofors, the MGB's a 2 pounder pompom.

The approaching boats appeared as a series of white ticks against the dark sea, six of them, three Italian Mat boats and three of the big new Diesel Schnellboot. The ambushers opened their engines up on Bill's signal, all pretence of secrecy now gone. With a roar of power the Packard engines opened up and the guns started chattering; tracer forming patters across the night sky.

Peter watched in awe as the *HMS Kintyre* opened up with her forward guns. The noise was incredible, the white columns of water rose off the bow of the enemy boat on the far side which swerved violently towards her nearest neighbour, which in turn veered to her starboard to be peppered with shells from 808's Pompom. The other guns from the MGB concentrated on the unfortunate boat which happened to be a MAT boat, very fast but currently suffering from the pasting Peter's boat was giving her. Suddenly the MAT boat dropped off the plane and with smoke rising from her aft deck she stopped and wallowed in the wake of her companions.

"Target E boat left ten degrees," the guns swung onto the new bearing and the destroyer fired once more this time with at least six of her heavy guns. It sounded to Peter and his crew like the world had exploded the salvo of shell howling over head on their way to the elusive target. They were receiving hits from the E boat's guns and shooting back, though with her heavier armament the German boat was hurting them. It all suddenly stopped as one of the destroyer's shells hit the E boat on the centre line of her deck and the boat literally blew apart.

Relieved, Peter looked for a new target, but to his surprise, the survivors of the raiders were all making off back towards their base on the Sardinian coast, two boats missing, the E boat and the MAT boat that had been boarded by Bill Hamilton and was now under tow back towards the approaching convoy. Peter flashed the destroyer "Thanks for the hand, big brother."

"It's what big brothers are for!" The destroyer turned with a flurry of foam and raced back to her place in the escort screen. Peter called out "Number One: check for damage and causalities."

The boat turned to rejoin the convoy in company with the others. None of the boats had been disabled though one of the MTB's had a long splinter ripped from her rubbing strake on the port side, and several had bullet and splinter damage. They had suffered several men wounded though mainly with light injuries.

The convoy went through the next few days in a blizzard of shot and shell. All of the small craft managed to run low on ammunition and the convoy lost three ships by the time it reached Malta.

It was decided there that the MGB group would continue to Alexandria independently, taking the repaired MAT boat for use by the Special Boat Unit there. Accordingly, with a resupply of ammunition, the three MGB's departed under the independent command of Acting Lieutenant Commander Peter Murray RNVR.

The journey was largely uninterrupted, except for the discovery of the forty-foot Greek fishing boat which was hovering on the brink of sinking, her mast shattered and her hull riddled with bullet holes. There was one survivor on board, wounded but able to direct the recovery of a sealed package from the semi-submerged cabin. Peter watched the fishing boat slip under the waves finally, having valiantly kept afloat long enough to save the life of its last survivor. He was surprised to see the survivor on the bridge of the gunboat just ten minutes after being brought aboard almost at his last gasp.

"Captain Murray, the package I have is most important I must get it to Alex as soon as possible. There are seventeen men on Aros Island waiting for pick up. They have provisions for another three days but if they are spotted by the Italians they don't have enough ammo to survive for long. If they are captured they'll all be for the chop as they are all out of uniform."

"That's tough! We have fuel to get us to Alex in 36 hours but only enough at this speed; if I put the hammer down we would be dry with 60 miles to go. That's no good to anyone. I'll get there as soon as possible but we are looking at over another day."

"Trouble is I'm not sure if they will last that long I'm already two days overdue. There is strict radio silence in this area; the enemy keep a close watch the whole time, mainly because we keep upsetting them with raids on their outpost islands. It's the reason for my poor old boat being wrecked. There was no give away; they just shot the boat up for the hell of it."

"Who fired on you?"

"Sorry I should have said it was a pair of Italian fighters. They flew past, and then a few minutes later they came back and strafed the guts out of us. My crewman who was a Greek islander was on deck and didn't have a chance, he was cut to ribbons. They came round twice before they were satisfied. The only reason the boat stayed afloat was that the floatation created by a trapped tarpaulin in the cabin was full of air. Your men cut the tarpaulin when they retrieved the package for me. You saw how quickly she went after that. By the way I'm with the Special Boat Flotilla; my name is Gardiner, Jason Gardiner, Major RASC. Stationed in Alex. Is there no way we can get this boat to Alex in a hurry?"

Peter looked hard at the Major. Then, making up his mind, called up the other boats by light to come alongside. When they were close enough he had the other skippers aboard for a conference. After introducing the now rapidly tiring Major he explained the position and asked for suggestions. Charlie King spoke "Why not pump the fuel from the MAT boat into this boat's tanks? She's the newest boat, she should be able to leg it to Alex in good time. The empty boat can be towed in turn by the other two boats. Using reduced revs we should probably make it to Alex, even though it would take a little longer than under our own power. Then, if you like, when you arrive you can pick up some fuel and nip out and meet us, though as I said we should make in time anyway!"

The other Skipper, Lieutenant Mark Wharton RNVR was a dour man but he nodded in agreement, "That should do it, Boss. If you pass over some of your ammo it will lighten your ship and give us a little extra to play with if we meet those Eyetie fighters."

Peter Murray nodded "Right, we'll do it. Get the MAT boat alongside Mark, and let's get the show on the road. Charlie, lay off and circle us while we get on with things here. Leave me two men to transfer ammo.

Chapter Four

As the Motor Gunboat approached the pontoon, the rating waiting there took the first line while his mate grabbed the stern lime and ran back with it. The boat came alongside with a squeal from the fenders. On deck Major Gardiner waited to be helped ashore. Peter turned to Sub Lieutenant Malcolm Easton, known by his contemporaries as 'Emmy'. "Refuel and ammunition for immediate turnaround; take spare fuel for the other boats."

Not waiting for the acknowledgement he jumped ashore and hurried after the Major. who was hobbling towards the building at the shore end of the pontoon.

The office occupied by the Special Boat flotilla was scruffy, but practical. The Warrant Officer in the outer office had a lined face and medal ribbons covering WW1 plus some odd ribbons from between the wars. He leapt to his feet when he saw the Major and had the sick bay called to attend the Major's injury. Within the inner office the lean, tanned figure of Lt. Colonel David Canning RM, officer in command of the flotilla was seated next to a Naval Officer with the two and a half rings of a Lt Commander RNVR. The Naval Officer was immediately recognizable to anyone who had sailed in the Cowes series of Regattas. Charles Bannington was not only an expert yachtsman he was also an Archaeologist who had over the past three years published two books on the treasures of Greece and the Classics of the Desert Nations. Peter knew him from the Cowes races, having crossed swords on several occasions. They were acquainted but not friends as such.

Peter saluted the Colonel and helped Gardiner to a chair.

Before Gardiner began he asked permission to meet his other two boats and the MAT boat at were still labouring on their way to Alexandria. "Wait one, Major; the package?" The sharp voice was impatient as he eagerly held his hand out for the package that the Major had brought back with him.

He took the extended box and opened it. Inside was a small figure and a bundle of papers, he opened the papers, reading swiftly, after a few minutes he said, "Okay, get your boat fuelled and ready; we'll need to get to Athos as fast as possible."

"Sir," Peter spoke sharply "Before we do anything else my other boats must be recovered, I have left three boats without much ammunition wallowing along at 10 knots over one hundred miles from here. Until they are relieved we cannot do anything, my first priority is to recover the rest of the flotilla, after that I will be glad to go to Athos."

"I would like to remind you young man that I command here." The Colonel's voice was cold and the manner angry.

"And I would like to remind you, sir; that I am not under your orders until I report here to you with the boats under my command, and until that time I will carry out the orders of the Admiral who sent me here." Peter's voice was equally icy and his face reflected his determination.

Charles Bannington held up his hand to stop the Colonel's response. "Gentlemen please, let's not get carried away; we are all here to fight the same war. Colonel, Lieutenant Commander Murray is perfectly correct, and no matter what you may feel about the present situation we cannot afford to lose those boats. The reason they are not here at the moment is because he had to scrounge their fuel to bring Major Gardiner back in a hurry."

He turned to Peter. "Commander Murray, can you carry enough with you to drop off to your other boats and still carry on to Athos and back?"

Peter thought for a few moments, working out the distances in his head. "Given some means of carrying the extra fuel and ammo for my other boats, yes!"

"Good, we have some things here for fuel that should do, they're like big bladders, so they can be dumped anywhere without sharp edges. I'll get two organized—each takes 300 gallons. It will slow you down on the way out, but it will still be much faster than any of our present boats."

He turned to Colonel Canning, "Sir, I suggest we send Pluto our ML out to meet the incoming MGB's, she can help to give them cover once they are on the way again."

The Colonel nodded/ "Very well, Jason, are you up to another sea voyage?"

Gardiner nodded "With my leg wrapped up and some sleep I should be okay." He added hastily, "I can sleep on the way if that's alright with you?" He looked at Peter who nodded,

"I think we can find a bunk for you if you can stand the noise."

The Colonel spoke "Right, that's settled, then. Off you go to get your leg seen to. Charles, see to the refuelling and provisioning, I'd like to get the show on the road as soon as possible. Lt Commander Murray, hang on a minute." When they were alone he stood up and limped round the desk and rested against the front edge. "Your brother John is here," he said "He is with the LRDG, and he has done a few jobs for us, I am pleased you have come to join us. We are all amateurs here, and we all get things wrong sometimes. I would just like to say that none of us are frightened to admit it. Our work is often made up on the run and because of it we get away with things the regulars wouldn't even consider. Go back to your boat and report to me officially when you get back."

He put his hand out and Peter shook it before saluting and striding off to the pontoon where his boat was being fuelled from a mobile fuel bowser. A second bowser was filling the odd-looking blimps on the deck; as the fuel went in the balloon-like objects swelled.

As he approached, the overalled figure of Sub Lieutenant 'Emmy' Easton approached and saluted him. "Ammo is aboard, Skipper. They're still topping up the blimps, but we'll be ready in half an hour to slip. By the way, the Major is back aboard. I put him in your bunk and I noticed he was asleep before I closed the door." He grinned. "I guess some people can sleep on a rope." He saluted once more and dashed off to shout at the man filling the blimps, shouting to him to watch he didn't spill any on his deck.

Peter walked the length of the pontoon studying the boat from end to end, noting the odd scars, making a mental note where he felt a lick of paint was needed. All in all, he was well pleased with the way she performed.

The mutter of the engine as the boat slowed made him suddenly aware of the sounds of the wind on the sea, the slap of water against the flare of the bow, and the subdued mutter of PO's voice as he gave the torpedo man a sharp reminder to keep alert.

The forward lookout called quietly, "Boats ahead sir, three points on the port bow."

Peter acknowledged and altered to bring the three slow moving craft onto the starboard beam of the MGB. The Radio Telephone squawked, and the voice of Charlie King could be heard suggesting coming alongside bow to stern. 'Emmy' acknowledged and the boats came together, with a flurry of white from the stern of the two boats under power.

Peter manoeuvred, pushing the bow forward beyond the stern of King's boat, his bowman grappling the lines of Wharton's boat. The MAT boat was hauled up alongside Peter's and a hose was passed to the waiting men who pushed it through the fuel cock. The gurgle of the hand pump moving fuel was quite audible from the bridge. Peter went down to the foredeck and squatted down to brief his other two skippers on the situation.

The MAT boat was being driven by an RASC Lieutenant who had volunteered for the job hoping to get attached to the Special Boat Service. The crew was a pickup bunch of villains, three of whom were returning to Alexandria after recovering from wounds. He confided to Peter that he anticipated keeping most of them as permanent crew for the MAT boat, once it was available for operations.

When the boats had been fuelled and provisioned he left them to make their own way to Alex. There; they were to carry out the repairs to the craft that were needed, and sort out accommodation etc.. He expected to be back in three days' time. Before leaving, the deck crew rolled up the now empty blimps, and passed them over to Wharton to return them to Alex, then the four boats parted company.

The engine on the MAT boat starting for the first time in three days, following Charlie King's boat under its own power once more. Peter watched them departing, seeing the guns rotating on their mounts as the gunners, tested them.

The approach to Athos was cautious, under engine power. There was always going to be some noise so they approached past a particularly rocky spit that created plenty of noise to cover the sounds. Major Gardiner, having slept most of the way over, was on deck, his bandaged leg covered with a long dark stocking.

Peter noticed and smiled, "What particular lady lost that piece of equipment, I wonder?"

Gardiner grinned, "I'd love to spin you a yarn about how I came by it, but truth be told the sister in the medical centre offered it since she realized I might need to keep my presence low key. She did say she had a stock of singles handed in by nurses who had laddered one of the pair. As you may have noticed their uniform includes black stockings." His grin was followed by the wry comment "I had wondered whose leg it was on before. Then I saw that old battleship matron in the main Hospital and stopped wondering."

Gardiner had a used face. Working as he had over the past two years in the Eastern Mediterranean had not been easy and it showed. This landing on Athos was his sixth since the fall of Crete, which had been his first experience at escape and evasion. The schooner that had brought him out was now one of the many wrecks that littered the seabed. The skipper, a Greek fisherman, had risked his life on several occasions. He shrugged, *best to put the past to one side and get on with it.*

Colonel Canning was inclined to be 'gung ho' but was always willing to jump into the fray himself when the chance arose. With a wry grin he thought he could have been stuck in a depot in Wick counting socks. While it would have been safe, it would not be much fun telling his kids what daddy had done in the war.

Peter mentioned the RASC Lieutenant in charge of the MAT boat, and his hopes of staying with the SBS.

"He should be useful especially since he has handled the boat already. We will need someone to crew the boat once she becomes ours. I'll keep it in mind."

The shore line neared and the engine stopped, on the foredeck. The rubber dinghy was already prepared and Jason Gardiner, ex-Oar at Oxford. was prepared, in roll-neck sweater and overalls, to row ashore. The Sten gun hung over his shoulder ready, in case of trouble.

"I'll signal two blue flashes when we return. If the others are with us I'll repeat the blue followed by a green. If I send a red at any time, leave it until tomorrow night at the same time." He held out his hand and shook Peter's hand firmly. Shouldering his own Sten gun and patting his hip to reassure himself his Browning was secure in its webbing holster, he cautiously lowered himself into the waiting dinghy. With a small flurry of foam the oars bit the water and the dinghy disappeared into the night.

Keeping in position was not easy, the wing engine was started periodically to bring the boat back on station, the water was too deep to allow anchoring and the tide too strong for a sea anchor to be effective. After about forty minutes an engine was heard in the distance. Headlights appeared on the shore as a truck drew up. The engine was switched off and all was quiet once more. CPO Walters said "I don't like the sound of that. D'ye reckon it's them. sir?"

"We can't take the chance Chief/ Ready engines and close up action stations quietly."

"They're already there, sir; ever since Mr/ Gardiner went ashore… Green light, sir, there just over to the right."

Following the Chief's pointing hand, Peter saw the green light flash for a second time. It was followed by a blue. "'Get the other dinghies in the water, Chief and make for the light. I'll bring her in as close as possible. As the Chief dropped down to the main deck he spoke quietly into the voice tube to the engine room. "Taffy, just a touch of engine, quiet as possible, we're a bit close to the beach."

In the cramped engine room Ifor Williams was muttering to himself, "Chust a touch of engine, how the bloody hell do I give him a touch of engine from an 800 horsepower monstrosity like you four buggers?" Je patted the block on the nearest Packard affectionately. "Come on, darling, quietly now, you heard what the skipper said." He pressed the starter button and the engine purred into life. "That's my girl." He wiped his hands on some cotton waste and leaned back against the bulkhead. The stoker, who was touching the oilcan to control linkage thought, *'stupid old bugger talking to himself again.* The fact that the stupid old bugger was 28 years old merely highlighted the fact that the stoker would be 21 next month.

"Shift your arse, you lazy bugger." The voice of the engineer caused him to start and bang his head against the deckhead. "Shit, not again!" he cursed the deck, the engineer, and the fact that he was here in this glorified death trap instead of sitting things out in a cushy number at home. It was the second time that morning he had bashed his head. He rubbed it ruefully, and got on with his oiling.

On deck Peter was listening to the mutter of a boat engine that seemed to come from everywhere at once. The Chief and the other dinghies were out of sight still heading for the shore. Around the point a MAT boat appeared, the Italian MTB idling along obviously patrolling the shore line. Peter spoke to the gunner down below on the fore deck. "When I say, I want his wireless disabled, got it?" "

Got it, Sir, the radio." The gun swung to cover the approaching boat. The light came on and wavered about finally settling on the last of the dinghies as they reached the beach.

"Open fire," Peter ordered, and he was shocked at the volume of fire that seemed to engulf the Italian boat. There was a flicker of flame then a hesitation as the boat began to respond to some unheard order and rise onto the plane. It swung round and headed for the rocky shoreline on the far side of the bay, the helmsman hanging in tattered rags over the wheel. The boat was rapidly building up to its top speed, over forty knots, still pursued by the tracer from the MGB which was also speeding now, following the MAT boat.

"Half speed ahead," Peter ordered. "Bring her round to pick up the shore party." The boat turned in a graceful arc and cruised over to the first of the loaded dinghy's and the men started hauling the occupants on board, Gardiner reported to Peter that they would need to make a second trip and started to pull for the shore once more. Peter took the boat in as near to the shore as possible to speed up the operation.

Across the bay the MAT boat met the beach flat out, the hull hurtled out of the water at high speed and smashed itself against the unyielding face of the cliff. The explosion brought down a great slab of the cliff face that buried the wrecked boat and obliterated the flames in seconds. Peter was puzzled at first; he could not understand why the explosion had cut off so sharply. However he was distracted by other things so he put it out of his mind and concentrated on the matters at hand.

At the top of the cliff line, the sparkle of gunfire could be seen and the crackle of small arms fire was audible. Since the cliff top fire was directed down towards the beach, Peter ordered the Quadruple .303 Browning's in their swivel turret behind the bridge to open up on the cliff top.

The shattering sound of the multiple machine guns echoed off the cliff faces, and the splatter of the bullets along the ridge made the riflemen on top get their heads down.

The second boat load arrived alongside and the occupants hauled aboard. With the dinghy slung on deck the MGB swung round towards the open sea and, with the roar of the four powerful engines, the shores of the island were swiftly left behind.

Handing over to Easton, Peter went below to confer with Major Gardiner.

The main cabin was full of talking men who became silent as soon as Peter appeared. Gardiner stood and called them to attention. "This is Captain Murray—the skipper of this boat and the man responsible for getting you lot back."

Peter nodded to the assembly and asked Gardiner to join him. They stepped out of the cabin and into the cubby hole that was the Captain's cabin. "Is everything all right?" Peter asked.

"We lost one man on the way down the cliffs; he was wounded and slipped falling thirty feet to the rocks. When we got to him he was dead. He is on deck beside the torpedo tubes. Otherwise everyone made it without more than the odd scratch."

Gardiner sat on the bunk leaning against the side hearing the wash of the water as the boat parted the waves. "We were lucky I know, to get away with it in the first place, but also because of you getting here when you did, and risking the boat in the bay saved a long awkward row under fire. Thanks."

Peter was embarrassed and shrugged uncomfortably, "I just played it as I saw it, nothing special. We should be back in Alex by tomorrow midday, so tell the men to get their heads down." He turned and retraced his steps to the bridge.

They nosed through the entrance at Alexandria and puttered quietly across to the Pontoons occupied by the Special Forces. The Colonel took the bow rope himself and lashed it to the bollard as the boat settled alongside behind Charlie King's 618 boat.

Peter sat in the bar at Shepherds' Hotel nursing his drink and watching the ebb and flow of people through the open doors leading to the sunlit terrace.

She walked through the door, her uniform whites crisp in the subdued light, out of the direct sunlight. Another girl was with her also in uniform. Peter stood up and called out "Claire."

She stopped and looked around, eyes still adjusting to the dimmer light indoors. He stepped forward and she was in his arms gripping him, holding him close. "Marvellous! When did you arrive, I thought you were in Malta, at least that was the last I heard."

They sat down and Claire suddenly remembered her companion. "Jenny, I'm sorry; this is Peter Murray."

Jenny turned out to be a dark-haired WREN Second Officer, with blue eyes and a pretty smiling face. "Hullo, Sir, I have heard an awful lot about you over the past several weeks. I'm surprised to find that you're an actual human being. According to legend you should be seven feet tall and able to fly on demand." She giggled as Claire turned on her; mouth open to tick her off, it was spoiled when she burst out laughing, too.

Peter took control, "Sit down both of you. I presume you would enjoy a drink?"

He called the waiter over and ordered drinks for the ladies. "So how is it you are here I thought everyone was being evacuated in the face of Rommel's advance?"

"We are Britain's secret weapon, Jenny said with a wicked smile."

"Silence, woman, you'll get us hung," Claire was quick to hush her up. The waiter came with the drinks and the conversation was steered away from sensitive subjects.

It seemed that the two women had been brought to Alexandria to support the code-breaking team intercepting the Wehrmacht radio traffic. Both had established their worth in UK and since there was a definite shortage of staff in the section they had been seconded despite the current policy for the region.

Claire was keen to hear all Peter's news but it was hardly the place or time and, much to the disappointment of Jenny, they decided to meet that evening for dinner when there would be time and the opportunity to bring each other up to date. And, as far as Peter was concerned, re-establish the easy relationship they had enjoyed in England.

It seemed that Claire had seen little of her brother Paul, but it was Jenny who appeared most interested in his current whereabouts. Her interest caused Peter to smile quietly to himself, it appeared Paul had an admirer.

Far from the administrative drag Paul had hinted at; his job entailed him travelling upcountry with the Long Range Desert Group, currently surveying the ports and harbors on both sides of the lines for future use. Peter had found out about it through the SBS contacts with the Long Range Desert Group who seemed to roam the reaches of the desert country with if not immunity certainly with remarkable ease, creating mayhem and collecting intelligence

That night Peter and Claire met for dinner in a small club restaurant in one of the other hotels, away from the throng of uniformed personnel that gathered at Shepherds'. There Peter found out without the distraction of Jenny's presence that things had not changed between them. If anything, Peter thought their bond was stronger.

The flat Claire shared with Jenny had two bedrooms and when they returned after their evening out Jenny's door was firmly closed.

They made love with an intensity that shook them both, and as they lay in each other's arms Peter mentioned the future for the first time. The subject had not been mentioned before since neither had felt the immediacy of the current situation. Here in Egypt, with Rommel knocking at the door, there was a feeling of urgency neither had felt before. It caused Peter to speak "Claire, I want you to know that I love you and I want us to be married, I realize we will probably have to wait some time before that becomes possible but I wanted you to know."

Claire looked at him in the dim reflected light from the street lamp outside, "If you really mean that I had better warn you I will probably keep you to your word, but in our jobs tomorrow is a long time ahead so let's not make plans we may not be able to keep."

Peter was taken aback by Claire's direct comment. It was not that he never thought about the possibility of dying or getting injured or captured even; it was just the bald statement that things can change regardless that threw him for a moment.

He held Claire close and kissed her ear whispering "I mean it. I think I knew the moment you poked your head out of the cabin in Paul's ML."

With a sigh Claire wrapped her arms round him and whispered, "Sold to the gentleman on my right," and kissed him.

It was the following morning when Peter mentioned that he would need to return to Alex the next day. Claire turned to him as they lay in bed together "I know there's a war on, but why must it always separate people? Jenny is besotted with Paul, and having just found each other, he gets sent off into the blue. No way of contacting him, and I think it is possibly the most dangerous assignment in Egypt. Paul was delighted to get the chance; luckily Jenny doesn't know, and I'm sworn to secrecy. So I get to worry privately. So how did you find out?"

"My job at the moment is with the Special Boat Flotilla at Alex. We liaise with LRDG as well as the Port survey boys. I happened to see Paul's name on the list."

Claire leaned back and studied him, "Special Boat Flotilla, and just what does that entail? I thought you were on normal MGB duties. That's bad enough; but Special has a sinister ring to it, does this mean I have you to worry about as well? Damn it, Peter, both of you on special duties, it's just not fair." She buried her head in her hands and he reached out and held her close, murmuring softly to her that it was no worse than normal duty in the Channel.

Chapter Five

Back in Alex, the boss—David Canning—was busy with a new operation plan involving Charlie King's boat. The crew were all busy loading boxes of ammunition and cases of rifles and submachine guns. A supply truck was offloading fresh provisions, and cases of tinned food.

"Peter, have you got a minute?" The Colonel called from the other side of the quay, where a dusty truck had just pulled up.

Peter looked at the truck curiously as he hurried across the quay. There were twin Brownings mounted on the cab roof, and what looked suspiciously like an 18 pounder gun disguised as a box trailer hooked to the rear of the truck.

On the other side of the truck, the driver was leaning on the wing, drinking a bottle of water. He had spilled some, it made tracks in the dust that seemed to cover him from head to foot.

"Captain York–Mike, meet Commander Murray–Peter; You two get together and sort out how you can get the Harbor Spotters off. I'll discuss your proposals when you're ready." Canning turned and strode off to the loading party beside Charlie's boat.

"He's a busy bugger, isn't he?" the Captain observed. The Australian accent sounded exaggerated to Peter's ears.

"Is there anywhere me and my boys can wash up and get a drink other than water?"

"Sure, bring the truck over to the building over there." He indicated the two white painted blocks that housed the Officer's and the other ranks' mess. "One question before you disappear; what part of the coast are we interested in?"

Peter decided to take a look at the area before he needed to start planning an operation.

The laconic voice of the Captain said one word only "Bardia."

The coastline of North Africa showed little of the romance spoken of in some novels, the grey and ochre of rock and sand offered a view of undulating skyline. The distant heights of the Libyan Plateau were seldom to be seen from sea level, the low line of sight causing the distant hills to become part of the undulating skyline with nothing to indicate their height.

The 806 boat cruised at economic speed paralleling the coastline, the sky grey, the clouds hiding the sun and casting a gloom over the land and water, surprising to the crew who had expected the weather to continue to maintain the blue skies and hot sunshine they had enjoyed over the past days at Alexandria.

On the bridge Sub Lieut. Emmy Easton stood on watch, glasses sweeping continuously across the area ahead of the MGB, the lookouts on both sides were equally occupied, the air of tension was heightened by the fact that they were sailing in enemy waters, though no other ships were in sight.

The risk of being spotted by an aircraft was slim as this close to the coast the sky was the province of the Royal Air Force; the occasional sighting of a Hurricane or a Blenheim, giving reassuring support to this belief.

The sound of activity from below caused an easing of the tension and the sight and sound of the mess-man with his Dixie of kye, the rum laced chocolate drink so beloved of the wartime navy.

Collecting his mug of kye, the skipper joined him on the bridge. "What's happening, Number One, anything moving?" Murray placed the mug on the rim behind the windscreen and raised his own glasses and swept the horizon. In the distance the flicker of light against the sky indicated the current front line the guns in action pounding away at the axis defences round Sidi Barrani.

Murray looked at his watch and ordered an increase of speed, changing course to give the beleaguered area a wide berth. At 26 knots the MGB made a fine sight with the moustache of white water thrown up on both sides of the bows, her stern tucked down and the entire boat atremble with the vibration of the 4000hp produced by her Packard engines.

"Alarm starboard!" The cry came from the starboard lookout. "Boat in sight 25 degrees off the starboard bow. I can see her bow wave."

Murray cut the engines from the control beside his right hand. The bow dropped and the white water dissipated, washing away as the sound of the engines reduced to a murmur. The boat was a German F boat used to transport goods to small ports and in situations where secrecy was required.

"Any sign of other boats in the area?" Peter Murray had been caught out that way before.

"Nothing in sight, sir; the area looks clear. I don't think she has spotted us yet."

"Good. Ket's keep it that way. We have other fish to fry tonight. Let me know when she has passed over to port, and resume our mean course at that time."

He picked up his kye and was surprised to find it still hot. He appreciated the warmth of the thick glutinous brew that seemed to penetrate his entire body.

He looked at his watch again; the gunfire ashore was off to port and the boat was now gently easing towards the coast once more. The speed eased off and the shadowy shape of a moored ship appeared outlined against the faint loom of the shore, the noise of hammering came from the direction of the harbor and it was soon clear that the ships moored in the outer reach of the harbor were preparing to move. The boat idled forward the murmur of the engine unnoticed in the clatter of the ships preparing to move.

Two E boats were moored side by side as their Captains conferred. Their position on the seaward side of the assembled ships made them vulnerable to an attack, which Murray decided would need to be a complete surprise to succeed.

Whilst he was wondering how this could be done the answer came in the form of a high speed launch which could be heard coming out from the shore between the moored ships.

"Depth charges stand by shallow setting." Without waiting for the reply he spoke to Ifor Williams in the engine room. "I will be going to full power in a few moments, give me all you've got."

"You shall have it, sir." Murray grinned; the Welshman was not capable of answering a simple question simply.

The power boat was approaching fast, the engine noise rising to a crescendo as it closed the two E boats. Peter felt rising excitement tinged with apprehension as the moment approached.

"Full power, all guns open fire, standby depth charges." When the orders came despite the nervous excitement Peter was feeling, it was in a clear calm voice sounding almost disinterested, all the doubts gone now the time for action came. The response to the order was immediate—the bows lifted sharply as the throttles were opened and the speed rose. The sound of the engines rose to a crescendo blending with the noise of the approaching launch. The chatter of the quadruple mount behind Peter was deafening, quickly joined by the steady thudding of the Oerlikons, and the pompom on the forward deck.

The two E boats were still tied together, though the hurriedly-opened door in the bulkhead of one of them allowed the light to stream over the deck, lighting the men running to cast off the lines. The waters began to boil as the engines began to move the two boats, still side by side, away from the threat of the MGB

"Depth Charges, fire!" The MGB curved across the stern of the two boats, guns spitting raking the decks now bloody from the men caught in the savage fire.

Two depth charges followed by two more rolled off the rails, where they were flung below the sterns of the two craft.

The MGB shuddered with the pressure of the explosion of the first salvo. The second blew the bows off the approaching high speed launch, which was seen back-lit by the flames from the burning wrecked E boats. Still moving, the launch dived under, screws still spinning, down to the bottom of the outer harbor.

Not for the first time Murray wished he had torpedoes in addition to his gun armament. He expended the remainder of the Depth Charges under the sterns of two of the moored freighters, with satisfying results, as the lightening sky revealed the havoc he had wrought in the anchorage off Bardia.

As they left the stricken ships, he turned to his Number One. "Well, Emmy, have we got what we came for?"

The face of Sub Lieut Malcolm Easton was a picture, flushed and excited he could hardly speak coherently. "I got the soundings as you ordered, sir. I have plotted the approaches and since that launch had no problem coming out in the main channel I reckon we would have no problem, running into the harbor as and when we need to."

The boat was not followed; the enemy were far too involved in rescuing their own people to worry about chasing them along the coast even if there were any boats available capable of catching the racing MGB.

After an uneventful cruise back along the coast they returned to their base in Alex, Peter reported the results of their raid and reconnaissance. With the chart on the table he pointed out the channel into the harbor, and indicated where the most prominent wrecks were sited.

The operation to place watchers was carried out using the cover of hit and run raids along the coast from Bardia to Tobruk, while the LRDG made excursions along the coast roads identifying targets.

The normally elegant figure of Lt Commander Paul Waterstone was clad in dusty khaki drill; the only visible signs of his naval origins were the fades gold stripes on his shoulder epaulettes and the dingy greyish shade of his cap, the blue equally covered in the pervading dust. He sipped a drop of the tepid water from his water bottle, and screwed the cap on once more. He said wistfully "It would be nice to think that we were just about to turn into the driveway of Shepherds' Hotel to collect a couple of dewy glasses of IPA."

His companion in the front seat of the Bedford 3ton truck smiled without humour. Captain Robert Walker. MC, once a stalwart of the Kings troop of the Life Guards, swore to himself as the truck bucked over yet another lump of the Sahara, then "You Matelots don't understand the science of the Sahara. Out here the one thing you don't ever talk about is ice-cold beer on a hot day."

Paul looked across at his companion as he negotiated another of the lumps that seemed to comprise the whole length of the so-called coast road. They had been out for three weeks on this occasion and would not be back into Cairo until after dark. The remainder of the group was spaced out behind them at intervals, trying to avoid the dust thrown up by the wheels of the racing vehicles in front of them.

The mission had been successful; in the centre truck were three German prisoners, a Colonel and two Captains;

all three captured from a survey party found in the Great Sand Sea. It seemed the Axis were also interested in the alternatives offered by the use of the dreaded uncharted area. On this occasion they had found pieces of Roman armor and a perfectly preserved Gladius, still encased in its ornamental scabbard, property of some grandee who perished, judging by the other remains found in the area, alongside his soldiers; victims of the desert.

The German party had been camped at one of the few oasis in this part of the desert. All the enlisted men in the party were deployed in defensive positions, but they were not really prepared for the skilled craft of the LRDG men, the short sharp skirmish had resulted in one of the raiding party killed, two minor wounds and six of the twelve man German party killed, three badly wounded. All were now in the convoy ready to be passed over to the interrogators, or doctors depending on their importance or needs.

Three hours later the convoy drew into converted car park, part of the HQ of the LRDG. The ambulance waiting with open doors was loaded with the casualties and drew away. The prisoners were escorted off by the MP's for examination.

Paul and Captain Walker gathered their gear and, while Walker went to report, Paul walked over to the Jeep with the RN insignia standing over by the wall of the admin building. He threw his kitbag and Sten gun into the back and climbed wearily into the driving seat and stamped on the starter. It was almost an anti-climax when the engine started. He drove off to the house on the Alexandria Road where he was living whilst here in Egypt.

He entered the cool hallway of the garden house beside the waters of the Delta. Calling out for Khamsin—his general factotum—he dropped the dusty kitbag to the floor and threw his cap at the corner hallstand missing the hook but trapping the hat between the stand and the wall.

There was a patter of bare feet on the fitted stone slabs of the floor; and Khamsin appeared in a rush. "Oh. welcome back, sir. It is good to see you once more." He seized the bag "I will run the bath immediately sir, and the lady called several times since you left and will you call the Colonel sir…" At this point he ran out of breath and stood panting slightly, happy that his boss was back.

"First a beer, then the bath; then I will worry about the people who have been calling."

"Yes sir, immediately sir, I go." Khamsin turned and ran off with the bag leaving Paul standing thinking as he did every time this happened that it was just like one of those comedy plays seen at the little theatre near home, in Somerset.

Later, washed and refreshed with the third cold beer standing beside his chair, he listed the calls he had to make.

He called his sister at her office to let her know he was back. Jenny answered the phone and passed him over to Claire. "Glad to hear you made it okay, Peter Murray is in Alex with his boats, and—by the way—would you ask my pal Jenny to be your partner for dinner when we all go out together?"

"What's that all about?" He asked, "Who, what?"

"Oh shut up, Paul. You know as well as I do: Jenny shares my quarters and works with me here in HQ. Her surname is Melville if you want to send flowers."

"Why would I want to send flowers to a woman I don't know?"

"Oh, Paul, you are a complete idiot. How many gorgeous brunettes do you know in this God forsaken country? Jenny is being chased by every male in HQ except the Rear Admiral, and I'm not too sure of him."

"I would of thought that you might be the quarry in that particular hunt. Why this other girl?"

"They think I'm engaged and my boyfriend is stationed in Alex, likely to visit at any time."

"Why should they think that?"

The question was a blunt one that demanded an answer, so Claire decided he should get one. "Peter is stationed in the Special Boat Flotilla; for some reason they have decided that he is my fiancé."

"Well; is he?"

"He hasn't said anything, so I suppose not." She didn't sound too pleased with the situation.

"I don't suppose you have given him any reason to think he should be engaged to you; have you?" Paul deliberately introduced a stern note to the query.

"It's no business of yours what happens between Peter and me." Claire replied tartly, "Stop changing the subject, and send Jenny a bunch of flowers, and invite her to join Peter, you and me for dinner as soon as you can arrange it with Peter." Her voice had taken on the bossy tone he knew only too well, so he decided to end the conversation as quickly as possible, and after a few comments on family at home he gratefully ended the call.

After a break for a beer, he rang the SBS Base at Alex. He was known to the CPO in the office so he had no problem getting a message to Peter to call him back when he was free. It was less than twenty minutes before the phone rang once more and Peter was on the line

"Hi, Paul, how's the Sahara?"

"I wouldn't know, old chap. I just swan around the vicinity escorting the odd bigwig. When did you get in?"

"Just a few days ago, so when can we get together? I've been in touch with Claire already. I'm told we are likely to be dining together, so it would give us a chance to relax a bit and have a chat before the social scene overtakes us, so to speak."

Chapter Six

At the base in Alex, Peter Murray had been busy vetting
the reports from the observers dropped along the coast when
Paul's call came through. As he put the phone down it rang
again almost immediately. It was Claire fixing up a date and
time to have dinner with Paul and Jenny. When he replaced
the receiver he found it difficult to concentrate on the pages
on the desk in front of him so he gave up and rose, collecting his hat and walked out of the office into the bright sunshine. He looked around adjusting to the glare then walked
purposefully down the quay to the boats moored alongside.

He was staring at the handiwork of Stoker David Martin
as he completed his latest painting—the small replica of the
Italian MAT boat destroyed on the last trip to Bardia had
just been finished, bringing the total number of kills for the
MGB twelve. The tall languid figure of Martin uncoiled
from his position on the deck beside the bridge and
stretched, his once pale face and body now tanned bronze.
He was a changed man from the pale artist who had replaced
Stoker Dean killed at his post on the portside mid-ships Oerlikon. In civilian life David Martin had been a recent gradu-
ate of RADA, where he had found his niche as a set de-
signer. To the surprise of everyone including CPO Ifor Williams, he had settled into his work as Stoker quietly and ef-
ficiently, rapidly becoming accepted by his messmates. His
unassuming cheerfulness and his willingness to listen and
learn had earned him the friendship and respect of the rest of
the crew. As he stood back to admire his handiwork he saw
movement out of the corner of his eye and realized he had
an audience. He snapped to attention and saluted with the
brush forgotten; still in his hand. The black paint left a stripe

across his forehead. "Sorry, Sir. I didn't see you there." His voice was cultured and betrayed his gentle upbringing; his father was a Curate in a village in Buckinghamshire, who had spared nothing in the Education of his elder son.

"Carry on, Martin, good work." Peter observed and turned back towards the office and his unfinished paperwork.

"Looks like we've got company, sir," said the Stoker, nodding towards the half-track that had just drawn up outside the office.

Back at the office Peter found CPO Walters talking to a middle-height Army Captain in dusty khaki drill shirt and shorts with webbing, belt and pistol holster, plus a short bayonet on his hip. The Captain turned round as Peter entered and saluted, "Captain Aaron Black, Sir. I wish to speak to Commander Murray."

"Come on through," Peter said as he returned the salute and walked into his office. "Like some tea?" without waiting for an answer he called to Walters "Lay on some tea, Chief, and see if you can find a biscuit for our guest." He waved the Captain to a chair and sat down. "What can I do for you, Captain Black?"

"I am not too sure; I was told by Commander Waterstone that you may be able to help in a project I would like to organize, rescuing some special people from the Italians. They were taken at the first battle for Tobruk, and information has come to me that they have not yet been recognised for who and what they are. Much more important, I understand that the prisoners are to be transported to Italy out of the way of the Army here. We really must stop them being taken if we can. If we can't do something then I will have to try to silence them before the Gestapo get hold of them."

The orderly knocked on the door then brought in a tray of tea and biscuits. Peter sat back in his chair; he looked at the tea tray and thought, *We are discussing the possible killing of our own people over tea and biscuits.* He shook his head, "So where do I come in to this problem of yours, Captain?"

"The Germans have a supply convoy en route to Bardia. At least one of the ships will be used to take 1500 prisoners to Italy on its return trip. My people have to try and get the special party out before they leave North Africa. I was told you might have some ideas on how we can approach the problem; I understand that you have actually been ashore at Bardia and that you know the harbor approaches well."

"I do know the harbor approaches providing the Germans haven't put in a few booby traps since my last visit. My shore time consisted of a short sojourn down the quay at one point, I'm afraid. Who are you and what outfit do you represent; LRDG, David Stirling's SAS?"

"We, my group and I are attached to Major Stirling's group. We are used generally for special operations as we are all German and Austrian Jews, and can pass among the enemy as German troops. My real name is Schwartz. It can be useful when gathering information."

Peter nodded his head in understanding, "I can see the advantages of your group, but what about these people you wish to rescue, have you any ideas in mind?"

"Well I was hoping that our rescue could be disguised by a larger scale breakout. I'm just not too sure of how we could approach that problem." Captain Black sat back with his tea and looked at Peter with icy blue eyes.

"How many men have you in your unit? Enough to form a platoon and more important will they be able to act like trained soldiers?"

"All are trained soldiers; they are fully equipped and armed with all the weapons used by the Wehrmacht. The half-track outside is a captured Africa Corps vehicle and we have two Daimler trucks and three Kubelwagons. I have thirty men in all: one Lieutenant, one Warrant Officer and two Sergeants. The remainder were all trained soldiers in the Wehrmacht who escaped in 1938; they all lost most of their families and all hate the Nazi government. My sister and I are all that is left of our family; Sarah is currently working for SOE in London."

"Right. Leave me all the information you have on the ship for the prisoners. I have a idea in mind that might work but I would like time to talk it over with my people first. Can we get together again tomorrow? Not here. I think."

"We have a house on the beach. It's away from any neighbors; perhaps that would be a suitable meeting place."

Peter rose to his feet "Good I'll see you tomorrow at 1400, with some ideas that we can discuss."

The beach house was as Black had mentioned; isolated, standing in its own grounds, facing the sea over a wide sweep of sand. The nearest other building was over half a mile away, occupied at present by the RAOC. The house was the home of an Egyptian club owner who had a close friendship with a member of the Abwehr. It had been requisitioned for the use of the Jewish contingent because of its isolation. It was lavishly appointed, complete with swimming pool and private cinema. The collection of pornographic films had been confiscated.

When Peter arrived in Jason Gardiner's Fiat car he was greeted at the door by a big blond Sergeant who was expecting him. He followed the man into a large lounge overlooking the Mediterranean.

Dressed in white shirt and grey slacks, Aaron Black came in and shook hands with Peter. He was followed by a fair-haired girl, perhaps twenty-four or five, in a cotton print dress. Peter was surprised when she was introduced as Sarah, Aaron's sister. She looked at him with big blue eyes, and smiled. "I have heard a lot about you Commander."

"Please call me Peter, and if I may I will call you Sarah. I thought you were based in London with SOE."

"I was and I am still in SOE. I have been seconded to help in the debriefing of prisoners here in North Africa, and since Aaron was here, I came to see him as soon as I arrived." Her voice was low and musical, Peter felt guilty at his reactions to Sarah and he turned hastily to Aaron, indicated his briefcase and suggested they get down to business.

Sarah left them to it, mentioning something about a swim.

The open case sat between them but Peter didn't need to refer to the papers there. The entire proposal was in his head and he sat and detailed his proposal.

"Taking into account my last visit to Bardia, it should be possible to land a party on the quay without detection. If we can have a platoon of German troops on the quay when the prisoners are marched down to board the ship we would be in a position where it should be possible to take over control of the ship. Then when the prisoners are boarded we could sail the ship out of the harbor and if my boats are in position, conduct it to Alex and repatriate the prisoners here."

Aaron was intrigued and for the next 30 minutes Peter explained the wreckage at the seaward end of the pier and the sunken ships along the pier. He pointed out that there was only one place where boarding from the pier would be possible, in the gap halfway along the pier where a burning ship had burnt through its mooring ropes and drifted off shore until it hit the bar in the centre of the harbor. The fortuitous accident provided a windbreak for the ships on the quay and a threat to any ship using the mooring, as the guns in the wreck were still useable.

Between the two men they planned an operation to cut out the prisoner's ship from under the noses of the Axis forces. As Aaron pointed out, the probability was that Italians would be used to move the prisoners and this could make things a little easier. It was also decided that the SBS should take over the guns of the wreck on the bar, using their rubber dinghies, timing their attack to be over by first light. Aaron's platoon would be located within the wreckage at the pier end. They would emerge and form up whilst the last of the prisoners were being loaded. They would march a group of Peter's seamen under CPO Walters to join the prisoners being embarked. Aaron would insist that they be embarked as a separate unit for security reasons. Once on board they would disperse with their escorts and take over control of the ship. Major Gardiner would lead the shore party and take the guns; the naval party would be led by Paul Waterhouse, with Peter commanding the boat flotilla. Ifor Williams had experience with Marine triple expansion engines as well as diesel; he would run the engine room on the prison ship. Black's platoon would handle the ship's guns. Despite his other commitments it was decided that Commander Paul Waterhouse would command the captured ship for the voyage back to Alexandria.

Finally the two men sat back, the ETA of the convoy was in four days time.

As the men sat back with cold beers Peter looked out of the window to see the bathing-suited figure of Sarah Black and another girl with dark hair running out of the water, laughing. He forced himself to turn away, only to find Aaron smiling at him knowingly. "You wouldn't know there was a war on here, would you? The other one by the way is Lieutenant Hazel Worral, Special Operations (Signals & Ciphers). She is also Austrian, married to and widowed from Michael Worral, a Boffin in the Cipher business. Killed in an air raid on London, I'm told. She has been attached to us for the past two months. Insists we all speak German in her presence so that we don't get caught out when we are operating."

Back in Headquarters, the planning group—consisting of Lt Col David Canning, Major Jason Garland and Lt Commander Peter Murray—sat around the table in the Colonel's office. The charts of Bardia, suitably updated, were lying between the three men and model boats were strewn about the map where suggestion and counter suggestion had left them. Now all three had decided on a final workable plan; the outline was written in longhand on several sheets of paper.

From here the section commanders concerned would be advised and the plans submitted for their comment and amendment if necessary. The phone rang and Col. Canning lifted it and answered gruffly, "Canning." The voice at the other end said something. Canning replied "Good show, thank you, Bill, it could be worthwhile."

"LRDG are in, they will be prepared to take 40-50 if it all gets chancy and some lads get a chance to do a runner." The Colonel smiled; "It looks like we're good to go."

Over the next three days the SBS base was a hive of activity as preparations were made for the forthcoming raid. For Peter the evening spent with Paul, Claire and Jenny Melville turned out to be like the 'Curates egg', good in parts. Both girls were tired and though they stayed the course bravely through dinner, both left Paul and Peter early to get some rest before another busy day. Peter was relieved for some reason that he himself would not admit, and it did give the two friends a chance to get together and chat. Paul was aware of the forthcoming operation and mentioned he would be in the shore party of LRDG for their part of the raid.

"I thought you would have been involved with the boats out here." Peter commented.

"I would have but when I arrived I was involved with the pick-up of stranded soldiers from the beach. Their commander said that they had miscalculated their position, hence they ran dry 60 miles from home and they had to make a run for it on foot. They were very short of navigators and trainers in navigation; the desert is one of those places where the compasses go wild because of all the fields of varying force that throw the magnetic versions off. Gyro-compasses would be better but the terrain can cause the gyro's to tumble, so they also are fairly useless. Stellar and Solar navigation is the only fairly sure way to travel from A to B in the blue. I offered to help and here I am."

The operation got underway with the forward placement of the coastal observers. At 1700 the flotilla set out, the MGBs and ML followed by the lean rakish shape of a fleet destroyer, *HMS Defiant*, her two forward turrets mounting 2x4.7inch guns in each of the twin mountings moving smoothly from side to side as the Gunnery Officer tested his controls.

The entire group moving at a sedate ten knots expected to arrive by 0300 the following morning. The leading element would separate to take position as close to the mid harbor shoal as possible to give the dinghy parties time to take over the guns of the stranded ship before the other landings were made.

Major Jason Gardiner stood looking through night glasses at the faint outline of the ship stranded on the shoal in the middle of Bardia Harbor. As he watched he saw the glint of light as a door opened and swiftly closed. He grunted with satisfaction, pleased that he was able to confirm that they were still on course for the stranded ship. The ML drifted towards the high stern of the derelict; the engine off, the boat silent. On the foredeck Staff Sergeant Stavros Papadopoulos was crouched, waiting to cast the padded grapnel onto the vessel.

With a grunt of effort S/Sergeant 'Poppy' as he was called in the SBS threw the grapnel overarm and with a satisfied grunt hauled the line tight, the hooks of the grapnel firmly lodged through the stern rail of the ship.

He hauled the rope to bring the ML under the counter of the derelict. The worn letters of the name of the ship were visible *Aurora* port of origin Palermo. The boat was drawn up against the fenders already in place round the bow of the ML. By this time Poppy was already aboard the ship and was standing waiting for the others to board. The Tommy gun was hanging from his shoulder by a sling, ready to hand if needed. Gardiner joined him followed by the remainder of the men, and Poppy led off down the sloping deck to the accommodation amidships.

HMS Defiant stopped outside the Harbor and dropped her boats, Captain Schwartz and his men climbed into the boats and they made their way to the tangle of wreckage at the end of the quay.

Having delivered their cargo, the boats returned to the waiting destroyer silently waiting for the raid to commence. The gun turrets were all trained towards the shore, with crews standing ready at their action stations.

Peter Murray was seated in the chair wedged in place on the bridge of the MGB; the lookouts were all concentrating on all round watch. He was worried that E boats may be returning to escort the ship loaded with prisoners, for the trip across to Italy. His concern was based on the fact that there were no escorts in port apart from an Italian MAT boat, and a repaired E boat from his last raid.

Onshore a long column of POW's came winding down to the quay, escorted by Italian soldiers. On the quay the gangways were rigged and the column split to allow two streams of men to board at once. The columns were directed down the port and starboard companion ways into the forward and after holds.

The platoon of German troops marched down the quay to the forward gangway. A large Feldwebel armed with a slung machine pistol bawled an order and the platoon halted with the crash of boots on the dusty concrete. The officer with the rank of Hauptmann stepped up to the Italian Major, standing watching the boarding, and saluted with his arm extended. "Hauptmann Schwartz 10th Grenadiers reporting with the escort party.......Sir." The deliberate gap before the word sir was a reflection of the difference between the German and Italian forces. There was no doubt that the Wehrmacht were not impressed with their allies and it showed.

The Major lazily returned the salute, "Escort party, I was not told of this. Who ordered it?"

"I have orders from Generalmajor Richter to report for escort duty to the ship. I believe he was concerned that there might be an attempt to rescue some or all of the prisoners so he wishes extra precaution to be taken. My men were due to be returned to Italy, so we were given the job." He stepped back a pace and saluted once more.

"Have I your permission to board my men, sir?"

The Major thought for a moment then with a casual wave of his hand and saidm "Very well, Hauptmann, get your men on board.

The German troops boarded the waiting ship carrying their kit and slung weapons. They made their way to the crew mess room directed by one of the crew.

Out of sight of the Italians on the quay, the crewman was seized and lodged in one of the storerooms in the mess. The three other crew members seated in the mess room were similarly treated. Captain Schwartz gave his orders and his men went round the ship collecting the crew members wherever they were to be found. Commander Paul Waterstone in the garb of a Gefreiter in the Wehrmacht, made his way to the bridge where he found the big Feldwebel leaning against the binnacle with his machine pistol trained on the Skipper and helmsman of the ship. *MV Gerona.*

Paul found himself in command of the biggest ship he had ever tried to handle, and decided he would keep the Captain on the bridge whilst leaving harbor. He had been expecting to be with the LRDG in the shore-based party, but the shortage of sea officers available at the time meant he was grabbed to sail the *MV Gerona* out of Bardia.

Chapter Seven

The loading of the prisoners progressed smoothly enough until the last group were being marched onto the quay. They were accompanied by a party of Africa Corps under Leutnant Kohlmann. Now Leutnant Kohlmann was one of those enthusiastic ex-Hitler Jugend Officers who was always trying to impress. He marched smartly over to the bored Major and sprang to attention with a snappy salute. "Leutnant Kohlmann reporting with prisoner's, sir."

"You're the second party of Wehrmacht I've seen today. What is wrong? Perhaps you don't trust you allies to handle this simple task?" He waved at the ship "We already have the platoon of extra escorts on board with your Hauptmann Schwartz."

"Hauptmann Schwartz? I'm sorry sir I don't know him. Anyway, I was the only Wehrmacht officer ordered to be here this morning. Can you tell me where he is now.... sir?" He added hastily.

"Why, on the ship of course; Where else do you think he would be?"

Kohlmann swung round and called to the grizzled Oberfeldwebel standing waiting while the last of the prisoners boarded the ship. "Rascher come here quickly."

Oberfeldwebel Rascher spat into the dust at his feet, *What does the little turd want now?* he thought, he turned to Gefreiter Wohl, "Look after this bunch of rubbish while I go and wipe the idiots arse for him."

"Jawohl, Herr Leutnant, coming." He trotted over to his officer and stood at attention.

"Rascher there is a detachment of troops on board the ship under the command of Hauptmann Schwartz. Find him and ask him to bring his orders here."

Rascher drew himself up to his full height. "Sir, can I suggest that the Lieutenant speaks to the Hauptmann personally. He may not be interested in what a mere Oberfeldwebel has to say."

Kohlmann looked arrogantly into the bleary eyes of his subordinate. "Did I ask for your opinion, Oberfeldwebel?"

"No sir." Resignedly Rascher turned and walked up the gangway after the last of the POW's.

On board Gemeiner Holz fingered his Schmeisser machine pistol, a little nervous now they seemed to have got away with it.

He got a shock when the figure of Oberfeldwebel Rascher appeared. He didn't recognise him so he snapped to attention.

Rascher looked at the soldier he was surprised at the man's smart appearance,

"Where do I find Hauptmann Schwartz?"

"In the mess hall forward, Oberfeldwebel."

"Good turn-outm Gemeiner, carry on." With a nod he walked through the door into the mess hall. In the confusion of activity collecting and locking up the crew members, nobody noticed Rascher when he went in, and it took a little time for him to sort out what was going on. Spotting the Hauptmann at a table at the far end of the hall he started making his way there. An Unteroffizer turned and saw him looking around; he picked up his Schmeisser and casually pointed it at the Oberfeldwebel. "Vorsicht, (careful) Oberfeldwebel, put your weapon down on the table."

Rascher looked into the eyes of the Unteroffizer and carefully put his pachine pistol down on the table.

"Komm" the cold eyes never shifted as the head nodded to the table at the far end of the mess.

Silence fell as Rascher made his way to the table where the Hauptmann was sitting, sorting out paperwork.

"So who have we here, Gottfried?"

The Unteroffizer stood to attention and spoke. "Herr Hauptmann, this man was found in the mess hall without authority."

The Hauptmann looked at Rauscher "What have you to say for yourself, Oberfeldwebel?"

"Sir I was ordered to call Hauptmann Schwartz to the quay to see Leutnant Kohlmann."

"Who is Leutnant Kohlmann, pray?"

"He is my commander, sir." Rascher was becoming more and more uncomfortable under the cold stare of the Hauptmann.

"So when does a Lieutenant send for a Hauptmann in the Wehrmacht?"

"Normally never sir."

"Good. Inform Lieutenant Kohlmann that I will see him here if he desires an interview and in view of my orders I will decide what to do with him at that time. Understand?"

"Jawohl, Herr Hauptmann." Rascher saluted and spun round and—followed by the Unteroffizer—marched out of the mess hall. On the quay a Kubelwagen stood with an Oberstleutnant sitting talking to the rigid figure of Leutnant Kohlmann.

Unteroffizer Gottfried tapped Rascher on the shoulder and steered him to one side.

"Holz, guard this man and shoot him if he twitches."

Holz unslung his Schmeisser and pointed it at Rascher and told him to sit down on the deck by the bulkhead.

Rascher cursed the Oberstleutnant whoever he was, another minute he would have been on the quay and away.

In the engine room of the *MV Gerona* CPO Ifor Williams was ready to start engines. On the bridge the telegraph rang and the indicator stated 'Engines - Standby.

Paul looked to see that the POWs were all aboard. The Italian deckhands fore and aft were waiting to cast off. The Italian Captain switched on the communications and gave orders to cast off forward. Paul rang for engines "Slow ahead, starboard helm." The bow of the ship started to swing out from the quay, the stern still held by the mooring lines. He nodded to the Captain, who ordered the aft lines to be taken in. From the quay came a burst of gunfire. The seamen fore and aft, still coiling the line both collapsed thrown to the deck by a storm of bullets.

From the stranded ship on the shoal a brief burst of fire pattered against the hull of the moving ship, and then ceased. Along the deck of the ship, several weapons opened up and the Kubelwagen subsided on bullet shattered tyres and blew up with a satisfying bang, as the fuel tank exploded. The soldiers on the quay were all firing now. Muzzle flashes of the various weapons flickering along the length of the quay. As the *MV Gerona* cleared the quay and reversed into the channel out of the harbor the guns on the stranded ship opened fire on the quay; with insane chatter, the machine guns swept a hail of 9mm calibre bullets along the length of the quay.

From the shore above the harbor the first mortar bombs splashed into the water and the bow of the ship was peppered with shrapnel. From out at sea a screaming salvo of 4.7 inch shells hammered onto the shore, shaking the ground with the impact; a second salvo came in being directed by the LRDG on shore. The mortar fire stopped, and did not restart.

In the outer harbor the *MV Gerona* swung through a 180 degree turn and set off to the open sea.

Peter watched the activity ashore as the sky lightened, as the dawn broke the mutter of high-speed engines came from out to sea. The Starboard lookout reported "Power boats to starboard, high speed, bow waves in sight; three vessels, sir."

Peter called for engines and picking up the boat to boat intercom called the other waiting MGB's "Action starboard, attack, attack, attack"

The engines of the three boats roared and all three hurled themselves forward the path of the approaching E boats.

The Destroyer *Defiant*, opened fire on the E boats with the aft turrets, and the three MGB's opened fire with everything they had, ignoring the lines of tracer fire that were arcing towards them. The action was short and vicious; the leading E boat ran into one of the salvo of shells and disappeared in the column of water blown up by the explosion.

The other two boats continued on their course zigzagging to avoid the shell bursts now regularly falling around the enemy boats.

Peter saw the end boat in the British line stop suddenly with smoke pouring from her hull. The pompom on the fore deck was having effect on the second E boat which suddenly lost its wheelhouse in a burst of smoke and flame. The boat swung to starboard and slowed down. The forward pompom smashed a row of holes down the port side of the E boat, which was now emitting clouds of smoke and being shaken by a series of small explosions as her ammunition was overheated by the growing flames. Peter could see the survivors leaping over the sides and at the stern a dinghy was thrown into the water, but the man who threw it disappeared in a sudden gush of flames that burst through the after deck.

The last of the E boats was looking the worse for wear and decided that he had enough. The boat turned sharply to starboard and made off in the early morning twilight towards the Italian coast.

Mark Wharton's boat was no longer on fire but his progress was reduced to the power from his wing diesel engine.

Peter ordered the four wounded to be transferred to Charlie King's boat which continued with the task force while Peter stayed to escort Mark Wharton's boat back to Alexandria. They passed a towline to speed up progress and, as they followed the coast, the sounds of action on land were heard as the LRDG clashed with elements of the Africa Corps who were upset at the audacious lifting of their carefully assembled prisoners.

They caught up with the *MV Gerona* off Matruh. She was being taken in tow by *HMS Defiant,* her engine having suffered unseen damage during the shooting as she left harbor that had cracked a coolant pipe. The overheating had occurred and despite Ifor William efforts the engine had succumbed.

The operation was being watched and commented upon from the crowded decks of the *Gerona*. The freed POW's were taking full advantage of the open air.

Peter accompanied the *Defiant* for the rest of the way to Alexandria, the two craft towing the two lame ducks.

The POW's had to be landed at the main quay, as there was insufficient water at the SBS quay for the *MV Gerona* to come alongside. The small boat flotilla crowded into the SBS base and the various groups landed. The group under Major Gardiner had vacated the stranded ship, leaving the guns dismounted and the entire area mined. The borrowed ML had risked her own safety to come as close as possible to the derelict to make the transit for the men as short as possible.

During the process she had lost her radio mast, which had been shot off whilst she was in range of the shore.

Lt Col David Canning, RM, stood and watched the boats coming alongside to land the wounded and the eight dead, mainly casualties of the mortars, plus those from Mark Wharton's boat.

"How many did we rescue?" He asked Peter as he stepped ashore.

"The entire column, as far as I know. Captain Black will be able to confirm when he gets ashore from the freighter."

"Well done, Peter/ The powers that be said we couldn't do it, but there you are. As Nelson always believed, you have to dare to win sometimes."

"Nelson?"

"Well... I'm sure someone did. The main thing is it worked. Come and tell me all about it." He turned and walked back to his office followed by Peter.

The preparation and the aftermath of the raid kept Peter and in fact the entire SBS unit busy for the next three weeks, and apart from a few hurried phone calls he had no chance to talk or see Claire. He received a message from Jenny Melville suggesting that he should try to get away to see Claire as she had been told Claire was being posted. They worked in different sections so she could not be sure. Jenny was now running the crypto-analysts section in the bunker in Naval Headquarters in Cairo, so was no longer sharing the flat with Claire.

Claire swung round on her chair and gave Peter a long look. "I see you made it back in one piece. How is Paul, is he alright." Her manner was distant.

Surprised and taken aback Peter went over and bent to kiss her. She almost turned her head away. Puzzled and offended, Peter drew back, wondering what he had done wrong.

"Is something wrong?" He asked "Am I missing something?"

She looked at him steadily for a long moment. "I'm sorry, Peter, something happened whilst you were involved with this last operation. I'll be going to Malta to take over the cipher office in Valetta; I won't have time to see you before I go so I'm afraid it's goodbye." He saw the glint of tears in her eyes.

He said "It's not the end of the world for us; we'll get the chance to meet again when I call there with supplies."

"No, Peter, I mean it. It's all over between us, there's someone else I'm afraid, stationed in Malta, I am going to Malta on transfer; I am due to leave tomorrow night on the Catalina. I have written to you to explain. I'm sorry, Peter, I did not intend this to happen." She looked at him miserably, shaking her head; "I really did not want this to happen."

Peter stood quiet for a moment then said low-voiced. "I'll say goodbye then; good luck with your new posting. It was fun while it lasted." He turned and walked out of the office and down to the reception area. To the Transport officer he said "I'll be off then." He went out to the forecourt where the driver waited with his jeep.

As the driver steered his way through the Cairo streets Peter realized that apart from the feeling of being abandoned he was actually relieved at Claire's news. He had been feeling guilty about his relationship with Claire, it had not felt right to become involved with her when he was involved in such hazardous duty. Perhaps when it was over he could think again about marriage and settling down. He shrugged then sat up in his seat and said "Right. Let's get on then."

The driver looked at him quizzically, then seeing the slight smile on his passenger's face, shrugged his shoulders fatalistically, officers were an odd bunch at the best of times, this one wasn't too bad. He drove on and Peter said nothing else until they arrived at the seaside villa occupied by the Jewish Company.

"Call for me in three days time." He said to the driver, and, picking up his bag, he walked through the front door, waving to the sentry dressed in an orange shirt and white shorts and sandals; carrying his Schmeisser on a sling over his shoulder.

Inside the house Captain Schwartz was supervising the collection of equipment being gathered in the centre of the lobby. He waved Peter over. "Just in time; I hoped you would get here before we left."

"What's this; a pier head jump, I thought you were here for the next week?"

"Last minute call, I'm afraid, Rommel has lost Tobruk and we're needed in a hurry so we'll be off now. Could you please explain to Sarah. Look after her for me—she is due today for a little R&R. The servants are here they'll look after you; there is plenty of food and drink so just enjoy. I'll see you when we get back."

The roar of an arriving truck came through the open door and while he spoke the equipment all disappeared through the side door to be loaded onto the truck that had just arrived. With a final Schwartz was gone.

Chapter Eight

"That's my brother; come and stay, then watch me run away." Peter spun round to see Sarah Black standing there with her suitcase beside her.

He smiled at the forlorn look on her face. "I have been charged with the task of looking after you in his absence." He picked up his own bag and reached for her suitcase, only to have both removed by the houseman who appeared from nowhere and signalled them to follow him up the wide staircase.

They looked at each other, shrugged, and followed him up to the bedrooms on the first floor.

Having explained that they required two rooms not one shared, they both changed and headed for the beach.

Peter noticed that Sarah looked tired, but to his eyes she was still the beautiful blond he had been introduced to several weeks ago. Having set up the umbrellas and loungers on the sand, both went in for a swim then returned to relax under the shade. The houseman brought out iced soft drinks to the two house guests and informed them that lunch would be served at noon and would be Nile Bass with salad.

The next three days were idyllic. No work, no pressure good food and good company. Both found pleasure in the other's company. When the break was over there was an unspoken acceptance that they would meet again. Peter realized why he had not been as shaken as he might have been at parting with Claire. The meeting with Sarah on the first occasion had disturbed him, and he had hardly spoken to her on that occasion. This time being thrown together as they were, both had got to know each other as friends, and though neither had mentioned it, both were aware and accepted the friendship between them.

The next months were busy for Peter as the Africa Corps were pushed further along the coast towards the advancing Americans. The focus of action was concentrated more and more on the Greek islands and the coast of Sicily. Partisan activity in Greece had tied down large numbers of German troops and the increasing unrest in Italy and Sicily was causing the enemy problems they could well do without.

The flotilla spent considerable time running weapons and supplies to partisan groups in both areas, and the collection and landing of agents had become a regular event.

Peter and Sarah did manage to get together on occasion during this period but only on hastily arranged last minute occasions. Basically Sarah's work in SOE was a closed book to Peter; it came as a complete surprise therefore when he was told by Charlie King that he had dropped off Sarah Black at Sciacca, on the southern shore of Sicily. The pick up three weeks later was scheduled for Menfi, at a place that had been used before with some success. She was supposed to be bringing back an Austrian scientist, Walter Schroeder, who had been working on research in a lab on the island. Peter decided that he would do the pick-up himself and accordingly the rendezvous was approached under the quiet mutter of the wing engine. At 2300 the boat drifted to a stop and lay rocking gently on the quiet waters. It was full dark by this time and the light signal from the shore was on time and in the correct sequence.

Peter took the dinghy in himself with CPO Jim Walters armed with his Thompson sub machine gun and Stoker David Martin who favoured the German MP40 as his preferred weapon.

The boat grounded on the small beach and contact with the shore party established. Sarah saw Peter and smiled with relief. She came over and took Peter to one side. "We have a problem," she indicated the hunched figure seated on a suitcase beside the low cliff face. "The Professor refuses to come without his daughter, Major Gardiner has gone to fetch her, but he has been gone too long. Maria, the Professor's daughter, is a loyal Nazi and she doesn't approve of her father's attitude. The Major has two partisans with him, but I am worried that they have run into trouble."

"Where have they gone, do you know?"

"Their house is along the road towards Ribera about two miles; they should have collected her and been here by now." Sarah sounded anxious.

Peter called Walters over and explained what was happening, "We will need to go and see what has happened to the Major and Maria. Tell Martin to get the Prof and Miss Black out to the boat, and pass the message to Lieut Easton to beat it and come back at the same time tomorrow night. Then come back with two more of the lads with some grenades and another SMG for me and we'll go and sort out the Major."

"I'll be coming with you." The quiet voice of Sarah Black was firm and uncompromising. "Neither of you speak German, I do, neither of you know the way or the house. I do."

Peter looked at Walters and shrugged. "Right. Tell him to bring an extra SMG for Miss Black as well. Sarah, tell the Prof we'll be back with this daughter tomorrow."

Stoker Martin returned with two men the other guns, and a bag of grenades. The party left the beach and moved off down the road.

The truck carrying a party of German soldiers passed them as they hid in the ditch beside the road. It stopped about half a mile further along the road and the soldiers debussed and spread out in a line across both sides of the road. They started to advance towards the house that was just visible silhouetted against the night sky.

"How many do you think there are?"Peter asked

"Twenty-five, at least," said CPO Walters.

"There will be more the other side of the house," Sarah said, "but if we can get past them quickly they may not have closed in yet. There may be a chance to warn them."

"Is there a telephone in the house?"

"Yes, but I don't know if it works or not." Sarah replied "Why do you ask?"

Peter pointed to another house just across the field beside them. "I thought perhaps we could warn them. It's worth a try." He set off across the field to the house he had spotted.

The others followed running quietly across the short grass.

The house seemed deserted, or rather unoccupied, but there was a wire running to a terminal on the corner of the roof. Walters broke the glass in the back door and reached through the gap and opened it with the key that was in the lock.

Inside using shaded torches they searched for the telephone. Located on the wall, beside it was a list of names and numbers. One number had the name scratched out and another name written in.

Peter looked at Sarah, "What do you think?"

"It's the only new name there so it's a good bet that it's them. Shall I try?"

Peter nodded, "Ask for Argonaut."

Sarah lifted the phone and rang the number written on the wall. After a few moments she said, "Argonaut."

She spoke "It's Sarah, here's Peter Murray," and handed over the receiver to Peter.

"Jason the place is crawling with Germans on each side of the house; I will create a diversion so that you can get out and join us."

"Peter; Maria is being a pain, she refuses to leave, I didn't see the phone until you rang, I presume she called in the dogs. I will do as you suggest, I'll have to gag her I think. Give me five minutes."

Peter told the others what the Major had said and led them out across the field to the right, the seaward side of the Professor's house. They approached the nearest Germans cautiously. The soldiers were lying down and one was smoking concealing his cigarette in his hand.

Martin said in a whisper."They think this is a waste of time as usual."

Peter said "You understand German?"

Martin smiled "My family used to go to Germany every year for the Oktoberfest, we all had to learn German at school; I have been visiting Germany and Austria for years, skiing in the Harz and the Alps. Yes, I speak German."

"Good. When I tell you I want you to shout a warning in German that the people from the house are escaping to the shore. First," he turned to CPO Walton. "Let's wrap these two up so that they can't give the game away."

Walton turned to the two extra hands "Right, lads. Quietly now; a good clout to shut them up then tie them up with their own webbing."

The two seamen placed their weapons on the ground and disappeared.

Peter whispered "Will they be alright?"

Walters whispered back "They are both ex-poachers, they will only be heard when they want to be. Don't worry, sir."

There was a rustle in the bushes and a voice said "Coming in." The two shadowy figures appeared and picked up their weapons. "There are four more about ten yards over to the right and there's another over on the left. 'avin a crafty fag."

Stoker David Martin made his way down towards the shore and a few minutes later Peter and his group heard shots and a voice calling in German. There was immediate response from the other three sides of the house, and the area was suddenly full of the noise of the troops crashing through the bushes as they congregated on the seaward side of the house and made for the shore.

A bedraggled David Martin appeared and the whole party made their way to the road where the truck was standing. The driver was peering towards the shore, wondering what was happening.

As the party under Major Gardiner left the house, the driver stood and lifted his weapon.

CPO Jim Walters stepped up behind the man and slid his arm round the soldier's neck.

The man struggled for a short while then slumped unconscious. Walters dropped the man where he stood and the whole combined party boarded the truck and drove off. After a hurried consultation with Peter, he stopped the vehicle beside the drive of the house Peter's group had broken into, everyone got off the truck except one of the two partisans who drove off to eventually dump the truck near Marsala. The two poachers trailed the party up to the house carefully removing traces in the gravel of the footprints and scuffs made by the passage of the group.

Having sought and found another way out of the place, the party settled down, watching the to and fro of the searchers, who were collected by another vehicle. The place did not settle down until dawn was breaking.

In the daylight it was possible to see the object of all the trouble. Maria Schroeder was 23 years old and pretty with big dark eyes that she inherited from her Jewish mother. She was not happy and it was obvious that the object of her anger was Major Jason Gardiner.

Peter said, "If you promise not to make a noise, I'll remove the gag." He looked at her steadily for a moment while she digested this piece of information, then she nodded. Peter removed the cloth bound round her mouth. Her hands were still bound in front of her and she lifted them in silent appeal.

"The same rules apply?" Peter said. Once more she nodded, so Peter cut the rope round her wrists.

"Thank you." She said quietly in accented English, "Where are you taking me?"

"To be with your father in Alexandria, at his request, and before you ask, he is aware that you don't agree with his politics, but he is convinced that the only reason you both are not in a Concentration Camp, is his value as a research scientist." Peter said "His worry was that if you were left here as you wished you would be arrested and sent to Dachau because of your Jewish mother. For what it's worth, I agree with him."

She sat in silence for a long time only speaking during the rest of the long day when asked about food and drink or answering a question.

As darkness fell that night the two ex-poachers went out to check the area between them and the pick-up point; the remaining partisan went with them.

When they returned the partisan was not with them, he had remained behind to make sure that they would not be surprised. The entire party set out with Major Gardiner bringing up the rear with Stoker Martin and one of the poachers while the other led the way.

The ambush was sprung less than a mile from the beach.

The German spoke in English. "Halt! Stand still, you are all under arrest." The click of bolts being cocked was sufficient for Peter to call a halt. He looked around, and realized that the small group with Jason Gardiner were not with them. He thought that at least they'll know what happened back in Alex. The ambush party came into view in the lights of a truck parked beside the road. "Put your weapons down on the ground at your feet." The order came next and the entire group bent to the ground including Maria who was pulled down by Sarah. As they stooped the guns of the rearguard opened fire, wounding the officer in charge and several of the soldiers.

The voice of Gardiner rang out "Run for it, all of you."

The entire party ran for their lives from the disorganised ambush party.

The voice of the wounded officer was heard as he shouted in German "Shoot the Jewish bitch one of you, kill her, don't let her escape." There were several shots fired but the soldiers were confused and were scared of hitting their own people.

Outside the area of light Peter and Walters turned and opened fire on the soldiers milling about under the lights of the truck. They wounded several more of the ambushers, including the officer, who stopped talking abruptly.

The party made their way to the beach where Sarah had already started the signal to the MGB offshore. The entire party were picked up without injury, apart from a sprained wrist suffered by Maria when she was dragged away from the ambush by Sarah.

It was significant that she cooperated with her captors from that time onwards; Sarah believed that she had heard the German officer's comment about killing the Jewish bitch.

Sarah disappeared as soon as they arrived in Alexandria. The Professor was at the quay when they tied up. Jason Gardiner took Maria, Sarah and the Professor off to some secret destination while Peter was sorting out the rest of the party.

His interview with the Colonel was uncomfortable, "What the blazes did you think you were doing, landing in those circumstances? Your job is to get your boat there and back safely, not go stumbling around the countryside in the dark. Your capture would have been of real value to the enemy, since you have an intimate knowledge of how this department works and the codes we use."

"So, sir, does Major Gardiner and, I presume, Sarah Black!" Peter shot back.

"Do you carry a pill, Commander Murray? I thought not. Are you trained to counter interrogation methods? No you are not. Are you getting the message, Commander Murray?"

Peter had no answer to that, so he kept his mouth shut.

The Colonel sat back in his chair and looked long and hard at the erect figure in front of him "Having said all that, you did bloody well, and I have put you in for a decoration for the operations over the past few months. I suppose I should have expected you to act the way you did, it's probably what I would have done in your place. It would still have been wrong, except in this game thinking on your feet is what things are all about. You were on the spot and it was your decision. I'm just stressing that you must know the full circumstances when you make a decision like that."

Sensing a slight softening of the Colonel's manner, Peter brought up the subject of Sarah. "Do you know what has happened to Sarah,.. ah, Mrs Black Sir?"

"I'm afraid I can't tell you that, that information is strictly on a need to know basis I'm afraid." He noticed Peter's disappointment at this comment, and opened the file on his desk. He made a point of looking at the contents before confirming his last statement. Then he rose to his feet and banged his leg, "Excuse me for a moment I must flex my leg otherwise I get too stiff to move," as he walked out of the door he called, "Sit down and order some coffee I'll be a few minutes, we'll discuss the next operation."

Peter looked at the open file and read the contents of the topmost memo. He wrote down the telephone number on a scrap of paper, then sat down and called the orderly to order coffee.

Chapter Nine

The weather grew hotter as the summer advanced and the activity at the Base in Alexandria became more and more administrative as the North African coastline was gradually retaken from the Africa Corps.

The setback for the US forces at Kasserine was now over and Rommel had been posted back to Germany, so the concentration of activity had now swung even further to Europe and support of the Partisan activities in Italy, Greece and France. In Yugoslavia there were still political problems between the Partisan factions, resulting in bitter conflict that favoured the Occupying forces. There were signs there now of the increasing influence of Tito's Communists in the struggle though much of the support was being stage managed from London direct.

The MTB half flotilla had rejoined Peter's MGB's and the six craft were now under Peter's command. His acting rank of Lieutenant Commander had been confirmed and he was now Acting Commander, replacing Bill Hamilton who was promoted to full Commander and sent home to command a new flotilla of Fairmile boats operating from Ramsgate.

The entire flotilla was at present cruising at economical speed up the Adriatic abreast of Brindisi. Lieut Easton currently on watch commented to the helmsman.

"I went on holiday to Brindisi with my parents and my sister in 1936; we had a villa on the beach front and spent most of our time in the water. I remember that the sun shone most of the time." He sighed and raised his glasses to sweep the horizon, trying to spot any signs of wake from possible enemy craft. He also remembered the Italian girl in the next cottage, she used to swim when he and his sister were out swimming, he had fallen desperately in love with her. He had in fact never spoken to her. Now he wondered as he had many times since just what had happened to her. He sighed again and made another sweep of the horizon.

At the helm Able Seaman Allan Hodges sucked his breath in and flexed his broad shoulders. He was remembering his last leave in England. The bank where he had worked prior to call-up had been moved from its old premises after it had caught a bomb during the heavy raids in spring. He had been on embarkation leave before being sent out to Alexandria.

Hillary Watson had occupied his attention ever since she had joined the staff as secretary to the Manager. The trouble had been that he was called up within days of her joining the bank; there had been no time then to get to know her. His first posting after training had been to a mine-sweeper on the East Coast, and though he had seen her briefly when he came on leave it was not until he had been posted to Egypt, and was at home for a week prior to boarding the AA cruiser that was joining the Mediterranean Fleet for convoy duty that he asked her out. He would be carried as supernumery as far as Malta, where he would join the regular convoy between Malta and Alex.

His first day home he had met Mr Harris. his former Branch Manager who had invited him in to the new Bank premises to say hullo to his old colleagues. He had bumped into Hillary by surprise as he walked through the door. He didn't have time to be embarrassed, he was too busy helping pick up the papers she had dropped. As they both squatted heads close together picking up the papers it had just come out. He still couldn't believe it. He had whispered to her

"I was going to ask you out when I got called up. Would you like to go to the pictures sometime?"

She blushed and then said "Why not? I would love to go." She looked around. "Tonight if you like."

Mr Harris tut-tutted as he came over to them "Come on, Miss Waters; we can't have our lad on leave crawling round the floor, now can we? Come on, Mr Hodges, come and see your old colleagues at the counter.

With a wink and a nod of his head, Allan had mouthed the word tonight; confirming the date before getting to his feet to greet friends behind the counter of the new branch.

He had been waiting for Hillary at closing time and they had gone off to the pictures as arranged. They had been out every night of that week, and by the time he was due to report back to duty she had promised to write to him, and although there was no formal arrangement he was certain in his own mind that she was the one.

He had received her first letter in Alex. It must have come in with one of the flights. She had said that she missed his company already, and to please come home as soon as possible.

He sighed, it was the first of many over the past three months and though he enjoyed this posting he did miss Hillary.

"Did you speak Hodges?" Number One was still peering through his night-glasses.

"No sir, I was just remembering my last holiday in Seaford."

"Bloody war, eh?"

They both nodded at this profound comment and then returned to their own thoughts.

Peter Murray stepped onto the bridge at 0300 hrs.

"What's happening then?"

"Nothing so far; all our boats still in contact, cruising speed 20 knots." Easton reported quietly.

Murray nodded and looked around the horizon with his glasses.

The clatter of mugs preceded the arrival of the Kye. Even here in the warm seas the thick cocoa mixture was gratefully received in the dark hours of the night.

The radio bleeped and crackled, the signaller came to the bridge with the message.

Peter read the words and then turned to Easton and said, "Turn them round, Number One; they've changed their minds again."

Easton picked up the handset for the RT and switched on. He pressed the squelch switch three times the signal to reverse course and switched off.

This was the second time they had made this run, and the second time it had been cancelled at the last minute. The boats all turned in response to the signal and the flotilla began the long run back to the rendezvous with their refueller—a 200 ton coaster currently sheltering in a quiet bay in Othanol one of the Greek islands north of Corfu.

"Let's get nearer to the coast on the way back, bring her five degrees starboard on my mark. Bunts, call the course change, radio silence is no longer needed."

When the signaller reported all boats in contact; Murray gave the order and all the boats changed course to approach the Italian coast.

The Dry Dock moved ponderously northwards towards Bari. It had over the past nights managed to move from Taranto round the heel of Italy to Brindsi, it was now making its laborious way to Bari. Only travelling at night, it was the only dry dock capable of use with the larger units of the Italian Navy and the bulk transport ships still in operation. At present there were two German destroyers needing repair in the yards at Bari.

The escort was an armed trawler and two Schnellboot; E boats with four big powerful high-speed diesel engines heavily armed, but only carrying two torpedoes; boats that could attain speeds of up 40 knots in a straight line. They were currently lazing along on either side of the big dock. The trawler that led the group was heavily armed with 20mm and 50mm cannon, plus a Vierling multi-barrel anti aircraft gun on the foredeck.

The trawler saw them first; Lt. Ed Hammond's MTB on the starboard wing of the Flotilla was one of the new Fairmile boats, but it was inclined to have problems with its fuel system, he had fallen back a little during the past half hour as his engineer cursed the fuel and changed the filter once more.

The storm of fire from the trawler nearly caught them completely by surprise, the starboard lookout just saw the glint of light off the metal of one of the weapons swinging into line as the first hint of dawn diluted the blackness of the night.

The cry of warning caused Ed to swing the wheel to port and hit the action stations klaxon. This was not normally used during night operations because the raucous sound could be heard for some distance across the water. Ed used it to warn the rest of the flotilla, as well as to bring his own men to full alert.

The lookout and the Oerlikon gunner took the brunt of the first salvo, both men killed where they stood. The splinters from the damage to the boat wounded the hand on the Depth Charge, rails throwing him across the deck to the port side where he scrabbled desperately to grab a hold to stop himself going overboard without success, and he was lost in the boiling wake of the rapidly accelerating MTB.

The multiple machine gun turret behind the bridge opened fire with all four Brownings hosing bullets at the now visible trawler.

Ed Hammond was calling the warning to the other boats that by now were all wheeling to see what the fuss was about. The Dry Dock had now been outlined against the faint dawn light and the menacing shapes of the E boats were becoming visible the increasing white curve of their passage through the water marking their increased speed; both now opened fire on Ed Hammond's boat.

Ed had turned towards the enemy group to reduce their target and bring his port Oerlikon into play. The other MTB's had deployed into line with Ed's boat and, like Ed, were preparing torpedoes. They concentrated on the Dry Dock, leaving the escorts to be dealt with by the MGBs.

Peter called Charlie King and Flash Gordon on the R/T to spread out and attack in line.

"Charlie, take the trawler while Flash and I look after the E boats, Christ, they are fast!"

The three MGBs worked up to full speed, weaving to avoid the fire from the E Boats. All three had their Pompoms in action—the thump, thump of the discharging shells heard under the shattering rattle of the Oerlikons, now beginning to find their targets, the tracer lashing back and forth in the still dark sky.

The almost lazy arc of the tracers which seemed to suddenly speed up as they approached picked and smashed at the craft on both sides. The E boats, both released their torpedoes to lighten their craft and give them extra speed. The torpedoes ran harmlessly until their motors ran out and sank to the sea bottom.

The leading E Boat ran into the concentrated fire from Flash Gordon's boat and stopped suddenly. It sat wallowing in the water spitting fire from its guns until it burst into flame at the stern, Flash became overconfident and approached too near, his boat appeared to hesitate, then it roared forward as flame appeared on the foredeck, the Pompom crew were dead sprawled on deck around the gun, which was blown onto its side. On the bridge Flash leaned against the screen gazing fixedly at the burning E Boat. Under his hand the throttle was wide open, the engines of the MTB screaming. The E Boat was throwing everything at the approaching MTB without apparent success. It began to move as the engineer got the engines going once more, but it was too little too late. The MGB, out of control hit the stern of the E Boat and the fuel exploded.

Peter saw the last moments of Flash Gordon and his crew, and he winced as the two boats collided, the bow section of the E Boat separated from the stern settled back on the water where it hesitated for a moment then it sank quickly, disappearing beneath the waves.

Stunned for a moment, Peter was brought back to his own problem when a bullet hit the rim of the helm, causing CPO Walters to swear as a splinter 4 inches long stuck into his arm. He did not lose control, but Peter took over the wheel and ordered the Chief below to get his wound looked at.

The SBA in the wardroom took one look at the wound and called Stoker Martin who was assisting "Get me the tin snips from Chief Williams. Jump about, lad, we can't have the Bo'sun laid-up while we mess about." He grinned at the Walters. "I'll not take it out, but I'll have to trim it off to get a dressing on it."

The Bo'sun looked at him for a moment. "You're a sadistic bastard, Mathews. Stuff your tin snips up your arse." He gripped the end of the splinter that protruded through his arm and tore it free, leaving the gaping wound bleeding and raw.

Mathews grabbed him as he fainted, easing him onto the cloth-covered bench. "Stupid stubborn sod, they never learns, everyone's a bloody hero." He grabbed a sponge from the clean bowl beside him and went to work on the wound, cleaning it as best he could but concentrating on sterilizing the area as well as he could, and packing the wound with gauze. Martin returned with the tin snips and was told to take them back as they were no longer needed. He looked at the wound disbelievingly, "Bloody nuts, the lot of them." Mathews muttered but he took great care with the dressing nonetheless.

On deck Peter was aware of the explosions from the torpedoes striking the floating Dock, which was leaning hard over to port, the E boat seemed to bear a charmed life as it continued to absorb the fire from fhe MGB. Two of the MTB's came up from the other side of the E Boat and attacked with their two pounder guns, twin Oerlikons and machine guns. The stern of the E Boat sank in the water as the full power of the engines was applied. The boat shot forward under full power and made for the coast breaking off the action, and abandoning the trawler and the Dock to their fate.

The Trawler had its deck awash as she sank with guns now silent. The surviving members of the crew were being picked up by Charlie King's boat, as they leapt into the water.

The crew of the sinking dock were being taken off by Peter's number two, Lt Com Bill Manning, the commander of the MTB section. While Peter watched, the dock tipped right over onto its side, then briefly upside down. From that position it quietly sank to the seabed, the great torn hole in the hull visible to the end.

In Alex once more Peter sat in his office thinking. He had finished the letters to the families of the crew of Flash Gordon's boat; he had recommended Flash for a posthumous decoration for the action. The Depth Charge hand had been picked up by Tiny Miller in the number three MTB, and was recovering in the hospital from his wounds. CPO Walters had been operated on to remove the rest of the splinter from his arm, and luckily would not be permanently disabled by it. Back on duty in three weeks was the M.O's guess.

Peter signed the posting for A/B Hodges A, recommended to attend the Midshipman's Course at HMS Alfred, in Brighton. His recommendation had been based on the observations of Lt. Easton and himself. Hodges would be leaving for England in two days if the place in the Liberator was not lost to someone more senior. Lt Col David Cumming RM seemed to know all sorts of people in this area, and as a fixer was second to none. He had arranged the seat, which meant that Hodges would have time for some leave before his course commenced.

The details of that last excursion were fresh in his mind, the picture of Flash Gordon's boat exploding taking the E Boat with it; the battered flotilla regrouping and making the rendezvous with the tanker. The long haul back to base, Hodges had confirmed his choice on the return trip when the two Messerschmitts came out of the sun guns blazing. The gunner on the twin Oerlikon mount was killed immediately, Hodges had leapt up and released the body from the harness and strapped himself in. The returning aircraft had separated and Hodges had picked the nearest, a machine with a snarling mouth painted round the engine. The cannon and machine guns of the aircraft were patterning the water in line with the boat. Hodges held his fire to the last moment, then he opened up, the tracer reaching for the attacking aircraft. Peter could see the holes appear along the wing and up to the cockpit. The fire from the plane ceased and the aircraft flew without veering at all straight into the sea. The cheer went up from Peter's boat but Hodges swung the gun round seeking the other attacking aircraft. It had concentrated on the MTBs off to starboard. Caught as it climbed from its strafing attack across the line of boats, the fire from the twin Oerlikons punched a row of holes in the aircraft from nose to tail. Smoke came from the wounded engine and the nose dropped as the Messerschmitt made its way towards the distant Italian coast. The crew of the MGB grabbed Hodges out of the harness and carried him around the deck, the bewildered young man finally escaped to find himself facing his Captain.

Peter looked keenly at him "Where did you learn to shoot like that?"

"Duck, Sir." Seeing Peter's puzzled expression, "My dad and I used to go duck hunting in the marshes at Dymchurch. He had a family hut in the area and every year we would take his gun, a 12 bore, and the .22 rifle for me, and he would shoot duck for the pot and I would shoot for the butchers. They preferred my duck because there was just the one bullet."

"I see." Peter nodded. "Well while you're with us your action station will be the foreword Oerlikon, O.K.?"

"Yes sir," Hodges turned and went below to receive the extra tots he would be given.

They had made it home without further problems and the boats had now all been patched up as had most of the men. The loss of Flash and his boat and crew had been a real blow as the flotilla up to now had borne a charmed life; now nobody felt quite so secure.

Chapter Ten

The Khamsin was blowing a fine dust over the SBS base. The moored boats banged and bumped against their fenders with the restless movement of the sea. Looking out of the window Peter could see the layer of dust lying on the water turning the surface grey. Through the window it was a grim prospect, the figures moving about had cloths wrapped round their faces to allow them to breathe.

Along the window ledge there was a layer of fine dust that had penetrated the sealed frame and as he looked around the room lit by the centre light he could see the dust motes in the air despite the precautions taken to keep it out.

"God, I could do with a cold beer." He mopped his brow and realized that he was speaking aloud. Making a mental note to watch himself in future he turned and sat back at the desk facing the pile of returns that seemed to grow whenever he looked.

The knock at the inner door was followed by the creak of the hinges as his writer came in. The little WRNS 2nd Officer Penny Sergeant came through the door with another handful of files for his attention.

There was a small smile on her face as he looked at the papers in her hand. From behind her back she triumphantly produced a mug of beer with a frosting of dew down the side.

"Voila!" she said, "Compliments of the Australian Army."

He took a grateful drink of the cold beer, then "Australian Army?"

"In the outer office waiting to see you, he has his mate with him."

He picked up the bundle of paperwork from his desk and gave it to her. "Be a love and get rid of this for me. Then send them in."

Penny took the proffered papers and spun round to return to her own office, managing to give her bottom a little wiggle as she went. She smiled when she heard Peter say "Nice" as she went through the door.

She was still smiling to herself as she shut the door, she knew she had a trim figure, and that most of the officers appreciated the fact; albeit from afar.

Peter smiled to himself, it did no harm to let Penny know she was appreciated; it was a game they played. Penny was firmly engaged to a six foot six Colour Sergeant in the Guards who was a Rugby player of renown; he was up country at the moment with the Long Range Desert Group. She in turn was aware that regardless of the friendly flirting, he was committed elsewhere. She thought once that it was the posh WRNS sister of Commander Waterstone, but that seemed to be over. There was obviously someone else but she was not sure whom, yet!

The two Australians came into the office carrying a small bath filled with melting ice. The collection of bottles nestled and clinked invitingly as they carefully put it down.

The stocky Captain pushed his hand out, "Captain Martin Jones, from Burramungee, and this lanky drink of water," he nodded at his tall thin companion, "Is RSM Willie Chapman, Royal Australian Rifles."

Peter shook the extended hand and waved them to chairs; the Captain lifted a new bottle from the bath and uncapped it pouring the contents into Peter's now empty mug. "It's only that Egyptian piss but it is beer." He and the RSM collected bottles, opened them, and took a long swallow.

"Christ, it's hot, and dusty." He looked at Peter and said "I suppose you're wondering why we came to see you?"

At Peter's nod he carried on, "As you may have guessed we're with Stirling's SAS doing similar things to the SBS but on land.

Peter listened attentively; Captain David Stirling had been largely responsible for the formation of the Special Operation groups currently working in the Middle East. He had managed to set things up despite opposition from the regular pfficers in the area and even now the Special Forces had to battle with the administration on a regular basis.

Captain Jones continued "We have an operation on at the moment, but we will need some help if we can get it. I'm told you have conducted several raids along the coast of Sicily and Italy. We need to get in and out in a hurry, most importantly without being detected. The boats we have at present are ideal for Greek Islands work but not much use in a fight. We have an excursion on the go which will need a certain amount of firepower if things don't go right; so—first, would you be interested?"

Peter looked keenly at the Australian, "Where would we be operating?"

"Probably from base in Malta up into the Tyrrhenian Sea; it would involve a landing and a pick up. We have been promised the landing in a sub on offer from the Free French, but they cannot guarantee a pick up because of prior commitments. That's where you would come in; we have probably as many as twenty to move—possibly some injuries."

"I'll need to clear it with the boss, and I suggest we do both in and out. With the distances involved it would make sense. If the timing is right we should be able to help. There would be one condition; we would have to be briefed on the whole operation. The man on the spot must be able to assess the odds if there is a delay or other problem arises. We have found that there is no point in going to all the trouble of an op if there is no leeway with the planning; no one wants to

leave survivors on the beach because of a hiccup in Comms
or a barrier on a road. Know what I mean?"

Jones thought for a moment, "Agreed!" He said and got
to his feet. I'll call you with estimated dates, and all that;
meanwhile if there is any problems give me a shout at HQ."

When the pair had taken their departure Peter picked up
his hat and two of the remaining cold beers and stepped out
to see the Colonel.

The Port of Valetta was looking battered in the sunlight.
The three MGB's were tied in parallel alongside the long
quay which was crowded with craft of all sizes. The town
always seemed packed with troops and people, and the
clamour of the cries of the beggars and traders anxious to
relieve the troops of their money.

The gangplank was guarded by sentries who were quick
to challenge anyone approaching the boats.

In the smoky atmosphere of the office located on the
quay the small group of men discussed last minute details of
the proposed foray into enemy territory. The group studying
the chart and sketches strewn on the long table were interrupted by a knock on the door. The RSM Willie Chapman
turned and opened the door, his bulk filling the entry. There
was a short exchange between Willie and the newcomer then
he stepped to one side and admitted two people, a Naval
Commander and a WRNS First Officer. Peter looked up
from the chart and saw the two strangers. The WRNS was
Claire, the Commander was RN.

"Hullo, Claire." Peter said "How have you been?"

"Hullo Peter; I'm well; and you?" She glanced at the
medal ribbon on his tunic, "You've been busy, I see."

Peter saw her glance and shrugged, and said quietly
"Off and on, off and on." He noticed the ring on the third
finger of her left hand. "I see you've been busy too." He observed dryly.

She flushed and the Commander spoke, "We have been sent to observe. The Admiral is interested in the outcome of this operation and since he is in Malta at the moment we were sent to report on how the cooperation between the Services works out."

The sharp Australian tones of Captain Jones cut across the comment, the sarcasm in his voice not lost of the listeners. "At this point we're all doing fine, so if you don't mind standing back and keeping quiet we can finish what we've set out to do."

There was dead silence at this, the Commander who was apparently named Wilson, looked as if he was about to explode.

Colonel Cummings stepped forward and suggested that the Commander and the lady wait while they finished the planning session. He would then take the newcomers to his office and explain what was going on, within the bounds of their security rating of course.

The pair stood back obediently and remained quiet whilst the rest of the details were discussed.

After the session ended Peter collected his charts and left the office with Bill Manning to return to their boats.

Outside the office Claire was waiting, "Can I have a word, Peter?"

Giving the charts to Bill, Peter said "Surely lets walk down the quay we talk on the way."

They walked for a few yards before Claire spoke "I am sorry, Peter, I didn't want things to turn out like this."

Peter said nothing he was upset and realized that he still had lingering hopes that things might work out between them, but her attitude told him clearer than any words that it was all over. He felt angry and relieved at the same time.

"What is happening with you now? I see you are engaged."

"Yes, I see you have a DSO, how did that happen?"

"Oh it was nothing much really we helped get some prisoners out of Bardia, that was all."

"That was you? Well I heard all about the operation but I was not told who was involved." She looked keenly at him "I see you are a Commander now, congratulations."

"I'm only acting." He glanced at the three wavy stripes on the shoulders of his Khaki drill shirt.

"I haven't heard from Paul for a while, do you know how he is?" Claire's voice had the hint of worry in her tone.

"He was fine the last time I heard, he is currently in the forward planning section in Cairo, chafing at being stuck indoors. Look, don't bother about things, I am fine and I have no real problems, I am glad you've found someone and I hope you will be very happy." He turned and they walked back down the quay to his boat." He stopped and turned to her and, tipping up her chin, kissed her chastely on the lips. "Bye, Claire, look after yourself." Turning once more he strode up the gangway without looking back.

The muted mutter of the wing engine of the lead boat reflected back from the walls of the sea cave. The second and third boats hauled in their tow ropes and drew alongside until all three were linked together.

Captain Martin Jones, dressed entirely in black from head to foot, with face streaked with black greasepaint, stood with the tall figure of RSM Willie Chapman, similarly clad, standing beside him checking weapons; in this case German MP40 sub machine guns with several magazines. The others of the raiding party were all appearing and collecting their equipment, and loading it into the rubber dinghies being thrown over the sides of the three gunboats. Peter stood watching the arrangement of the raiders sorting themselves out with practiced efficiency into groups for each boat.

CPO Jim Walters had the MGB's own dinghy ready to collect the raider's boats and return them to the cave until they were needed for the return.

Peter, also in black overalls, climbed down into the lead boat, having decided that he would like to inspect the landing site personally so that the return could be covered properly. In the event of things going wrong he wanted to know just what he could do or not do to make the re-embarkation as swift and safe as possible.

The entire group of boats made their way out of the cave and round to the bay to the north. The men paddled carefully, keeping the noise to a minimum.

One of the paddlers missed a stroke and was quietly told of his noisemaking error by the RSM. The fact that the man would have found the self infliction of the action impossible was not reassuring as the promise of the RSM's assistance if necessary followed immediately, all conveyed in a whisper that could only be heard by those in the immediate vicinity.

Off the beach the party checked and Captain Jones shone a blue light towards the dark mass of the land.

Almost immediately a red light flashed twice, and the entire party moved forward to land.

When the dinghy scrunched onto the gravel of the beach, Peter stepped ashore and, looping the sling of the Sten gun over his shoulder, he made his way up the slope to the broken face of the cliff. The vague figure of the contact on the beach, said "This way" and with a brief flash of shielded light led the way up a rough path to the cliff top. Peter realized that it was a woman leading the party and there was something familiar about the voice that rang a bell in his memory.

The raiding party went straight to the path leading up across the face of the slope and carefully crossed the skyline to disappear into the countryside beyond.

Pater climbed the cliff and encountered the female guide at the top.

"All clear up here?" He asked.

The vaguely familiar voice replied, "It all seems quiet. It's Peter, isn't it?"

"Ah. I recognise you now. Hazel, isn't it?"

"Yes it is, that's not bad considering that we only met for a moment months ago." Her tone was light and it was obvious she was smiling.

Peter was suddenly aware that they were having this conversation on enemy ground in the middle of a dark night. He shook his head and pushed the picture of the bathing-suited figure from his mind. He recalled the details of the raid strategy and started working out times for the third time since landing. "They should be there in ten minutes roughly." He observed.

"Providing there is no problem." Hazel sounded doubtful.

"Is there likely to be?"Peter asked.

"I am not too sure. There is a man I am unhappy with among the Partisans. He seems all right but I have this feeling about him. I'm probably jumping at shadows but I am just not sure."

Peter thought for a moment then turned to Stoker Martin his runner. "Get hold of Lt. Easton and tell him I want ten men from the boats armed with Stens and pistols up her as fast as possible, under the command of the Cox'n." He looked at Martin steadily, "Quietly now!"

David Martin nodded and disappeared down the path, with a slither of gravel, quickly lost in the darkness.

"You are taking a chance." Hazel said quietly.

"I have learned to trust my instincts." Peter replied and they both sat down side by side to await the arrival of the party. Peter felt the woman beside him shiver in the chill of the night. She was wearing a thin coat over a summer dress.

Without thinking he put his arm round her and drew her close sharing the warmth of his body. She started to resist, then snuggled gratefully into the shelter of his arm.

They sat comfortably together without moving or comment until they heard the footsteps coming up the path. Then regretfully Peter stretched and rose to his feet to greet the men from the boats crew. He held his hand out to Hazel who rose in her turn with murmured thanks.

CPO Walters arrived dressed in dark overalls following Martin up the path. Martin was wearing his tin helmet and he had brought Peter's with him.

Peter turned to Hazel "Wait here in case I miss the party in the dark, I'll go direct to the house and spy out the land. If you hear firing. go down to the beach and get aboard one of the boats."

Hazel looked at him for a moment, then took him to one side. "Peter, my place is here at present, I have established my local identity and I have a local address where I am known and accepted. I will come with you and see what is happening. All being well I will return to my house and take up my work without anyone realizing who or what I am, do you understand?"

Peter took in what she was saying then nodded. "Look after yourself. I would like to continue our conversation a later date and I would be most upset to find that I had been the cause of your not being able to."

In the faint light Hazel looked up at him, studying him in the starlight, then she rose up to her toes and kissed him, "Take care, Peter, and I'll look forward to it."

The party set out following the path taken by the raiders.

Hazel led the group quietly along the road until they reached a fork. Here she stopped and turned to Peter "We should scout from here; there should be a lot of noise by now unless things have gone seriously wrong. I suspect they have. So I think we should take a look very carefully and see where the party is."

Peter turned to CPO Walters. "Split the men into two parties, I want a very quiet check up of the road edges both sides. Silent removal is what I have in mind. We think the others have been betrayed and the Germans may have left men to see if there is a follow-up party. So let's take it easy."

Walters turned to the first two men immediately behind him. "You heard the Commander, off you go." The two men turned to the men behind them and passed over their Sten guns and webbing. They separated, armed only with their knives, and each took a different side of the road and disappeared.

"I thought we would be better off letting the experts clear the way sir, it's our two poachers and they are not accustomed to being caught. If they can't find anyone; there is no one to find." He looked at Peter quite determinedly.

Peter looked at him for a moment, then nodded "Good thinking, Chief, I didn't think of that."

The group settled down at each side of the road and waited for the two men to return.

It was over half an hour before the men returned within a few seconds of each other.

The first back was a man named Mathews, who came over to where Peter and Hazel were seated. "Sir. the party are locked in the barn beside the big house." His partner returned at that point. "No watchers on this side sir, but three guards at the barn by the house, and a half track outside with a gunner at the machine gun, who looks half asleep.

The man, Corbett, said "The Captain is inside the house being interrogated by a nasty-looking man in a black leather coat. He is visible through the window, there is a gap in the blinds and I was able to see into the room."

"Chief!" Peter called Walters over. "We haven't time to get more men so we'll have to deal with this ourselves."

The Chief nodded gravely and when Peter drew a sketch of the layout in the dust and using the shaded torch showed the Chief what he wanted to do."

Hazel added her input about the interior of the house and suggested that after they had released the men from the barn, they should be able to rescue the Captain and continue with the mission.

Mathews and Corbett collected their guns and webbing and led off down the edges of the road. The party approached the buildings carefully, Corbett taking off to the side and coming up behind the half track that stood in view beside the front door of the house. There was light coming from the front door that spilled out highlighting the bonnet of the truck.

There was a shadowy movement beside the truck and a thud, the silence. A figure made itself visible on the truck, it was Corbett, he returned to Peter's position and reported. CPO Walters sent one of the gunnery hands to operate the 20mm gun on the half- track.

Walters then took Corbett, Mathews and David Martin to the barn. The three guards had slung weapons, not anticipating problems here. With guns levelled the small party marched straight up to the three men and Martin ordered them in German to put their hands up. Mathews and Corbett went forward and disarmed them. One of the men tried to lift his MP 40 and his hand was round the butt when Corbett punched his knife upwards into his heart. The others hastily discarded their weapons and allowed themselves to be roped and gagged.

Chapter Eleven

The barn was laid out with two rooms in the front and a large room to the rear currently being used as a cell to hold most of the captured party. There was a passage between the front rooms leading to the main room at the rear of the barn that was lit by a single bulb.

The door to the rear room was barred with a drop bar made of metal. There was a small dirty glass panel in the door to allow the interior to be observed. The murmur of voices could be heard speaking from in English from within the locked room.

There was no one visible, though lights were on in both front rooms; the ill fitting doors spilled a shaft from under each door.

CPO Walters waved Peter forward and indicated the doors. Stoker Martin pointed to a labelled panel on the left hand door and nodded.

With his Sten gun ready Peter went to the door and waited Martin turned the knob and thrusting the door open shouted 'Attention'! in German to the men within. Peter stepped through the door, gun up, and faced the two men within, both of whom had leapt to attention in response to Martin's shout.

They started to react then froze as Peter waved the Sten at them. The officer a Waffen SS Obersturmbannfuhrer (Lieutenant Colonel) Manfred Von Triere looked at Peter with cold angry eyes. Martin went behind the pair and frisked them both disarming them, placing two pistols in his shoulder bag. Walters produced cord and tied them both at the wrists and gagged them with their own handkerchiefs. The second man was a civilian with a small swastika badge on his lapel. His leather coat flung across the back of the chair suggested he was probably Gestapo.

David Martin asked if there were guards in the rear room but only received a shrug in reply.

Peter said in English "Don't worry about it we can shoot them if they lie to us, it will be put down to the Partisans anyway."

The Gestapo man spoke in accented English. "There are no guards in the room but you will be captured very quickly. Fhe company of SS will be back shortly with equipment so you might as well give up now."

Peter smiled, "Let's get the others quietly, then we'll clear the house." He turned and left the office and turned down to the rear room door. At his nod Walters lifted the bar and swung the door open. The men inside were sprawled on the floor in various attitudes trying to sleep. When they looked and saw the uniforms they got to their feet excitedly. Mathews came into the room and reported that the men's equipment had been stacked in the second room under guard of an SS Scharfurer. Peter looked at him with the unspoken question; Mathews drew his finger silently across his throat in answer.

The RSM Willie Chapman came over and called the men to attention quietly and reported to Peter. "Skippers in the big house, sir; they took him and the lady about an hour ago."

"Arm the men RSM and join us outside; quietly now. We have a man on the half–track gun. Replace him and send him back to me. We will go and see what's happening in the house. Meanwhile, send out scouts, I'm told that Company will be arriving pronto and I would rather know sooner than later."

The RSM saluted and turned at his order. His men filed out and collected their weapons and equipment from the room next door, ignoring the dead SS man on the floor. Peter called his team together and they assembled outside the front door of the house. Walters sent men to cover the other door at the rear while they went in. Corbett and Mathews disappeared immediately upstairs while the others crept down the hall to the big room at the front of the house. Voices could be heard through the thin panels. At the door Peter knocked, a voice called out impatiently. Peter looked at Martin who nodded and opened the door standing to one side to let the group in, as before he shouted 'Attention!' in German at the top of his voice, startling the occupants of the room. The five people on their feet were standing round the two seated figures. The woman sagged in her seat. head down, obviously unconscious. The man—Peter recognised as Captain Jones—had a bloody face but was awake and aware of what was going on. His cry "Behind the door" caused Walters to slam the door against the figure lifting a gun to fire at the intruders. Martin slammed the butt of his Sten gun into the man's face and he collapsed to the floor unconscious.

The others were quickly disarmed and tied up. All now sat in a row on the floor. The woman had been released from the chair and was now in the care of Hazel who had her carried through to another room where there was a bed so that she could look after her properly.

Corbett and Mathews reported that there were rooms in use upstairs but all were empty.

There were several servants in the kitchen, all local, all under control.

Peter went outside and called the RSM. "Your boss is okay, a bit battered but otherwise alright. Is there any sign of activity about here?"

"So far all quiet. I have men posted at the roadsides in both directions."

"According to the Gestapo the company that captured you will be back shortly, I would like to prepare a proper welcome for them. First, how many were there? Did you get a chance to see?"

"I would estimate about forty. They had two heavy machine guns mounted on their truck. Otherwise all were armed with these." He held up his MP40. "my man found a mortar in the half-track. We can set up as soon as we know where they are coming from."

"Good. By the way, how did they catch you? My impression was that you all knew what you were about."

"Bloody Partisans led us right into an ambush, we had no chance. They stood and laughed and smoked the German's cigarettes while we were being disarmed and pushed around. The woman called them everything and they didn't like it much—one of the clouted her with his rifle butt, knocked her out. The Nazi's were not pleased, they thumped him about and kicked them all out pronto. Don't know where they went but they were pretty pissed when I saw them last."

"Perhaps they forgot their pay." Peter suggested.

Just then Captain Jones appeared. "Hi, Willie y'okay?"

Willie grinned "We're right, Skip, how about you?"

"I'll do." He pointed to Peter "Can we talk?"

In the now cleared room where the interrogation had been conducted the two men sat discussing the situation.

"My problem is that the people who were here are now gone, I was due to lift the electronics expert who lived in this house with his housekeeper and three kids. It seems they were transferred to a place called Lamia about ten miles inland. I would prefer to finish the job if I can."

Peter looked at him in astonishment. "Are you suggesting we stroll into Lamia and collect them? An unknown town with thirty men in Allied uniforms?" He stopped at that point as the idea occurred to him. "Let's sort out the returning company to start with. I have an idea how we could deal with Lauria, providing there are not too many German troops there"

"What have you got in mind?" Jones asked.

"Leave it until we've dealt with the returning company. It will depend on how things go."

"Right. I'll get things organized outside." Captain Jones went off to prepare the ambush of the German company with the RSM.

Peter returned to the house and ordered the uniforms to be stripped from the SS officer, and Sergeant. He took the Gestapo man's black leather coat and trilby hat for himself. German-speaking Martin tried the officer's uniform whilst CPO Walters tried the sergeant's clothes. Minor differences in size were not too noticeable. Peter then ordered that the other uniforms from the captives be used to clothe three other members of his party. The remaining uniforms were bloody and could not be used.

The sound of a laboring truck was heard in the distance, so the men dressed in German uniforms were kept in view although in positions where they could not be easily identified.

The remainder of the men were positioned to surround the returning Germen troops in the shadows around the area in front of the house.

The truck crawled up the last stretch of drive and stopped in front of the porch of the house.

David Martin appeared with his face in shadow as the Sturmbannfuhrer (Major) Hans Keppler stepped down from the truck and clicked his heels and gave the Nazi salute standing rigidly with his right arm out until his salute was returned with a casual wave of Martin's hand. He then swung round and shouted for the men to dismount and watched while they jumped down from the bed of the truck to the ground and formed up in two ranks.

There were twenty-two men in ranks and the Scharfuhrer (Sergeant) called them to attention. The men stood in their ranks with their right hand gripping the sling of their MP40, left hand rigidly at their sides in line with the seam of their trousers.

A whistle blew, and behind the rank of soldiers appeared the party under the RSM whilst from the house Peter and the other men in German uniforms appeared with weapons displayed pointing at the ranks in front of them.

Martin stepped forward into the light and ordered the German party to ground their arms. Such was the discipline of the SS troops they as one bent at the waist and laid their weapons on the ground beside their right boot and rose as one back to attention. The major—realizing that the man in front of him was not his colonel—wrenched at his pistol holster; only to feel the heavy hand of RSM Willie Chapman clamp round his hand removing it from the holster flap. The gun was taken from him and he was led into the house, grim faced, to be questioned. The Scharfuhrer and the other men were marched into the barn and told to strip off.

This allowed the entire party of raiders to be dressed in enemy uniform. In the house the Gestapo man Otto Kraus rank Oberfuhrer (Brigadier) was talking quite freely, certain that the insolent intruders would all be captured quickly. His eyes when he glanced at Hazel made it clear that interrogating her would give him great pleasure.

It seemed that the object of the raid, the electronics engineer and innovator, Professor Michael Di Marco. and his housekeeper and three children had been removed to the local town for safe keeping when the information of the raid was passed on by the traitors in the Partisans.

Within the house, the Germans had set up a radio in one of the bedrooms. Hazel went up and tuned the radio to a frequency from memory. She looked at her watch it was 0100;

the Partisans should be on watch. She keyed a sequence of letters in code, then sent her message in plain language.

The acknowledgement came in one letter A. she switched the radio off and went down stairs.

'She had considered calling Alex and informing them of the situation, but decided against it, preferring to trust the commander on the ground with the decision.

Below in the living room, the location of the Professor and his family having been established, the plan was finally completed. The naval party minus David Martin and Peter would escort Von Triere back to the boats. The remainder of the party including Hazel—who would be dropped off at the edge of town to maintain her cover—would travel to the local town of Lauria to try to collect the Professor and his family.

"According to Kraus, the other men of the company have been left as security for the Professor and his family in a safe house under command of the Obersturmfuhrer (Lieutenant) he has twenty men including the other Scharfuhrer." Captain Jones summed the situation up and looked at Peter.

Peter considered for a moment or two then, "I suggest this is a case for a bold approach. We go to town at 0600 and take over control of the house and the Prof. and his family. Since this arrangement was 'last minute' I would guess there is still no one entirely sure of all the details of the situation."

The discussion was interrupted by the arrival of the Partisans summoned by Hazel. The leader, a small wiry man with greying black hair and a cigarette in the corner of his mouth, looked at the uniforms of the group and said in broken English "I would have shot you all if I had not seen the beautiful Signorina Scorpio with you." He looked warmly at Hazel addressing her by her code name.

"Ciao, Franco, these are friends come to collect the Professor." Hazel smiled and waved at the group. The soldiers are in the other room. We will need the captured soldiers to be kept quiet for two days. Can you do that?"

"No problem, Signorina. I have a place, and if they give trouble." He drew his figure across his throat suggestively.

Two of his men came in and were ordered to collect the soldiers from the other room. Meanwhile the rest of the raiding party sorted through and donned the discarded uniforms of the captured soldiers.

The night seemed to pass all too slowly for Peter. The female agent who was being interrogated was able to leave with the naval group for the shore. Arrangements for a rendezvous in the evening were sent with CPO Walters and his prisoner.

Otto Kraus would be going to town with the disguised raiders. His rank and presence would ensure their safety. To make certain that he stayed in line he was linked to a big Aussie with a handcuff set used in the interrogation room.

The early morning chill was welcome to Peter who was now sitting dressed in the uniform of a private in the Waffen SS. The butt of the MP40 nudged him in the ribs he moved from side to side with the motion of the truck.

The Gestapo man Kraus sat beside him with a big Aussie Mike somebody on the other side of the German.

The truck negotiated the streets into the awakening town nearing the centre where the safe house stood.

The house stood back from the road in its own grounds. The hedge effectively hid the building from the view of the passing traffic. At the gate the sentry leaped to attention and saluted the truck. As they passed through two men dropped off the truck and replaced the astonished man who was bound and gagged before he could protest.

The truck reached the front door of the house and the men climbed off. David Martin, enjoying his role, stepped through the front door as if he was made for the part and he snapped at the Scharfuhrer who leapt to his feet at the sight of the Obersturmbannfuhrer standing in the doorway.

"Call your men together. You are to be relieved. There is activity on the road to Naples. Where is the Obersturmfuhrer?"

The Scharfuhrer stuttered "He is resting, Herr Obersturmbannfuhrer."

"Fetch him now!" The tone was icy and the look combined to send a chill up the spine if the rigid man.

"Well?"

The frozen Scharfuhrer snapped out of his trance and raced off to fetch his officer, shouting for his men to assemble in the lobby forthwith.

On the landing above, the figure of a woman appeared. Peter who had entered the lobby with their Gestapo prisoner looked up to see the blue eyes of Sarah Black looking down at him. Martin looked up at the same time and said in German. Madam, please arrange for the children to be returned to their home. We will be taking the Professor back now we have captured the British spies."

She nodded and hurried off calling softly to someone as she went.

The Scharfuhrer returned and shouted at the assembling troop to form up.

"You can collect the sentry at the gate when you leave." The clipped tones of the Sturmbannfuhrer reassured him. Where are the servants?"

"We do not allow them in until 0700, Sir."

"Good. I will brief them when they arrive." He turned as the Obersturmfuhrer arrived hurriedly adjusting his uniform. "You are?"

The officer straightened his uniform and saluted; "Obersturmfuhrer Baron Eric von Mitterwald Herr Obersturmbannfuhrer."

Martin returned the salute, "Parade your men outside I will inspect them before they leave."

"Jawohl Herr Oable Obersturmbannfuhrer" he saluted once more and called the Scharfuhrer to assemble the men outside.

The entire group of soldiers broke ranks and ran outside to form ranks.

Martin turned to Peter with a lifted eyebrow. Peter nodded and accompanied Martin outside where they marched up and down the ranks inspecting the men.

Then standing back, Martin ordered the parade to place their weapons on the ground. They acted without question placing the guns beside their right feet and standing upright once more. "Scharfuhrer, collect the weapons."

The NCO ran down the ranks collecting the MP40's by their slings and presented himself to the Obersturmbannfuhrer, loaded with nineteen MP40's and the Obersturmfurer's pistol.

One of the raiders ran forward and took the weapons from the overloaded Scharfuhrer, who gave them up grateful to relieved of his burden.

"Right. Lads. bag 'em and bind 'em" called Peter and stood back while the disarmed soldiers were bound and gagged and bundled into the house out of sight.

He retained the frightened Gestapo Oberfuhrer Kraus whom he decided worth taking as a prisoner back to Alex.

Meanwhile the bewildered Professor and his family assembled in the lobby with their luggage.

The loaded truck left the small town without further incident leaving the furious Obersturmfuhrer and his men struggling to release themselves from their bonds.

When the loaded truck drew up outside the Professor's home once more the raiders, the Professor and his family and housekeeper re-entered the house.

The prisoners held by the Partisans had all disappeared in the interim, the barn now empty of bodies and the room used for the interrogation emptied of the furniture, and the bloodstains scrubbed away. The troops occupied the barn; Peter and Captain Jones used the front room of the house as a temporary base. The Professor was told to camp for the day, not to unpack as they had to be prepared to leave that evening.

The rotation of German uniformed sentries was arranged with Martin still in his full regalia on standby to step in if and when needed.

The day stretched out endlessly, the men passing the time playing cards, then behind the barn an impromptu cricket match commenced with rude comments and a lot of banter. When the children appeared they were roped in to play by the men. The noise became so loud that Captain Jones had to intervene to quiet them down.

Unfortunately he was too late to stop the English comment being heard by unfriendly ears. The turmoil already created in the little town of Lauria with the discovery of the bound and gagged SS troops added to the report of the activities at the house created reaction from the German army headquarters.

The Fieseler Storch appeared in the early afternoon, and despite the fact that the men were inside by the time it arrived, there was obviously more than a suspicion of their presence. The little aircraft buzzed about for twenty minutes before departing.

Peter was concerned; the appearance of the aircraft had been unexpected and unwelcome, and the possibility of further action from the occupying forces was worrying. Between them the party only numbered twenty-three men, plus the family. The problem of making the rendezvous that evening in safety was a becoming a real concern.

The half track was in running order and, combined with the truck, they had plenty of transport, plus the extra fire-power of the mounted machine gun but the reaction of the Germans was likely to be overwhelming.

Jones contacted the Partisans. The leaders arrived on a motor bike within twenty minutes. They went into an immediate huddle with the two officers working out how to get round the possible reactions of the Area Commander.

"He is not a front line soldier." The Partisan leader was a grey-haired, vigorous man with a stiff leg—from an injury gained in the other war, as he described it. He was known as Senor Lupo (Mr Wolf). They never discovered his real name. "But he is not a fool" he continued. "One of the reasons he has done well here is that he has not targeted the local people. I believe he was a policeman before he became a soldier." He paused then "I think you should move out immediately, on foot; we will take you to another place that is secure within our area. You will need to contact your pick-up people to collect you further down the coast at Scalia."

Peter looked up from his study of the map of the area. "Scalia is a fishing village. Surely it will be guarded and controlled by the Germans. How can we just stroll in to meet our boats there?"

Senor Lupo looked at Peter and smiled. "In this area there are many Fascisti, they control the fishing and collaborate with the Tedesci, you say Germans; we have been considering their removal for some time. We are now strong enough to do so, with the help of the 'Famiglia' (Mafia).

Peter had been told that the Americans had enlisted the assistance of Lucky Luciano, the Mafioso from the US, to recruit the help of the Italian family against the Fascists and the occupying Germans. He had not realized that the influence of the New Yorker extended this far.

He and Jones conferred and compromised. agreeing to the move. but because of the times and distances involved decided to use the truck for most of the journey. Lupo agreed and admitted they could use the truck themselves afterwards. They also decided to take the half-track, to deny it to the Germans and also to back up the Partisans' efforts to clear out of the Fascisti in Scalia.

Captain Jones was briefed to take and hold the boom across the harbor mouth. This would be vital so that the MGBs could enter and leave the Harbor without delays. With their wooden hulls they would be vulnerable to gunfire from the shore. It would also mean that the lift off would be simple and fast from the quay, the boom link was on the outer arm of the sea wall and it would be possible to pick up Captain Jones and his men on the way out.

Chapter Twelve

It took nearly one complete hour to organize the move and it was nearly three in the afternoon before the two vehicles moved off to the South in the direction of Scalia, ten miles along the coast.

For obvious reasons they could not drive directly into the village and the convoy, led by the motorcycle, ended up driving into a barn in a farmyard on the outskirts of the fishing village.

Peter contacted Alexandria to let them know what was happening and asking them to contact the three MGBs currently in hiding and ask for the pickup in Scalia at ten that night, when darkness would make visibility difficult. Alexandria was able to contact Charlie King through a watching fishing boat lying off the cave where the boats sheltered.

The men changed back into their own uniforms, just in case they were captured. In the early evening they split up into several parties each with a partisan to lead them, then they began the final part of the journey to the boats.

In the Area Headquarters in Lamia, Generalmajor (Major-General) Manfried Schuppe, sat looking at the man standing in front of him. He recalled the last time he had seen the man Obersturmfuhrer Baron Eric von Mitterwald, strutting arrogantly into this office looking down his nose at anyone who was not a member of the SS. He had arrived as part of the unit lead by an Obersturmbannfuhrer whose name he could not recall, charged with special protection for some Professor and the arrest and detention of the growing band of Partisans in the area.

They had refused to have any dealings with the local area command and had billeted themselves and set up their own headquarters in the small town with their own transport and administration.

Now this stuck-up little Prussian idiot was standing in front of him asking for help. He has lost his boss and half the men and wants someone to hold his hand.

"Am I to understand, Obersturmfuhrer, that not only have you lost your Sturmbannfuhrer but also half your men, as well as the Professor and his family who were your re-sponsibility?" He continued; driving home the message causing the man in front of him to squirm with embarrass-ment. "Plus all your transport I understand. How did you get here, by taxi?"

The red-faced Obersturmfuhrer said nothing but looked helplessly at the Generalmajor seated behind the desk in front of him.

Taking pity on him the Generalmajor made his mind up. "I will allocate a company of infantry to your command, perhaps you can arrange to round up these impudent intrud-ers. According to the pilot's report they were still at the pro-fessor's house at midday, though they have probably left by now. It would seem to be a good place to start your search." With a wave of his hand he dismissed the Obersturmfuhrer.

The confusion of collecting the men together and orga-nizing transport died down when the three vehicles departed. The Wehrmacht officers and men were not happy under the command of the SS and they reacted sluggishly to the orders of the impatient Obersturmfuhrer.

The Feldwebel (Colour Sergeant) allocated to the com-mand muttered under his breath that the SS idiot could not organize a shag in a brothel, and proceeded to drag his feet even more.

The convoy made its way to the house occupied by the professor, where they found nothing.

After considerable study of his map von Mitterwald decided that the raiders would make for the coast and ordered the trucks forward once more, now needing the headlights as the evening was well advanced. They made their way towards Scalia, but were halted when the lead truck got a puncture and stopped effectively blocking the roads for the other vehicles. By the time the wheel was changed it was discovered that the other front wheel had also been punctured. The second truck provided its spare wheel as a replacement. They then discovered that the road had been strewn with three-way spikes causing the punctures. This required the deployment of the two men with mine detectors followed by two men with brushes to sweep the vicious spikes from the road wherever found.

The sound of automatic gunfire from up ahead caused the Obersturmfuhrer to leap into action, ordering the men to dismount from the trucks he set off along the road to find out what was happening; and if possible capture the gunmen.

In Scalia the partisans had upset a hornet's nest. Peter hurried his party down to the quay as quickly as possible, Sarah Black who was acting as nanny to the professors kids, bumped into Peter as she slipped on the greasy cobblestones. He caught her and she whispered, "Give me a gun if there are too many for us. I don't waste bullets."

Peter grinned tightly and nodded and they ran on urging the others on to the fisherman's quay. At the far end the Partisan leader Lupo was flashing his torch out to sea.

Everything happened at once, the murmur of engines came from the sea and the shadowy shape of the MGBs ghosted through the entrance to the harbor. Down the hill into the village came the sound of army boots running into the village. Gunfire could be heard from several different points in the village as local scores were settled and Fascisti and Partisan fought it out.

German orders were shouted to the running soldiers who were ordered to halt and take aim and fire at the retreating raiders running toward the end of the quay. Peter shouted to the group to drop flat and as they all tumbled to the ground the volley passed over their heads. Before another volley came their way the stutter of the quadruple Brownings mounted in the turret behind the bridge on the lead MGB started stitching a pattern across the street where the soldiers were taking aim. The fire sent the survivors stumbling into cover as the bullets sang and struck all around them. The machineguns were joined by the Oerlikons; both added their fire to the now bloody mess on the sloping village street. The occupants of the houses had locked their doors and put shutters up to the windows. It did not give the soldiers much chance for shelter.

The boat nosed up to the quay and Peter hurried the civilians onto the decks where they were swiftly taken below by the waiting sailors.

Lupo turned to Peter "Leave us to clear up here; now that the soldiers are stopped we will manage by ourselves." He held out his hand and took Peter's. "Come back soon, we will be waiting." He released Peter's hand and loped off down the quay, slipping the gun from his shoulder.

The crowded boat left the quay wall and backed off shore before it swung round to head out of the small harbor. The number two boat had already picked up Captain Jones and his men from the sea wall where the boom equipment had been smashed; the net now lying on the bottom of the sea, and sections of the boom itself were now floating on the seaward side, the punctured pontoons used sinking rapidly to the bottom.

The boats gathered and sorted out the passengers between them. Peter had a chance to speak to Sarah and reassure her that Hazel was alright as far as he knew.

In Lauria; Generalmajor Manfried Schuppe listened to the report of the Feldwebel Weber standing before him. There was a bloodstained bandage around the Feldwebel's wrist, and he was dirty and sweat-stained. He was also tired out.

At the end of the recital the Generalmajor sat back and waved the man to a seat. "Tell me, Weber, what happened to Obersturmfuhrer von Mitterwald?"

"Regretfully sir he was killed in the firing from the Schnellboot that picked up the raiding party." Weber's face was sad as he mentioned this, but then he was a good actor. He failed to mention that when the first hail of machine gun fire swept over the men—killing seven—von Mitterwald had been cowering on the ground in a blue funk. He had then screamed at Weber to get the men down to the quay and arrest the escaping people. Weber told him to fuck off, and von Mitterwald had been furious promising to court martial the whole company; so Weber shot him. He had then withdrawn the surviving men, bringing the wounded and dead with them.

The truck party had caught up with them, at least to the top of the hill and the party had been loaded on and carried back to Lauria to lick their wounds.

Schuppe looked keenly at the man sitting across the desk. "How many men did you lose?"

Weber thought for a moment "I lost seven killed and four wounded two badly."

"Plus the Obersturmfuhrer, I presume."

Weber nodded "I believe he was inexperienced in the soldiering sir."

"Quite Feldwebel quite." He was already thinking of what he would write in his report when he dismissed the Feldwebel. After thinking for a few minutes he picked up the telephone on his desk, and ordered the operator to contact him with the naval base in Naples. He was connected to the operations officer Korvettenkapitan Wassermann.

"This is Generalmajor Schuppe from Lauria, we have I am told, three Englisher Schnellboot on the way to North Africa from Scalia carrying wanted people from here. They have raided the area and are now escaping and I have no boats that could catch them or stop them even if we could find them. Is there anything you can do for me?"

In peacetime Schuppe had been a police officer, he had risen to the rank of Commissioner through talent and hard work. He was respected within his profession, and had over the years learnt to be tolerant and humane. His arrival in this area of Italy was orchestrated as support to the local administration. He had assumed command in the area when Italy started showing signs of wavering in its adherence to the Axis cause.

One of his major problems had been the arrogance of the Nazi members of the staff around him who failed to realise that more can be gained with honey than with clubs.

The Korvettenkapitan demonstrated his efficiency in the reply he made. "Sir, we have three Italian seaplanes here that may be able to locate them, but I have no boats. I will have to contact Messina to see if they have anyone to spare. Please excuse me, Herr Generalmajor' I will call back if my aircraft find the boats."

With a sigh of relief that he had found a professional and not one of these amateur idiots the Generalmajor sat back to wait.

In the lead boat the passengers were all trying to sleep below in the wardroom and the crew mess, the crew were on watch. The occasional squeak of the mounting of the twin Oerlikon as it was rotated reminded Peter that they still had a long way to go in dangerous waters.

They were due to rendezvous with two of the island schooners, operated by the SBS this evening. Both were carrying fuel bladders for the MGBs and since they were coming independently from different directions it was hoped that if one were lost the other would make the rendezvous.

The distant hum of an aero-engine came from the north east. Bad news at any time it was especially unwelcome now. There was not sufficient fuel in the boats to race around at full speed and evading air attack could be tricky. Peter ordered the alteration of course to starboard away from the sound of the approaching aircraft. Unfortunately almost immediately the sound of another aircraft was picked up ahead in the new direction. Peter altered course back to their original heading hoping that the aircraft would pass them without spotting them.

The port lookout reported the aircraft in sight, a seaplane, the biplane with the big underslung float was immediately recognisable as the RO.43 reconnaissance aircraft, the Italian markings showed up clearly against the pale paintwork of the tail. Peter ordered the boats to stop so that there was no white wake to show up against the choppy grey sea.

The three boats rocked uneasily in the water as the plane droned past on its way. The sigh of relief from 'Emmy' Easton was heard throughout the bridge.

Peter commented "Don't clap too soon, the planes will probably be coming back soon."

Easton's face fell as he realized the truth of that comment, and it was not long before they heard the sound of the aero-engine once more, nearer this time.

Once more the boats stopped and they lay uneasily rocking in the water while the seaplane droned across the grey sky, the two crew members were visible through the glass canopy. The aircraft did not deviate from its course as it passed out of sight once more, this time to the north-east.

The boats set off once more though Peter altered their course to the west towards the track of the RO43. He also chanced increasing speed to get beyond the range of the plane that he guessed came from Naples.

The answer to the question about whether they had been seen or not came swiftly after the disappearance of the seaplane. Over the horizon almost at sea level two RO43's appeared roaring towards the position the boats had occupied earlier. They altered course to allow for the change of position of the trio. The move had made just enough difference to allow the trio to split up and prepare for the attack that was coming. Peter thought that the planes with their armament consisting of two machine guns each may well have assumed that the MGBs were actually torpedo boats, and not realized that the gunboats were much heavier armed. The deployed boats now turned to bring their foredeck gun to bear, the 2pdr Pompom mounted there was a powerful weapon for surface or AA, The twin .5 machine guns in the power turrets either side of the bridge plus the extra two twin .303guns mounted on the bridge could put up a fearsome barrage. Added to fire from the twin 20mm Oerlikons behind the bridge passing of the MGB could be a painful process.

The planes came swiftly toward the three waiting boats, all poised to open throttles and turn out of the line of fire. Both aircraft opened fire with their machineguns and one started to climb Peter presumed, to drop a bomb. The fire was short, the range too long for the 7.7mm guns on the aircraft. All three boats opened fire—the tracer shells from the Pompom seeking out the climbing aircraft, leading it and finally shattering the propeller and engine, tracing a pattern of damage the full length of the fuselage. It blew up = the fuel causing the bomb to detonate. The pieces of the RO43 fluttered down over a wide area of sea.

The second aircraft made it past the boats inflicting slight damage on Charlie King's deck and wounding the starboard turret machine gunner. Then—when it seemed it had escaped without damage—the twin Oerlikons from the behind the bridge picked him up from nearly vertically overhead and tracked him down into the sea. The seaplane managed to put down after a fashion on its centre float but the starboard wing mounted float was gone and the wing dropped and the plane spun round in the water and began to sink.

Peter's boat reached the wrecked aircraft first and they rescued the pilot and his observer. Neither had been wounded, though the observer had sprained his knee in the landing.

The boats continued their journey to the rendezvous meeting first one then the other schooners during the evening as arranged.

The replenished MGBs recommenced their long voyage before midnight; the refuelling had taken place off the island of Levanzo, located at the west end of the island of Sicily. With full fuel tanks and 120 miles to go they could afford to speed up for the rest of journey.

Sarah came up to the bridge as they left the schooners behind; she looked at Peter "Will it be all clear now to Tunis?"

Peter hesitated for a moment thinking about what he would tell her. Then it occurred to him that this was a woman who had been risking death and torture for months behind enemy lines, so he told the truth. "We could be clear, but I believe the aircraft would have got a message away about our location back to their base. If they did we could have problems. My guess would be an ambush not too far from the island of Marettimo" he pointed to the loom of land up ahead. "At least that is what I would do."

"I wondered why you had ordered the other boats to spread out to the right like that. Is that to give them room to manoeuvre?"

"Actually yes; it's always a toss-up in case like this. Together we have more concentrated firepower – apart we have freedom of action and can react to whatever they try to throw at us. Like all action in war it's guesswork and the best commanders guess right. I just hope I have tonight."

Sarah gripped his arm and rested briefly leaning against him, "You like Hazel, don't you?"

He looked down at the woman beside him "Was it that obvious?"

"It's something that you tend to know, especially when friends are involved." She spoke quietly. "We are friends, like brother and sister. You look at Hazel in a different way, that's all. I envy you both but I am also happy for you." She squeezed his arm and left him standing there in the darkness, alone with his thoughts.

The brief flash of white

in the wrong place gave it away. Charlie King spoke quietly on the RT to the other boats warning them that the enemy were out and in the area. The three boats slowed down to a crawl, the movements causing hardly a ripple in the water. With the engines shut right down they could hear the thrum-thrum of the diesels of the enemy craft. It was possible to locate them by the noise. The Chief was on the wheel and Peter turned to him "What do you reckon, Chief; three or four?"

"Sounds like three to me sir."

"Well let's go and find out, shall we?" he called below. "All you've got, Chief."

"Full speed, Skipper," the Welsh voice came up the pipe as the engines roared, driving the stern down as the boat rose onto the plane and built up to top speed at 31 knots.

The bow waves of the other boats appeared as if by magic against the dark water. The diesel boats also became more obvious building up speed, but all three of the British craft were already in action, all guns blazing.

There were three of the big E boats all powering up, with tracer smashing into the upperworks, their own guns answering the fire from three directions. The German boats were all together and for the British boats firing from the beam, shots over the nearest craft were striking the other craft running abreast of them. The Pompom on Peter's boat concentrated on the lower hull of the near E boat which suddenly stopped in the water as the concentration of fire penetrated the engine room turning it into a charnel house as the shells penetrated the metal hull hit and shattered machinery filling the room with flying shrapnel killing the engine room crew instantly. The diesels died and the boat was dead in the water. Power to her guns was cut off and only the light machine guns were now operating.

The three boats turned on the two surviving German craft concentrating their fire on the bridge of the two surviving craft. The centre E boat with shattered wheelhouse veered off to port causing the other boat to veer also; both continued the turn and headed back toward the third craft bobbing helplessly astern of the action. Peter signalled his craft to break off the action and resume the mean course to Malta.

Chapter Thirteen

The Professor and his children were bundled off to board a flight to Britain. Sarah stayed with the MGBs for the trip back to Alexandria.

Back at base the Colonel appeared to be heavily involved with details of an operation to backstop the small islands in the Aegean Sea, whilst the Major had disappeared somewhere mysterious up country.

At a loose end Peter tried to contact his brother John, who was attached to the LRDG, but his friend Captain Jones was only able to tell him he had been sent on detachment. No further information.

Aaron Black called and invited him to take a few days leave at the beach house, and finally that's what Peter decided to do. As he handed over command to Bill Hamilton, leaving the villa as his address, he observed "I doubt if anything will be happening for the next few days, in fact for the next few weeks. Action has shifted from this area and I would not be surprised to get orders to move on. If anything does come up let me know."

Bill nodded "Don't worry. I prefer to let someone else carry the canm thank you very much. I'll see you in a seven days time, and don't get too much sun."

With a cheerful wave, he watched the car disappear in a cloud of dust. He sighed with relief; Peter had been in continuous service for the past thirty months and the strain was beginning to show. A few days and nights in the company of that gorgeous blonde would do him good.

He turned and entered the dusty office and contemplated the paper on the desk. "Sod it, I'm off for a drink."

At the villa there were only the servants to greet Peter when he arrived. He was greeted by the Major-domo who ushered him to his room and ran a bath for him. When Peter dried off, he found shirt and shorts laid out on the bed with a pair of sandals to slip onto his feet.

Down the stairs the table was laid on the veranda overlooking the sea, the sunshade adjusted to keep things comfortable and a jug of iced tea and glasses set out.

He collapsed gratefully into the chair and for the first time for weeks started to relax. Lunch consisting of cold chicken and salad followed by fresh fruit with a water ice helped the process.

Through the long afternoon he dozed and did not notice the small services he was given. The adjustment of the sunshade, the replenishment of the tea jug, always there when he reached out in his waking periods.

At dusk he enjoyed a Whiskey and Soda before going up to his room to change into slacks for dinner.

When he came down, he found to his surprise that the table was laid for two. He was unaware of anyone arriving since his own arrival, perhaps while he was sleeping during the day.

He shrugged, mildly annoyed that this peaceful period was being interrupted, and lifted the bottle of champagne from the ice bucket and commenced opening it.

The ceremony accomplished he heard a quiet step behind him and said "May I pour you some champagne?" He half turned as he spoke.

"You certainly can." The familiar voice nearly caused him to drop the bottle, and he turn round fully to see the figure of Hazel Worral standing hesitantly dressed in a simple linen dress.

Recovering himself Peter poured the champagne and turned to her with a glass in each hand,

Instead of giving her a glass he stepped close to her and put his arms round her, drawing her close and kissed her firmly on the lips. He let go, stood back, and said "I've been dying to do that since we first met. He held up the glasses still full and presented her with hers."

Hazel said nothing, just looked at him with steady eyes. "My name is not Hazel Worral." She said. "It's Caroline Cartwright either Cissy or Carrie, either will do between us. My husband was Captain Robert Cartwright of Spennymoor, somewhere in Yorkshire I believe, I never knew quite where." She was gabbling on and didn't know why; all she knew was that she did not want the moment to pass.

Peter put down his glass and took hers from her hand placing it on the table beside his. He put his finger to her lips to stop her speaking drew her to him once more and kissed her again. She slid her arms round his neck and returned his kiss hungrily. They stayed locked together for what seemed ages, before a quiet voice outside the room announced "Dinner is served."

The spell broken for the moment they parted, but Peter took her hand and they walked together to the dinner table where the Major-domo, seated them brought their drinks to the table and served dinner.

If asked Peter could not have recalled what they ate, being here with Hazel/Carrie was enough. When they moved back to the Veranda to share the second bottle of champagne they talked quietly together.

Peter discovered that Carrie was in fact Grafin Caroline von Witzenburg, daughter of the Graf Anton von Witzenburg, an Austrian Count from a line extending back to Charlemagne.

She had been in England improving her language skills when Hitler marched into Austria. Her father had ordered that she remained in England and he would join her there. The family estate in Wiltshire would become their home until the interloper had been evicted, was the way he put it. He had been arrested at the Swiss Border; he was tried and executed within two days as an example to other Austrian aristocrats.

The Wiltshire house had been turned into a rest home for officers returning from Dunkerque

Robert was there briefly, to recover from an injury received on the beach. When it healed properly he returned to duty at Salisbury training his new company of Engineers. They had continued the friendship begun at the house and she visited Salisbury several times. He was under orders to go to the far-east, one thing led to another and they got married with a special licence. He was sent to Southampton to embark on a troopship to Ceylon. She was quiet for a moment then "He was killed on the dock at Southampton in a bombing raid, Robert and most of his company. The Colour Sergeant came and saw me to let me know personally, Robert was popular with his men. It's odd; at the time I felt nothing but later it sank in and I felt guilty. I suppose I realized that whilst I liked Robert I had been swept up in the fervour of the time, in love with the idea rather than the man." She had looked at Peter "I know now what I didn't know then, what I felt then was not what I feel now."

Peter leaned across and took her hand in both of his. "I know what you are feeling; I felt it the moment I looked at you that first time in this house. I didn't recognise it at the time and it wasn't until I saw you in Italy that I knew. I thought you felt the same way, but I could not be certain. When you walked in today, it all became clear. No more doubts, fears or worries nothing, just you and me together from here on."

"Oh yes, yes." Carrie gripped his hands fiercely.

The week passed too quickly for them both, they swam together and dined under the stars and when Sarah appeared on the fifth day she joined them in their happiness, taking pleasure in their joy.

Peter returned to the base at Alex to discover that everything had changed. He had been promoted to Substantive Commander awarded a bar to his DSO for his action in Italy and posted to Command an MGB Flotilla operating from Harwich on the East-Coast of England.

He had two weeks to sort out his affairs and hand over to Bill Hamilton, who—to his disgust—fad been given the flotilla at Alex, with as he put it 'bugger all to do' whilst the war went on without him. Charlie King had been hiked up to Lieutenant Commander as 2i/c.

It took two days to find Carrie to let her know what was happening, only to discover when he did find her that she was packing to leave herself having been posted to London HQ of SOE for special duty. They had no time to meet before she was due to go and both were desperately unhappy saying goodbye over the telephone, with the irate operator making rude remarks about using official line for their private affairs.

England was raining there was no other way to put it as far as Peter was concerned; winter and spring had melted into one and the rain was just there to see that no one had a chance to interfere with the arrangement.

Peter got off the train in Harwich railway station and lugged his bag towards the barrier. There—having proved he was a serving member of His Majesty's Royal Navy--he was able to call for a cab.

"No cabs ere sir." The voice came from the Petty Officer with the armband declaring him to be albeit temporarily on watch for unruly naval personnel. "Need a lift to the Base, sir?"

"I could do with one, PO; this is my first time in Harwich."

"If I might suggest a cup of tea, sir," he indicated a tea stall on the station forecourt. "In five minutes a vehicle will be here to collect me and return me to the base."

"Thanks, PO, much appreciated; tea it is." Peter went off to the stall leaving his bag with the PO.

He had been home to see his parents at Christchurch. The few days spent there had been mostly hard work in the yard, but he had enjoyed the feel of tools once more and the smell of timber and resin. His mother was looking tired and she was worried about his father overdoing things. She pointed out he was not getting any younger and by now he would have been retired in normal circumstances.

Peter had new uniforms; his old ones had succumbed to wear and tear and the hot climate of Egypt. The three new gold wavy rings on his sleeves felt oddly permanent, the ribbons of his African service and his DSC and bar occupied their place on his best uniform jacket. The hat felt odd with the scrambled egg on the peak, but he would get used to it he had no doubt.

The trip to the Docks took a little time, the gate security insisted on examining all passes and warrants despite the fact that he knew the PO personally. As they drove through the docks Peter was surprised to see so many craft packed in, some under repair. Out in the clear water the row of MTBs and MGBs nodded at their moorings, they looked spick and span compared with the tired look of his flotilla in Alex; but then they were not being continuously bombarded with the sand that eroded the paint almost before it had time to dry.

The truck finally drew up beside the gangway to the Depot ship allocated to the submarine and coastal forces flotillas. When Peter got out of the cab the sentry leaped to attention and called to a colleague on deck to come and take Peter's bag.

When the man clattered down the gangway Peter was able to board the former cruise liner where he saluted the duty officer and the ensign reporting his arrival formally.

The duty officer escorted him to his cabin and informed him that the Captain would expect him in his office in 30 minutes. Peter nodded and thanked the Lieutenant, and started to tidy himself up.

Unaware of the name of his new commanding officer Peter's heart sank when he reached the Captains door. The sign read Captain Michael Hawthorne. DSO. RN. O i/c Coastal Forces. Knock and enter.

Peter knocked and entered the cabin stepping forward and stopping in front of the desk,

"Commander Peter Murray reporting for duty as ordered sir."

Captain Hawthorne looked up from his desk and studied the man standing before him. Then he sat back in his chair and said "You've moved up in the world since we last met. Commander now, two DSC's you have been busy." The familiar sardonic voice was as he remembered it. "Well we still do things the navy way here, and I expect you to carry out my orders to the letter. You are the most senior Commander in the flotilla and will of course be in overall command of both MTBs and MGBs, there are two acting Commanders at present but you are expected to take control of the MGBs directly. Cummings has only been with us for two weeks so there should be no conflict with you taking over, he will be your number two on the MGBs. I do go out occasionally with the MTBs and I will continue to do so; understood?"

"Of course sir" I will command the MGBs, very good sir, will that be all sir?"

"Yes, carry on, Commander."

Peter about turned and strode out of the office thinking that there would be tears before bedtime with Captain Hawthorne in charge.

In the wardroom several officers were sitting about reading the papers. others with drinks in their hands and three were playing snooker on the table at the far end of the room. He put his hat in the rack provided and strolled over to the bar where several men were concentrating on a set of poker dice. He looked round the group, "Are there any real sailors here?" He asked innocently.

There was a deathly silence at this question then the entire group turned on Peter with evil intention. Spotting the three wavy gold rings stopped the men in their tracks. Peter stood there waiting as the group shuffled their feet and tried to decide what the question meant.

Peter took mercy on them "Real sailors would not let a lonely survivor die of thirst, not even a bunch of layabout amateurs; at least not in my watch."

The barman produced a pink gin which he presented to Peter. "I take it this is on the account of these gentlemen."

"As you say sir, and welcome to the wardroom."

"Thank you, Wallace. I wondered where you would end up. Enjoying it here?" Peter recognised his former servant from Portsmouth.

"I would be happier working back with you sir, if it could be arranged." It was apparent that Wallace meant what he said.

Thoughtfully Peter turned back to the group of officers in front of him. "Would you like to introduce yourselves, I am Peter Murray."

The big Lieutenant at the rear of the group pushed forward, "I'm Roberts, sir. I served with you in Weymouth."

"Ah a familiar face. Michael, is it not?" His eyes moved over the group of men, stopped at another familiar face. "Hodges, Midshipman Hodges?"

"Yes sir I'm number three on your boat."

Peter shook the hand of the Midshipman who had left his command as an AB. in Alex thirteen months ago to attend Officer Training in Brighton, "How is your young lady these days?"

"Hillary is fine sir; we are getting engaged when I take off the tabs." He referred to the white patches on his uniform collar; they would be replaced by the thin gold ring worn by Sub Lieutenants when he finished his qualifying period as Midshipman.

The other officers introduced themselves one by one and Peter had his first real chance to start to assess the men under his command. Lieutenant Commander Tony Cummings RNR came in shortly before dinner and introduced himself to his new Skipper, and like most of the knowledgeable officers present took note of the ribbon and bar of the two DSCs. Like the others he realized the youthful looking Commander Murray probably knew what he was about.

After dinner that evening he called Tony Cummings to show him the Flotilla offices, and spent the next two hours trying to make sense of the system initiated by Captain Hawthorne.

The following day Peter went off early to inspect his new command. The row of boats nodded to the wash of a departing destroyer, on the workboat going out to the MGBs he could now see quite clearly the two submarines tied up side by side to the pontoon alongside the Depot ship. From the water he could now appreciate the lines of the ex-cruise liner, the name still faintly visible through the layers of Battleship Grey paint '*Western Star.*' At his boat he noticed that, though it was a Fairmile D., the Forward deck gun was a single 2 pounder Pompom in a power turret, a twin Oerlikon aft of the bridge and a Holman Projector. No forward Oerlikons and the boat was fitted to discharge torpedoes if carried. The cooking was by electric power no longer paraffin, though despite being fitted for shore link-up, being moored offshore the stove could only be used when the engine was running. Hodges took him round the boat showing her off to her new Captain. The Cox'n and the Motor man were both acting until the men posted to these positions arrive later in the day. Both men had been transferred to Captain Hawthorn's MTB, as soon as the replacements were signalled.

Chapter Fourteen

The crew members on the boat were already at work when Peter boarded that morning and he made sure that he got to know them all. He had spoken to the Wardroom secretary last night about transferring Wallace back to his boat. There was no problem and Wallace was even now handing over the bar inventory to his successor. The 6000 boat was new and in good condition, the engines much better baffled and insulation more effective, allowing quieter running than his old boat. The quarters for his 12-man crew were roomy and judging from the comment of the men they would have preferred to stay aboard rather than in quarters on the Depot ship. Peter made a note to enquire into it as soon as possible.

When the new Chief Petty Officer and the Chief PO Engineer arrived, Peter was strangely not surprised that they were Jim Walters and Ifor Williams. When they reported on board the Chief commented that they were both surprised that they had been transferred to Peter's boat. Jim Walters explained to Peter when they discovered where they were going they presumed that someone had arranged things so that they could keep an eye on the Commander and see that nothing happened to him. This was said with a completely straight face.

Peter's comment was short and pungent and fell upon deaf innocent ears.

The 6000 boat crept off the mooring on the wing engine; it made its way out through the harbor boom passing the harbor service launch on the way in. The North Sea outside was choppy without being particularly rough. The boat rose and fell and then as the throttles opened the boat rose onto the plane and started to really move through the water.

The spray rose and was thrown over the screen spattering the men on the armored bridge. RT squawked and the voice of Captain Hawthorn came over slightly distorted. The acid in the voice scarcely concealed

"Since you are already outside the harbor, there is a report of an aircraft down." He gave the position; "Take a look while you are out' it will give you a chance to settle in with your crew." The RT snapped off with a click. Peter looked at the Mike in his hand ruefully.

"Alter to Starboard. steer 125 degrees."

"25 degrees of starboard wheel, sir" the helmsman repeated as the boat heeled round in an arc to the right and the throttles were opened wide. The white wake widened and spread as the speed increased.

As the search area approached the speed dropped and the lookouts were doubled. It was not long before the yellow dinghy came into view, beside the semi-submerged hull of a Walrus seaplane.

As they approached it was clear that the survivors were all uninjured and as soon as they were brought inboard, the wreck was sunk, its remaining buoyancy tanks punctured. The pilot of the Walrus could not wait to tell them that they had spotted a Hipper Class German heavy Cruiser racing along the Dutch coast.

They had time to report by wireless the position of the Cruiser before the Arado seaplane carried by the ship found them and chased them, finally hitting the engine of the Walrus and causing them to land with the top wing ablaze and a dead engine. The Arado left as soon as they hit the water. As the pilot finished his story a shout from the lookout directed their eyes skywards to the aircraft approaching from the West. Twelve Swordfish biplanes all armed with torpedoes hanging between the stick like undercarriages.

"It looks as if your signal got through." Peter commented as the men on deck waved the aircraft on.

By the time the boat reached Harwich with the survivors, the sound of aircraft was heard once more. Five only of the twelve returned the fifth being escorted by the others as it trailed smoke from some damage received from the raid.

They heard later that the Cruiser had not been hit. The squadron of Swordfish had been attacked by the Arado seaplane; he shot down three. Of the others three were hit by flak. All remaining torpedoes were launched; three struck the bottom and exploded prematurely. One was launched at too low level, and its motor failed to start. The other two despite being launched and running properly were avoided by the cruiser's swift manoeuvring. Another Swordfish was lost when its engine stopped as it passed over the cruiser and it crashed into one of the sand dunes on the Dutch shore. There were no survivors. The smoke trail on the final casualty was caused by the oil leaking and dropping onto the hot exhaust. The aircraft and the crew survived.

The days passed and over the next two weeks and Peter got to know his new flotilla. Relations with Captain Hawthorn did not improve during this time, the Captain's arrogance and lack of understanding of the temporary officers under his command caused friction that Peter did his best to deflect from his crews, but he not always successful.

The flotillas record was not the best up until now and determined to improve matters Peter discussed the problem with Commander Harris RN, a contemporary of Captain Hawthorn but a much more relaxed individual, who had been recalled for duty having been axed during the 1930s as part of the reduction in personnel that decimated the Royal Navy. Having worked outside the establishment for some years Commander Ronald Harris had a far better idea how to handle people in general; he was regarded with affection by the officers of the flotilla and a source of irritation to the Captain.

Without so many words Peter and Ronny had worked out a system of circumventing the Captain whenever possible. As the end of the year approached, an opportunity for a raid to cover a landing for SOE in Holland, came up. The Captain had been summoned to the Admiralty for a conference; his return was not forecast for at least seven days.

One of the biggest conflicts between the Captain and Peter had been the Captain's insistence on due notice for operations, and his continual interference with Peter's planning in urgent situations had caused two near disasters.

With Commander Ronny in charge Peter had a free hand to arrange matters and he organized a combined operation using both MTBs and MGBs staging two diversionary raids. Fortuitously an enemy convoy could be targeted at the time; and a raid, a shore incursion by a Commando unit contemplating an excursion to the Dutch coast to sort out a radar repeater station recently established there.

The SOE group were due to land at Zandvoort, involving four people in two separate operations. Peter had decided to use his 6000 boat for the landing and had arranged for a squad of five Commandos to land first to clear the ground as the SOE group would not be met on this occasion.

All the boat Skippers and their Number Ones were assembled in the briefing room for the initial schedule to be produced. Commander Harris had the stage and was busy pointing out the salient points off the Dutch coast especially the new mine fields that had be laid three nights ago.

"Remember the Ramsgate boys were busy earlier this week and the new areas covered are here, here and here." He tapped three purple patches on the big wall map. "All the other features are as before; updates will be notified by tonight's final brief.

"All questions about the operation to Commander Murray." He stepped down from the stage leaving Peter and Captain Van Doorn, RM Commando to carry on. Peter rose next and detailed the various tasks of the flotilla. Acting Commander James RNR who commanded the MTB flotilla was assigned to task of dealing with the convoy. He turned to Bill James "You will take two of the MGBs to help out with the escorts. Lt Commander Cummings with two MGBs you will take and land the commando party under Captain Van Doorn. I will take my MGB 6000 and 5989 commanded by Lieutenant Roberts to make the SOE landing and pickup at Zandvoort.

As soon as our landing is complete and clear—if time allows—we will rendezvous with Commander James for the return trip. I stress that at the rendezvous point you do not wait longer than one hour. I expect you to be back here by 0800." He turned to Captain Van Doorn, "I will leave you with Commander James, I will liaise with Lieutenant Depp directly he arrives."

With that Peter left the briefing room following the others leaving Bill James and his Number One, with the Dutch Commando to organise his landing.

The SOE party arrived at 1400 hours, the small Morris van with the five commandos following the Wolseley Saloon onto the quay. They were ushered directly onto the 6000 boat which was moored alongside the pontoon now located by the quay for the purpose of easy boarding.

Commander Harris had arranged for the pontoons with the connivance of the Captain of the Depot ship. It meant that the MGBs that were fitted for it, could be linked to the electricity and water supply and the crews could live aboard. This did leave extra room available in the Depot ship accommodation. The older boats using the 24volt system already accommodated their crews; the newer boats like Peter's 6000 series were fitted for the shore connection with the 220 volt system. It allowed Peter and the crew to live aboard, a much more acceptable alternative to the Depot ship accommodation.

Peter anticipated trouble when Captain Hawthorn returned, as did Ronny Harris, but—as he pointed out—it was task of the First Lieutenant to take the humdrum detail off the shoulders of his Captain whom he had confided to Peter on one occasion from within his seventh gin, "Was still the little shit he had been when I first knew him as a Snotty on HMS Marlborough."

The small group from the car boarded the boat without fuss. The woman took off her shoes as she stepped down to the deck and entered the cabin on stockinged feet. All four went into the wardroom and seated themselves without being told. The officer in charge of the Commandos ordered his men into the crew's mess and came into the wardroom to join the others. Peter stepped over the coaming into the wardroom to greet the passengers.

He saw the stockinged feet of the woman first and with a start he recognised Claire Waterstone. He looked around at the others, no one he knew so he introduced himself, then turning to Claire last he said "Hullo, Claire/ booked for the cruise, I see?"

Claire smiled and said lightly, "Well, you did say that when the chance offered I would be welcome; so here I am."

The Lieutenant in the army battledress uniform came aboard and saluted, "Lieutenant Depp Royal Netherlands Navy reporting sir."

He was followed by five Commandos led by a Sergeant, The five soldiers disappeared below.

Depp grinned, "My personal pirates." He said. "We will do the initial survey of the landing site."

Peter led them below "Maps of the landing area have been issued to you, I understand, but for my benefit I would just like to go over the arrangements one more time."

Peter laid out the chart of the Dutch coastline and pointed to Zandvoort.

"The beach here runs all along the front below the new racing circuit, it has been mined and wired but we do have a way through marked out for us by the visitors who did a recce last week. They were not spotted; they did nothing but peg out a route and check out the fortifications. It seems that the Huns are depending on their minefield for their main protection at the moment.

"In the meantime I understand that we have someone to collect on the second beach here." He indicated the southern stretch of beach beyond the racing circuit where the coarse scrubland came down to the beach, there was no seawall as such but the moorland rose to a higher level and the beach did not appear to get the scouring effect noticeable on the northern section.

"I propose having the pickup carried out by the second boat that will be travelling with us while the troops do their recce of the landing site. Then I will land the SOE party, pick up the troops and depart for points west; any questions?"

The three men were sitting in a row on the starboard bench. The older man took an empty pipe from his mouth and spoke. "I am John, at least for the present anyway." The others chuckled.

"Why can we not land with the soldiers, it would save valuable time for you while you are close in to the beach and be less dangerous for you."

"I have been informed that there has been a mass roundup of SOE personnel in Holland recently. We have no way of knowing how much the enemy know of our movements. When we collect the agent from the south beach we will know more but until that time we take no chances. The troops go first and check the area out then we send you ashore when we know it's clear." There was no question of argument; Peter's tone said it all.

"I see" said John. "Well, I think I'll get some sleep." He turned to the other men as he said this. He ignored Claire and put his pipe away and moved along the bench and lay down.

Peter returned to the bridge and gave orders to cast off. He called across to Mike Roberts in the 5890 boat to follow him out.

As they left the boom behind Claire appeared. "Have I permission to come up to the bridge?"

"Of course, you're welcome." He took over the wheel "Cox'n find the lady a duffle. I'll take the wheel."

Walters returned "Here we arem Miss." He passed over a duffle and a scarf to Claire. She put them on gratefully. "Thank you, Cox'n."

Jim Walters resumed his place at the wheel, grinned to himself as he thought, *The boss kept that one out of sight, though now I think of it, she had been in Alex hadn't she?.*

Peter looked at his watch. "Four hours to landfall, it will be dark in three hours." He called for cruising speed of 25 knots, which was enough to cause the boat to bounce a little, sufficient Peter thought, to make sleeping on the bench in the wardroom difficult.

"So what's up with the three wise men below?" He asked.

Claire liked up at him "You noticed?"

"How could I miss it?" Peter replied. "You didn't exist as far as 'John' was concerned and neither of the others took any notice of you. Bluntly speaking that is not the normal reaction of red-blooded men."

"Why, thank you kind sir. In fact I am not the flavour of the month with them. The operation was planned before the German mopping up commenced. As a result every agent who returned around the time of the operation was suspect.

"I was detailed for this job at the last minute, I speak Dutch and I am cleared to a high level now. My job is to keep an eye on things and I have the authority to abort the job if I am unhappy about anything, before we lose any more agents."

"I see, I can imagine that did not win any popularity prizes. But surely they are professional enough to grin and bear it and get on with things?"

"Obviously not."

Chapter Fifteen

They were silent for a while; Peter did a sweep of the horizon with his glasses, noting automatically the white moustache of foam from Mike Robert's boat. As he passed over the racing image something caused him to swing the glasses back and examine the area around Robert's 5989 boat. There it was; the thing that was wrong. Behind 5989 there was something in the water that was wrong. He swung round picked up the RT and clicked twice on the send switch. The reply was immediate. "Sir?"

"Behind you Mike on your starboard quarter; there's something in the water. Come about and I will direct you to it."

The wake behind Mike's boat dropped to nothing as the throttles were closed and the boat reversed its course. Peter had stopped his boat and was concentrating on keeping the mystery object in view.

"What is it?" Claire asked "What have you seen?" She was turned looking in the direction that Mike Robert's had taken.

Peter did not answer immediately, "Cox'n follow Mr Robert's boat but off to one side so that I can keep a clear view."

"Aye aye sir." It was the calm voice of CPO Jim Walters realising something was up now back at the wheel.

Over the RT Mike Robert's voice came calmly verifying that he could now see the object in the water.

The two boats closed the gap and finally they could see clearly what they were looking at.

It was a boat, a dinghy half awash. There were three figures seated slumped on the cross seats, all quite still with the water lapping around their knees.

"They are boys; schoolboys." Claire said with a catch in her voice. "What are they doing out here, so far from land?"

The boat had been dragged alongside by one of the hands on Robert's boat.

He called out "This one is still alive, he reached into the dinghy and lifted the small figure in his arms and placed gently on deck, two other men lifted the remaining figures out of the dinghy, while a third searched the boat thoroughly for any clue to their being out here nearly 80 miles from land.

At Claire's insistence the three figures were passed over to Peter's boat and she had all three brought below, stripped and rubbed down thoroughly to dry them off and wrapped in blankets to get some heat back in their shivering bodies. They turned out to be two boys and a girl, all about twelve years old, thin and a little undernourished. The first, one of the boys regained consciousness while he was being scrubbed with the rough towel. He was Dutch but he spoke good English. His story was simple.

"We three had borrowed the dinghy from the sailing club in Vlissingen, it should have been kept without its mast and sails, but the owner had made sure that they were hidden nearby in case he needed them.

"We were all orphans—our parents had all gone and we were being kept in the orphanage in the little local town. I am the oldest I learned to sail with my father before the war, Angela the girl had sailed on the Zeider Zee during the last holiday with her parents. We both had lost our families in the German advance into Holland. Henry the other boy had been abandoned as a baby; he had become friends with us when we came to the orphanage three months ago. Henry knew all the ways out of the orphanage, and was happy to share his knowledge with us.

"We had spotted the boat on one of our night time escapes, and Henry found the rigging and sails. We made plans to escape from Holland using the dinghy, reasoning that between us we could sail the 120 miles to England in two days, or at most three.

"It took over three weeks to collect provisions and bottles to fill with water. We chose a night where there was wind and darkness to hide us."

The cocoa and corned-beef sandwiches arrive at this point and they let Martin tuck in before continuing his story.

"We launched and rigged the boat in the dark, stowed our provisions under the thwarts, and set sail, four nights ago. I had a compass that I had been given as a Boy Scout."

Martin paused at this moment to wolf down a second corned-beef sandwich and another mug of cocoa, before continuing his story.

"We made good progress the first night and when dawn broke we could hardly see the shore line. It was at that point that Angela pointed out that we were being pulled along northward by the current. Though the sail was full and pulling the boat the current was too strong for the boat to stem it.

"It was then the trawler appeared. The armed vessel was one of the many in use by the Germans along the coastline of the Channel and the North Sea."

The skipper of the trawler thought it was a huge joke for these kids to attempt to escape in this way. When he heard they were orphans he decided that he would teach them a lesson before he returned them to land. He had the mast removed from the dinghy and left them one bottle of water. He then towed them beyond the line of the current and set them adrift in the open sea. He said he would return for them when they had learned their lesson. They watched him sail away towards the now invisible coast.

All three were devastated, they had been caught so easily and now they could not go anywhere without sails or oars they were stuck waiting for the trawler to return and take them back into captivity."

At this point Angela took up the story. "We had watched the trawler disappear over the horizon, and we heard the stutter of machine gun fire. A small cloud of smoke appeared from the direction of the trawler, then nothing.

That had been, she thought, three days ago. "We had tried to make progress by paddling with one of the dinghy bottom boards but it did not make much of an impression. Yesterday the sea got rougher and we had trouble keeping the water out of the boat, we ran out of drinking water and though it rained we still suffered and got very cold. We tried huddling together to keep warm, but as we got colder and colder we started to lose hope and we had all resigned themselves to dying, then you came along."

Claire relayed Angela's part of the story to Peter as they continued to their destination at Zandvoort, unlike Martin; Angela only spoke Dutch.

"The worst part for Martin had been when they passed through the wreckage floating on the water during the night. A section of a mast with the peculiar gooseneck from their own dinghy, shattered and in amongst other bits of boat timbers that he guessed must have come from the Trawler that had stopped them.

"We realized at that time that there was now no hope of being picked up unless a passing craft saw us."

The Group arrived off Zandvoort beach after midnight and the two boats separated, each to their own task. Peter took the 6000 boat as close to the beach as possible, and the small group of Commandos slipped down into the dinghy and rowed off to the shore.

The MGB sat at a light anchor waiting for the signal from the shore before attempting the landing of the group of agents.

On the other boat Mike Roberts had diverted to the area to the south of Zandfoort to collect the returning agent. He was having a bad night, the collection of the returning agent went like clockwork, but the news he brought was worrying. Once the man had given his information Mike turned his boat and raced back to join Peter at Zandvoort.

The agents from Peter's boat were still aboard when Mike Roberts came in range and signalled his Commanding Officer.

"Whatever you do not land the agents at Zandvoort, it's a trap." Mike's terse message took them all by surprise.

Peter called the group of agents together and told them of the message from the other boat.

"The agent they picked up sent the message that there had been more arrests and the rendezvous at Zandvoort was compromised. I am wondering about Lieutenant Depp and the Commandos; we still have no report from them and what is more important no contact at all so far.

"If we cannot contact him then in the face of this information I will have to take you back and perhaps try another time." He turned to Claire. "What do you think?"

Claire was quick to reply, "I think we need to speak to our returning agent, we can perhaps make up our minds what to do when we have the full story."

The rest of the group grudgingly agreed that it was probably the best idea, though the agent John; still thought they should have landed already, but since the other boat would be contacting them direct shortly anyway, he agreed they should wait for it at least.

The discussion was interrupted by a call from Lieutenant Easton, "Signal from the beach, sir. Red flash repeated twice."

"Don't acknowledge." Peter's voice had an edge. "The signal is a warning. Keep your eyes peeled, Number One, the brown jobs will be back with us shortly. Make sure the men are alert—we may have to make a dash for it."

Easton called softly to the Middy Allan Hodges, "Take a stroll round and make sure the men are all awake I want no jumpy trigger fingers. Keep an ear and eye out for the landing party returning." Hodges walked off and made a circuit of the boat the murmur of the voices, questions and answers faded as he checked each man at his post.

The second MGB came alongside with a quiet grumble of the throttled down wing engine. The recovered agent was helped into the boat by Hodges who brought him below to the cabin where the others were gathered.

The newcomer looked around the Wardroom at the assembled agents, his eyes settled on Claire then drifted on to Jones. He was slim, about 5ft 11in. dark hair with a side parting. He smiled and his face lit up. "Well, the good news is that I found you in time. If the operation is going to continue you have to land elsewhere. I think further south, nearer Rotterdam. There is a lot more commercial activity, and security, but at the same time a lot more opportunity to get in and out safely.

The entire group began discussing whether an alternative landing was possible. Peter came down and interrupted the meeting. "I have to tell you that time is running out for a landing tonight."

The dinghy with Lieutenant Depp and his men has returned to the boat, boarding quietly one by one. The Lieutenant had looked at Peter and shook his head; "No chance of getting ashore here. Whoever suggested it must be either mad or in the pay of the Germans."

"Bad was it?" Peter said quietly.

"There were sentries and posts all along the sea wall. If we hadn't been prepared they would have had us in a minute. Where is the team?"

"Below in the wardroom; come on down, you can explain to them directly.

In the wardroom the group of agents were discussing their options. Peter was pleased to see that the group included Claire, the earlier pique forgotten in the face of this new emergency.

The returning agent, who called himself George, was speaking as they entered. He stopped as they came in, but reassured by recognizing Peter, and the uniform of Depp. He continued speaking, "If you use the place where I was collected there should be no problem." George spoke English with hardly any accent; he had an easy manner and Peter assumed he was one of the many European members of the SOE ranks who ranged from Austrian to Norwegian, Dutch, French and Belgian.

Lieutenant Depp looked at George with a puzzled look on his face. He turned to Peter and said quietly "Where does George come from, do you know?"

Peter shrugged "I'm afraid I don't. Why do you ask?" He replied equally quietly.

The boy Martin came in while they were talking, Claire turned and saw him and immediately went over to usher him out. Peter joined her and took Martin by the hand "Come on. lad, this is no place for you just now." Martin was looking at the group with horror in his eyes. Peter noticed and took him from the room pulling Claire with him.

"What's wrong boy? What scared you?"

Martin spoke quickly the words tumbling from his mouth, "That man! It's him, he is the one!"

"What man? Calm down, boy. No one will hurt you here." He sat Martin down on the helmsman's seat and Claire put her arm round the boy protectively.

"That new man in the cabin is Gestapo. He took my mother with a lot of other women from the town. The soldiers laughed as they were taken; they made rude signs at them when they were loaded onto the trucks. We heard later they had been taken for the men. No one explained what it meant, but in the Orphanage the nurse told us that we would never see the women again, so we thought they were all killed." The simple tale from the small boy brought tears to Claire's eyes.

Peter said "What makes you think this man is the man you remember?"

"I heard his voice, I will never forget it. Then I saw his face, he had a black hat and a long black leather coat on and an armband with the crooked cross on it in red I will never forget it; and his eyes looked right through me as if I wasn't there."

Lieutenant Depp came out and joined them. "This man George, I think I know the accent, where does he come from?" He looked at Claire with the question.

"I am not sure myself, but Martin here says he is the Gestapo man who took his mother away."

At this comment Depp's head jerked up "Gestapo? German – that's it! He comes from the region just over the border with Germany. Near Herzogenbosch. The people both sides of the border speak both languages. I knew a man from Geldorf in Nordrhein when I started working at Phillips in Eindhoven. That is the accent I could hear in his voice. Give me a few minutes to talk with him. We will soon find out who he really is."

Peter stopped and spoke to Emmy Easton, then he and the Lieutenant went back into the wardroom. As they entered the sound of the engines rose and the boat turned and accompanied by Mike Roberts' 5890 boat commenced the long passage back to Harwich.

In the wardroom the Lieutenant's entry had stopped the conversation for a moment. Depp said "What was it like when you were making your way to the beach tonight?"

George answered easily "There were no guards about they must have all been deployed where you were meant to be operating."

Depp nodded thoughtfully "You're Dutch, aren't you?"

"Indeed I am." George's voice was controlled/ "I come from Den 'Bosch," He used the familiar name for the southern city.

"Well, we have someone here that you may know in that case." He turned and called Martin to come in.

When the boy appeared George wrinkled his brow, puzzled. "Well" he said with a smile "Who have we got here?"

Depp removed the pistol from his holster on the side away from the agent, keeping it out of sight.

Martin walked in head high and looked directly at the agent, "What did you do with my mother?" He said and ran forward with his fists raised. He was caught by Peter who had followed him in. "In Oostvoorne, you took her with the other women; for the soldiers, you said."

The boy was in tears and struggled to get away from Peter who held him close.

George's face was a picture. At the mention of Oostvoorne he went white and Depp saw it. Depp brought up his pistol and pointed it at him. George had reached for his pocket but stopped when he saw the gun. Peter told the agent John to get behind George and frisk him. John cautiously did as he was asked and drew out the gun from George's pocket, and laid an array of objects including the gun, on the table. Claire looked at the objects from the man's pockets. She stepped forward and picked up two items from the objects there. The cigarette lighter and a small silver locket engraved with initials.

"She showed the items to the other agents. As she lifted the lighter she moved the base and a small red light could be seen flashing. She quickly closed the flap covering the light again. John said "Is that the famous camera?"

"It certainly is; it the *Minox*. And this is the locket that Mark Wharton wore every day everywhere; he told me that he had promised his wife he would never remove it." She opened the locket and showed the group the photograph inside.

George said desperately "That is my wife."

"What color is her hair?" Claire asked him.

"Why, sort of fairish blonde." George replied.

"Wrong, her hair is red." The instant reply came without hesitation.

"I meant red." George said hurriedly "She sometimes dyes it."

The people round the wardroom were silent as the boat moved with the action of the waves against its speeding hull, all were looking at George, nobody said a word but the distrust in the atmosphere was tangible.

George looked around desperately "You've got it wrong, all of you; I am Captain William Harper REME. I have been with SOE for three years."

At this, John, the agent with the pipe, took a pistol from his pocket and pointed it at him. "You tortured him didn't you?" John's voice was toneless and the more menacing for it.

"What do you mean? Tortured who? I haven't tortured anyone; we are all friends here, why the gun?" George was not looking so good, he was sweating now and his eyes darted round the room looking for a way out.

John said "If you were who you say you are you would know what I mean. In training we were all taught to say certain things under interrogation. One of them was to claim to be Nurse Sadie Smith if you were female and if you were male, Captain William Harper REME. SOE was not in being three years ago. The trick was to stretch service to one year past our start date. Do you still claim to be one of us?"

Without another word he shot George.

Chapter Sixteen

As the body fell there was dead silence, the execution was so sudden Peter reacted first reaching out and snatching the gun from John's hand.

From her place beside the body of George, Claire looked at Peter and shook her head "He's dead." She said.

"Pull up his right sleeve." Depp said. Claire undid the shirt cuff and pulled the sleeve up. On the forearm was a tattooed number. Seeing it she said "SS." Tight-lipped, she pulled the sleeve down covering the damming tattoo. "They must have worked fast, they would normally have prepared him much better than this, I suppose they were depending on us being in a muddle with losing agents all over the place and frankly if Martin had not been here he would probably got away with it.

"He was a plant taking the place of our man, a last minute switch here to lead us into a trap. Probably because he spoke English and there was no one else available."

Two hefty seamen carried the body of George away. The Bo'sun made a note of the tattoo number and the clothes were removed. The body was wrapped for examination in Harwich and lashed to the deck rails.

Claire reached out to Peter and took the pistol from him; she turned and pointed it at John.

"Now, John, perhaps you can explain this gun."

"I always like to have insurance." John was quite calm.

"We were all told no guns; all weapons would be supplied ashore. Where did this come from?"

"I collected it after we were cleared to leave during the delay caused by the panic over the round up of agents."

"You joined at Waverley Station when we came down from Inverailort, now perhaps you will tell us just where you came from so conveniently."

"I was ordered to join you by London." Jones was still quite calm and ignored the pistol still held in Claire's hand.

"Now convince me that you are who you say you are." The steel in Claire's voice surprised Peter, who called the Bo'sun to standby.

For the first time Jones showed a little nervousness. "I don't understand, I am not the odd one out here, you are."

"But I can prove who I am; I am inviting you to prove who you are. Do any of you know this man?" She swung round to question the others; as she turned Jones reached for the gun.

The shot caught him in the shoulder and spun him round, he fell to the floor. Claire looked at him coldly. "Now why would you do that?"

"I suggest we examine John's arm since he knows so much about our dead friend."

One of the others ripped the sleeve up John's right arm, then the left. There was no sign of a tattoo. There is nothing there, you must be wrong Claire."

"Oh, I don't think so." She reached down and removed the pen from the pocket of John's jacket. Putting the gun on the table she balanced against the rocking of the boat and twisted the top of the pen. The short aerial that popped out of the barrel of the pen took the others by surprise. "Set in the base is a homing device that is supposed to bring rein-forcements as we speak."

There was a deathly silence; she spoke again "Fortunately we found it and modified it without Mr John know-ing"

She turned to Peter "Sorry about this, we had to find out who the insider was. W thought it might be John but having found our friend decided to let him run to see what happened." It seems George had done his job and was now expendable. They were using him to confirm John's credentials with the other agents."

"So this whole operation was set up to trap the spy?"

Claire grinned "'Fraid so, even the others didn't know." She waved at the other two agents seated in the wardroom.

With John secured Peter was back on the bridge for the rest of the trip home, three small figures kept him company. The Cox'n stood a stool by the wheel so that Martin, Angela and Henry could take turns steering the boat, their cries of delight could be heard every time the spray burst over the bow.

The final stretch to Harwich was done with the three well-fed children fast asleep on the wardroom benches, all wrapped up in soft blankets, and lashed in to stop them rolling off their berths.

The arrival in Harwich was an anti-climax not assisted by the presence of Captain Hawthorn DSO RN standing on the pontoon waiting for the return of the boats. The main party under Bill Manning was already back, mission accomplished.

The Captain was not amused to see the passengers being offloaded. He sniffed "My office, when you've finished offloading."He stalked off, immaculate uniform without a crease showing a contrast to Peter's scruffy battledress.

An unmarked van collected the enemy agent and the body of George, the other SOE personnel were taken away in a saloon car.

Before she left Claire spoke to Peter. "Thank you, Peter, I knew we were in safe hands with you." She reached up and kissed him, her breath soft on his face, "I'll see you again, I think." Then she was gone. The car drove off into the grey morning and Peter turned with a sigh to face Captain Hawthorn in his office.

Peter leaned against the bridge screen and looked out at the line of scruffy merchant ships nodding along in two lines down the swept channel towards the Thames Estuary. Only a few more miles and he could hand the Convoy on to the Ramsgate flotilla for their final trek up the River. He was thinking of Caroline, of their time in Alex, when he had realized that she was the woman he wanted to spend the rest of his life with, where was she now he wondered, he had had no word from her though he had written care of SOE. He lifted his eyes to the ships around him the angular shape of the old fashioned coaster abeam reminded him of John Masefield and his 'Dirty British Coaster with its salt stained smoke-stack'.

The other MGB's were stationed along the seaward side of the slow moving group of ships, many of which looked as if they should have been en route to the scrap yard. He hated convoy duty, as he knew only too well defending a convoy was always a chancy business, though now it was daylight it was much easier to spot E Boats coming in.

He raised his weary body from the rail standing upright and stretching his arms high over his head. As he turned, he saw the twin engine aircraft coming towards them at sea level, so low the propellers kept causing the sea spray to fly into the air like rooster tails behind them. The Port lookout called out a warning and Peter stabbed the action stations button. The clangour rang out over the water; he called out at the same time "Gunners action Port, enemy aircraft at nought feet."

All the deck armament swung at the same time as the gunners acquired the target. Across the water the sound of the action bell was repeated to the other escorts. The Hunt Class destroyer commanded by the escort commander blew its whistle, the signal for the convoy to scatter. The ships really had no place to go, and all they could do was break up the pattern they so painfully maintained.

The three aircraft turned out to be Messerschmitt 110's all arriving with guns blazing. The escort Destroyer and MGBs all opened fire sending up a storm of fire in the path of the three aircraft.

Beyond the convoy all three climbed sharply still pursued by the 4.7 guns of the destroyer and the combined pompoms of the other escorts. Two of the coasters were leaking smoke from fires started by the cannon fire from the strafing planes.

As the aircraft turned to continue their attack one of them suddenly staggered and the port wing dropped the port engine bleeding smoke and flame. The sound of machinegun fire came faintly from the sky and suddenly the air seemed full of aircraft as several Hurricane single engine fighters came into view pursuing the two surviving Messerschmitts over the horizon.

Lieutenant Commander Max Cummings on the Starboard wing of the convoy picked up the survivors from the shot down enemy aircraft.

The Convoy reformed, both the damaged ships managed to get their fires out and were able to resume their positions.

The flotilla made several other convoy trips through the summer of 1943, The invasion of Sicily happened and the talk in October was of the further invasion of Italy, and the stop go progress of the Allied army since its start in September.

For Peter Murray, the biggest event in the life of the Harwich Flotilla was the replacement of Captain, now Commodore Hawthorn DSO RN newly detached to command the base at Leith, with the welcome arrival of Captain Gerald Harper DSO RN.

The sight of the short dapper figure gave the entire Coastal Forces Unit the sort of shot in the arm that was sadly needed.

His arrival was followed by the replacement of Commander Ronny Harris RN who had surprisingly been promoted to Captain and posted to take over command of the Ramsgate Coastal Forces Base.

The farewell party for Ronny was in full swing when the mess door opened and the neat figure of Captain Archer appeared followed by another taller officer with the three rings of a Commander RNR on his sleeve.

Peter saw the Captain and immediately called the mess to attention, an order immediately countermanded by the Captain. Peter who had gone to meet the Captain saw the Commander clearly for the first time.

Captain Archer Smiled as he introduced his newly appointed Executive Officer, who was grinning at Peter, hand held out. "Commander Waterstone I see." Peter grabbed his hand delighted to see his friend once more.

Archer said "If you chaps wouldn't mind I'll get a drink and circulate, I won't hang around too long."

"I would say you'll be lucky to escape that easily from here, Sir." Peter grinned as the dapper Captain was suddenly surrounded by three WRNS Officers two of whom carried pink gins. Both were gravely presented to the Captain who courteously bowed his thanks and allowed himself to be carried off leaving a hint of perfume from his charming escort.

"You survived the desert, I see." Peter said as he dragged Paul over to the bar.

Once Paul was supplied with a drink the pair brought each other up to date. Peter told Paul of his last encounter with Claire. In his turn Paul was able to tell Peter that Caroline was now in England and currently in London working with a Colonel Buckmaster, whoever he was.

Paul had met Caroline while he was in London, had been given her telephone number in case Peter was interested. He smiled smugly when he said this and laughed aloud when he saw the look on Peter's face as he gave him the news.

The train pulled into Liverpool Street Station at ten o'clock Friday evening. Peter pulled down his weekend bag from the rack above his head and stepped down from the first class compartment on to the dark platform. He gave in his ticket at the barrier, The Ticket Collector's eyes flicked over the medal ribbons on Peter's jacket. "Good evening, sir, enjoy your weekend."

Surprised but touched Peter smiled at him. "I'll do my best, thank you."

He took two paces and he was suddenly face to face with Caroline. There was no hesitation, no shyness she was in his arms and he swore then and there he would never ever let her go.

He felt her tears on his cheek as they kissed.

The ticket Collector watched smiling thinking, *good luck to you both,* as he closed up his box, finished for the night.

Sub Lieutenant Allan Hodges was already enjoying the tea and biscuits in the drawing room of the Seaford Hotel. Hillary sat opposite with a broad smile on her face. She had been so proud when Allan had called at the bank for her. In his officers uniform he looked handsome and more assured than the young man who had left her two years ago. The letters had always been warm and affectionate and full of interest. She had been happy to claim him as her boyfriend, though she had been approached by several men since he had left, there had been something about Allan that had made it easy to reject the various advances made.

Her friend Gracie had said she was daft to remain faithful to someone overseas for so long, "He'll be having it off with all those girls sailors pick up when they are abroad." She was insistent, but Hillary had refused to be drawn, determined to wait, and now he was here.

"I suppose you've been to a lot of romantic places since you joined the navy."

"Well, you may think of them as romantic but mostly they were hot, sweaty and swarming with flies. The streets stink and the noise is horrific" his voice softened; "But the night can be like a velvet cloth scattered with a million lights. The moon is so big it fills the sky and you can read the headlines by its light, the waters of the Nile are suddenly silver with scattered Feluccas moving here and there, and Palm trees silhouetted against the horizon."

For a moment he was silent seeing the picture he was creating with his words. Hillary sat entranced also by the imagery.

"Oh, Allan I've missed you." She couldn't believe she had said that; she had not intended saying anything except perhaps in response to something he said. Gracie had told her, "Don't give anything away, make him commit himself before you say anything!"

Allan looked at her wonderingly, "Do you mean that?"

"What?" She answered not quite sure of what he meant.

"What you said about missing me."

That did it "Of course I did, I've missed you from the day you left, and I've waited for you to come back to me..." The rest of her words were lost as Allan rose to his feet and swept her into his arms in front of the assembled people gathered for tea in the Hotel Lounge.

Ignoring the rustle of interest he kissed her, until finally to the patter of applause from the watching audience he released her and hesitantly sat down once more. "I-I'm sorry" he said stumbling over his words "I just..."

"I'm not!" Hillary said, blushing, but certain of his feelings now she was determined to make sure that he knew how she felt. "I did not intend things to happen like this but I'm glad they did. You are only home for the weekend and I would hate to waste our time when it's so short."

He reached for her hand, and almost with surprise found it willingly ready to hold his. "I fell in love with you the day you joined the Bank, the first time I saw you. For me there is no one else, there never will be. I have wanted to marry you for the past two years and I want to marry you today or tomorrow, as soon as it's possible, unless you want to wait. If you do I'll wait as long as you need."

She reached across and laid her hand on his cheek, "As soon as it can be arranged is fine by me." She said no more, she didn't have to. They sat holding hands until the waiter coughed politely to ask if he could clear the table.

The weekend leave was an interesting time for the new CO. Captain Gerald Harper DSO RN was a busy man; and that first weekend was the prelude for the beginning of a series of actions that would lead up to what was now being whispered as the Invasion of Europe.

He was sitting in his office considering the prospect when the signal came in advising that an operation would be mounted requiring coastal forces for reconnaissance and escort duties with a mixed fleet of craft initially exercising in Loch Linnhe. The flotilla would be temporarily stationed at HMS St Christopher in Fort William whilst the training was undertaken.

He was pleased to note that the movement order was not until next week end and as far as he was concerned there was no need to bring people back early from leave this weekend.

Chapter Seventeen

The return to Harwich was a relief to some, and a wrench to others. For Peter it was an opportunity to review his feelings about Caroline. Seeing her again and being with her for the first time on their own, away from the distractions of work was good for them both. It was evident that neither was sure enough of the other and the first hours they were together in London were marked by restraint. They dined at Lyons Corner House for want of anywhere else at that time.

Thankfully by the time they had both talked and eaten the unwinding process had worked for them both. Caroline had suggested that accommodation in London was difficult at the time and she had a spare room in her flat he could use.

Neither mentioned what was obviously on their mind, though it surprised neither when during the night they finished up together in the same bed.

From that time onwards there was no tension between them, both found a peace in each other's company and they spent the rest of the weekend in the flat together.

Now back at work with a movement to plan and accomplish within the week he had to take his mind off Caroline and concentrate on arrangements for the trip to Scotland.

The coastal trip was quiet, the escort of a convoy to Leith was the usual slow drag, but the rest of the trip to Inverness provided an exhilarating dash through choppy seas making the entry into the Beauly Firth via the Moray Firth a contrast. The calm waters against the backdrop of the rising land of the Black Isle were followed by the smooth waters of the Caledonian Canal.

To most of the crew the journey through the canal was a magical experience, the waters of Loch Ness allowed them to make an exhilarating dash the length of the famous Loch. The mountains on both sides were patterned in autumn colors of green and gold. To the Subby Hodges the transition from the soft countryside of Sussex to the rugged scenery of the Highlands was a revelation and as they transited the final stretch of the canal through the woods and moorland beneath Ben Nevis he swore he would one day bring Hillary to see this amazing scenery.

HMS St. Christopher was the Coastal Forces training establishment based in Fort William. The whole region was in use for various aspects of training, the Commandos at Achnacarry and Inverailort, the mini submarines at Kingairloch, and the Royal Marines at Mallaig.

The waters of Loch Linnhe were ideal for the exercise to train in combined tactics against heavy warships; it was also the first opportunity to give the Flotilla rest from the continuous pressure of action. The fact that the majority of the officers and crews were Volunteer Reserve placed them in a different category to their counterparts in the regular navy.

The arbitrary regular two-year rotation of duties applying to the regulars did ensure some relief from the continual pressure of active service. In Peter's case he had been in continual action for over three years and the effects were beginning to show.

The break from operations was a tonic for the entire flotilla. They had to work but without the pressure of enemy activity the men gradually relaxed and in the varied series of tasks they were required to perform they operated throughout the islands of the Hebrides as well as up and down the Atlantic coast.

They had been in the area for close on three months when the report came that the *Valkyrie* the Hipper Class

Cruiser, encountered by the crew of the Walrus Peter had rescued from the north sea, had broken out of the Stavanger Fjord. She had been lying there behind a series of anti-torpedo nets, for nearly one year and was popularly supposed to have grounded on the empty food and drink tins and bottles dumped over the side.

She had left Stavanger Fjord on the Norwegian Coast, without being noticed during a snowstorm. The first evidence of the presence was a frantic sighting report from a convoy escort that had just turned towards the cruiser, to match her puny 4 inch gun against 8x8 inch guns, set in 4 turrets, capable of defying all but the largest of the ships of the Home Fleet. At 14260 tons this heavy Cruiser, had a top speed of over 32knots. She was a truly formidable opponent. The convoy dispersed but the losses were catastrophic. Seven ships out of twelve plus the corvette that had made the report.

She was believed to be heading north.

The progress of the *Valkyrie* was followed closely. While the weather was clear enough for the reconnaissance aircraft they could keep her in sight; and the trio of light cruisers from the Home Fleet who had sailed from Rosyth to shadow her hoped to catch up with her and take over from the aircraft as the weather worsened.

The problem was that the shadowing group had been sent out far too late to have a chance at catching the enemy ship unless she was delayed, she dropped out of sight for several hours.

The next sighting of the *Valkyrie* was north of the Faroe Islands, just a glimpse through a torn curtain of scudding cloud. The Liberator was returning from Iceland, the pilot saw enough to estimate course and speed. It confirmed that any shadowing force would need to be in a better position to catch this ship.

In Fort William the flotilla had exhausted the patience of their training officers; and the enthusiasm of the boat's crews. Peter was beginning to feel that it was time to return to regular duties before he had mutiny and desertions on his hands.

The Staff Officer (Training) Lieut Commander Michael Stephenson caught him as he was leaving the wardroom at HMS St Christopher "Can I have a word, Peter; something has come up."

They sat down in the ante room—once the lounge of the Highland Hotel—and while Peter waited Michael loaded his pipe and lit it. Satisfied finally that his pipe was going well he began.

"The *Valkyrie* is headed towards the Atlantic; sadly there are no capital ships in place to stop her between here and the mid-ocean convoy gap. (a gap between the air cover from the American ports and those of the UK, the gap was currently regarded as the killing ground for the U Boat wolf packs.) If she gets there she could cause absolute mayhem with convoys both ways.

"We cannot commit Swordfish to the job because we have no accurate fix on her whereabouts and they don't have the range for an extended search. It occurred to me that your boys have the range and the speed and if you all get fitted up with torpedoes you might be able to slow her down."

Peter looked at his companion; the initial shock at the suggestion now replaced by the tactical problems of the suggestion. "I think it's risky but possible; provided the seas are not too high and the weather is suitable…" He thought for a few minutes "We'll need to attack after dark if we can. It would give us the best chance of success and also a chance to get away again afterwards."

Michael held up his hand. "Hold on a minute. I was just floating the idea in the air as it were. If you think it possible and are willing to have a go then get it on paper and I'll send it on up to the powers for their blessing. You're sure you are willing to try this?"

"If I were not I would have turned you down from the start. Give me until after lunch," he looked at his watch. "About three hours and I'll have some answers. One thing I'll need Radar on the other boats, we still have two without and we will need it to keep in touch and to locate the *Valkyrie*."

Peter called all the boat skippers to assemble in the wardroom of the flotilla leader and put the problem to them. The next three hours were spent on the problem. Charts of the North Atlantic were produced and the logistics of getting the flotilla into the right area by the time the enemy cruiser arrived. All were conscious of the urgency and the risks involved.

Max Cummings admitted to Peter that the idea scared him to death, but at the same time he wouldn't miss the opportunity for worlds.

The call came to Peter that evening. The men had been involved in practice loading torpedoes on all boats. The MGB's crew's were not accustomed to having the tubes used and all the circuits and mechanisms had to be overhauled and tested. When the call came the orders specified volunteers only were to be used.

The PO's mess was full of the buzz as soon as the orders were received. There was an air of nervous expectancy that raised the normal level of noise.

"Volunteers, that's a laugh, nobody volunteers in this navy unless they are already round the bend."

Jim Walters looked around the mess to who had spoken. It was a burly TGM a regular one of the base training staff.

The immediate hush that followed these words said it all to Jim Walters who laughed out loud and said. "If you can't take a joke you shouldn't have joined." The roar of laughter that followed this comment sent the base PO off with a red face and the firm conviction that all Coastal Forces personnel were completely crazy.

The following day the entire flotilla cruised round to Mallaig, to be ready in the event that the go-ahead was given. Peter thought the boat felt heavy with the added weight of the two torpedoes, he realized that it was just imagination, but he also knew that the top speed would be affected. It was evening by the time the boats had all been refuelled. The electricians finished the installation of the radar in the two boats that had been, up to now, without, and the sets were being tested as they cruised out into the Sound of Sleat. The order to refuel at Kinlochbervie away up on the North West Coast was received and the flotilla set off once more up the Sound to Loch Alsh, then through the Kyle and northwards to the little fishing village just 20 or so miles south of Cape Wrath. The boats pulled into the shelter of Loch Na Claise, the first boat coming alongside the quay to refuel at 0300 hrs.

The reports of the progress of the *Valkyrie* came in at intervals, still no decision from the Admiralty to commit the flotilla to the attack.

A squadron of Blenheim bombers droned over the hills to the east while the flotilla lay at anchor. Three only returned.

The orders came through at last. The *Valkyrie* was expected to be passing Rosemary Bank on the north side of the Rockall trench by 1800. The flotilla would proceed to intercept and if possible sink her with torpedoes. Radio silence would be observed on the way as no warning should be given of the Flotilla's presence.

As Peter would verify, it is no fun waiting at a rendezvous, so he adjusted the speed of the flotilla to put them there as near to the expected time of arrival of the enemy ship as possible allowing for lead time in case of any updates. On the way Peter had the flotilla exercising changing attack patterns to take into account speed and course of the target, but also to scatter the pattern of boats in case the enemy had radar on board they could possibly be mistaken for the fishing fleet.

The long swell of the Atlantic waves lifted the boats in succession rising and falling scattered over an area of a square mile, all six boats on all round watch. Mike Roberts sent the signal by light, the first flickering image of the *Valkyrie* had appeared on his screen, the escort destroyers appeared shortly after, having difficulty keeping up with the speeding cruiser. By threading the needle and chancing the gap between the Faroes and Shetland she had caught the Navy on the hop. Running the Strait at high speed they had saved time and eluded their shadowing cruisers.

The waiting boats prepared, scattering to the positions arranged more or less both sides of the mean course of the German ship. The report of the first sighting of *Valkyrie* and her two consorts came from Lieut Commander Cummings 5890 boat.

The first torpedo hit one of the escort destroyers; the speed it was moving meant it had no chance of surviving. It lost the bow as the torpedo hit below the gun mounting on the foredeck.

With the loss of its bow the speeding destroyer drove straight under the sea the pounding engines allowing no chance of survival. The other torpedoes were in the water and the guns of the cruiser and the remaining destroyer were blazing all around at the attacking force. Two torpedoes struck the cruiser, slowing its progress immediately but the strikes seemed if anything to increase the level of response from the various gun mountings. Another torpedo hit the remaining destroyer staggering it and causing it to sink by the head. It remained afloat but by the time they stabilised things the propellers were almost cutting the surface of the sea and her speed was reduced to a crawl. The remainder of the flotilla were circling around seeking a firing position, but the accurate gunnery of the *Valkyrie* and her wounded escort was making it difficult, the boats having to react to a barrage of fire from the Main and secondary armament from both ships.

When the wounded *Valkyrie* started to turn Peter realized that they had done enough. On her reverse course, Peter worked out that of its only two options, the *Valkyrie* had elected to return to Norway, it had been either turn back or make for Brest on the French coast. The second of his torpedoes had slowed the cruiser down but the attackers had suffered as well, despite the advantage of surprise the enemy had reacted fast and two of the boats were now under tow. Peter's boat had been damaged, the Oerlikon behind the bridge looked like metal spaghetti, the gunner was laid out on deck stunned but not otherwise hurt; the gunner and his weapon had gone from the starboard gun position, the shell had just swept the entire section away, the boat otherwise was peppered with shrapnel holes and to his surprise Peter found he was bleeding from a wound in the top of his shoulder. He hadn't felt it and it was only now that the Doctor was cleaning the wound and dressing it, that he was aware of the pain kicking in. He ordered recall over the RT and radioed the report of *Valkyrie's* new course and the fact that she had been hit by two torpedoes to base, and took his battered flotilla south to the repair yard at Corpach, Fort William.

He was grateful when the Doctor finished his work and injected him in the shoulder, the pain reduced to a dull ache and he was too busy to bother with it.

They had not lost a boat though there were fourteen men wounded and six killed and all the boats were damaged.

When he reported to HMS St Christopher he was told that as soon as his boats were ready they were to report back to Harwich. The operation that had brought them here was cancelled. He was also told that there would be a second bar to his DSO and that he was to recommend five others for decorations after the action against the *Valkyrie*.

Chapter Eighteen

The wound was not too troublesome and it had healed quite well over the next three weeks. The scar was still tender but wearing uniform was no longer irritating.

Peter sat in the office on the Depot ship wishing Paul Waterstone would get back from leave and allow him to get back to his boat. He was fully aware that Sub Lieutenant Allan Hodges DSC RNVR was enjoying his temporary command, chasing the new Midshipman Martin Wendover and practicing the role he had been yearning after ever since he had volunteered for the navy.

He had received his DSC for his conduct during the action against the *Valkyrie* when he had been in command of the forward pompom. The gunner had been injured and Hodges had taken over the gun and despite injuries to himself had carried on keeping the gun in action throughout the action. He had finally collapsed and been relieved as the *Valkyrie* disappeared into the mist smoke billowing from her wounds.

The Doctor had removed the piece of shrapnel from his side where it had lodged against his ribs; Peter guessed it was from the shell that had removed the starboard turret. Two weeks later he was back on duty his wound much less of a problem than Peter's.

Despite the rude comments about old men taking longer to heal than the young, the temporary posting to Paul's job had been a break for Peter, though he would not acknowledge it. He felt almost guilty sitting at a desk when he was perfectly fit to return to his beloved boat. Turning back with a sigh to the work on the desk Peter reflected that with Christmas on the way there would be some pretty uncomfortable nights ahead. Of course there was always a chance of a little leave around that time and since Max Cummings had drawn the short straw he was scheduled to be on duty over Christmas, while Peter looked after the New Year stint.

In the ward room later he greeted Paul who had returned early from his leave.

"So what's all this then, Paul? I could not believe you would come back early so what is happening?"

Paul was looking serious and having checked there was no-one within earshot he spoke quietly "Ever heard of Langsund in the Telemark area of Norway?"

Peter nodded "I've heard of it. I sailed past it en route to Oslo when I was delivering a yacht, it must have 1938, summer."

"Well, early this year a party of the resistance with commando support raided the power station where they produced something the boffins call 'Heavy Water'. It's something they use in some secret process that no one will talk about. They thought that they had stopped the production; but it seems that the Germans are active at the plant again so they may have got things working once more. Whatever this 'Heavy Water' is it has our boffins and the Yanks in a panic."

"We have been tasked to do a diversionary raid and drop off and pick up from Langesund. The landing and pick up will be by ML escorted by the MGB section, the MTBs are doing a dash into the Oslo Fjord to stir up the ships anchored there. There will be air cover and a naval excursion to Narvik Fjord to keep the pot boiling while you take the visitors in and out; you can work on landed time of three hours maximum." He took a pull at his drink and looked around the wardroom. "All the lads back yet?"

"Last one came out of hospital two days ago, the new boy Ronnie Harris has settled down well as Max Cummings' Number One." Max's Number One had been injured, in the last attack and would not be out of hospital for another three months to make sure all the repairs to his shattered body knitted together properly. He also had been decorated for his part in the action against *Valkyrie* and when he came out of convalescence he would be offered his own command.

Christmas came and the boats suddenly sprouted decorations and mysterious activities among the crews. The ML arrived in time to be included in the pre-Christmas arrangements. It was commanded by Lieut Commander Charlie King who slotted into the wardroom as if he had been there all the time. From him Peter found out that the flotilla at Alex had been recalled and the officers and men distributed between the new boats coming off the slipways. They provided the stiffening of experience among the raw crews. For Charlie himself things had gone well and his current command was one of the newest of the Fairmile boats.

Armed as well as the MGBs, it was faster and had better accommodation than the other boats, and was longer by ten feet.

The boat was ideal for the purpose of delivering and collecting the party, provided that the arrival and departure could be covered without too much hassle.

With a smaller crew and extra length the ML had ample room for the fifteen man party she would be carrying.

Peter had managed to contact Caroline and arranged to meet her and take her down to his home in Christchurch for Christmas day, they would return to London on Boxing Day and have two days alone together before he had to return to Harwich.

He thought things might be awkward with the family having been with Claire the last time he had brought someone home. He was quite wrong; he discovered that Claire had stayed in touch with his mother and that she had visited when she had the time twice during the past months.

When he arrived with Caroline his mother had kissed him and turned to Caroline, "You must be Caroline Cartwright. Claire told me all about you. Do come and I'll show you where to put your things." Caroline looked helplessly at Peter and followed Grace from the room. Peter walked down to the yard, the smell of the raw wood a familiar perfume bringing memories of all his younger days here, working the plane and shaping the ribs of boats long gone.

Mike Murray was there as he knew he would be. "Hi. Dad, still busy I see." He indicated the frames for the rather square looking hull sitting awaiting completion on the extended stocks. "Making them bigger now I see."

"Hullo, son, good to see you, lad." He put his hand out and shook Peter's hand warmly. "Yes, they came and stretched the boatshed, free of charge, so that I could build the bigger boats."

Peter was concerned, his father was looking tired and he had aged over the past year since he had last seen him.

"See you've got your third stripe now, is that official not temporary anymore?"

"Substantive yes, not a permanent thing though, I'm not planning to stay in the navy after the war." He smiled "So all the men away for Christmas are they?"

"Yes I was just clearing up a bit before I went in to meet your lady and have dinner, I suppose we'd better go in but hang on a minute more." Mike went over to the bench and ducking down he retrieved a bottle of Scotch covered in sawdust. He carried it over to the sink where he washed two of the mugs used for tea. Pouring a healthy tot into each cup he gave one to Peter and lifted his own, "God bless you, son, I'm proud of you, good health." He clicked Peter's mug and drank it down. Peter raised his own "And you, Dad" and drank. "Whose bottle is it?"

"Charley Watts keeps it there. He thinks I don't know." His father grinned and put the bottle back. "I'll tell him one day, now let's go and eat, she's been cooking for hours so we'd better do it justice." He put his arm round Peter's shoulder and strode through the door and back to the house.

On the train to London they managed to get seats in a First Class compartment and on Boxing Day the train was quiet. Caroline said "I like you family and I think they like me." she smiled at him, "I felt at home for the first time since I left Austria."

Peter smiled at her, "You are home. I want you to become part of the family, I want you to marry me, please."

"Do you mean it; seriously?" She looked at him intently.

"I was never more serious about anything in my life." Peter answered her "I think I knew when I first saw you in Alex. I wanted to ask you in London when we last met, but I thought I might scare you off, and now... I couldn't help myself." He shrugged.

"Oh Peter of course I will marry you, I've known for over a year that you were the only one for me. I decided if you didn't ask me I would ask you."

The early planning was kept secret until the operation was approved finally.

Intelligence had reported the little settlement at Langesund, had no soldiers stationed since the place had been cleared during the big raid. The few people who now occupied some of the houses cleared at the time were not regarded as a threat, and few fishing boats used the once busy quay.

The plan was for the boats to enter the harbor and the ML would go alongside the quay and offload its passengers. The meeting was arranged at Brevik, just up the valley where the scientists would compare notes and information. The Commando party were given the task of a rescue raid on the Gestapo HQ at Skien. The recent activities of the Gestapo had resulted in several arrests of people important to the resistance, and to the Norwegian people. Latest information indicated that the people were being held but not at present under interrogation. Their value was believed to be as hostages rather than suspects, so it was vital to rescue these people before the enemy became aware of the true value of their captives.

So once again the two sections of the flotilla were separated and Max and his section of MTBs were briefed separately, no hint of the tasks of the other boats was given in case they were captured and interrogated.

The MGB briefing was based on the security for the ML and back up for the MTBs on the return journey.

The destroyers *HMS Whippet* and *HMS Aries* would accompany the MTBs to Oslo, both had the speed to keep up with the MTBs and their own torpedo tubes and their 4.7in guns could do a lot of damage. Finally the RAF and the Fleet Air Arm both would be taking part on the occasion Mosquito bombers from the RAF and Albacores from the Fleet Air Arm would be raiding targets in the Oslo area to keep the enemy forces occupied.

The assembled force rocked at their moorings awaiting the signal to proceed. In the ward room Paul sat with Peter drinking coffee, the 6000 boat was alongside Peter was fully kitted out it would take a few moments only for him to board and get under way. Paul was uncomfortable about something and he was trying to think of a way to tell Peter what was troubling him.

"Peter, I have been told something in confidence that may come as a shock." That was as far as he got as the Signals PO came in with the go signal for the operation. With a sigh of relief Paul decided his news would have to wait until the raid was over.

"What were you going to tell me?" Peter asked.

"I'll tell you when you get back, there's no time now. It will keep, don't worry." He called as Peter boarded his boat.

The early morning departure was a cold occasion, the wind was northerly and there was sleet and snow carried on it. "Just to make things bloody perfect," observed Walters, who was wrapped up like a teddy bear with balaclava helmet and a scarf round his neck, the duffle coat done up to the neck over a towel already damp, and an extra pair of socks inside his seaboots.

Lieutenant Allan Hodges beat his hands together to try and get them warm, "Mathews, see if you can find a brew for us." He took over the wheel while A/B Mathews went below in search of hot drink for the Bridge and lookouts.

Allan looked around at the company of boats scattered around the immediate area, over in the distance. To Port the MTBs and the two destroyers were bobbing and swaying at low speed, while close-to on the Starboard side the other MGBs and the big ML cruised in a an equally scattered formation. the more distant boats were difficult to distinguish in the current weather conditions. "Good job, too," he said aloud.

"Pardon sir, what was that?" Walters asked.

"Just thinking out loud, Chief. It's a good job that visibility is bad today, we'll be better off without the attention of our neighbourhood E Boats."

Mathews came noisily up from below carrying a Dixie of tea and a bunch of mugs. He started handing the steaming mugs of tea round and the duty watch accepted them gratefully, warming their hands against the hot enamel.

The trip across the North Sea had begun at 03.00hrs and the speed maintained at 25 knots had been tiring at best. There would be refuelling at dusk this evening, otherwise the relentless regime would continue without let up all the way to Norway; with the operation commencing at 0400 local time.

Peter came on to the bridge and lifted his binoculars to make a sweep around the horizon.

"So what's happening, Number One; any problems at all?"

For the second time that day a group of aircraft swept across the collection of boats searching for any sign of enemy activity. A single aircraft at high altitude had kept them company during the transit of the North Sea.

"Well, so far – so good, sir. We did think we might have had a problem with refuelling, but we got the confirmation signal in time. All is otherwise quiet and all watch stations manned.

Peter nodded in acknowledgement "I'll take over now, go and get your head down; you can take over again at 18.00 hrs. Before you settle down make sure the men are fed and organize sandwiches and hot soup prepared before the start time for the operation."

"Aye aye, sir," and Hodges went below.

"How about you, Chief, do you want to get your head down?"

"Perhaps later sir. I'm feeling just a little edgy at the moment, I would rather wait for darkness if it's okay with you."

The boat was carrying extra crew on board to allow the ML to carry all the landing parties, the chief had accordingly been relieved of his standard watches.

"The arrangements seem to be working out well." Jim Walters commented.

Peter grunted, unwilling to chance comment too soon. "I'll be happy when the others leave us; we make too big a target for my liking." He lifted his glasses and swept the horizon once more.

The steady rumble of the engines had a soporific effect on Allan Hodges, he hardy had time to think about Hillary before he was fast asleep. He awoke at the clatter of running feet and the reduced noise from the engines. Alarmed at first, he realized that it was the crew refuelling from one of the submarines sent to act as tankers to the boats.

On the bridge Peter was watching the refuelling in the dim light of the moon through the clouds, although there was no direct light the loom of the moonlight was present. The two destroyers were circling the thirteen boats and the three submarines that were refuelling them from the long containers strapped to their decks.

He examined his watch in the light of the binnacle: 21.00 hrs. The confirmation signal should be received any time now. He sighed and leaned over the bridge wing, "How is the fuelling going, Number One?"

Down on the deck aft Hodges straightened up. "About full up sir, topping out just about now."

"Good. I would like to get going again as soon as possible." As he spoke he heard one of the submarines submerging, and from the other noises the others were preparing to follow suit. Over the RT the reports came in from the flotilla confirming their readiness to proceed.

As Commander of the transit to Norway, Peter gave the order to proceed and the armada, as Lieutenant Hodges insisted on calling it, got under way for the final part of the voyage.

The confirmation signal came in at 21.15 hrs and it was a both a relief and a worry. It was a relief because now the uncertainty was over, but a worry because the operation was fraught with danger. There were still many unknown factors in both parts of the raid, and for Peter the raid on the power plant was a serious risk for the men and the partisans involved.

The force separated at 01.30 hrs. The Oslo raiders increasing speed to complete their journey before the 03.00
deadline.

Peter's force crept in to the coast line to complete the
final stretch to the village at Langesund.

The first part of the operation went like silk; the ML
slid up to the fishing quay and moored alongside. The two
separate parties landed and were met by their guides, swiftly
disappearing from view. The dying sound of a truck engine
was a distant reminder of their passing.

"Now we wait." Peter spoke to the Chief who was on
the bridge, ready to go into action wherever he was needed.

"How about I check the local Gestapo HQ, sir? It
wouldn't do to be surprised-like, by a last minute reinforcement of SS or suchlike."

"Good idea, Chief, take your cattle thieves with you and
contact that man on the dock." He pointed out the shadowy
figure of a man on the dock; liaison with the partisans.

"Aye aye sir," Walters called softly below and as two
men appeared fully kitted out for night action ashore Peter
realized that Walters had guessed he would approve his suggestion and he had wasted no time being prepared for instant
action.

"Take care, Chief; they aren't all idiots here."

"I will, sir." The words drifted away as the dinghy that
had been tied up alongside was paddled swiftly and quietly
away from the boat towards the nearby quay wall.

The three men climbed up the ladder to the quay and
Walters approached the shadowy figure waiting there. As he
approached he gave the password "Narvik"

The answer came back, "Churchill"

"Can you direct us to the local Gestapo HQ? We want
to make sure there are no unpleasant surprises."

The voice replied in accented English, a feminine voice. "I had better take you there myself, it could be tricky in the darkness. Come!"

The party of four left the quay, Walters and his men following the small figure of the woman through the streets of the village.

They stopped as Walters encountered the outstretched arm of their guide who whispered "Slowly now, just round the corner ahead."

Walters came up alongside the woman and peered round the corner. There was a square, obviously the centre of the village. There were lights showing through the open front door. The steps were highlighted in the shielded headlamps of the truck parked there. The driver was leaning against the radiator smoking a cigarette, and warming himself against the hot metal.

As he watched he saw several armed men carrying boxes into the building, and an officer came out and shouted an order, and the driver hurriedly dropped his cigarette and stood to attention.

Walters was suddenly aware of the faintly perfumed scent of the crouching woman next to him. She said quietly "They are going to move out to intercept a suspected raiding party."

Walters asked "Are there any more of your people available?"

"Not here. I am the only active member left here, the others are all out with the two raiding parties."

"I'll need to contact the skipper. Corbett, can you find your way back to the harbor?"

"No problem Chief."

"Report to Commander King on the ML, he can call our skipper on the RT. Tell him we need more men, at least 12. They should be armed with Stens and grenades, bring them back with you. Got it?"

"Got it, Chief!" Corbett the poacher disappeared without a sound.

"Mathews, I want you round the left side of the square. If that truck or any truck moves, shoot the tires out. Understand? Then go." He didn't wait the reply he turned to the woman. "I will have to stop them moving out."

In the dark he saw the pale shadow of her face turned towards him. "Of course we must." The click of the cocking handle on the MP40 smg underlined her simple comment.

He reached out and took her small hand in his, "Stay with me unless I am hit. In that case, get out fast. Don't let them get you, understand?"

"Got it!" she said, purposely copying Corbett's reply.

Chapter Nineteen

Commander Peter Murray RNVR, appeared beside CPO Jim Walters, followed by a file of armed men, all wearing their battle gear and armed with Sten guns and grenades.

"What's the situation, Chief?

"The Gestapo HQ is that building with the truck outside. There has been some activity and I think there are more men there than we expected, possibly as many as thirty."

Peter turned to the woman. "Are there any prisoners there that we should worry about?"

The woman looked up at Peter in the semi darkness of the street "Call me Christina. No one as far as I know, and if you are worrying about problems for the local people, the only people living here in town are the traitors who collaborate with the Nazis."

Peter smiled "I'm Peter Murray, shall we pay them a visit?"

"Why not?" Christina replied quietly. "I've put it off too often in the past.

"Chief, we're about to cross the square. Are the men in place to cover us where necessary?"

"Yes sir, and I will be right behind you both, but if I may, sir, I would like Corbett and his mate Merryweather to clear the way, if you wouldn't mind."

"Of course, Chief; glad you reminded me."

The three watched as the two figures drifted into view, out of the shadows on the far side of the square. They openly walked over to the driver and NCO standing smoking by the truck. Corbett waved cheerfully to the driver and Merryweather slapped the NCO on the back then grabbed the body to stop it falling and propped him over the bonnet of the vehicle. The startled driver had no time to do anything but gape in astonishment as Corbett slid the blade of the Fairburn knife acquired from the Commandos in Fort William across his throat.

The squad under Peter moved out with Christina well to the fore as the two bodies were hauled out of sight behind the low wall surrounding the building.

Walters signalled his men to cover the other exits from the building and Peter and party walked in through the front door.

"Capture any officers you can find, but don't put yourselves at risk to do it. These people are the scum who massacred the local people here so don't worry about hurting their feelings." The others in the party grinned at this comment and started opening doors.

The clatter of the first burst of Sten gunfire roused the building and soon the crack of Grenades and submachine guns echoed through the building.

The surprise was complete; though once the Gestapo and SS men in the building realized what was happening the resistance was bitter. Corbett and Merryweather found two people in the cellars who had been undergoing interrogation, a man and a woman. Both were attached to electrical wires and both were apparently unconscious. The naked figures were slumped in chairs facing each other. As Corbett entered, a tall man in the white overalls was throwing a bucket of water over the man. A uniformed officer was bent over the woman stroking her cheek with his gloved hand.

The first sound of firing came as Corbett and Merryweather burst through the door. Both men were caught by surprise, Merryweather called out as he saw a third man behind the door pulling his pistol from his holster. The thunk of the thrown knife as it was embedded in the third man's throat was followed by the crash as his falling body collided with a trolley of surgical implements as he fell to the floor.

The other two men recovered and raised their hands as Corbett lifted his Sten gun.

"Frisk them, Merry." He said tersely.

Merryweather lifted the Luger from the officer's holster, then ran his hands down the overalled figure of the other man.

The seated man had been roused by the water thrown over him and he was stirring in the chair. Merryweather removed the leather straps holding him in the chair and unclipped the electric cables; he then carefully lifted the man up and onto the hospital trolley standing in the corner of the room. Then he roughly pushed the officer onto the chair and strapped him in. He then gently unstrapped the unconscious woman unclipping the cables from her body, there was a cot in the corner of the room and he placed her there. He indicated to the overalled man to remove his overalls before pushing him into the other chair in his underwear and strapping him in.

The man on the trolley was sitting up, grimacing in pain as Corbett went to help him. He said something neither of the sailors understood. Then noticing their uniforms. he said in English, "How is Margit?" Then seeing the woman on the cot covered with the overalls he tried to get up.

"Hold on there, mate." Corbett said kindly. "Take it easy, we'll soon sort you all out."

Boots sounded in the passage outside the door and the door bust open. The SS man stepped in, MP40 up and ready. The butt of Merryweather's Sten caught him on the side of his head and he collapsed in a heap on the floor. More feet pounded down the passage and a voice called in English, "Corbett, Merryweather, where the fuck are you?" The familiar voice of CPO Walters rang out and Corbett answered "Here, Chief; we need a medic."

The face of Walters appeared through the doorway, taking in the scene swiftly he said "Right. Let's get the show on the road." He detailed two of the men with him to carry the injured male victim and told Corbett to get the woman onto the trolley; they would take them to the medic just in case they had to move out fast.

Slipping the unconscious woman into the overalls, they laid her on the trolley and, while Corbett and Merryweather went back to clearing the rooms. the men with Walters took the prisoners and their victims out to the truck in the square.

The building was cleared with four casualties among Peter's men, one serious. The enemy suffered thirteen killed and four wounded, seven survivors taken prisoner, three of them officers. The Gestapo man taken from the cellar was the senior officer present. Peter had all the prisoners and the wounded taken to the boats in the truck, which then returned to the square.

Christina suggested that they remove all the records from the building for study in England. The doctor came and reported that the two people being interrogated had both re-covered consciousness and though sore and bruised, both were mobile and wished to talk to Peter and Christina.

The two were properly clothed once more and they were both clasping mugs of coffee laced with rum. When Christina saw Margit she recognised her immediately. "What happened, how did they get hold of you?" She asked.

Margit smiled wryly "By accident. They caught us out after curfew in Brevik. We played at being lovers, but they brought us here anyway, I'm convinced it was so that they could play with us. The Gestapo man is a pervert and his companion is as bad. They were asking questions for effect, not in any way relevant. I am convinced they were amusing themselves and experimenting on us because they were bored; they made no real attempt to gain information from us." She looked at the man, Robert, who was sitting half asleep in the other chair. He woke up with a start, then catching up with the conversation he agreed with Margit.

Christina suggested that since they were able to clear the records and held the arresting party prisoner the two local people could return home if they wished, otherwise a place was available in the boats. They elected to return home but Margit and Christina went off to compare notes and debrief before the party returned to UK.

In the approaches to Oslo the diversionary party caught the defences completely by surprise. HMS *Whippet* and HMS *Aries* opened fire on the shore batteries whilst the six MTBs raced into the harbor. Max torpedoed the tanker linked to the shore refinery by pipes, loading oil. The explosion of the ship created a fireball that rolled along the pipeline to the refinery causing further explosions as the nearest storage tanks blew up in turn. The other boats with all guns blazing were lining up the big destroyer and the freighter at anchor in the centre of the harbor. Two boats separated and both released torpedoes before they turned away heading for the waterfront. As they turned two more torpedoes hit the destroyer from the flight of Albacores that had appeared over the headland to the west. On shore the army barracks received a series of bombs from the Mosquito fighter bombers that swept in over the city. Other Mosquito aircraft were strafing the anti aircraft guns that had begun to open up.
Two of the boats released their torpedoes at the dock gates where ships were being worked upon. The explosions blew the gates away and revealed the ships inside. The next two boats launched their fish into the dock creating mayhem among the ships under repair.
HMS Whippet was now concentrating her gunfire on the trot of E boats moored together in the bay beside Bygdoy Island. The boats where activity had begun suddenly were shattered and smashed by the destroyer's 4.7in guns and the pompoms depressed to their stops pouring a blizzard of 2lb shells among the moored boats.

Lieutenant Commander Max Cumming smiled at the mayhem they had created in the harbor. His Radio Operator monitoring the radio traffic said that there were panic calls going out for reinforcements to come to the aid of the Oslo Garrison who believed that they were facing an invasion force.

Max took a last look round. The sinking ships, the burning refinery and the smoke and flames following the air attack gave the entire scene the look of a war zone. Satisfied, he gave the order to withdraw, and was gratified to receive the acknowledgements from all the craft in the attacking force. One of the Albacores had crash-landed in the water offshore; the crew members were recovered by *HMS Aries* as she turned to leave the harbor. Her guns were still firing at targets on shore and as Max watched something blew up with another massive explosion.

The MTBs tucked in two by two behind *HMS Whippet* and were followed by *HMS Aries*. The guns of the two destroyers continued firing until the defences of Oslo were out of range.

The flotilla cruised back to the region off Langesund, where they waited to link up with Peter's force.

Peter was delayed, waiting for the return of the two remote sections. Reports of the delay caused him to order the Oslo force to join him in the harbor.

The ships entered the fjord and moored. Nets were strung over the MTBs who moored alongside the various buildings by the shore and the destroyers retired to the disused fish factory where they tied up alongside the long landing quay and strung up the warehouse doors to partially cover the ships alongside. Peter had decided that they would be better leaving in the evening so that they could take advantage of the dark hours to get well on their way home.

He called for the marine detachments from the destroyers to reinforce the defence force in town. Though it was not needed at present, there were German forces in the neighbouring towns and the risk of them coming through the town was a serious possibility.

The return of the scientist group from their journey up country was a cause for relief, although the Commando group were still absent. A call had been received saying that things were progressing well and if the boats had to leave sooner than expected they would join the Norwegian Partisans in the mountains and carry on from there.

Peter sent a runner back on a motor bike inform the Commando Captain that they would be there until dark that night.

CPO Jim Walters had set up the aid station for the doctors from the flotilla, and arranged for the injured to be cared for. In addition patients had been coming in from the country region bringing an assortment of complaints for treatment, from children with childhood ailments to broken limbs and one difficult pregnancy.

Christina had been of assistance in arranging things and seemed quite happy working alongside the big Londoner.

They stopped to eat when things were running properly and Jim seized the chance to talk with her privately. "So what are you going to do when this is all over?" He asked.

She looked at him eye to eye and smiled. "Why, I am not sure. I have been studying accountancy, but they closed the College, I suppose I will go back to it after all this is over."

"I heard the skipper say to you that you should return with us tonight, will you be coming with us?"

Something in his voice must have given his more that idle interest away.

Smiling slightly she said "He did mention it, and I am thinking about it. Are you interested in whether I come or not?"

The direct replay took him by surprise; he blushed and confused stuttered slightly "I was concerned. After all, you have been seen by several people with us. and… and…" He ran out of things to say and stood there unusually tongue tied.

Taking pity on him she grinned and said "I will be coming with you and if you don't mind I was going to ask you to keep close when we arrive. I have never been out of Norway before and I would prefer to have someone I know I could depend on," she blushed in turn. "To give me moral support when I get there."

Jim sighed with relief, smiling back. "I would be very happy to stay close when we get back."

He bowed deeply to her. "I would be honoured to escort you wherever and whenever I can. How about dinner the first night home?"

She swept him a curtsey "Why, thank you kind sir, but what will your wife say?"

Confused for a moment Jim blurted out "Wife? I have no wife, nor girlfriend for that matter. I've been moving around too much to make friends." His voice tailed off as he realized the girl smiling at him had been checking up; just in case!

She said "I do understand. My last boyfriend left school to join the resistance, he was shot and killed in the first landings. I found out two months later. I joined the resistance and have had no time or inclination since." She hastily added "Not that I am looking now…. Oh bother."

They both burst out laughing and the atmosphere between them relaxed and a tacit understanding was reached without another word spoken.

The Commando group returned mid-afternoon. Three times German aircraft passed over the town but none made any indication that they had seen anything. Peter had a long discussion with the local Partisan leaders who had come down from the hills to collect weapons and stores. The collected weapons and stores of the captured and killed German troops were an unexpected bonus, and the chance to talk face to face with the allies was welcomed.

Several of the scientists in hiding were rounded up to go back with the party. Whilst further north there was regular communications through the services of the Shetland Bus, here in southern Norway things were more difficult.

Working with the leaders Peter arranges a system of communication and a rendezvous point to deliver arms and supplies in the future.

"So" he summed up "If we load supplies in sealed containers we can buoy them and drop them at night in one of the three bays between here and Kragero, an announcement on the BBC will let you know when a drop can be expected." He looked at the three men sitting round the table, one by one they nodded in understanding.

Nils Nielson the leader of the south Norway Partisans made to rise then sat down once more. "One last thing," he said. "The Gestapo man you have prisoner here has been responsible for murdering 84 people over the past three months, including the men of this town who refused to collaborate. We have sentenced him to death in a properly constituted court, and I would like to have him executed here for his crimes."

"I sympathise, but if we do that there will be more reprisals against your people. As it is if we have the record of his trial and conviction, and he is removed by us to England, Your own Government can confirm the sentence and he can be hanged there, without repercussions here."

The other two Norwegians were nodding in agreement. After a moment Nils also nodded. "Ja, okay, you are right. They cannot blame us for what you do." He rose and put out his hand, crushing Peter's in his big paw. "Thank you, friend, and goodbye. Be careful on your way home – they will be out looking for sure."

In turn the others also left.

Peter stretched and sat back in the easy chair falling asleep immediately.

Charlie King woke him an hour later. "Sorry, Boss; we've got company."

Peter was instantly awake. "Company?"

"A column of personnel carriers coming over the road from Kristiansand heading for Oslo I should think, but they may call in for extra men if they suspect we're here."

"Right. Get the Captain in. How long have we got?"

"Half hour, maybe more. I'll get the Captain." He left in a rush and was back in minutes with the Captain,

"He was already on the way here." Charlie said. "The destroyers' Captains will be here in a few minutes."

Peter nodded and turned to the Captain Martin Talbot, RM. "Som Martin, what do we do? Fight or run?"

Talbot was thinking. "Four AP carriers – probably 100 men, plus the small armored car. Let's speak to the destroyer Captains."

The two Commanders came in just a few moments later.

The German convoy crawled over the hill and came into sight of the town below. The Kommondant was seated in a Kubelwagen, following the small armored car that was leading the way.

Suddenly the armored car rose in the air as the charge buried in the road went off. The driver of the Kubelwagen wrenched the wheel over to avoid the crater and nosed down into the ditch. Behind them the convoy stopped and the men began to debus. The concealed ambushers opened fire and the troops in the convoy started suffering losses immediately. A shell arrived and obliterated the last truck which was attempting to turn in the road.

The radio in the Kubelwagen issued a shower of sparks as a burst of fire stitched a row of bullet holes across the face of the instrument.

The Kommondant crawled out of the vehicle and lay in the ditch. He seized the MP40 handed him by the driver. The Hauptmann who had been seated beside him still sat erect in his seat, eyes open, anchored in his seat by the barrel of one of the Vierling machine guns from the wrecked armored car.

The reinforced company of Marines under the command of Captain Talbot assisted by the local Partisans and a platoon of armed sailors from the gunboats added their weight to the ambush using a Spandau machine gun captured from the German HQ in Langesund.

The troops in the third carrier dismounted and threw down their weapons while the remaining occupants of the first two carriers were mopped up.

The Kommondant was hauled out of the ditch, furious but helpless in the circumstances. The surviving soldiers were put to work clearing up the mess of dead and wounded while the Partisans collected the discarded weapons. The empty third truck was undamaged and used to transport the partisans and their weapons on their way back to their place in the mountains. The other mobile truck was used to take the wounded for treatment while the remaining men were marched down to the town under escort. The forty-two uninjured prisoners were taken on board *HMS Whippet* and *HMS Aries.* The Kommondant, to his disgust, was placed with the Gestapo officer in the ML. The civilians leaving with the party were accommodated amongst the MGBs and MTBs.

The flotilla sailed at dusk, having made its mark on the Norwegian coast.

The high speed departure over a day after the raid on Oslo gave the flotilla a small breathing space and by dawn the following morning they were well out into the North Sea.

They were found by the Luftwaffe in the afternoon and were under attack from a succession of Me 110 and Junkers 88 aircraft. The storm of fire that greeted the aircraft cost them dear, two of their number were destroyed in the first attack. Several of the craft were damaged during the attacks but all managed to keep going. A squadron of Mosquitoes arrived in time to cause the remaining Axis aircraft to disperse in a hurry, leaving three of their number in flames. The remainder of the journey was made under the reassuring drone of friendly aircraft. The entire force made it back to Harwich without further loss. There were casualties in several of the boats including four on Peter's MGB. Christina was quickly involved in helping the doctor dealing with the wounded, and followed him to the other craft that were without a doctor when the shooting stopped.

She rejoined the flotilla leader shortly before reaching the English coast, much to the relief of Jim Walters.

Chapter Twenty

The wound suffered by Jim Walters was not really seri-ous, but it did mean he had to be sent to hospital. It also meant that he was not there when Christina left the base to be accommodated with the free Norwegians near London.

It was during the last attack from the enemy aircraft on the way home from Norway, a piece of the shattered Perspex from the machinegun turret behind the bridge had lodged in Jim's back. The same shattering Perspex had wounded the skipper at the same time. Peter Murray was in the same hos-pital with a similar back injury. Both were due out after two weeks, both scheduled for ten days recovery leave. But whereas Peter was visited by Caroline: Jim was unable to contact Christina, she had been taken off by the Norwegian people in UK.

When Caroline discovered Jim's dilemma she had got in touch with the authorities to find Christina and was able to bring her down on her next visit.

For Jim that first visit was difficult initially, Christina was shy and neither could think of anything to say. When Jim started to ask about the place where she was being ac-commodated, she answered saying that the people were kind. As she got up to leave she turned and took Jim's hand. The contact seemed to act as a trigger and she burst out cry-ing "Oh Jim, I was so worried about you and no one seemed to know anything. People had arranged everything and I could not get anyone to understand that I wanted to see you. I told them we were engaged." She blushed "I didn't think you would mind, but it made no difference. When Caroline appeared I was at my wits' end. She was terrific; in no time I was out of there and into her flat. She introduced me to her boss at SOE and I have decided to join them."

Suddenly the awkwardness between them had gone and the words flowed both ways. Before Christina left Jim arranged to see her when he left hospital.

Taking her hand as she was turning to leave, he kissed her. "By the way, when I see you next we'll need to get a ring. After all we can't be engaged without an engagement ring, now can we?"

Her arms round his neck as she kissed him once more gave her answer.

He lay there alone once more and realized that he had meant every word he had said, never ever had he felt like this about anyone. He lay there realizing that that thing others kept telling him would happen to him one day had happened. He was in love with the little Norwegian girl. Christina had just crept into his life without warning and without asking. He fell asleep still confused, but happier than he could ever remember.

There were things happening while Peter was on leave, The Allies were fighting their way up the length of Italy, and the battle to relieve Leningrad was being won by the Russians.

Caroline was apparently unable to get time off as the level of activity in her department was rising all the time now. Though there was nothing actually said, the feeling was that an invasion of the mainland of Europe was in the air.

The engagement of Peter and Caroline was celebrated at Christchurch. Jim Walters and his new fiancée Christina attended the party. They had been staying in the house of Jim's aunt in Littlehampton, who had received them with open arms. Having no children of her own she regarded Jim, her sole nephew, as the son she never had.

The two men returned from leave at the same time to find the base in a frenzy of activity preparing for the transfer of the flotilla to Weymouth for operations in the channel.

Commander Paul Waterstone stood behind the desk in his office with his hands in his pockets. His brisk voice was an indication of his current harassment. "Good leave, congratulations by the way. Now, Peter, this move is in preparation for the big push." He strode over to the door and made sure it was closed. "Between us it's the invasion of France this time. Everything is building up for it. The Yanks are sending their troops across in massive numbers and the Powers that be are having a hell of a job keeping the whole business secret.

"Our job will be to keep things stirred up so that they don't know where we will be coming from. Personally I don't know either, but I'm willing to bet it's not going to be the Pas de Calais. Somewhere further down the coast would be my guess."

Peter sat stunned for the moment. Of course they all knew it would happen at some time but he had no idea that it would be so soon. Trying to maintain his calm acceptance of the news he said "So I take it the move to Weymouth has nothing to do with the fact that your home is just round the corner from there?" He leaned back in the chair and stretching his arms up then clasping his hands together behind his head he said "I suppose we will be getting quite busy again. What about the refits?" he referred to the promised maintenance of the boats of the Flotilla.

"That's all taken care of; your own boat came off the slipway yesterday. When you get back to her you'll see there have been a few upgrades while they were at it. I grabbed you to make sure that you realized the urgency of the whole business. So get off back to your boys now and let me get on with my panic in peace."

As Peter boarded his boat, he was received by Allan Hodges who was looking more harassed than Paul Waterstone, "Welcome back, sir, we've had our refit and are just getting things organized."

Peter looked around" You seem to have things well in hand, Number One, I'll let you get on with it. We can have our chat when the hands break for tea. Carry on."

He went below to his cabin where he found his gear already unpacked and put away. As he sat down with a sigh, Mathews appeared with a tray. "Thought you could do with a cuppa after your trip, sir. The lads asked me to pass on their congratulations to you and your lady, sir." He put down the tray to withdraw.

"Thanks Mathews and thank the lads, the tea will be just right." Peter poured out a cup and sat back facing the pile of documents waiting his attention.

The next two weeks were busy for the Flotilla HQ staff as they battled with the problems of moving the men and maintenance teams in advance to Weymouth. The boats were the least of their problems, there was no depot ship at the Weymouth base so all the facilities were shore based. The fleet of trucks fought their way across the south of England at a time when the armies were moving into position; and other teams of men scattered around the Southeast and East Anglia were producing all sorts of strange assemblies. Made up to look like tank parks and artillery squadrons, the strange collections were being created to convince the enemy that the invasion would be attempted at the Pas de Calais. The apparent build up of equipment lending credit to that belief.

All this activity caused the communications between Harwich and Weymouth great difficulty and frustrating delay. It was only after three weeks of unremitting work that the transfer was completed.

For the transit, the boats left loaded with last minute stores and staff. Paul Waterstone travelled with Peter, the Captain having been called to the Admiralty en route to Weymouth regretfully gave up his place in the boats and settled for being taken in a staff car to London with the prospect of a train journey for the balance of the trip.

The first week of operations from the Weymouth base turned out to be almost disastrous for the MGB section. The full six-boat section set out on Tuesday, the second day at their new base in company with the MTBs; the entire flotilla taking a shakedown cruise along the Dorset and Devon coast.

When they encountered the collection of ships assembled in the Seaton area of Devon, to Peter's dismay, the nearest craft opened fire on the gunboats and only stopped when hurried signals were exchanged establishing that the approaching craft were in fact Allies.

No one in Peter's Command knew of the successful attack on the practicing landing fleet that had been carried out by German Schnellboot two days before on the 28th April 1944. The news blackout had been complete. 749 US soldiers and sailors had been lost to the enemy attack. The successful suppression of this news contributed to the success of the invasion.

Apart from some unsightly bullet holes in the starboard echelon of boats no harm was done, and the matter was passed off as itchy fingers on behalf of the practicing landing fleet.

In the de-briefing session the fact of the presence of the landing craft was down-played and the crews were briefed to keep their presence to themselves.

Paul Waterstone had a long list of maintenance tasks to be carried out and though patrols were to be mounted the main effort of the enlarged flotilla was to be on building up to top efficiency, for what was to come during the next few weeks.

Because of the proximity of Weymouth to Christchurch, by borrowing the MG Roadster currently owned by Paul Waterstone Peter was able to get home to see his parents a little more often than before. The last weekend was special because his brother John had returned from the Western Desert, a Captain now in the SAS, en route to Scotland for a refresher course with the Commandos.

As far as he was aware, the SAS would be involved in advance strikes in some new operation scheduled for some time later in the year.

His parents were showing increasingly the effect of the pressure of work imposed by the demands of the War Office. His father particularly suffering now with back trouble and depending more and more on the efforts of the ubiquitous Joe who had been with him now for over 30 years. Peter could not help noticing his bent shoulders and the grey in his hair so much more than last time he had called.

John disappeared with a rush and a roar on a motorbike for his course up north, and Peter felt the vacuum left by his passing.

The work of keeping the flotilla on the top line took a lot of ingenuity and it involved co-operation with the RAF Rescue boats and the increasing number of convoys up and down channel. During the period up to the end of May the ever increasing activity on land made more and more speculation occur and it caused problems with maintaining the security blanket over the south of England.

In the base the invasion was now a general topic of conversation, it was just where and more importantly when, that occupied most of the crews in the flotilla.

The meeting at the Admiralty was very discreet. Those present were all in uniform including Caroline who was wearing the uniform of a First Officer WRNS. The others present were a Vice Admiral a Captain, a Marine Major and two Commanders RN. A Chief Petty Officer, WRNS was taking notes.

The Admiral spoke first "No names, please; this meeting never happened, and we do not know who attended." He turned to the WRNS Writer "I want your notebook when we finish."

The Writer nodded in acknowledgement.

The subject of the meeting was the use of two captured E Boats, both of which the Germans had good reason to believe destroyed.

The Admiral opened the discussion "Where are the boats now?"

The smaller of the Commanders spoke. "Both boats are in Poole Harbor, disguised as coasters at present. They have gone through the complete range of trials, always after dark and covered by destroyers."

"Excellent, we are ready to proceed then?"

The taller Commander answered. "Crews, sir; we still need crews, we have no trained crews for the boats."

"Good god, man, we have MTB's and MGB's scattered all around our coasts. They are all trained. Get crews from the nearest base, Weymouth or Portsmouth." The Admiral sounded irritated. "We have known about this operation for the past three months. There is no excuse for further delay. Get on with it, man. Now, which shall it be; Weymouth or Portsmouth?"

The Commander was not pleased to be put on the spot like that so he answered hastily, "Weymouth, I suppose. The Flotilla Commander there is VR and has handled most small craft, has two DSO's so he knows his way about, chap named....."

Before he could finish the Admiral broke in. "Damn it; what did I say about names? None to be mentioned here in this room, and I bloody well meant it; sorry, my dear." He apologised to the woman beside him.

The Commander, now red-faced, shut up.

The Marine Major spoke in a cultured lazy drawl "My chaps are ready to deploy as soon as the target is nominated. The nature of the target will dictate the equipment they carry so the sooner I know the sooner I'll be ready."

He looks about sixteen, Caroline thought, *but the rows of medals tell their own story. This languid young man has been places and though he is not in fact sixteen, he is still young to be a Marine Major.*

The Captain spoke next, hastily. "The target has now been selected. Ooint Y has been chosen, refer to the original brief, please. It had been selected despite the difficulties in approach to divert attention from the main purpose of the manoeuvres next month." He referred to the forthcoming invasion.

Caroline spoke then, immediately taking the attention of the entire room. "Since we started researching this project we have had agents operating here, here and here." She indicated three places on the wall-map. "Our latest reports indicate that the enemy are near enough convinced that we will go for the short route; the Pas de Calais. Because of the swept channel into the harbor the E boats will be particularly suitable for landing the Commandos. The targets are the new radar units either side of the harbor entrance. Unfortunately the boats will need to get into the harbor to land the raiding parties but since they will be there, the opportunity can be taken to destroy harbor features and sink the ships presently sheltering there. The support group of MGB's and MTB's will be off shore and they will drift in rubber dinghies to the beaches on either side of the harbor entrance to take off the raiding parties when their work is done. If the E boats are lost the crews have the rendezvous points to escape using the same rubber boats as the commando." She sat down carefully, troubled now knowing that Peter would be kn the thick of the forthcoming action."

"Thank you, my dear, very clearly put; any questions?" He looked around the group "Good. I know you have all worked hard on this exercise and I want to thank you all for your individual contributions. Good luck, Major, I will see you when you return." He stood, followed by everyone else, reached out his hand for the Writers notebook, which he took and thrust into his pocket. He left the room followed by the others.

Chapter Twenty-one

The orders to report to Poole harbor came at 1200 hours from Captain Archer himself, and they were verbal. "I don't know what's up but they want a boat and two spare crews to report the Yacht club in Poole Harbor by 1800 tonight. I think in the circumstances you will want to be there yourself, so I suggest you get under way as soon as possible. Take your own crew and another experienced crew, I have an idea you'll be using some different boats, so make sure the other skipper is a seaman."

With the Captain's words still rattling round his head, Peter called on Mike Roberts to bring his crew and join him on Emmy Easton's boat for the trip to Poole.

The MGB rumbled into the Poole Yacht Club anchorage at 1545, the flashing light ordering the spare crews to report to the clubhouse ashore.

Inside when the business of identities and crew members sorted out the men were split into their individual branches and taken to different rooms in the building. Peter and Mike Roberts finished up in the CO's office once the office of the club secretary.

An Admiral and a Commander were already there waiting when they were ushered in.

"Sit down, please, and listen. Your task tonight is to acquaint yourselves with the workings of a captured German E boat; the members of your crews are all being shown their parts of boat so that they can operate the systems in action. All the controls have been relabelled in English so that should be no trouble. The boats are fully armed and will be used for a special operation. I have arranged for German-speaking men to attend to communication whilst you are under German colors. You have three nights to become fully acquainted with the boats then the operation will be on. Any questions?" His keen eyes stared at the two officers sitting in front of the desk. He took the immediate lack of response as their answer. "Good. I'll be off then, down to you now, Commander." He picked up his hat and left the office leaving the faint scent of cologne as he passed through the door.

The dour-faced Commander didn't bother to introduce himself. He produced a plan sheet with details of the deck layout and the cabin layout of the big German diesel-engine E boat.

There were other sheets covering the schematics of the internal communications system. All was as fitted in the Blohm and Voss yards except the RT system which was the same as that used in the British boats.

The gruff voice of the Commander spoke. "The boats are constructed round bilge for seaworthiness and the triple diesel engines are powerful enough to get up to speeds of over forty knots. The bridge is armored and the range at 30 knots is 800 miles. They are armed with two torpedo tubes, and carry four altogether, with twin 20mm guns and a single 20mm, in addition they have a 37mm flack gun. Normal crew numbers 20-30 men. Study the plans we will give you a test run at 2200 hrs."

The Commander abruptly left the office leaving the two men with the drawings.

The two men looked at each other and burst out laughing. Then they got down to the study of the documents before them.

At 2200 hrs they boarded the boat correctly designated Schnellboot. The E boat designation being the name for 'enemy' boat only; both men found their way round the boat from the drawings provided and they were impatient to get under way and see how the boat handled.

The surly Commander appeared and ran over the controls with both Skippers, The Cox'n of each crew was already aware of the location and operation of the controls. All the other members of the two crews were already practiced at the operation of their parts of the boat; though they none of them had been under power yet.

Finally the order was given to cast off and the motors started. The deep rumble of the diesels sounded strange after the accustomed roar of the Packard's they were accustomed to.

Gingerly they moved off out into Poole Harbor then swinging out between Sandbanks and Shell Bay and out into the waters of the Channel. Peter let his breath out as he got to grips with the 114 foot length of the boat juggling the throttles of the three engines feeling the balance between them before opening them wide to experience the surge of exhilaration that came with the kick in the back as the engines wound up the revs to full power. Taking turns at the controls and the helm the two Skippers and the Cox'ns got to know the feel of the boat whilst the rest of the crew exercised with their own jobs.

After an exciting two hours they brought the boat back to her mooring at the Yacht club, both Skippers were happy with their ability to control and, if needed. fight the boat and the crew seemed equally happy with the jobs they had to cover.

The entire party was accommodated on the site and they were told they would not be returning to Weymouth until after the operation was completed.

The second night Mike Rogers took his crew aboard the other boat and the two boats exercised together, communicating through the RT being shepherded by two destroyers, just in case!

The briefing was on the third day and Caroline gave the run down on the location and the method of the raid. The boats were expendable and the alternative escape plan was detailed. The remaining MGB's of the Weymouth Flotilla would be assembled to take off the returning men from the raid' the rendezvous would be the Plage at Le Touquet.

Obviously if possible the boats were to be recovered as there were other uses they could be put to. The Skippers got together to decide if any extra equipment was needed and both agreed proper smoke floats should be taken to complement the generators that were carried on board.

Small arms also would be required if they had to escape across country, Peter had been astonished to find there were none on board. Apparently there had been none on board when she was captured. Both items were provided promptly, and the weapons distributed around the boat so that they could be grabbed on the run if needed.

Lectures over, Caroline was able to see Peter briefly before she returned to London, but it was sadly too little for both of them. To her eyes Peter was looking tired and she hoped he would have a chance to wind down soon. For Peter seeing Caroline was like a refreshing breath of air. Holding her in his arms had been wonderful though he wished he could just keep holding her long after she had left. He stood watching the road long after the car had disappeared.

Standing on the bridge was still an odd experience for the British officers; the alien feel of the area, armored and spacious after the cramped confines of their MGB's was odd and somehow made them feel exposed. The different sound from the engines – Peter had never expected to feel nostalgic about the tearing scream of the big Packard engines rising in tune to the increasing revolutions as more speed was demanded.

The diesels seemed to get the speed without the dramatics demanded by the petrol engines.

The two boats made steady progress across the channel at a steady 30 knots. CPO Ifor Williams appeared on the bridge, "Just reporting, sir, the engines are doing well. I've left my oppo in charge for a bit, give him a chance to get to know them, just in case like." He lapsed into silence gazing about the bridge and over the surrounding darkened seascape. "Bit different up here, isn't it? Don't normally get the chance to see 'ow the other half live like. Windy, isn't it?" He shivered.

"Well, Chief. how do you like the view? And the boat?" Peter asked with interest.

"Funny you should ask, sir, I was just thinking, she's a good boat, well-built like, and the engines are great; but I prefer our own Fairmile, since you ask. sir. And as for the view, it seems just the same as it always does to me, sir, so I'll go back to engines, if that all right, sir." With that Ifor Williams, Chief Petty Officer Engineer went below calling for something hot for the bridge as he passed the galley.

As the coastline approached the boats slowed down and the startling white wakes reduced. Under half throttle the boats eased into the estuary of the La Canche River with the town of Le Touquet sitting along the southern shore above the sands of the plage.

The evening sun cast long shadows across the waters and as the two boats approached the buoyed channel, the challenge was being flashed from the signal tower. Peter never knew where the information had come from, all he was aware of was the message that had come through only five minutes before giving the correct replies to the challenge.

The tension did not ease until both boats had actually entered the area of the north side of the La Canche where there was enough water to anchor among the assembled small craft. Over by the quay a larger ship was moored. From the look Peter decided it had to be the mother ship for the smaller craft in the harbor. As darkness fell, a bugle sounded. All the craft in the harbor hauled down their ensigns and depending on the type, men stood at attention at the salute or in the case of a scruffy trawler the deckhand hauling down the flag discreetly spat over the side.

For Peter standing on the bridge watching, it was a scene played out in just about any port with a naval presence. The difference here was he was wearing a clean white cap cover, affected by sub mariners and coastal forces in the German navy, otherwise he was in his own battledress uniform ready for the forthcoming action.

The signal came from the mother ship for the Captains of the new arrivals to report aboard.

The signaller replied with the affirmative and the bustle of the boat being prepared and launched focussed attention on the visible side of the boat. The other side was a hive of concealed activity, as was the deck of the second boat screened from the shore by Peter's craft.

The Commando force on board were busy boarding their inflatable boats and as each filled they set off across the dark waters for their tasks on the southern side of the estuary.

On the dark, hidden side of Peter's boat, similar activity was going on out of sight of the shore. Mike Rogers and his crew, armed to the teeth appeared in sight, the small dinghy containing the Mike in his white covered cap with three others in the boat driven by an outboard engine, phut phutted towards the quay, whilst round the stern of the shielding boat came three heavily loaded boats with the remainder of the crew, quietly pulling to the shore. The outboard pulled alongside Peter's boat and hooked on, giving the impression it was picking up the senior skipper to bring both to shore together.

Mike called up to Peter. "We'll never get out of here with the boats so I've left a scuttle crew on board to block the channel. We can connect with the landed party when all your men get to shore. I presume you will want to perform a little mayhem first."

"Come aboard, Mike, and enjoy the show. We are just swinging the boat for the best effect."

The skeleton crew was all that remained aboard when the impatient signal from the mother ship demanded their presence forthwith.

"Oops, we are getting tetchy, are we not?" Peter grinned at Mike Rogers who was standing by the twin 20mm mounting. Taking a final look at the bearing of the bow, he pressed the firing button for the two loaded torpedoes. He called "Open the ball, hoist battle ensigns; let them know we're here."

As the torpedoes left their tubes with the hiss of compressed air the hammer of the twin and single gun mountings began. Even the ack ack gun played its part as the 37mm shells shattered the windows of the signalling tower on the north bank of the river, and then started to gouge out the brickwork on the structure with devastating results, causing the near wall to crumble and start to collapse. The aerials on the roof folded gracefully and hit the ground. A power cable flashed and sparked before causing the structure to burst into flame, illuminating the administration buildings beside and below the knoll on which it stood. The torpedoes hit the mother ship and it rose in the air with the force of the explosions. It had little clearance below and the effect of the explosion was magnified by the reflected downward force. The ship literally disintegrated, giving the people on board no chance of survival. Debris rained over the entire harbor area, causing fires on other boats and coastal craft, moored in the area. Both of the E boats were damaged and the two skippers were only saved from injury by the armor behind which each had sheltered instinctively.

The shaken voice of Mike came up from the fore deck. "Wow, that must have stung! Is there anything left?"

In reply the spatter of machinegun fire hitting the armor round the foredeck guns assured him that there certainly was.

On the other boat, which had been veered to point at the southern side of the estuary, the torpedoes were fired off hopefully. Tere were no targets visible, but you never knew. Mike's Number One was doing the final preparations for the final disposal of the boat and had decided that he should do as much damage as possible before abandoning ship.

The roar of the engines announced that he was preparing to go and block the channel, the clink of the anchor chain as it was slipped could be heard and the bow of the boat swung back to point towards the sea. The surge of speed as the boat moved off, guns spitting fire, took the enemy forces on shore by surprise. The guns on Peter's boat were now ranging over the other craft moored at the harbor. There was little return fire as most of the crews were ashore. Many were in flames already and others were adrift colliding with the boats still at their moorings, setting them on fire in turn.

To Peter the scene was like some depiction of hell, fire and tracer bullets, rockets, all were adding to the confusion they had created.

The second boat had been spattered with fire and was aflame in several places, the gunner on the foredeck was sprawled in a pool of blood and the gun was being operated by the Cox'n who had a bloody bandage round his head. He was swearing in a continuous monotone swinging the mounting from side to side spraying 20mm rounds across the area causing woodwork to splinter and shattering the hulls of small boats within range. The single 20mm was concentrating on the pillbox that was causing them most trouble and having managed to get a burst through the gun port of the pill box he was concentrating on stopping the men from remounting their machine gun, showering them with the scatter of broken concrete chips from the edges of the gun port.

As the boat approached the spot where they had decided to scuttle her, an explosion caused both guns to cease fire. When Lieutenant Jimmy Manners, Number One of the boat, looked over the foredeck he saw both the Cox'n and the other gunner were both sprawled unmoving on the deck. There was a hole in the deck and the smoke rising told him that things were about over for this trip. He hauled the engine controls back and switched off before jumping over the forward panel of the bridge to the deck below to check up on the Cox'n and the gunner. Both men stirred and got to their feet groggily and allowed themselves to be led over to the Port sheltered side of the boat where the dinghy was alongside. In the dinghy the other two volunteers who had survived were already seated and they helped the two wounded men to board. "Where are the others?" Manners asked.

The engine room motor man said, "The Chief bought it as we came up from opening the valves. He stepped on deck and a piece of debris from the shell hit forward took his head off."

The motor man got the engine running and the dinghy left the side of the boat, keeping well clear of the stern. They watched it settling more or less on an even keel as another shell landed in the water not too far away.

"Okay, let's get going." Manners had no wish to stay around while the boat was sinking, the shells were just too close for his liking. They set of across the harbor to join the remainder of the party on shore.

The racket was horrendous, with all guns blazing the E boat was creeping in towards the southern shore. There was a scraping sound under the keel, "One of the sunken boats, sir." The CPO commented calmly.

Peter had thought his heart would stop when he felt the scrape under the keel but the boat cleared the obstacle and continued slowly to come alongside the quay. All through the boat charges had been laid and when all the remaining personnel were safely ashore the trigger was pressed.

The entire group were well clear before the charges went off.

They linked up with the others who had waited for them to arrive and set out for the rendezvous point on the Plage.

The well-armed party met little resistance to start with as they made their way through the town. The elegant Hotels and the Casino were looking careworn and tired from lack of attention over the past three years, the streets were deserted and houses locked and barred. Peter guessed that many of the houses were unoccupied as they were owned by people who lived elsewhere and used them during the summer months. They started to meet resistance when they met several soldiers from the garrison led by a Feldwebel who called them to halt. The Chief lifted the Sten gun he was carrying and opened fire, causing the entire party to duck and seek cover. Ifor Williams threw a grenade over the wall concealing the German troops. As the grenade exploded the entire party moved forward; by-passing the group. They depended on the shock of the explosion to keep the enemy heads down while they made a run for it.

By the time the Germans had recovered they were well on their way once more.

The next problem came with the arrival of the armored car and a platoon of soldiers who were waiting between them and the beach.

The first signs of trouble came with the spatter of bullets that caught the leading party by surprise; two men went down before the party could react. The remainder of the group took cover and replied to the firing but the situation was not good. It got rapidly worse when the armored car came round the corner. Its 20mm machine gun chewed the corners of the building where the British party was taking cover.

The armored car took position in the middle of the street, firing regular bursts to keep the British heads down and cover the advance of the infantry. The bullets of the British party bounced off the armor having no effect whatever.

One of the trailing party spoke to CPO Walters, who turned to Peter "One of the lads had seen something. I'll check it out and be back in a few minutes if that's okay, sir."

Peter looked at him decided that it must be worthwhile "Be as quick as you can, we are going to have to move off soon."

Walters disappeared around the corner.

Five minutes later there came a roar from an engine and a half-track lumbered round the corner. Mounted on the vehicle was an ack-ack set up, consisting of a mounting containing 4 Vierling heavy machine guns that started firing as soon as the vehicle turned into the street. The guns were fully depressed and the smashing combined impact of the hail of fire at that range drove into the armored car at the joint where the turret was mounted on the body causing the turret to actually lift and jam as the bullets hammered the spot until the turret was driven off its mounting exposing a gap through which the Vierling bullets poured. The smoke poured from the now silent vehicle, and it burst into flame. The Vierlings swung round to sweep the positions of the German troops who hastily dived for cover.

The cheerful voice of CPO Walters called out "All aboard for the Skylark, mind the step as you board the vehicle.

The rear-most group of men ran out from their cover and boarded the half-track, as it drove forward the men on board provided covering fire for the remainder of the party who left their positions and fell in behind the truck. Through the town the party progressed slowly. Local people appeared to see if this was the invasion, only to retreat back into their own houses when they found out it wasn't. They met several small pockets of German soldiers, though in the main they were what CPO Walters called garrison troops, "It's lucky that they are garrison troops, if they had been front line troops they would be much harder to get out of our way."

They reached the Plage where the pick-up was scheduled to take place. There were several explosions from points above the town which were the sites of the Radar stations. The Commando troops were already assembling on the beach.

"Blimey bach, it's just like Dunkirk." CPO Ifor Williams said as they filtered down to the beach to join the men waiting there.

Offshore the four MGBs sat, engines grumbling quietly. The dinghies were already shuttling between the boats and the beach. The half-track was now manned by Commandos who were in position to oppose any attempt by the enemy to interfere with the evacuation. When the last pick up was due they drove the truck down to the water's edge and wrecked the gun action by blowing it up with a grenade. The men tumbled down and boarded the boat to be taken out to the waiting MGB.

With a derisive roar of the engine the boat turned and made off across the channel towards the safety of the British coastline. The roar of engines from the overflying Hurricanes drove home the fact that the whole exercise had been a success.

Chapter Twenty-two

The de-briefing after the raid was carried out in the Royal Poole Yacht Club. The dour Commander was not pleased with them for not returning the Schnellboot. Peter explained "The choice of Le Touquet for the raid made it impossible for the boats to get out of the harbor safely, there were shoal waters all about the anchorage and the arrangement of the boats already within the harbor made the entrance tortuous. By the time we had wrecked every boat insight many of the possible escape routes were blocked by sinking craft, the limited space for manoeuvre gave the enemy every opportunity to range on our two boats; the number two boat was badly damaged, and scuttled herself in the main channel on my orders. We collected the survivors from the other boat and made our way across the harbor to the south side."

He paused and collected his thoughts before carrying on

"We landed and issued weapons before landing and were able to fight our way through to the beach where we were able to join the Commando units and get picked up safely by the MGB contingent who were waiting for us."

He sat down and mentally ran through what he had just said. Satisfied he sat back waiting for comment.

The Admiral came into the room followed by Caroline. "Well done, Commander. Our information is that the German Army is reinforcing the area with three Divisions of Panzer Grenadiers so it appears that the operation achieved its objective. You and you flotilla will return to your duties." He added as an afterthought, "In seven days, I think. Your entire contingent, have seven days leave. Then you will be busy for a while." He turned to the dour Commander. "Arrange it." Then he left, with his aide dashing along behind him.

Caroline joined him, "Well at least we have a week." Peter looked at her "You, too?"

Caroline nodded "The old boy knew you were my fiancé so he gave me the week off too."

The waters across the Channel were dark and grey and to Peter it looked as if they were covered with ships of all shapes and sizes. In the lead the huge blocks that were the called Mulberries were being towed into position and set in formation to provide a harbor for the invasion forces.

The astonishing part of the whole operation was the lack, the complete lack, of enemy aircraft. The only aircraft seen by the coastal forces group were Allied, all wearing the triple white stripes on their wings and fuselage to make them recognisable regardless of nationality.

The buzz of the R/T interrupted his thoughts the voice of Captain Harper came through, calm and clear. "Peter we have a small problem at Villers sur Mer. Some of our airborne got blown off course and they are currently trapped in a hotel on the sea front. Pick up an anti tank group from the nearest landing craft and pop over to give them some support. Apparently they suspect they will be under fire from tanks sometime soon."

"Right, Sir, we will get moving; over and out." Peter called Martin Cummings CO of the MTBs section, "Fox to Huntsman over."

The reply was immediate "Huntsman here."

"This is Master, Martin nip across to the nearest LCT and collar an anti-tank group. Take them on board and rendezvous with me at Villers sur Mer as soon as possible. We have an airborne group pinned down on the seafront and armor is on the way; Master out."

The lead MTB over to starboard sheared off and dug its stern in the water as it powered up to full speed, direct for the line of transports carrying the reserve landing parties. Cummings voice came over the R/T "Huntsman to Fox; on my way, Master. Huntsman out."

Peter called for full speed and the remainder of the flotilla turned to head for the small resort on the coast east of Caen.

"Allan, check the chart and the tides for this place, Villers sur Mer, I'd like to know how close inshore we will be able to go?"

Lieut Hodges ducked his head and took a last look at the chart on the table. "We should be able to get within 20 feet of the beach, there is no harbor unfortunately, but the tide is currently in our favor."

"That was quick, Allan; well done. Chief, start collecting the pirates together we may need to winkle out some of the enemy while we're waiting for Commander Cummings. Warn the other boats we might need reinforcements." Peter turned and lifted his glasses to study the coastline ahead. The eleven boats made a fine sight carving white grooves in the grey water.

Meanwhile Jim Walters was busy telling off the men he wanted as a landing party. He opened the arms chests and issued the Sten guns and rifles to the selected men. He had the signal flashed to the other boats to make similar preparations, calling for two men from each boat.

As they approached the long beach the sound of firing could be heard and some of it was directed at the approaching boats.

"Open fire at targets you can see. Let's shut down as much of the opposition as we can."

The regular thudding of the foredeck gun and the Oerlikons added their racket to the noise, and it was possible to see the effect as the German troops occupying the buildings around the trapped paratroopers started taking casualties from the fire. The building occupied by the Allied contingent had a Union flag hanging from a pole overlooking the sea. The fire on the seaward side dropped off to just the occasional shot so Peter gave the order to start landing. The other boats started to launch dinghies collecting into groups of six men before making for the shore.

Allan Hodges, complete with tin helmet and webbing, his Sten gun over his shoulder, went ashore in command, with CPO Walters and two men from the command MGB.

Peter scanned the shore as they reached the coast line watching for any signs of reinforcement for the German forces. The Chief Yeoman called "MTB approaching sir, signal states, am carrying consignment requested, will land them immediately with your approval."

"Send 'carry on'. All quiet at the moment but could get sticky in a hurry."

The MTB roared up to the other boats and a dinghy appeared with several soldiers crammed in, carrying what looked like a length of stove pipe. When they reached the beach the group raced up the sand to the occupied building where they were met by Lieutenant Hodges and an airborne officer. The anti-tank team went along the beach under the cover of the sea wall to a position where they could cover the front of the former Hotel where the airborne troops were dug in.

Puzzled by the lack of any attempt to evacuate, Peter was about to signal the landing party when the R/T buzzed. He picked up the microphone himself. "Fox flotilla, Master speaking."

The voice of Captain Harper came over, calm as ever. "Peter, the brown jobs have decided to stay if they can, they have reason to believe the Huns have something up their sleeves and they think they'll be able to hang on and develop their position and cause the Germans a problem when they try to reinforce defences on Sword Beach at Caen. They ask if you could stay and support where you can, over"

"Fox here; wilco, sir; have reinforced with 25 men from the pack. Can extend our input if necessary; over and out." He put the mike back "Signal Mr Hodges to return to the boat to take command." He turned to Sub Lieutenant Peters, who had been posted in just before they left Weymouth to join the invasion fleet. "I will be going ashore myself to co-ordinate with the senior officer there. Lieut Hodges will return and take command in my absence."

The new Sub nodded "Yes – er – aye-aye, sir."

Peter looked at the Quartermaster who had taken over from the Chief on the bridge. They exchanged glances and Peter felt reassured, the Quartermaster was a PO waiting to rise to Chief, and had been in the Navy since the Subbie had been in rompers. He would keep an eye on things till Hodges came back; he would then be there to help Hodges out if he got in trouble. Peter wondered often what would happen to the navy if the POs weren't there to oil the wheels.

As the dinghy came alongside he jumped down and took delivery of the webbing and Sten gun from Hodges. "Take over, Number One; don't know how long I'll be. Commander Cummings has the Flotilla in my absence."

As he stepped ashore, he had that feeling of déjà vu, gazing along the beach. Similar to Le Touquet, the sands stretched seemingly for miles to the estuary of the River Orme, where the landings were taking place on Sword Beach, the mutter of small arms gunfire mixed with the heavier crump of shellfire from the ships, was quite clear. He was reminded that this was a war zone when a bullet hit the ground at his feet, and he sprang forward, striding up the beach to the hotel at the run.

In the hotel he was greeted by CPO Walters who took him to the CO of the airborne troops, a Major Armstrong.

The Major greeted him and indicated the maps on the table in front of him. The military map was only of use for half the area, the troops had not anticipated being quite so far off course. The Major had managed to collect local maps to cover the area, albeit without the minor convenience of the location of the local German units.

"Perhaps these will help." Peter said and tossed his own set of maps on to the table, they at least indicated all the coastal bases and gun sites.

"My name is Murray, I've been asked to give whatever help I can. I brought another 25 men with me, all armed. They have all spent time in shore actions, so what do you want from us?"

"I thought we would be evacuated by now, I've just received orders to create as much mayhem as I can, though what I was supposed to do with 38 men I don't quite know. With your extra 25 men I suppose we have now become a diversion force to relieve the pressure at the landing beaches, so now we try to find some targets within our capacity to stir the Hun into activity." Armstrong looked enquiringly at Peter. "By the way my name is Charlie." He held out his hand and the two men shook.

"I'm Peter, so let's see what we can do."

Both men studied the maps on the table before them. While they were still engrossed one of the patrols sent out by the Major returned with the news that there was a column approaching from inland that contained at least eight vehicles. The Sergeant in charge commented "Sir, they are not in any mad rush, I reckon if we shift a bit we could cause them aggro. Number one platoon reports that the tank is immobilised at the moment with a broken track. The crew are repairing it, Lieut Horrocks says he'll wait until it's been fixed than snatch the tank for us to use." Finished. he stood and looked at the two officers, waiting.

Charlie looked at Peter, "What do you think? Shall we open the ball?"

Peter shrugged "Why not? How are we off for explosives?"

The Sergeant answered "We have a box of dynamite in the corner there, and the chute with the plastic stuff is here but we have no one who can use it."

Peter smiled "My torpedo gunner will be in his glory, he hasn't had a chance to play with real explosives for a long time. Take the dynamite and find PO Hanson. He'll be happy to look after it and your other explosive as well. I'll come and join you when we decide what were going to do. Before you go, take a look at the map and put us into the picture."

After the Sergeant left hauling the box of dynamite, Peter turned to the Major. "Charlie, if you like I'll follow the sergeant and sort out the reception for the trucks. I'll try to liberate some of the transport while I'm at it."

Charlie scratched the bristles on his chin "You're on; stop the reinforcements and get me a couple of trucks. Good luck!" He grinned "Got to start somewhere."

Outside, Peter looked at the road inland. The convoy was just in view in the distance, the trucks distinguishable within the cloud of dust they were creating. PO Hanson, the Torpedo Gunner, came over, saluted and reported. "Sir, I've put together a couple of bangers to take out the trees in front and behind the convoy. We thought we would let the small vehicle though first. Then drop the tree to block the rest off. The sergeant has two Bren's sited and most of our lads set up in the ditches either side of the road. If you would like to follow me I'll take you round the set up."

The firing in the immediate area had ceased completely, the local troops being no match for the highly-trained paratroopers. Some of the remaining local people were out and about talking excitedly and holding French and British flags.

Where they came from Peter could not imagine, guessing they had to have been hidden well out of sight.

Two of the soldiers were herding the civilians away, pointing out that there was the convoy coming and they wanted to prepare to deal with it. Unfortunately the French did not seem to be able to understand the strong Yorkshire accent of the two soldiers involved, Peter yelled out in French that the Bosche were coming and they needed to be stopped. That seemed to convince them to return to their houses and reluctantly they returned to their houses.

With a roar the Tiger tank that had been having its track repaired rolled into the area opposite the hotel. The big gun traversed the entire 360 degrees then the lid opened and the Red Beret of Parachute ERegiment appeared. followed by the round smiling face of a Second Lieutenant. "It's hot in here." He said to no one in particular and dropped back into the tank. Another hatch opened and a private got out with a tin of paint and a moulting paint brush. He proceeded to paint three white stripes across the tank. "Choost in case bloody air force decide to bend it while I'm inside." The broad accent was alien in the little French town. The officer appeared through the top hatch, "Get on with it, Boothroyde, we haven't got all day. The bloody blue jobs'll be over before you get your arse in gear."

"Ah'm dooin ma best, boss, give oos a break like."

With a muttered; "Idle bugger," The boss disappeared once more.

"Ah heard that." Boothroyde did not seem too worried about it; but then neither did his officer. Peter grinned at the exchange and thought to himself that as long as men like Boothroyde served in the army there was little to worry about. He followed the figure of the PO down the road and walked with him round the ambush layout. The Para Sergeant Marshall, was placing the naval party amongst his men giving the ambush a high incidence of firepower between the two target trees. CPO Walters sighed as the convoy rumbled into view. Peter was watching through binoculars as the vehicles approached. The leading vehicle was a Kubelwagen occupied by an officer, driver and two others. The troop carriers were trundling behind with clouds of dust and smoke making it difficult to see the full length of the convoy. From his position ahead of the mined tree Peter watched the Kubelwagen approaching at about 30 mph. As it passed the tree, the charge exploded and the tree fell across the road, trapping the convoy behind it. Nothing happened for what seemed like minutes but was actually only seconds. Then the Kubelwagen stopped and started to turn. Halfway round Peter and his group opened fire and the driver, collapsed. The officer stood up and toppled over as he was hit; he collapsed over the side of the vehicle. The two soldiers in the rear fell out of the car to shelter behind it but discovered that there were other ambushers on the other side of the road. One threw his MP 40 smg into the road and dragged out his handkerchief waving it in surrender. His companion shrugged and threw his gun down as well and both men stood up.

As they took possession of the Kubelwagen and the two prisoners, the bodies of the driver and the officer, an Oberleutnant in the Wehrmacht, were carried off to the side of the road. Peter and Walters made for the trapped convoy where the shooting was all over. The main body of men carried were unarmed and the few with arms had been swiftly subdued. There was still a certain amount of firing further down the convoy but here at the head the tree was already being shifted by a group of prisoners. As he reached the first group, Peter heard the Para Corporal urging the prisoners on in German. The soldier/prisoners did not look like front line troops to him. The Corporal saw him and snapped to attention. "What troops are they, Corporal? What regiment?"

"They are pioneers, sir, they must have scraped the barrel for these men, I doubt if they've ever fired a gun in anger before." The sound of gunfire had now ceased and the trucks were all starting up once more. They drew forwards and one by one and parked in front of the hotel. The prisoners were formed up and counted off. There were 82 men plus 6 dead and 12 wounded. The ambusher's lost 1 man killed and 3 wounded. Five of the trucks had carried the pioneers, the other three were loaded with supplies and ordinance.

The wounded were taken into the hotel and the others under the command of their Feldwebel were marched down to the school where they were locked into the school hall with guards, though it seemed that the Pioneers would not need much guarding. Most of them were from Romania and Hungary conscripted for their use as laborers. The dead men were all recovered; wounded from fighting regiments sent to keep the pioneers ready to work wherever they were needed. The equipment in the trucks included picks and shovels, wheelbarrows and sand and cement. In addition there were two sets of the light anti-aircraft guns, with ammunition, presumably scheduled to be sited somewhere wherever they would do the most good.

Charlie Armstrong smiled."Good." he said.

Peter looked up. "What?"

"The AA guns will come in handy and added to the tank we can now cause some real havoc among the ungodly. I've got the pioneers working to mount the AA guns into the Kubelwagen. Luckily it has not been damaged so we can use it. I think if we strike inland and to the southwest. we can approach the suburbs of Caen and provided we scout carefully, we could stir things up a bit and take the pressure off the landing forces. We can try to convince them that there is another landing force in fact." He smiled, "And of course there is."

Chapter Twenty-three

There was silence in the office for the first time that day, the only person there was seated behind the desk smoking a cigar and relaxing with a glass of Schnapps at his elbow.

Generalmajor Manfried Schuppe had been busy all day, most of which was spent watching people running round in circles in panic. Orders and counter orders had been flying back and forth, demonstrating to the General that the landings around the area of Caen had taken the High Command completely by surprise, the expectation and the entire concentration of German effort being directed at the Pas de Calais, the Caen area was completely unprepared.

The resultant panic had led to contingents of troops being ordered to move apparently haphazardly without any overall direction. The local garrison of a hodge-podge of units had been assembled and allocated to places in the area formerly held by the regular Wehrmacht, all of whom had been sent off in a mad rush as reinforcements to the Caen defences.

The arrival of the paratroops had created a panic and the initial reaction had been to scream for help to the Western European Defence HQ. As Schuppe had been there awaiting reassignment, the immediate reaction had been to send him here to take over the defence of this area. He smiled ruefully to himself. '*This will be a chance to redeem yourself*' he could hear the voice of Rommel's aide in his head; he smiled once more. There would be no redemption; he had guessed that the so-called invasion was merely the landing of a group in the wrong place and being elite troops they promptly decided to make the best of things and get on with the war from where they were. He admired their attitude, good soldiers whatever army the belonged to, pity he had none like them under his command.

He had done his best, but the fact was the best-trained troops under his command were the Pioneers, who consisted of men from all over Europe dragged into service but not trusted to do anything other than build shithouses and repair roads. He seriously doubted they would be of any more use than the collection of clerks and orderlies that made up the other units here.

He shrugged and finished his cigar, he had done his best; asked HQ for reinforcements and unsurprisingly been refused. Now he had to get on with it.

He rose and stretched, tossed down the Schnapps remaining in the glass, and turned to the door where a rapid tattoo of knocks announced another emergency.

"Come" he called.

The door burst open and his aide came in and leapt to attention. "Herr Generalmajor, I have to report that the Allied force is approaching our headquarters being led by a Tiger tank; seven vehicles with no sign of the units that we sent to oppose them. The tank must have been taken before it could go into action." As the young man spoke there was a loud bang followed by the crash of falling masonry, the building shook from the impact quickly followed by another and another.

"Collect the men and get out of here now!" ordered Schuppe. "Regroup at the strongpoint at Mereville-Franceville-Plage. Now move!"

The young man saluted and turned and ran from the room. Generalmajor Manfried Schuppe picked up his cap and looked around the room that he had occupied for six hours and wished he was back in Dusseldorf Police Station sorting the latest case files. He had the distinct feeling that there would be no further postings for him after this debacle.

His last job in Italy had been a disaster through the efforts of those Gestapo bastards who were incapable of doing anything that did not entail beating, raping and intimidating helpless prisoners. There seemed to be no soldiers among them and though they had clearly been the cause of the debacle at Lauria, he had been blamed despite the fact that he had been deliberately excluded from the planning and direction of the operation from the beginning.

As Rommel had told him privately, "Don't expect the High Command to admit to failure at any time when there is some poor bloody soldier to be given the burden."

In the case of the Gestapo, run by Himmler, he would not allow them to admit to mistake or error. In Rommel's case he had been removed from Africa because—despite his brilliant campaign—lack of supplies and support from Berlin had forced his retreat in the face of Montgomery's reply at El Alemein. In Schuppe's case, after his return from Italy; he advised a low profile to save his neck.

With a rueful shrug, low profile indeed, he turned and left the room.

The crash of the 88mm cannon on the Tiger tank in the lead of the column caused the men in the trucks to cover their ears. Peter had a place in the Kubelwagen and they had circled round the houses to scout the line of retreat on the other side of the HQ building.

Walters at the Vierling gun called out as they rounded the last corner. "Over there, sir. The staff car." Peter swung round and looked. The gun above his head opened up with a shattering burst. The staff car had just started to move when it came to an abrupt stop, with steam pouring from the radiator. The Kubelwagen was alongside the stalled staff car almost before it stopped. The officers on the back seat were faced with the muzzle of the 20mm gun as they recovered from being flung forward when the car had slammed to a halt.

The older man put out his hand to prevent the younger from drawing his pistol. He realized they were helpless under the threat of the armed men in the Kubelwagen. He rose to his feet and raised his hands in surrender and stepped from the car through the door that had been opened by Peter.

Seeing the badges of rank on the officer's tunic, Peter realized that they had captured a General in addition to the Oberleutnant, who had just passed his Luger pistol over to PO Hansen. The General indicated his own holstered weapon and Peter held out his hand. The General lowered his arms and passed his own weapon over to Peter. He came to attention and said in passable English "I am Generalmajor Manfried Schuppe, Wehrmacht." He stood waiting, while Peter studied him.

"Commander Peter Murray RN. I recall the area commander in Southern Italy was named Schuppe a few months ago, was that you?"

Schuppe looked keenly at Peter and guessed, "You were with the Schnellboot that raided and stole the Professor. That was a well-executed operation. You cost us 37 killed and 2 aircraft and our own Schnellboot, I was not running that operation – it was a Gestapo mess."

One of the trucks came round the now wrecked building and the prisoners were loaded into the back under escort.

The Tiger came round the building and Major Armstrong jumped down from the deck, swinging his SMG behind him as he trotted over to Peter. He took in the wrecked staff car and watched the General climb into the truck. He nodded at the General. "What was that all about?"

"That was the General in charge of this area. I knew of him in Italy. His name's Schuppe and, from what I gather, better than the average Hun. Now, where do we go?"

Major Charles Armstrong was thoughtful. "I've been given a free hand to make as much trouble as possible before linking up with the main force once more, I'm inclined to head for Varaville, and then inland to swing south round Caen, it would be where we were originally intended to be when they dropped us. The rest of my units were scattered to hell and gone when their plane was hit by ack-ack fire. If they made it to the first target, we can possibly reconnect. If not, we'll go ahead anyway. At worst we'll cause the enemy grief as they'll have to watch their back, at least until they get rid of us. I believe they have everything they've got at moment in the line against the landing troops on all five beaches. Anything we can do to interfere with their effort will be to the good."

Peter was looking at the latest radio messages. "It looks as if we may get reinforcements; it seems that several of the gliders were sent astray by the same unexpected winds that you encountered. In the area in the grounds of the Chateau-de-Beneouville, six of them managed to crash land. They have only just found a radio that still works and checked in with HQ"

He passed the message over addressed to Acting Lieutenant Colonel Armstrong. "Parachute Regiment has been ordered to take command and combine forces with all other available units; independent unit formed to be known as the Villers Combined Force."

Charlie Armstrong looked at Peter, surprised. Peter grinned. "Virtue is sometimes rewarded, though it does help if you are the only one there. Congratulations, Colonel. We had better get moving, it looks as if we are going to be forced to demonstrate what can be done with this rag-tag army."

Peter signalled Commander Cummings to arrange the transfer of the prisoners, and shortly thereafter an LCT was commandeered from the landing force to collect the prisoners. It delivered an armored car and some heavier weapons, including an anti-tank gun towed by an armored half-track.

The armored car under the command of a Cornet in the Blues was sent off with six trucks to rendezvous with the Glider contingent. The Kubelwagen went along to report back as soon as the party arrived at Varaville. The Villers Force would set out to join them as soon as the dispersed men could be recalled.

The town of Varaville could not be described as a metropolitan area, just a small country town with a generally quietly obedient population. The arrival of the trucks containing the glider troop soon changed all that. The small contingent of German soldiers and the town officials were suddenly reminded that there was a war on. The sight of the trucks offloading British soldiers and the armored car bristling with weaponry convinced them that for them the war was over. They gladly handed over their weapons without protest, though it did appear that the local Gestapo man would protest until a burly Feldwebel clouted him with a fist like a ham and stretched him flat on the ground to the cheers of the other soldiers.

The town sprouted a crop of French and British flags and when the Villers Force arrived there was a delegation waiting to welcome them.

In the newly established HQ in the Hotel de Ville, a meeting occurred between the Colonel, Peter, and two scruffy looking men with MP40 SMGs stolen from the occupying troops representing the Maquis. Using maps from the local German unit they identified the lines of communication with the defending forces at Caen.

In the square the Tiger stood, now clearly marked with the Allied white stripes, with a Union Jack replacing the German insignia on the turret. It was covered with a heaving mass of children, all clamouring for sweets and chocolate.

Private Boothroyde was perched in the middle, handing individual squares of chocolate to the kids with scrupulous fairness. His voice rising up above the hubbub, periodically saying, "Now, lads, one at a time. Coomb on, you bugger, yow've already had a bit."

Lieutenant Horrocks was perched beside a pretty French girl exercising his schoolboy French and drinking wine from an enamel mug. In the street there were several women assembling what looked like a celebration feast for the troops. Peter came out of the building and saw what was happening. His first thought was to look up to see if there were any aircraft about: his second was to call out for the sergeants and Chief Walters. He caught the eye of Lieutenant Horrocks and beckoned him over. He looked round at the assembled men. "We are a small force in the depths of enemy-held territory; one battalion of Grenadiers could be enough to wipe us all out including the local people. One aircraft at the wrong moment could see all this with the same result. Get this square cleared and the Tiger under cover; make sure the defensive patrols are on their toes and report back to me, pronto." He waved at the group preparing the feast "P.S., be tactful with the ladies!"

He turned back into the building, hearing the protests from the first group as he went through the imposing doorway.

He joined the Colonel at the table where he had been briefing the partisans.

Armstrong looked up as he came in." Good. Peter, I'm glad you're here. It looks as if I'll need to let you go. Now that I have the reinforcements from the glider troops, I have over 200 men and I cannot justify keeping you with me. This message just came in asking me how long I will need your services. Unless you can think of something I've missed, I cannot justify you and your people staying here."

Peter felt a twinge of disappointment, he had been enjoying this sojourn ashore and he did not want it to end so soon; he shrugged. "Duty calls I suppose; just as I was enjoying myself, too. I'll get the lads together and we'll arrange a pick-up back at Villiers." He turned to leave

"Peter!" He stopped and turned back to the Colonel. "Thanks, Peter, without your help and backup we would have been in the soup. I appreciate the help and I'll buy you a drink in London when it's all over." He stood up and thrust his hand out. Peter shook it and with a grin and a wave of his hand, left.

Back on board the MGB Peter found nothing had changed and settled back into the day to day routine broken only by the odd message to dash off to another part of the invasion area, normally followed by a second message to abort.

The E boat flotilla caught them by surprise, the first Peter knew of their presence was when the screen in front of the bridge shattered, smashed by the blast of fire from the lead craft. The flotilla had approached in the lee of two of the Mulberry units that formed the harbor for the landing force. As Peter thrust the throttles forward the engines died and the boat settled down on the water lifeless. "All guns fire at will, choose your targets and let 'em have it." The guns started up with a crash of sound that startled Peter, until he remembered that the noise of gunfire in the past had been overlain by the noise of the engines. More fire was coming in and hitting along the deck raising splinters, driving them into the starboard Oerlikon gunner. He shuddered and hung in his harness, blood streaming from his wounds. Several bullets struck the armor round the bridge, and a ricochet hit Peter just above his right hip flinging him into a corner, head spinning. The helmsman landed across his legs, blood spurting from his neck. Peter looked at it for a moment thinking, *I should stop it.* As in a dream, he reached forward and clamped his thumb on the hole in the man's neck. He pressed hard and the blood stopped. He was still sitting there holding the man's neck when the Doctor arrived festooned with bags, Hanson with him carrying a bottle of oxygen.

They said afterwards that they had to pry his fingers loose from the helmsman's neck, leaving bruising there for more than two weeks before the colour faded. Young Mason the helmsman proudly admitted that the marks were where the skipper had strangled him to save his life.

The sunlight patterned the lower part of the bed when Peter woke, the partly-opened curtains allowed light in the room but left half the room in shadow.

He squeezed his eyes shut, then opened them once more; nothing had changed, he was in bed in a sunlit room and his hip hurt. He winced after touching it, causing a stab of pain in his side. Sweat suddenly stood out on his forehead. He carefully tried moving his legs Left then right. With relief he found both worked, though the movement of his left leg caused the stab of pain once more. He had a headache and for some reason the fingers and thumb on his right hand were aching persistently. As he lay there it all started to come back. He shifted quickly and groaned. From the other side of the room a figure stirred and came into view. The nurse took his wrist in her cool hand and checked his pulse. The she put her hand on his forehead checking his temperature. "So how are you feeling, Commander? Your pulse is normal and your temperature seems to have come down." Her voice was soft and her touch soothing.

"I have a headache but apart from that not too bad; how long have I been here?"

"Just a week. There were a few complications with the wound in your side but they seem to have cleared up nicely now; you did give us bit of a fright when you first came in, but it all seems to be sorted out now."

"Complications?"

"Yes, most unusual. The bullet seemed to have caused your appendix to burst during the operation to remove the shrapnel. Tor a while there it was touch and go. You were lucky we had the London Consultant here at the time and he spotted the problem and dealt with it."

"How is the young…." He hesitated trying to recall the name of the wounded helmsman.

"Young Mason is recovering nicely, thanks to you. You had a death grip on his neck, apparently stopping the loss of blood and making time for your ship's doctor stop the bleeding and keep the boy alive until the surgeon was able to repair the artery. He asked to see you as soon as you are well enough to see him."

Peter nodded tiredly/ "Any other casualties, do you know?"

The nurse looked at Peter directly. "Three dead and eight wounded, all minor except you and the boy Mason."

"Thank you, nurse?" he looked up.

"Weatherby, Sylvia, they all call me 'Webby' or 'Auntie' depending on their age. You may call me Webby."

"Thank you. Webby, I'm Peter."

"Well, Peter. Now I have news for you, good news and bad news; which would you like first?"

"I could do with some good news I think."

"Although you will be with us for some time you will make a full recovery."

"So that's a relief, so what else have you got to tell me?"

"I'm happy to say someone else will be the one to do that, you have a visitor and she will be with you as soon as I have tidies up your bed." The tall elegant figure proceeded to straighten and tuck in his bed covers before briskly walking out of the room to be replaced by the diffident entry of another woman.

Peter looked at her curiously, he did not recognise her. She was dressed elegantly in a smart suit, perhaps thirty years old, with a slim, toned figure. Her face was interesting though not beautiful in the accepted manner, but she would turn heads just walking down the street.

The lady looked at him searchingly and he suddenly realized he was staring.

"I beg your pardon, madam. I don't think we've met. What can I do for you?"

"I am sorry, I thought the nurse would explain. I received a letter from an unknown person and I thought I should correct the misunderstanding that this person had." The English was good but there was the trace of an accent that clearly indicated she was a foreigner, *European probably,* Peter thought.

"How can I help?" Peter was mystified.

"Perhaps if I just show you this," the lady passed Peter a letter which he recognised, written to Caroline several months ago. He had addressed it to Grafin Von Witzenburg because at the time Caroline was changing names once more and he was unsure which name would reach her at the time.

"I beg your pardon. How did you get this letter?" Peter was mystified and not a little upset.

"Perhaps I should explain, I am Grafin Caroline von Witzenburg. I work as an analyst with the MOD. This letter was found in the SOE offices during an investigation into a leakage of information from a suspect agent.

"I was contacted and the letter given to me to examine. I confessed I was completely ignorant of the things mentioned and had no idea of the identity of the writer or the recipient. Happily I managed to convince the investigators and as a result I was asked to cooperate with them in tracing the agent concerned."

She stopped and looked at Peter sympathetically; "I'm afraid you've been tricked by the agent concerned. A woman believed to be Anya Molotov, a Russian national working for the Soviet army intelligence."

Peter was stunned, "But what, why would the Russians need to spy on us? They are our allies. Surely there has to be some explanation. What does Anya say?"

"I'm afraid I can't tell you, she disappeared two weeks ago and we have no idea where she went. She took papers with her with information of the location and identities of several of our agents in the Netherlands. We have been trying to contact them to warn them but I'm afraid we were too late to save most of them. Can you make any suggestion as to her whereabouts? Has she been in touch?" The green eyes were trained directly on him as Peter struggled with the realisation that his Caroline had lied and used him.

"I.. I can't think of anywhere she might be. We always met at her place in town and apart from a visit to my family in Hampshire I have only seen her in Egypt and when on a raid in Italy. So I'm afraid the answer is no, I cannot help you."

The Grafin rose to her feet and looked at Peter "I am sorry to bring you bad news. The woman Anya was a fool to become involved whilst working as a spy. I hope you will soon be back on your feet." She rose and leaned across to shake his hand leaving a wisp of perfume in her wake. "Goodbye, Peter. If you are at a loose end in London, come in and say hello. I'm in the MOD in Whitehall." With a smile she left the room.

"Well, well. Aren't we the smooth operator? I shall keep an eye on you in the future."

The familiar voice of Claire Waterstone broke the silence following the Grafin's departure.

Then she was sitting on the bed, smiling before leaning forward to kiss him in a manner more appropriate to a lover than a brother.

"Wow! You are a sight for sore eyes, where did you come from?" Peter was surprised but pleased to see her friendly face. "The morning has not been one of my best so far."

Claire sat back and looked at him appraisingly. "She told you then?"

Peter looked back at her. "You knew?"

"I was the investigating officer, I'm afraid so I was detailed to make sure that there was no stone left unturned in the enquiry. Your Caroline was in fact Anya Molotov; Mrs Anya Molotov, wife of Colonel Yuri Molotov of the Soviet Army; currently serving on Joseph Stalin's personal staff. She has successfully worked in this country for several years on and off and I'm afraid her method is to take lovers where it is convenient, usually in places of strategic importance. Her latest was one of the translators in the Foreign Office. A woman of considerable value had she had time to suborn her." Claire stopped seeing the puzzled look on Peter's face.

"Sorry, you couldn't know. She chose her lovers from both sexes, targets of opportunity if you see what I mean; though if it's of any consolation to you, in your case the choice appears to have been one without political motive."

She sat back on the bed and reached forward to run her hand down his cheek catching the tear that ran down his drawn face. "Oh, Peter, I'm so sorry. I was ordered to break things up with you in Alex and I could not tell you why. There was too much going on at the time and the man I had to contact—ahe man I introduced as my fiancé was under investigation. He was exposed and shot in Malta, and by the time I returned to Alex you were already involved in the Italian job, and word was, seeing someone else. I felt I couldn't just walk back into your life."

She stopped and flushed confused and worried that she had said too much. She needn't have worried. Peter was still wallowing in his unhappiness, not really believing that he had been so naïve. He looked at Claire, suddenly aware that she was sitting on the bed holding his hand.

She squeezed it and said, "You really did not deserve this. You have enough to handle just getting better from your injuries."

Webby came in at that point and looked at the pair of them holding hands on the bed.

"Sorry, you lovebirds; time to kiss and say goodbye for the time being anyway. The surgeon will be round in a few minutes." She spoke to Claire "You can call whenever you like from now on, the boss thinks girl friends are good for the patients, but no rows, mind. Raised voices are not permitted in Libraries and Hospitals."

The two on the bed hesitated, neither sure of what to say in the face of this outburst.

"Well, kiss him goodbye for Pete's sake. I haven't got all day. I won't be embarrassed."

With a shrug and a grin, Claire bent over and kissed Peter thoroughly, under the approving eye of the tall nurse.

"There, that will keep you until next time." Claire said lightly and she left with a flirt of her uniform skirt.

Chapter Twenty-four

The office where Claire worked was typical of the standard in the Civil Service of the period with green walls and basic furniture and carpet according to rank. She didn't mind, the window she was looking through overlooked the park behind Buckingham Palace, rather than the featureless bricks and mortar of the majority of the windows shared by her colleagues.

She was thinking about Peter, an occupation she had thought pointless and counterproductive when they first split up. At that time she had thought that they were getting serious too fast, and was trying to think of ways to slow things down.

When she had been ordered to cultivate that Lieutenant Commander in Malta it seemed a good excuse to split up before things got out of hand. It had not been long before she started having second thoughts; missing him, his gentle humour, and the sound of his voice, his laugh sudden and infectious. It had taken her a long time to get that all sorted out.

Then when they had met once more, it had all come flooding back, and it had taken all her self-control not to fall on his shoulder and confess how she felt. Now his injury and the news about Caroline was an opportunity to set things right, but she would need to be careful, there might not be another chance if she blew it this time.

The fact that he was in hospital and unable to get out was irksome for Peter; happily Paul Waterstone and Charlie King had managed to get away and call in. They had wheedled the Sister in to allowing him out for lunch at the Bell and Dragon in Cookham, just down the road from the Hospital at Clivedon. It had been exhausting but the sort of change he needed. The shock of the news about Caroline had been pretty devastating, but not as crushing as he had anticipated. Claire had called on several occasions and she phoned to make arrangements for his convalescence when he was ready to be discharged. The Hospital was only the initial part of his recovery he was expected to spend at least another month at convalescence.

The wound healed slowly, the result—the doctor said—of too much stress for too long. He pointed out to the Admiral visiting the hospital that there were limits to the endurance of the human body, you could only push so far. The Admiral was not impressed, "We need the men, there are not enough to do what we have to do. There's no point in complaining about things.

As the three month period of healing reached its end Peter became more and more impatient to get back to his flotilla.

Claire's visits were more and more welcome, allowing him to keep up with what was going on in Europe. It also became clear that the empathy they had shared from the beginning had by no means gone; and over the period of her visits Peter became aware of the renewal of that initial attraction that had been so overwhelming from their first meeting.

When he realized that Claire had been ordered to Malta to investigate the Lieutenant Commander she had introduced as her fiancé, he thought that, had he known, he would have understood and waited for her; then thinking a little more clearly about it, he realized that he would have fretted much more had he known what she was doing.

As things were at the moment he was quite happy to take things slowly and see how things worked out.

Now he was back on his feet and walking every day, he no longer needed the stick the Hospital provided. The walks in the surrounding countryside became longer as his strength returned.

He was walking in the riverside woodlands in the hospital grounds when he saw Caroline for what he thought was the last time. He sat on a log and rested his chin on his crossed hands folded on the handle of the walking stick, he had grown accustomed to carrying it on a walk, it gave him something to slash the nettles with. The rustle of the autumn leaves on the ground betrayed the presence of another person. As he sat upright the woman sat on the log next to him. He turned and saw the auburn-haired woman who had joined him on the log, He caught his breath as he realized that it was Caroline or Anya as he now knew her.

"Hullo," she said. "I thought I would let you know that I really enjoyed being with you and I'm sorry that things turned out this way."

Peter laughed cynically, "I see, you're sorry. Well, that makes it all right then, Mrs Molotov; or whoever you really are."

She was silent for a moment, then "I did not intend things to go the way they did. You were not a target, I was at the Villa for other reasons, you just appeared and things just happened but I did not deliberately try to make you like me."

"What does your husband think about you sleeping with targets, was it?"

"He is my husband in name only, his preference is for men, I am just window dressing for the Party. They don't approve of homosexuals, at least not in Stalin's circle anyway."

Peter turned and looked at her "You do realize that I should turn you in, and you would be tried and shot as a spy?" As he spoke he realized that she was truly beautiful, and at the same time he knew he would never turn her in.

She turned to him "At another time, another place perhaps we could have made things work between us." She shrugged and stood. Turning swiftly, she kissed him lightly on the cheek, "Goodbye, we won't meet again." Then she was gone as swiftly as she had appeared.

Peter sat there on the log, he touched his cheek, and wiped off the hint of lipstick that remained, her perfume was fleetingly there then the breeze took it away.

He sat for a few minutes more and was preparing to get up and return to the hospital when Claire burst through the bushes, "There you are," she said. "They told me you would be…" She had no time to finish what she was going to say as Peter swept her into his arms and kissed her without holding back, all the pent-up emotion and frustration of the past few years suddenly resolved. After the initial shock Claire had joined in with enthusiasm. When they came apart Peter looked at her and she gazed directly back at him both of them knowing that this was the way things would be; whether they waited until the end of the war or married tomorrow, they would not be separated again.

That tacit understanding reached, they walked back to the hospital and had lunch, after being told off by Webby for being late.

Weymouth was still the same, the smell of high octane and seaweed, tinges of tar and anti-foul. And the boats – the sight of the long graceful hulls rising in turn gently on the quiet water brought a lump to his throat as the staff car drew up on the quay outside the office.

The rowdy reception from the officers of the flotilla was a reassuring reminder that he was home and for the next few weeks he was occupied with routine patrols up and down the Channel.

The call came at just after 9.00 pm four weeks to the day after Peter's return to duty. He was sitting at his desk clearing up paperwork that had accumulated while he had been out on patrol when the telephone rang. It made him jump, he wasn't accustomed to receiving calls at that time of the evening.

"Hullo, Murray here."

"Sorry to disturb you, Commander I have Brigadier Armstrong on the line for you." The voice of the female operator shut off as she put the call through.

Peter could not imagine who Brigadier Armstrong was or for that matter why he should want to talk to him anyway. Before he could take that thought further the vaguely familiar voice of the Brigadier was speaking. "Hullo, Peter, remember me? Charlie Armstrong. We invaded France together."

"Charlie, hullo." Peter suddenly realized he was talking to a much senior officer. "I beg your pardon, sir, Brigadier Armstrong."

The voice at the other end of the line blew a very un-officer-like raspberry "Don't be so bloody formal, it's always been Charlie and Peter and as far as I'm concerned it always will be; now to get down to business. I seem to recall that you and that crew of pirates you command have handled the odd German Schnellboot. Please correct me if I go wrong."

"I'm not allowed to comment on that subject, but so what?"

"What I have in mind is a visit that may require specialist support. Interested?"

"After the last few weeks trolling up and down the empty waters of the Channel, I'll listen to anything. You're place or mine?"

"Mine, I think. You'll not be so noticeable up here. Oh, and by the way, bring your small kit for a two-night stay; this could take a little organizing. I'll lay on accommodation. Come to room 84 at the War Office, we'll go from there. Say tomorrow morning 10.00 hrs. We'll get up to date then. Cheerio, Peter; until tomorrow."

Peter sat back, having replaced his phone, Charlie was a Brigadier then, but he still sounded the same old gung ho warrior so effective in the Normandy champagne.

After sitting and wondering what Charlie had in mind, Peter picked up the phone and called Paul, who was having a quiet night in the largely empty Ward-room.

When he came to the phone he said in a peeved voice "Tell me that the war is over or something equally important otherwise prepare to answer with pistols at dawn. This is my first peaceful night in a month."

Peter smiled, Paul had in fact just returned from a very active week's leave. "Well I cannot comment on the end of the war at the moment, it's still top secret, but I thought I had better let you know that I have been called by those on high to attend for a day or so. This does, of course, require you to act in loco whatever it is until my return. The result of this blessed relief from the current tedium is that I need not continue with this boring paperwork as my local incumbent can have the pleasure. Since this is a matter for rejoicing, I thought you could be depended upon to support me in a little celebration." Peter waited expectantly.

"You crafty bugger/ Claire's in London and you've wangled a chit on the company. I'll see you in the wardroom instantly or know the reason why. The drinks you will see arrayed will be in your chit." The phone went down with a bang, and Peter did not waste a second collecting his cap and making the dash to the wardroom.

As Peter mentioned before the evening became social, the call from Charlie had come completely out of the blue and with no prompting had to sadly pass all the current paperwork over to Paul whilst he departed on this urgent matter.

It was quite evident that the by now assembled group did not believe a word of it but all were interested in the possibility of getting out of the current boring routine they seemed to be landed with.

The traditional 'morning after' was, for Peter at least, a non-starter. Knowing he would need to be ready for anything, and anticipating meeting Claire, he had first of all called her and asked her to arrange somewhere to stay; he had then carefully kept his intake of alcohol to a reasonable level to avoid any problems in the morning.

He found the rail journey to London boring despite his attempts to read the book he had brought with him. The Major sharing the first class compartment had the habit of speaking in short bursts. The irritation of being interrupted at these irregular intervals created the need to re-read the same sequence several times over. In the end in desperation he closed his book to concentrate on the conversation, only to find that the Major had fallen asleep. He could not settle down to read once more so he watched the wintery landscape through the grimy window for the remainder of the journey to Waterloo Station.

There was a staff car waiting to meet the train, with a smart WRNS PO driver at the wheel. Peter offered the Major a lift to the War Office, but the offer was, with regrets, declined. The Major looked at the driver with a calculating eye and muttered "You matelots get all the luck." He made off into the crowd with another regretful look at the WRNS driver.

London was busy with traffic, Peter could not help noticing the number of new gaps in the rows of buildings. "Have there been many air raids lately?"

The driver said "It's not air raids as such, it's the bloody Doodlebugs."

"Doodlebugs? Oh the flying bombs, I didn't realize that they were causing quite such a problem. We have seen very little of them down in the West Country. They must be a bigger problem than I thought."

"Oh. they are a problem all right. They come without any real way of knowing where they'll strike. If you can hear them, you're OK. If you hear the engine stop, look out; it could be in your lap before you know it."

They arrived at the War Office where he was vetted and admitted and whisked down to an underground room, where he joined several other officers sitting drinking coffee and tea and waiting to be called. Several looked at him. their eyes dropping to the ribbons on his breast, the bars to his DSO caused the observant to look twice at the young man wearing the decorations.

He had no time for tea, sitting as he was with his back to the door, it was the heightened interest among the officers facing him that tipped him off that someone had entered and as he turned the hint of scent told him it was a woman. Claire's voice completed the picture as she appeared in front of him to escort him to his meeting.

For a moment he studied her; dressed in her uniform with the three blue rings in her sleeves she was every inch a Naval Officer and the smile she gave him made him the envy of every other man in the room. "Hullo, Commander Murray, will you come with me please?" She led the way out of the office and down the corridor, she looked about her quickly then opened the door beside her and dragged him in. It was a stationary cupboard and she was in his arms before he had time to think. The kiss lasted and the feel of her body against his was a long awaited confirmation that they belonged together.

"Oh, Peter." She said

"Well! I take it you're pleased to see me?" Peter said, still a little breathless from the assault.

"I'm sorry. I didn't mean to attack you like this. But it has been so long and I suppose I just flipped." She looked at him contritely "Have I upset you?"

Peter didn't bother answering, he gathered her in his arms and kissed her thoroughly and comprehensively for a second time.

When they broke apart, once more breathless, she gasped, "I take it that's a no, I'm forgiven?"

"Was there ever a doubt between us?" Peter looked at her tenderly "Never again."

"What do you mean, never again what?"

"Never again will I let you go, I do not intend to lose you now or ever again." Peter said "So write it down and make your arrangements, you are now stuck with me and I intend to make you Mrs Peter Murray as soon as the details can be sorted out. That's what I mean."

He looked at her a little anxiously, to see how she took this news. He needn't have worried the answer was there in her eyes and smile, "We're engaged then?"

"Just so." He kissed her quickly "Now where am I supposed to be going before you kidnapped me?"

"Oh, my god, we're late." She grabbed his hand and opened the door, as they exited the stationary cupboard she noticed his face. "Lipstick" she said pointing at his face, he hastily wiped his mouth with his handkerchief as they approached a door guarded by a sergeant who examined their passes before letting them in. The Sergeant noticed the way they were together and grinned to himself as they passed through the door. *Lucky bugger!* he thought.

Chapter Twenty-five

Brigadier Charles Armstrong, DSO.MC, looked no different than the Major Charlie Armstrong Peter had met and worked with in Normandy; a little greyer at the temples perhaps, maybe an extra wrinkle or two, but otherwise the same Charlie. The other two people in the room were strangers, both looked at him curiously.

"Peter, you haven't changed a bit, I see." He advanced across the room and shook Peter's hand warmly. "Fully recovered from your wounds, I hope. I think you'll be interested in this." He walked over to the table in the middle of the room with an arm round Peter's shoulders and waved at the model lay-out there. "These chaps have come to me with a problem that made me think of you immediately." He turned to the other two, "Morris Adler and Charles Lenz meet Commander Peter Murray DSO RNVR. This is the man who saved my bacon in Normandy and was responsible for my accelerated promotion to my current exalted rank. Peter, these two are scientists recovered after setting off across the Baltic in a rowing boat to escape from their place of work at the Heereseversuchsanstalt, Peenemunde; the German Army scientific research establishment, where they produce Doodlebugs and, what is even more important, the V1 Rocket." He paused and lit a small cigar before continuing. "The place has been targeted on occasion by our bombers, but the defences around the place are pretty tough to get through.

"I have been asked to see if I can arrange a landing for a sabotage attack on the establishment, to cover the extraction of the scientists currently employed there. It seems a large proportion of them are of Jewish extraction who face death regardless of the success or failure of their work. They have been forced to co-operate with the fate of their families being used as an incentive.

"Both Morris and Charles discovered that the letters they have been receiving regularly from their respective families were being forged by the Gestapo. Both families were sent to a Concentration Camp where they have now been reported dead. They received the news from one of the political prisoner's used for slave labour on the site. Apparently he reported that a whole group of women and children had arrived at the camp bewildered by their arrest as they said their husbands were research scientists who had been promised protection in return for their work for the Government.

"They managed to escape when they were sent out to Ruden Island range observation and monitoring station. They found the boat in an abandoned shed and took their chances on a cold dark night, aiming for Sweden. They were picked up half dead by one of our submarines that came up for air under their boat; gave the skipper quite a shock when he popped his head out of the hatch and found these two looking down at him."

Charlie stopped and puffed at his cigar while Peter thought about what he had just been told.

'I take it we are to get in close, drop your men off and while they play soldiers, collect as many of the scientist as we can. Then I take it, we pick your chaps up and come home. Is that it?"

"In a nutshell: yes. Though there will undoubtedly be more to it than that/ After all, as we both know from experience, if something can go wrong it probably will."

"Has anyone any suggestions for getting there—and back of course—or are we still at the planning stage?" Peter tried to keep the sarcasm out of his voice though it was difficult in the circumstances.

Morris spoke up in heavily accented English, "Off shore at the establishment there is a regular patrol by Schnellboot. To keep us in as much as anything, I believe. More important I am informed by the Brigadier that the allies have captured several of these boats that could possibly be used to approach the area. He also informs me that you are one of the few Naval Officers who has actually operated a Schnellboot under fire. In the circumstances I think the seemingly impossible might actually be possible, what do you think?"

To Peter the idea sounded feasible and his mind started to sort out possibilities.

Charlie broke into his thought train at this point. "Lunch, gentlemen. I believe you and Charles are booked to see some boffins for lunch so I will take Peter off to the Mess and we'll resume after lunch somewhere more comfortable." He ushered the two scientists out of the room in the company of one of the many messengers who had strict instruction to make sure they went direct to their next appointment without side trips.

When they had gone he turned to Peter. "You're all recovered, I hope, I don't want to dump something like this on your shoulders if you're not fully fit."

"I'm fine, I've been back on the job for over a month and I am dying of boredom. This sounds like a workable operation, provided that they are telling the truth."

"On that subject I still have my doubts, though I am inclined to believe them. After all, what could they get out of it? They are already here they've made it so they don't have to bother.

"That is really why I brought you in. I think it's a sound idea and I have confidence in you running the operation. I'll provide Commando for the whiz bangs and I am promised a company of Marines for the body snatch. Hopefully that should do the trick. Now lunch."

As it turned out The Marine detachment was replaced by the enterprising company of reprobates commanded by Major Schwartz, brother to Sarah, and last encountered in Alexandria when the mass rescue of prisoners was undertaken involving the theft of the ship in which they were due to travel. The operation that led to Peter being awarded his first DSC. There were obvious advantages with having a German force to carry out the assembly and snatch operation, and the fact that they were Jewish as well should make the whole process much easier; though from experience neither Peter nor Aaron Schwartz were convinced that it would.

As far as Peter was concerned, the operation was based on the E Boats that were supposedly available for their use. The timescale was now just over 30 days, which left them little leeway for repairs or modifications to any of the boats that might need work. A visit to Gare Loch to examine them was essential and needed to be as soon as could be arranged.

It was impressive the way Charlie got things moving, Peter, with his engineering team that included his two CPO's Jim Walters and Ifor Williams, were sent to Scotland within 36 hours on a commandeered Dakota aircraft that was tasked to remain and bring them back when they were ready.

The flight from RAF Hurn Bournemouth was bumpy but uneventful, apart from the continual murmur of complaint from CPO Ifor Williams who declared regularly that they were not bloody wings on his back and he wasn't a bloody angel or fairy for that matter and what was wrong with the trains. Jim Walters, sitting next to him was enjoying the flight watching the passing scenery far below. He ignored his friend's moaning until he finally told him to put a sock in it and be grateful that he was allowed to do this 450 mile trip in luxury in a couple of hours rather than spending 13 hours crushed into a train with a bunch of sweating squaddies for company.

From RAF Renfrew the trip to the Gare Loch in the firth of Clyde took just less than two hours. The tender that took them down river ate up the distance at high speed, delivering them to the Fleet Air Arm base at Rhu and into the charge of the Commodore in time for lunch.

The base was actually dedicated to seaplane operations. Catalina and Sunderland flying boats were the aircraft in use tasked with convoy patrols and anti-U-Boat operations. The use of tenders to access the aircraft taking off and landing in the waters of the Loch; had made it necessary to provide power boat maintenance for their own tenders, that also maintained the RAF Rescue launches operating out of the Firth of Clyde. Their location in this remote place seemed ideal to discreetly tuck away the six E Boats, captured before they could be scuttled in Cherbourg Harbor.

After lunch Peter and his men were taken up the Loch to the big boathouse and hanger further along the shore. Peter noticed two boats marked with RAF roundels moored on a trot out on the water. The PO Cox'n commented "Seemed like a good idea to make use of a couple of the captured boats." He shrugged "The others are all in here." He swung the wheel and deftly brought the tender alongside a landing stage just within the big hanger building that extended out into the water on pilings to permit access direct from the Loch.

The huge area of the hanger had the four E boats tied up at a jetty on the other side of the hanger while on the hard standing a Catalina sat on its wheels with a gantry erected around the starboard engine and two mechanics working inside the open canopy.

They made their way across to the boats and boarded the first. On the shore the Cox'n of the tender started up a big fan blower. Peter pressed the started button for the diesel engines on the first of the boats and was surprised and gratified to hear the big diesels start after a short turnover. The reassuring roar of the powerful motors was accompanied by a cloud of smoke that was swiftly whipped away by the big fan blower thoughtfully started up by the Cox'n.

The other boats were started in turn and all appeared to be in good order, Peter turned to the Base Engineer, an RNR Commander with grey hair and twinkling blue eyes.

"You'll be needing to give them a run, no doubt. I suggest you wait until dark and then we can take them out for a spin without prying eyes seeing what we are doing." The soft Highland accent betrayed the Commander's origins.

"Thank you. You are Commander McNeish, I understand, and I believe we have you to thank for this collection of transport." He waved vaguely at the assembled boats "We'll do just that. I think you have looked after them well from the sound of things."

"They're bonny boats and the lads were glad of the chance to work on something a little different. By the way the name's Angus!" He reached into his pocket and removed a well-used pipe; he took time to stuff it with black tobacco from a tatty leather pouch. He examined the result, and satisfied he lit it with a lighter made from a cartridge case from a .303 bullet. He blew out a cloud of smoke, coughed once then said, "It was really quite amusing; all six boats arrived at Dunoon having been towed by two tugs from Cherbourg. When they reached the entrance to Holy Loch the signals began to fly, no one knew what to do with them. I popped out to the leading tug. I knew the skipper well, and when I got on board he told me that no one knew anything about the boats and the latest buzz seemed to be that they should be dumped in Loch Striven until they could be stripped and broken up. He said it seemed to be a helluva waste as the boats were all in good condition.

That was when I thought that they could possibly be of use to us for ASR duty. I said there would be a bottle of Islay Malt for any tug skipper that managed to lose his tow at the upper end of Gare Loch." He puffed at his pipe once more "The rest is, as they say, history."

Peter looked at the Commander keenly "You're a canny bugger, Angus. I'll try and return the boats to you when we've done with them. Between you and me, it could be useful to have some passage crews at Inverness when we get back from our excursion. Meanwhile I'll leave my men to nose about and get back to the office to sort out the logistics, I've to find a way of getting these boats out without them being identified as E boats." He shook Angus's hand and returned by road to the offices, leaving the tender to bring the others back when they were ready.

His problem was crossing the North sea; the transit to the east coast was simple. The Caledonian Canal allowed the first part of the trip to be carried out discreetly. He was pleased to find that the second problem was solved for him by the quiet engineer, Angus.

By producing a weird arrangement of timber frame and canvas he changed the appearance of the rakish Schnellboot to that of a dumpy coaster complete with a funnel made from two oil drums welded together end to end to be guyed to the cabin roof. The others were similarly modified with suitable variations giving an overall appearance of the sort of scruffy assortment of ships that Peter and his men had been escorting along the east coast from time to time.

The arrangement for the transit of the North Sea was for the six disguised Schnellboot, a small tanker and six of the flotilla of MGB-MTBs to act as escorts. A Catalina and a Liberator would alternate as top cover.

With the return of the inspection team, crews for the German craft were selected and all were shown a collection of photographs of the workings of their temporary craft, to introduce those who had not been involved in the earlier raid using captured E Boats.

The crews were then transported to Renfrew in three Liberator aircraft to enable them to start training as soon as possible. Commander McNeish had gone ahead with the disguise for the craft and the result was that the motley fleet of scruffy boats were already transformed by the time Peter managed to get away and rejoin his men in their temporary base in Scotland.

Paul Waterstone would bring the Flotilla's remaining craft round to Frazerburgh to meet the tanker that would make up the small convoy, leaving Cummings in charge of the remainder of the flotilla until the raiders return.

The two-day training session soon passed, helped considerably by the labels pasted on all the controls. The entire flotilla left Rhu to sail up Loch Fyne to the Crinan Canal where they passed through the few miles to the Atlantic Ocean. Two by two they passed through the sea lock and made for the Sound of Mull and Loch Linnhe and the entrance to the Caledonian Canal, at Caol, Fort William. The enforced separation of the boats climbing the set of locks known as Neptune's Staircase enabled the six boats to traverse the width of Scotland without bunching at the succession of locks throughout the Canals length.

Along the shores of Loch Leven, Achnacarry Castle, the home and estate of the Clan Cameron chieftain was now the training base for Commandos. The raiding party of Commandos under Captain Willie Horrocks had been tuning up as he put it. They were waiting to board the flotilla as they passed through on their way to Inverness and Frazerburgh.

At the Gairlochy Lock they boarded the first two boats as they arrived, unseen and unremarked the men immediately sent below for the remainder of the transit of the Canal. As Peter observed to Captain Horrocks "Be grateful Major Schwartz doesn't join us until we reach Frazerburgh, you would really have got the chance to sweat with the other thirty-five men aboard."

"But we're all packed into two boats and you have six, there would have been no problem."

"The others are for the use of the people we're picking up, so you'll have to share until we rendezvous with the MTB's out at sea once more." Peter smiled at the dismayed look on Horrocks' face. His comment, "If you can't take the joke you shouldn't have joined" was not appreciated, though the sentiment was understood.

Peter lifted his night glasses and confirmed the cover party following their progress from the canal bank were still in place. When he turned back Horrocks had gone.

The big German Schnellboot passed through the canal, negotiating the locks for the short stretch between Loch Leven and Loch Oich, then the longer stretch to the series of locks at Fort Augustus. They saw few people on their journey and those they did see were by now well accustomed to seeing craft passing through.

The trip through Loch Ness made a welcome break, allowing the extended file of boats to stretch their legs a little on the 20 plus miles of the length of this famous loch. The final stretch through the outskirts of Inverness was an anti-climax after the complex negotiations of the past few days. From the final lock at Clachnaharry it was open water cruising along the Moray Firth to their next stop at Frazerburgh.

The boats tied up to the outer quay where they were met by Major Schwartz and his men. Claire who had accompanied the troops north brought up-to-date charts of the approaches to the site. While they did the final briefing for the raid and snatch Paul arrived with the MTB flotilla. He joined the briefing session still dressed in his seagoing gear, drying off his face with a fresh towel as he came through the door.

He unzipped his overalls and stepped out of them, leaving the wet suit in the corner and accepting the mug of tea from one of the stewards standing by the big urn in the corner of the room and joined them at the table in his shirtsleeves. The Brigadier entered before the briefing resumed and having satisfied himself that all were present that needed to be, he instructed that the doors be locked while he addressed the group.

"I have received word that the deadline has been moved up for the relocation of the scientific group from the Peenemunde base. The Russian forces are making moves towards Berlin but another group have been tasked with the repatriation of specific scientific personnel and they are actually advancing towards Peenemunde now. At the rate of present progress they will be there within the week. We cannot afford to delay, so I want this operation mounted as fast as possible, certainly within three days time. I believe the Reds have already got people in the area, just as we have. This operation is in your hands, gentlemen, I know you won't let me down!"

He rose to his feet and looked keenly round the group. "I know that if anyone can do it you will, good luck. I'll see you all again in ten days time." He saluted them with a lifted hand and swept out of the room to his next assignment.

Peter looked at the others round the table, "Well, you heard the boss; let's get on with it."

The waters lapped against the hull of the Command Schnellboot, Peter leaned forward, steadying the binoculars against the armor plated bridge screen, studying the dark shoreline ahead. The long journey across the North Sea had been accomplished without incident. The transit into the Baltic had caused a certain amount of havoc with the disguise, as the rough choppy waters had been extremely unfriendly to say the least. The gale force winds from the north had encountered the opposing tides north of Denmark creating a maelstrom of treacherous currents and spray. making progress difficult to say the least, and causing a collision between an MTB and one of the Schnellboot, from which the MTB came off worse. Luckily the German boat had not been damaged seriously. The MTB had been forced to limp back to UK with another MTB escort.

Once through the Skagerrak, the waters calmed a little and the disguise was dismantled as they passed through the Kattegat. It was with considerable relief that the clumsy woodwork and oil-drum funnels were discarded as the weight of the disguise tended to unbalance the boats, which made them awkward to handle at any sort of speed.

Their progress in the calmer waters of the Baltic had been easier and they had made up the time lost in the earlier part of the trip and now they were here within the time specified Peter was just taking a final look before sending the Major off with his Commandos for their diversionary strike at the Military Base and designated targets in the small town.

Major Schwartz and his platoon, suitably dressed in their Waffen SS uniforms, were poised to follow the Commando unit ashore to take over the camp where the scientists were accommodated.

Checking his watch Peter ordered the dinghy parties away and told the Cox'n to steer for the quay leading the first three boats alongside ready to evacuate the scientists released from their compound.

Chapter Twenty-six

The barracks where the scientist were held were in a guarded compound in the centre of the waterside area, the lights were dimply visible through the rising mist. Peter turned to Lieutenant Easton standing next to him, "We'll be back hopefully within the hour, keep your eyes open and don't take too many risks. If you need to, pull the boat out and wait for a signal from me. Green red green" He smiled at Emmy's enthusiastic face. "You have the watch, Mr Easton.

"Sir." Easton replied "I'll be here."

Peter left the bridge and waited on the deck with Aaron Schwartz and his men. Stoker David Martin, crouched beside him muttered quietly "If you can't take a joke you shouldn't have joined!"

The big boat slid alongside the quay, followed by the boat landing Horrocks and his men. The Commandos melted into the shadows towards the town centre. Peter and his party debarked and made towards the barracks close to the harbor. The challenge by the sentry was answered by Aaron Schwartz, who snapped at the man in German, causing him to leap to attention at the salute. The Major gave the soldier, a man no longer in the first flush of youth a thorough dressing down. "Have you reported the arrival of the three Schnellboot sent to evacuate the scientists?"

"No... nooo Sir" the sentry was now shaking in his boots.

"Where is your guardroom? Take me there now, dummkopf."

The shaken sentry turned and led his tormentor to the building at the rear of the warehouse on town side of the quay. The party under Peter followed at a safe distance, spreading out to cover the area to prevent any surprises.

In the guardroom the entire guard were brought out on parade by the angry Waffen SS Sturmbannfurhrer (Major), who gave them a thorough blistering inspection, and demanded to know where their officer was located so that he could personally report their casual approach to their duties.

The Unteroffizer in charge hastily pointed the way to his headquarters, a building a short distance away up the street. At that point Peter stepped forward with the others and took the unhappy Sergeant and his men prisoner.

Martin commented to Peter that the original sentry seemed very happy to be made prisoner, if only to get out of punishment for neglect of duty.

The prisoners secured; the company formed up and marched up to the headquarters building with Peter and Martin in their naval uniforms in the centre of the column. Outside the offices, the company came to a crashing halt on the shouted command and Aaron strode over to the door of the office which opened as he approached. A bleary-eyed Hauptmann who stood in the doorway peered at Aaron and seeing who it was snapped to attention saluting hastily.

Aaron returned the salute with a perfunctory wave of his hand. "I have been sent to remove the group of scientists to another place. Have they been prepared?"

"Why, no sir, I did not received any orders until this evening." The Hauptmann was nervous.

Aaron thrust his way past the man. "Show me your orders, they were quite explicit. Come on, man, I cannot waste time. The Reds are coming one way and the Tommy's the other, they won't wait."

The nervous young officer led the way into an office where a female officer in the Wehrmacht sat touching up her make-up. The Hauptmann looked at her nervously and reached for the order lying on his desk. "Leutnant Froehlich brought the orders from Division just within the hour."

Aaron turned to the woman now standing rigidly at attention. He smiled "Hullo, Leutnant Froehlich. Caroline, is it not?"

Caroline shrugged her shoulders and relaxed. "Hullo. Aaron' how is Sarah?"

"Well, thank you. I have an old friend with me. You remember Peter?" As he spoke Peter walked in.

Seeing Caroline was a surprise. He had not expected to meet her again; he was pleased to find that he was able to regard her quite dispassionately after the passage of months since they had last met. "Hullo, Caroline; fancy meeting you here of all places."

Caroline regarded him calmly. "You're looking well, Peter. I've missed you," she shrugged again. "This war plays hell with relationships."

Aaron studied the orders, "We had better get going, the Reds expect to be here by morning. Hauptmann take us to the barracks now!"

The young officer standing still bemused by the events around him straightened with a jerk and led the way out of the office, Caroline and the others followed. The entire group followed Major Schwarz and made their way to the barracks, a large building inside a wire compound erected in the village square. The sentries stationed around the perimeter came to attention at the shout of the Hauptmann and the Unteroffizier opened the gates. Aaron's men split up and gathered the sentries up and marched them to the Gatehouse where they were disarmed and tied up. The Hauptmann realized that something was wrong at this point and reached for his pistol.

Caroline put her hand over his. "Don't be foolish, young man; you have no chance."

Stoker Martin crossed the room and relieved the officer of his pistol. "Very sensible, Miss; the lads have a short fuse." He nodded at Aaron's men who were now deploying to round up the scientists who were already stirring, having heard the activity outside in the compound.

A seaman ran up to the gate. "I have a message for Commander Murray." He called as the gate was opened for him. He saluted Peter then passed a note to him.

Peter read the note and looked at Caroline. "Your people have been moving fast. A Russian destroyer is approaching. My MTB flotilla is currently in between the destroyer and us; they are all ready for action. Can I suggest you inform your people that we are supposed to be allies before World War three begins."

Caroline looked at him steadily for a moment, "I didn't know about this." She said, "I'll do my best but I can promise nothing."

Peter turned to Aaron " Have Caroline escorted to the boat to speak with the Russian." He waited for her to leave then "Post lookouts I have the feeling the Russians are closer than we have been told, and I don't expect them to let us get away scot free if they can help it. After all they can always blame the Germans for any injury we suffer."

Aaron nodded. "I agree." He turned to his Number two "Schaeffer, send out a screen around outside the compound. I want to know if a mouse farts."

"Zu Befehl, Herr Sturmbannfuhrer." He saluted and moved off, shouting orders to the remaining men standing by.

The growing group of scientists were assembling in the compound.

The soldier running down the street was the first indication that something was about to go wrong. His breathless report of a column of trucks led by an armored car sighted on the coast road to the east. He estimated that the sighting put them about eight miles away. His partner spotted a German position about two miles ahead of the Russians, though there was no sign that the Russians had seen them.

The faint mutter of ordinance in the distance to the east came almost immediately following the report by the observer. Peter looked across at Aaron who raised an eyebrow.

"I'll get in touch with Major Horrocks." He said, but I'll need one of your men to do it, mine are in the wrong gear for that task. Maybe we should try the radio?"

"We'll do that first." Peter decided "Martin." He called/ "Get hold of Major Horrocks and ask him to contact me asap."

David Martin muttered to himself quietly, but "Aye Aye sir," he answered and left the warmth of the room and set off down the street following the sounds of gunfire from the town.

Peter sent the assembled scientists down to the quay under escort, the remainder were still being collected and it appeared that the most important members of the team were actually on site and would need collecting. Commandeering two of the garrison trucks Peter left Aaron in charge at the Barracks and departed taking a sergeant from the company as interpreter plus squad of men.

The establishment building was on the approach road to the island offshore that had been used for monitoring the development of the V2 aircraft.

At the building there was a nervous sentry at the entrance who was quick to leap aside when the trucks drove up. Peter had him disarmed and bound, then entered the premises. In the main office several men were collecting documents and piling them into boxes, adding them to the increasing stack by the door. The Sergeant quickly ascertained that the place was being evacuated and the leading group of scientists were being held in the canteen at the rear of the building. Apparently two Gestapo officers had arrived that day and arranged for the evacuation.

Peter looked at Sergeant Mordeci Hahn. His lips formed the silent word, "Russians?"

The sergeant nodded in agreement and asked how many were in the Gestapo party. It seemed there were four. Leaving two men to gather the documents and load them using the staff on hand, Peter and Mordeci and the other six men went to the canteen to collect the remaining scientists.

In the canteen, the two Gestapo men in the almost regulation leather coats were lounging in chairs smoking while two Feldgendarmerie Unteroffizier strode back and forth between several bedraggled looking men of middle age, who sat dejectedly in the centre of the room. Two of the new arrivals casually ambled over to the military policemen while Peter and Mordeci approached the lounging Gestapo men. The MP40 sub machine gun hung from its sling over Peter's right shoulder, his hand steadying it holding the pistol grip.

One of the Gestapo lazily rose to his feet. Peter could not help admiring his acting. If he were, as they suspected, one of the Russians snatch party, he was acting the part extremely well.

Mordeci sprang to attention and saluted. He was acknowledged casually with a wave of the man's right hand and a snapped question.

Whilst his attention was distracted by the sergeant, Peter brought up his weapon and pointed it at the man's companion. "'Hande Hoch." The lounging man unfolded himself from the chair and rose to his feet, spitting German comments faster than Peter's limited German could manage. The other man was frozen with his hand half out of his pocket holding the butt of a pistol; he was facing the knife point that was two inches from his right eye.

"Carefully now, bring the gun out of your pocket and pass it to me with two fingers." The knife did not move while the pistol was withdrawn and passed over. The other man stood with raised hands under the threat of Peter's gun. The sergeant turned from his man and frisked him removing another pistol.

"Right. All out." Peter ordered, swinging his weapon around the room and the entire group including the now dis-armed Feldgendarmerie men moved out of the canteen and the building into the waiting buildings. *The contents of the boxes will be of interest to the boffins at home, and the Ge-stapo men?* He shrugged perhaps they were genuine, per-haps not.

Major Horrocks was in touch when they returned to the barracks. The scientists were sent immediately to the boats and Peter was put in touch with Major Horrocks.

"The Russians are coming, they had a snatch squad al-ready here when we arrived and now they've been spotted along the road to the east." He suddenly realized that the sounds of firing in the distance had ceased. "From the sounds of it, they have got through the German road blocks so they should be here soon. For obvious reasons I don't think we should get involved. How near are you to finishing up?"

"I can be done quickly now. I was not expected to start another invasion after all. Say the word and I'll pull my boys back straight away." The still youthful voice of the Major sounded clearly over the crackling static.

"Right. Withdraw now and we'll finish up here." Peter closed the connection and turned to Aaron "Let's get things organized. The two Gestapo?"

"Definitely Russian; they immediately ignored Caro-line, which means they know her or have ice water in their veins. They are Russian."

"We'll leave them with Caroline then. Let's get every-thing else sorted out and get out of here."

The two men swiftly gathered their remaining men and withdrew to the quay to await Major Horrocks and his men.

The report of the Russian destroyer came while the commandos were filing aboard the big E Boats, and as soon as they got under way, Peter got in touch with Paul and the MTB flotilla.

"Radar shows the Russian to be 10 miles away but other ships are approaching fast. She'll be with us within the hour, and we don't really have time to get away before she arrives." Paul was sounding a little anxious. "Remember we were ordered to avoid contact with our allies to make sure they were not aware of our interest in the scientists."

Peter thought carefully for a few moments before replying; then, "Paul, take your boats on a sweep down coast hunting for coastal craft, use the opportunity to shoot up the odd shore establishment. When you meet the destroyer make contact and try and find out what she is up to. Even if he won't tell you, it will tell us that he's on a secret assignment. After all, we are allies, aren't we?"

Paul chuckled. "And if he won't stop?"

Peter thought seriously for a moment. "Sink him!" He said distinctly "Kill his radio first, the last thing we need is a naval battle between us but this operation is too critical to hazard. I suspect the Russian is on the same job as we are, but we don't want them shouting from the rooftops, do we?"

The roar of the departing MTB's could be heard briefly fading into the distance to the east. All the boats had been refuelled from the accompanying tanker so they had plenty of endurance to play with. Meanwhile Peter urged the remaining people boarding to hurry.

Caroline appeared on the quay, released now that the party was leaving. She approached Peter, still standing on the shore beside the gangway.

"Peter, I would just like to say that I am sorry the way things turned out between us. I had no wish to let you down the way I did." She reached out and touched his hand "I'm not going back. By the time the ship arrives, I will be on my way to the south of France. I no longer have any trust in my Government, they have lied to me too often in the name of expediency, this is the last time. She took his hand and Peter felt the full impact of the extraordinary personality of the beautiful girl in front of him. "Take care of yourself ." She rose to her toes and kissed his cheek. "Goodbye, Peter."

"Goodbye, Caroline." Peter started to say , but she was already halfway down the now deserted quay. With a last wave she was gone, out of his life forever.

The call from CPO Walters shook him out of his momentary daze. "All aboard and accounted for; standby the gangway."

Peter took a last look round and mounted the gangway.

Chapter Twenty-seven

The group of E boats rendezvoused offshore, leaving behind the now mainly deserted establishment. As they left the quay the series of delayed explosions marked the work carried out by the commandos during their excursion ashore. The site was now out of commission and with the rapidly advancing Russian army closing fast there was little chance it would be reopened.

Happy that the job had been done with so few casualties; it was now time to go home.

Peter was worried about the presence of the Russian destroyer so he contacted Paul on the radio. When Paul answered, he asked for the situation.

"The Russian has pushed off to the north, He altered course before we made contact so as far as I can guess he does not have radar. He is approaching Borholm Island. I'm shadowing him at the moment, keeping out of his eye line. My operator thinks there are some other ships just over the horizon and that our friend is going to meet them. If he's right, we could have trouble getting through the sound past Zealand, without detection. Maybe we could take the other route through the Langeland Sound?"

"We don't have the fuel to make the diversion. I'll crack on speed, we should beat them to the channel. If you think you can make it past him and get ahead, do so; but only if you think you can make it without giving yourselves away. The tanker is already on its way through and will be waiting for us to top up. Otherwise, follow the Russians through and we'll meet on the other side in the Kattegat. We'll sort out any problems when we have more sea room. See you later." Peter put down the microphone thinking hard. The Russians were a complication he did not need, although things had gone smoothly so far; a factor—he had accepted—was down to good planning. The wild card of the Russian interference was one he could have done without.

In the chartroom, he bent over the chart, measuring off the relative distances. It would be a squeeze but he should be able to get the E boats through to the Kattegat before the Russians could enter the Sound from the south. According to the location given by Paul, the destroyer, even at full speed, could not reach the Sound for at least two full hours after the Flotilla passed through. The long night would be on the side of the raiding force, providing cover for passing between the Danish Island of Zealand and the Swedish coast.

The group of E boats kept close formation as they passed the Zealand shore at low speed, the throttled-down engines rumbling quietly; a contrast to the loud roar at high speed. the normal huge white wake produced at speed reduced to a transient wash of foam swiftly dispersed in the white caps of the windswept sea.

At Helsingor on the Danish Island a searchlight suddenly sent a hard beam of light across the narrows. The beam flicked across the stern of the trailing boat, catching the German ensign fluttering at the stern. The beam moved on then returned to bathe the boat in its light. Peter turned to Aaron "Get your signaller on the lamp tell them to dowse that bloody light."

The German signaller was in action before Peter finished talking, the signal light flashing its urgent signal to the shore station quoting a code reference taken at random from the code books captured with the craft. The light switched off hurriedly, the darkness seemingly more intense after the brilliance of the searchlight beam.

There was increased tension while the flotilla finally emerged into the Kattegat, a soft collective sigh of relief from the personnel on the bridge.

The radar operator seated in his temporary place in the chartroom below the bridge reported contact with the tanker group at a range of fifteen miles and Peter thankfully steered to intercept at increased speed, he wanted to get the flotilla refuelled before Paul arrived with the MTB group. The sixth Eboat was finishing off its refuelling when the first of Paul's flotilla came into sight, the white vee of the bow wave visible in the faint increase of light beginning to creep along the horizon. The radar operator had been following their progress ever since they entered the Sound, so the sighting was anticipated and as the remainder of the MTB flotilla appeared the order for refuelling was established and the first two boats came and hooked on, one on each side of the tanker to top up with fuel.

Paul came alongside and jumped over the gap between the two boats Peter greeted him with a grin.

"Well, that went alright." Paul commented as they descended the steps to the wardroom where Aaron had seated himself with the charts of the Kattegat and the Skagerrak. He was looking at them in a slightly puzzled way as he tried to interpret the various marks and figures printed on them. Across the table Willie Horrocks was smiling quietly to himself. Hhis first independent raid had gone well and the rest of the trip was up to the navy. Peter and Paul entered the room and the mess man appeared with a jug of coffee and a plate of corned beef sandwiches.

"Willie, you can tranship your men to the MTBs as soon as the first pair have refuelled. Aaron, you can send half your men over to the other E boat as soon as Willie's men have moved over. That will give us all a bit more breathing space."

Peter reached out absently and, selecting the top sandwich. took a bite and munched it looking idly at the charts on the table.

Paul poured out a mug of coffee and, looking at the other two men asked, "Everything go alright?"

Aaron tapped the chart, "How far do we have to go to get out of danger?"

Paul looked at the chart and then the second one. "Two more sections," he said laconically.

Horrocks looked up at him, "What does that mean?"

Paul turned to Peter who was still relaxing after the tensions of the past few hours. "Sad, isn't it? I was always told that taking Pongos to sea was like asking a matelot to march in formation." He turned to the two soldiers and touched the first chart. "The Kattegat" he tapped the second "The Skagerrak" he said. "The next is the Eastern North Sea, and finally The Western North sea including the Dogger Bank. Each chart covers an area of the seas of the world in detail. This allows for us to avoid any serious hassle with natural features and gives us room to enter any wrecks or other hazards to ships that may occur from time to time."

The two officers listened to this impassively; both accustomed to the rivalry between the services, both considering ways to get their own back on some suitable occasion.

"Using simple terms so that we simple soldiers can understand, how far do we have to go to be out of trouble?" The dry question was drawled by Willie Horrocks, who looked innocently at Paul with an eyebrow elevated in question.

Peter smiled. Having finished his sandwich, he was contemplating a second. He interrupted the conversation "Guess one thousand miles give or take; there is a strong possibility that we will have to dodge about a bit. We do happen to be in waters nominally controlled by the enemy, and as far as I know there is still at least one heavy cruiser in the area somewhere, and an unknown number of destroyers and other craft all of whom would be delighted to catch and cremate us at the first opportunity. Daylight, however short, is almost with us once more and there is a Russian destroyer climbing our backside if I recall correctly, so we are entirely on our own until we reach the North Sea, where it may be possible to get air cover. So, gentlemen, your question is answered to the best of my ability. We must be prepared to defend ourselves and use every opportunity to evade contact with the enemy from both sides of the border."

He chose another sandwich and sat back, picking up the mug of coffee poured out for him by Paul while he had been speaking.

"As soon as the refuelling is completed I want the Tanker and the MTB's on their way. These diesel boats have now enough fuel to make the entire journey without another refuelling, even if we need to speed up for half the journey. The MTB's will be in trouble if any action starts, as soon as they start high speed operation the fuel supply goes down faster than Chief Walter's beer, so that's the two main objects to start with. Make sure you have full ammunition status while the boats are fuelling. E boat six has extra ammo for your lads, Paul."

When the last MTB pulled away from the tanker her skipper increased speed to her maximum 14 knots, with the close escort of gunboats taking station around her. The MTB flotilla spread out across the track ahead and the E boats spread out in line across the rear of the mini armada, making steady progress north towards the narrows of the Skagerrak.

At first Peter marvelled at the lack of activity in the area, he had not realized that the action on the mainland reaching a critical stage had drained the resources of the Kriegsmarine. Since the concentration of forces would be repelling the advancing armies of the Russians on one side and the British and Americans on the other, naval personnel would be taken into the ground forces to bolster the numbers, leaving few to carry on the operation of fleet.

The winter day was darkening as they passed the Island of Laeso without hold ups or challenges. although the first signs of trouble were becoming apparent. The radar operator came up from his post in the chartroom to report. The young Leading Seaman, Teddy Johnson, was popular with the other hands because of his cheerful manner and willingness to lend a hand when he was not on the radar. He had not had a chance to distinguish himself so far and this made him reluctant to commit himself today, but his instinct was strong and he decided to risk making a fool of himself. "Sir?"

"Yes? Johnson, isn't it?" Peter turned to look at the young man directly.

"Yes Sir. I cannot be certain, but I've been keeping an eye behind us and I think we have acquired a shadow. So far I've had a glimpse of three ships. I cannot be certain but I am sure they are on the same track as us. I also think they have at least one radar set with them; they are too definite about minor course changes. I think they are ships as opposed to boats, with the radar aerial up a mast higher than ours, which gives them slightly longer range than ours." Johnson stopped at this point, waiting to see what reaction he got.

Peter thought for a moment. "How far?"

Johnson replied immediately. "About twelve miles, sir. I am only getting a partial return when the ships rise up the waves, I get a clear response when we and the ships behind us both rise at the same time. I cannot swear to it but I spoke to Commander Waterstone's radar man and the trace looks like the Russian destroyer they spotted last night."

"Thank you, Johnson. Keep a close eye on them and let me know if there are any changes. Well done!"

Peter sat down in the chair bolted to the bulkhead, and scratched his bristly chin thoughtfully.

That was all he needed, an international incident with the Russians Allies.

Then Johnson, the radar operator interrupted his train of thought with another report. " Sir, I have a contact to the north, just at the limit of our range. Are we expecting any-one, sir?"

"No, Johnson, we are not. You may be sure that if it is from the north it will be a German." These last words were scattered behind him as he made for the bridge once more.

Once back, he picked up the TBS mike and called Paul. "We have an intruder to the north, possibly more than one/ It's apparently at extreme range. Pop out and see if you can get some idea of what we are up against, will you? Don't take chances, but with our friends behind us and the enemy in front we could be in for an exciting time."

"Will do, Peter. Lucky we came out with a full inventory; mind you, the torpedoes are probably rusted in their tubes by now. See you later."

Three boats detached themselves from the group and spread out in line abreast, the vee of their white wakes disappearing into the oncoming night.

Peter altered course to the east to bring the group closer to the Swedish coast. If the worst came to the worst his passengers might have the chance to escape to Sweden, neutral territory at least, and hopefully beyond the reach of the Russians and the Germans.

The news was not good, the squawk of the radio brought the news of a German Heavy Cruiser, looked like the Hipper or the Blucher, one of the slightly older members of the Kriegsmarine. Nevertheless these ships, armed with 8x8inch guns and 12x4.1 inch, plus numerous smaller calibre guns, were no pushover, and with a rated speed of over 30knots, they were nearly as fast as the boats under Peter's command. The destroyer's escorts sailing with the Cruiser were the heavy fleet type. The force approaching them was formidable indeed.

Peter thought for a moment then turned to the signal rating standing by. "Message to the Commander of the Russian force, I don't have his name follows; German Heavy Cruiser approaching from the north with believed two destroyer escorts. Suggest you take evasive action immediately."

He picked up the mike, "Paul, I think the best idea is to leave me to approach and attack the cruiser with the E boats. We will possibly have some element of surprise. After all, I do have Major Schwartz with me to lend authenticity. I would like you to remain off to the west of the cruiser, lying doggo with engines off to show no sign of your boats. The dawn light will not reach you for some time and there is a good chance that they won't spot you until it's too late.

"I am going to approach across their course as if I am out on patrol legitimately. I'll fly the German ensign until I attack. When I go in approach slowly to give no warning, they should be too busy with us to notice you. Take the destroyer nearest to you I'll go for the cruiser, the other destroyer will be for any survivors to handle." Peter's voice was steady but his heart was in his boots. After performing the task they had been assigned to have the cruiser come on the scene was a bitter blow that could kill them all.

He turned to Major Schwartz beside him and started to explain what he intended in detail.

Chapter Twenty-eight

Vice Admiral-sur-See Manfred von Richter was not happy; the captain of the heavy cruiser *Hanover* was a hastily-selected U boat commander who had never served on a cruiser in his entire career, the crew were survivors of several damaged submarines and base staff no longer needed in the naval base where the cream of the cruiser's crew had been pulled out to join the ranks of the retreating army in the face of the Russian advance. The orders had arrived yesterday to bring the *Hanover* down from Oslo Fjord to the northern German coast to support the defence by the army. Her guns could play havoc with the enemy armor. In the mind of von Richter their chances of firing the guns, let alone hitting anything, were slim. Most of the men were completely untrained and they are even now having to be pushed to their stations by the few experienced Petty Officers remaining under command.

He leaned on the bridge screen gloomily, the newly-appointed Captain Hansi Gruber, Knights Cross, was a waste of time. After a long and successful war his nerve was gone. He smoked incessantly and could not control his hands. He jumped in alarm at the slightest noise and he did not want to be here.

The Admiral did not blame him. After all, the war was lost. What was the purpose of carrying on with the killing for the sake of it? He had been on the Russian front three weeks ago when the Russians finally began to break through. The savagery of the fighting had frightened him, there was no suggestion of quarter in either side. The German troops were no better than the Russians – the wounded savagely dispatched with whatever came to hand. He had himself seen a young sixteen-year-old bayonet a Russian then beat his head to pulp with his rifle butt' his companion finally pulled him off. The young soldier just wiped the butt of his rifle clean in the snow and carried on.

Lifting his glasses to his eyes he swept the empty horizon ahead of the three ships. He caught the starboard side destroyer in the corner of his eye. She looked alright but both the escorts were in as bad a way as the cruiser. Manned with pickup crews neither was in any state to perform with any efficiency; Admiral Raeder would be as appalled as he was if he knew the state of the three ships – all that was left of the once proud Baltic fleet.

He swept the horizon once more and nearly missed it, the flick of white foam from the bow wave of a ship. He leaned across and hit the alarm bell calling the men to action stations. The clangour of the bell was followed by the sound of the men running to their action stations.

The voice of Captain Gruber came from the other side of the bridge, "What is it, Sir? Why did you sound the alarm?" His voice shook and he sounded nervous.

"There is a ship ahead; I spotted it on the horizon. Since I have not been informed of any ships in this area I thought it would be better not to take chances." The pale blue eyes of the Admiral seemed to bore into the skull of the unfortunate Captain who blushed and turned away.

The Wireless Officer appeared on the bridge and snapped to attention before presenting a message to the waiting Admiral. "Sir, this message has just been received from the commander of the flotilla of Schnellboot presently crossing ahead of our course." He hesitated and lingered whilst the Admiral read the message.

The face of the Admiral reddened. He finished reading the message and turned to the Captain, "Did you ensure that our sailing was only known to Admiralty Berlin?"

At the Captain's nod he said, "Well, that explains it. The local naval forces have no knowledge of our presence here, but what is more important, the flotilla passing us at this time should have been allocated to us as part of our escort." Turning to the Wireless Officer he said "Take this message, to Admiralty Berlin, I am taking control of the flotilla of Schnellboot operating out of Kiel. I have reason to believe that the Russian Baltic fleet is at sea coming west and I require all the force I can assemble to cope with the fleet and the tasks assigned to me. Confirm my instructions to the Kiel flotilla headquarters; KorvettCaptain Schiller by return."

The Wireless Officer saluted, "Zu Befehl, Herr Admiral." He disappeared below with the message in his hand.

Within five minutes he had returned and he was standing white-faced, as he passed the message flimsy to the Admiral.

"What's this? Are they mad? The flotilla is in view." He pointed to the six boats still visible on the horizon to the west.

Just then the PA system came to life with the action stations gong once more. A messenger reported to the Admiral. "Sir, the Captain says that four Russian warships have been sighted to the south east and requests permission to open fire."

"Damn Russians! How did they get here so soon?" He was running to the closed section of the bridge as he spoke.

The forward guns rocked back in their mounts as the first salvo was fired, the cruiser started to turn on the suggestion of the Admiral to bring her after guns into action. The Russian destroyers spread out in line abreast to disperse the target and settled down to close the range as fast as possible.

To the surprise of the Admiral the first salvo nearly took out the leading destroyer, the fall of shot close enough to spatter the deck with spray. As the cruiser-s after-guns joined the action, the waters around the approaching ships were churned up with the successive salvos.

On the bridge of the lead E boat Peter heard the battle commence and did not hesitate, the Russians were after all supposed to be allies. He called Paul. "I'll be attacking with torpedoes, back me up at your best speed. This is one big cruiser and the escort destroyers are damn near as big as *HMS Belfast*; best of luck."

The six Schnellboot swung round onto a closing course with the German force. On the *Hanover* the message that was handed to the Admiral was ignored as the successive salvos continued to cause the Russian attackers to zigzag, delaying them and keeping them out of the range of their 4.7 in guns. It was inevitable that someone would get caught and it was the starboard-most destroyer that suddenly slowed down and belched smoke from her mid-ship. She came to a halt and rolled for the moment, dead in the water, while the crew frantically worked to put the fires out and get the engines going once more. The cruiser had diverted her fire to the remaining ships still advancing and now coming within range of their guns. They opened fire immediately, continuing to approach the cruiser and her escorts, both of which were in action now.

The Admiral was conscious of the approaching Schnellboot without being aware of their significance. He remembered the message forgotten in his hand and lifted it to read it. For a moment the significance of the words on the message did not register. Then it sank in and he swung round to look out to starboard in line abreast the six boats were approaching at high speed, as he watched the German ensigns on all the craft were pulled down and replaced with White Ensigns snapping and flapping in the 35 knot breeze. He opened his mouth to give orders when he heard the Captain, his voice calm and cool now they were in action, giving orders for the secondary armaments, the 4.1 inch guns to engage the approaching boats.

The whip-crack of the other guns joined the heavier noise of the 8 inch and columns of foam rose around the approaching Torpedo boats.

The Admiral looked at the Captain; he found it difficult to believe that this was the same man. The nervous uncertain man before the action had begun had turned into the calm man of action controlling his ship as the guns fired and the ship heeled to a zigzag pattern to confuse the aim of the enemy.

He listened to Gruber order the two destroyers to make smoke, then watched him calmly lift his binoculars to his eyes to study the approaching Russians.

The cry "Torpedoes starboard side!" rang through the bridge and the Admiral swung round to see what was happening. He was in time to see the starboard destroyer leap in the water with the impact of at least two torpedoes. She slowed immediately and heeled over, her guns still firing as she rolled completely over exposing her keel. She dropped behind swiftly, left astern by the cruiser now racing at her full speed of over 33 knots. The smoke from the other destroyer poured from her funnel wreathing around the two ships, obscuring and exposing the hard edges of the metalwork of the bridge wings. In response to the order of the Captain the *Hanover* heeled to starboard in the direction of the attacking line of Schnellboot.

A torpedo passed down the side of the ship missing it by a few feet. A shell from one of the Russian destroyers hit the deck in front of the bridge and the lethal splinters showered the area killing several of the men standing there. The Admiral jerked and steadied himself against the fore bridge screen. The shock of the impact of the piece of shrapnel at first gave no pain at all. Then the agony of the burning hot metal buried in his shoulder hit him. There was no way that the pain could be ignored, the Admiral fell against the armored screen, suddenly aware that there was a man beside him ripping back his jacket and thrusting a dressing onto the wound. He felt the prick of a needle in his arm and the edge of the pain was gradually blunted as the morphine took hold. The orderly bandaged his shoulder, lashing his arm to his ribs to immobilise it and prevent its movement opening the wound again. He lifted his head once more, Captain Gruber looked over at him and seeing he was still on his feet nodded and turned to order another turn towards the manoeuvring Schnellboot. The Admiral was thinking that the last of the great cruisers would die here in the Kattegat, although the ship was better armed and of greater power that any of the enemy, he realized they could only dodge the torpedoes for a limited time and with one of their escorts already gone the chances were there was a torpedo already on its way. His last command was doomed. The action had given Gruber his life back and he knew that though the ship would die Gruber had not let it down, he would go down fighting to the last man. He thought of his wife, killed in the bombing of Dresden, it would not be too long before he joined her *Soon my love.* He thought.

The torpedo hit just aft of mid-ship and the speed of the ship dropped sharply as the forward boiler room was suddenly reduced to scrap metal, the bulkhead doors were already closed and though the ships speed was cut she still had way and she could still manoeuvre, albeit hampered by the extra water that had flooded the wounded ship.

Gruber was fighting the ship like a man possessed. He gave helm orders and caused the secondary armament to be concentrated on the closest Russian destroyer on the port side. The starboard secondary guns were still savaging the waters around the Schnellboot that were being replaced by MTBs also flying their Battle Ensigns. He realized that there was little time left now, but—by God—he would let them know that the Kriegsmarine knew how to fight. The forward 8inch guns recoiled in their mounts and he watched with satisfaction as the trailing Russian destroyer disappeared in a welter of white water, only to re-appear, slowing and pouring steam and smoke from her mid-ship. As the ship slowed to a halt her guns stopped and through his glasses he saw the boats being lowered. A shocking explosion seemed to stop everything for a moment, when he looked again the Russian destroyer was gone along with the boats.

The second torpedo hit the forward section, throwing the great bow off course. As the bow smashed back into the water the sudden reduction in speed caused the next salvo of shells from the Russians to fall short. Gruber looked at the remaining Russians, one limping along and returning south away from the action the sole undamaged ship now turning to join her wounded consort. The German escort on the port side had now come round to the starboard side of the grievously damaged cruiser. Gruber gave several orders calmly before crossing to the Admiral.

Sir I have ordered the men to abandon ship, the destroyer is coming alongside to transfer your flag. The *Hanover* is finished we cannot hold back the water now the forward bulkhead has gone The British have broken off the action, and I suggest we return to Oslo to get the wounded proper medical attention.

Peter recalled his force, turning once more for the Skagerrak and home. The Russians seemed to have given up the chase and the German Cruiser was now down by the head, the surviving destroyer alongside taking off the crew.

Through his glasses he could see the German destroyer collecting a few of the poor wretches in the water. The two surviving Russian destroyers were stationary; the damaged ship carrying out some repair, the other waiting, somehow still threatening but at present harmless to the British force.

As they watched the Cruiser's stern rose in the air and it slid down, disappearing under the cold waters of the Kattegat leaving the last German ship to move off alone retracing its course north to Oslo.

The undamaged Russian ship turned to follow the British force now entering the Skagerrak. Peter shrugged, the destruction of the German force had taken some time but the British group would need to put on speed to keep ahead of the Russian force, the tanker despite having made a certain distance ahead of the group was still far too close to evade the Russians and without her fuel the British group would not make it home.

What was troubling Peter was why, what was the reason for the Russians stalking them?

The salvo from the leading destroyer was a shock. though the shells fell short. Since the battle ensigns were still flying on the E boats, but as Major Schwarz pointed out, in the heat of battle it's easy to make a mistake. "I think they were sent to do what we did, to collect the scientists, and I also think that they will cheerfully sink us rather than allow us to escape with them."

Peter looked at him disbelievingly, "You can't be serious? We are, after all, allies."

Aaron Schwartz looked at him pityingly. "You don't realise what this is about, do you? This is nothing to do with the war, this is to do with post-war development. The Russians have suffered enormous losses, but to a large extent they have no modern infrastructure. After the war it is the industrial capacity of the survivors that will dictate where they stand in the world. Stalin wants to bring Russia into the modern world with a bang. Up to 1939 he had one of the most backward nations compared with the Western world. By collecting all the experts he can, he hopes to kick-start Russian economy – before the end of the war if possible. Believe me, those destroyers would rather destroy your force and kill all the scientists than allow you to escape with them."

Peter looked again at the ship still approaching once more from astern. He was thinking hard. If he sank the Russians, he would be court-martialled; no one would believe that the Russians were trying to sink the British force. By using the E boats they had given them the perfect excuse, mistaken identity!

The signal was terse and to the point. "You have Russian personnel on your boats. Stop and hand them over immediately!"

"Russians, what is the man talking about?" Peter was astonished.

Schwartz was quick to point out that two of the scientists were Lithuanian, thus technically Russian.

"Right. Ttwo can play at that game. Reply to them. Who are you? And make sure they can receive a signal to Admiralty, Am being stalked by destroyers who claim to Russian, but they demand we stop and hand over our rescued personnel. I believe they are German. I intend to attack with torpedoes if they don't withdraw."

The Signals PO took the signal below and sent it off.

Almost immediately the after lookout reported. "The destroyer has increased speed Sir and has opened fire." The noise of the approaching salvo obscured his final words.

And the sea behind them was turned into a turmoil of yellow-tinged white water as the salvo landed.

Peter reacted turning to the bridge signaller "Signal Commander MTBs to take over escort of tanker and make best speed home, the E boats to increase to full speed and reverse course for flotilla attack on enemy destroyer with torpedoes.

The flashing lamps passed the messages on to the boats of both flotillas and the big E boat heeled as it turned to confront the enemy astern.

More spouts of water appeared as the Russian fired at the approaching E boats, now spreading out to cover the destroyer, which was firing all its guns to try and hold off the attacking E boats.

As the boats started to line up to fire their torpedoes the destroyer slowed down and for the first time raised the Russian ensign it started to turn and a lamp stated to flash a signal.

Peter ordered the flotilla to hold their fire.

It was not until the Russian had completed his turn and was making speed back to his surviving companion in the Kattegat that the boats reversed their course in turn, and made speed to catch the retiring MTBs and the tanker for the long voyage home.

The signal from the Russian was short, "Mistook you for the enemy. Dosdivanya,"

They had no serious problems on the return journey, the lone Messerschmitt 110 that came snooping around halfway across the North Sea received such a rousing welcome it turned for home, climbing hard and trailing a thin streak of fluid in its wake.

After the lengthy debriefing session the flotillas were ordered back to their normal duties.

For Peter life was changing dramatically. His position as Commander of the Weymouth flotillas was passed over to Paul Waterstone and he was transferred to the Admiralty as 2 i/c Coastal craft operations. He was appointed to work under Rear Admiral Sir Michael Thomas DSO KB RN (Rtd).

Describing himself as a retread, the Admiral was a cheerful man in his sixties who had piloted a Coastal motor boat in the First World War. He described it as being the equivalent of flying a Sopwith Camel over corrugated iron sheets at 50 miles per hour. He judged that the damage to his lungs, kidneys and bowels caused by the combination of the hammering and the ingestion of castor oil during his service, had contributed to his present inability to travel too far from the toilets for too long. This had all been retailed with great good humour by the 6 foot two inch beanpole of a man who seemed as fit as a fiddle for most of the time Peter knew him.

He was also responsible for the promotion that Peter was given prior to his posting to the Far East.

Peter and Claire were formally engaged at a party in the Weymouth Wardroom. The party that followed his appointment to the Admiralty had been a huge event, climaxing in the invasion of the mess by a column of other ranks bearing a cake made to the design of the Fairmile MGB that he had last commanded. Though the engagement was conducted on a much more sedate level it was a party to be remembered nonetheless.

The promotion to the rank of Captain had been projected on the basis that since he was being sent to Australia to advise on the use of the small craft in operation in the Pacific his enhanced rank would carry more authority than that of a Commander.

He arrived in Sydney after a four day flight on a variety of aircraft ranging from a Liberator bomber to an American Clipper for the final part of the Pacific journey.

Chapter Twenty-nine

The sunshine and blue skies were a tonic after the grey and damp weather of the past year. He gladly changed into the tropical whites that were the uniform of the season.

He was still unused to his new rank and was on occasion taken aback when he received salutes from Commanders, during his daily rounds.

Since his work was with coastal and light forces he was introduced to the Admiral in charge of the local training of the MTB and MGB forces.

Admiral John Arthur. RAN had climbed the ranks from Ordinary Seaman to Admiral over 30 years of service. His balding head had a thin skein of grey hair on top and a thick pelmet of pepper and salt hair that appeared to have been attached around his head at ear level. A full 5 foot 7 inches tall—Peter towered over him—there was no question his forceful personality made up for his lack of vertical inches.

Having received Peter formally, he tossed his hat onto the rack and sat at his desk, waving Peter to the chair opposite.

"You're welcome here, Peter. You don't mind me calling you that, do you?" He carried on, taking Peters answer as read. "We have some experience of small craft operations here though most of the MTB work has been with the Americans PT boats and early British boats, so the arrival of the 12 Fairmile boats has been welcome. I'll take you down to meet the boys after lunch. They are all learning to find their way round at the moment; I reckon the size of the Fairmile was the big surprise. They had the statistics of course but when you are faced with a 114 foot boat after playing around with 70 foot Thorneycroft and Higgins boats, well, you'll know better than me, I'm sure. Their biggest shock was finding that the Fairmile had the range and the speed to be really useful out here. So let's go to lunch and we'll play boats afterwards."

Peter rose to his feet and followed the little Admiral out of the office, having said no more than hullo all morning. Over lunch the two men chatted about everyday matters; at least the Admiral chattered and Peter listened, at some point the Admiral told Peter to call him John, but—brought up as he was in the Royal Navy—Peter could not bring himself to address an Admiral by his first name.

The boats were all assembled and armed, ready for the handover: the ceremony short and simple. The Australian Captain formally received the 12 boats from the British High Commissioner at the waterside in Sydney Harbor. The Australian crews lined up on the decks at the salute as they passed in order, en-route for their forward base at Port Moresby on New Guinea. They would shake down on the first stretch to Brisbane and carry out exercises before departing for the New Guinea base, where they would arrive in 7 days time.

Peter would be flying direct to Port Moresby in three days time to make sure that all was ready for the reception of the boats. A team of British mechanics would be working alongside the local maintenance crew until they were satisfied that they had everything under control.

As far as Peter was concerned, he would move on to be attached to the Admiral's staff of the South East Asia Command. He was not really expecting too much excitement as the major command in the Pacific was American. The carrier *HMS Victorious* was one of the 12 fleet carriers that were part of the British Pacific Fleet; her comparative small size compared to the US carriers made the American Admiral reluctant to include the British force in his main fleet efforts. The steel-armored decks of the *Victorious* and other carriers in the Fleet did permit them to continue operations during attacks by kamikaze Japanese aircraft, despite suffering direct hits. The US carriers required a six month refit if hit by kamikaze aircraft, and this did allow the fleet to saturate the airfields in the Sakishima Islands while the landings on Okinawa were undertaken by the US Fleet.

The base at Port Moresby was by comparison with the Sydney and Brisbane bases, hot and ill equipped. To Peter the abundance of food and other supplies were ample, and to begin with the clash of personalities between the British and Australian personnel was a problem no one had envisaged.

The first battle was to get the entire unit and its maintenance crew to the north side of the island. Madang was not the favourite spot for a restful life with its lack of amenities and the proximity of the dense forests inhabited by local tribes who regarded the practice of eating the heart of a brave enemy as a means of enhancing their own image and ability.

The arrival of the boats was a cause of great interest to the local garrison and the local tribesmen.

Peter found it necessary to take command of the No. 1 boat when they first arrived in Madang, as there was no one qualified to carry out the urgent pickup from the collection of small islands by-passed by the main fleet in their drive to Japan. On many of the small islands, garrisons of Japanese troops still ruled and the task of clearing these islands would take time. Meanwhile, on many of these islands, coast watchers had been stationed to keep an eye on the movement of the Japanese naval and air forces, giving warnings of raids and landings wherever they occurred. The urgency of the first task was created by the attempted collection of the coast watcher on Palap Island in the Solomon's. A boat had been sent to pick the man up but it had lost its engine approaching the island and the boat had been spotted by the Japanese force on the island.

Though the boat had been wrecked ashore before the Japanese could react, the enemy were now making a sweep of the island, looking for the boat crew and they were likely to find the watcher as well. The treatment of captured coast watchers was a nightmare to contemplate. The Japanese had a hatred for these people who spied on them and they made sure that any they discovered suffered accordingly.

The twelve boats, all carrying spare fuel, were making their best speed over the ten-hour journey to the island. All twelve boats were modified for general purpose use; all had torpedoes in their tubes but no spares. All had the main deck armament normally carried on the MGB format and all carried blimps of fuel that could be stashed on arrival to provide for the return journey in the event of an extended range search.

The dusk turned immediately into night and the radar operators were nervously operating their equipment, gingerly rotating their seeking beams, searching for any hard objects that could cause their frail craft damage and leave then at the mercy of the sea and the sharks.

It had been a surprise for Peter to discover that the majority of the crews—with the exception of the Commander, allocated to the boats—came from the heart of Australia. Whilst Commander Bob Henry RAN was from Perth and from a shipping family to boot; his experience had been in big ships rather than small. Coming from England where the sea is never more than 60 miles away it was difficult to understand that some of the crew had never seen the sea until they arrived in Sydney for training. The thought that some of the men lived over one thousand miles away from the water was not only surprising, it made training difficult since the programs were based on an assumption of certain basic knowledge that extended beyond swimming in the local Billabong.

The heat became intense as soon as the boats slowed down, despite it being early morning. The bay was in the east end of the island, the guidance beacon tucked into the fork of a tree. The dinghy was paddled across to the beach by two armed men. They hauled the rubber boat onto the sand and walked warily up to the tree with the beacon. The taller man reached up into the fork and hauled the beacon down. He switched it off then on again, performing the operation twice. The two men then sat down under the tree and waited.

Half an hour later the man came out of the woods and sat down to join the two waiting men.

It was twenty minutes later that the radio came alive and the voice of Lieutenant Greely could be heard.

Peter picked up the mike and answered.

"Sir, we have a situation here on the island. apparently the Japs have picked up the boat crew and they are holding them just over the river, while they carry on looking for the watcher. Billy Holmes, the watcher saw the capture while he was waiting for the pick-up."

"How many men are involved in the search party?"

"He says at least twenty. The garrison on the island stands at about 45 men and three women. The search party is under command of the deputy commander of the garrison, a Captain."

"Right. Greely, bring Mr Holmes on board. We'll decide what we can do here. Do you need any help with equipment or luggage?"

"No Sir, we'll manage. Over and out."

Peter turned to the Commander beside him. "Well, Bob, you heard what Greely said. What you suggest?"

I agree with you, Sir; have a pow-wow when Billy gets on board. After all he knows the island better than we do. If we can rescue the boat crew then let's have at it."

Peter grinned. "How are we off for personal weapons?"

"Pretty good, as it happens. Operations in the islands have always been risky, so all boats carry a proper weapon store – enough to kit out the entire crew. And on that sub-ject, the lads may not be much as sailors yet but when it come to shooting they are something else. When you're brought up in the outback, shooting is a way of life, if you take my meaning." He looked at Peter steadily, waiting for his reaction.

"Well, let's get to it and see that all hands are issued weapons and ammo, just in case."

The dinghy arrived with Billy Holmes and the two crew members who climbed aboard, passing up the bits and pieces of Billy's luggage as they came.

Billy was a small man, burned dark brown by a lifetime of sun and wind. He was dressed in shorts and a tatty faded tartan shirt. There was a gun belt round his waist with a hol-stered sixgun on his hip, he carried a Tommy gun on a strap over his shoulder. He came up to the bridge of the Fairmile and seeing Peter stuck his hand out and introduced himself in a cultured English voice. "Hullo, old chap; the name's Billy, or—if you prefer it—William Holmes, lately of this benighted island, formerly of Barton Coomb Somerset."

Peter could not resist grinning at this unusual introduc-tion, "How do you do, sir? I am Peter Murray, Captain RNVR temporarily in Command of this little navy. Now, if you wouldn't mind I would like to run over a few details of the geography of this island and the location of the enemy base and posts."

"I would appreciate a cold beer and then we can get started." Billy grinned in turn and the two went below to plan.

The first landing party went forward cautiously until the two scouts waved them down. The men stopped and sank down into the undergrowth. In the lead the Captain crept silently forward and peered through the bushes at the encampment below.

The Japanese party were seated round the fire eating. Off to one side a group of men were tied to bamboo poles, their arms painfully stretched over the ends forcing their heads forward. There was a guard leaning casually against the tree behind the prisoners. There was no other sign of guards. The whole party numbered twenty five in all. The officer was identifiable by the sword at his belt and the fact that he was seated at a small table on which stood a small bottle and an empty plate.

At a nod from the Captain, the two scouts slid off around the encampment, seeking extra guards. The main party waited until the signal came from the scouts. At that point the men started to slither round the encampment. For a moment everything stopped as two of the seated men went into the bush to relieve themselves; when they returned the encirclement continued.

Peter waited, his nerves wound up to breaking point. When the signal came at last he lifted his whistle to his lips and blew a single blast. The surrounding party all stood up, Tommy guns at the ready, aimed at the men below. One of the scouts rose behind the guard over the prisoners, slipping his hand round the man's neck. His other hand slipped the knife into the man's throat, and he died there on the spot.

The officer lunged to his feet reaching for his submachine gun. He never made it; the thrown knife from the second scout took him in the chest and he sank back into his chair with a sigh. The men seated round the fire just sat there. stunned at the totality of the disaster that had happened so suddenly. The two scouts were down in the clearing, skilfully removing the weapons from the seated men. When they finished they took time to cut the bonds of the prisoners, releasing them to swing their arms and get the blood flowing once more.

The Japanese soldiers were tied individually then linked together with a long rope. Eight of the men were detailed to carry the bodies of their officer and the dead guard, and the whole party trekked back to the bay where the boats were moored.

The stockade had been built by the remaining crew members instructed by Billy who was skilled in utilising the materials to hand. The prisoners dug graves for their dead men and resumed their bonds.

Peter studied the location of the enemy camp indicated by Billy. It was set in an inlet at the far end of the island. According to Billy there were several buildings and still at least 25 men plus three women there. There was also the gunboat used for the patrolling of the channel round the far end of the island that separated Palap from Salangm the small islet no more than three miles long that sat on the other side of the channel. Salang was uninhabited; there was no water supply apart from the odd rain sink in the rocky ground.

The prisoners were interrogated and one divulged the fact that there was a 25 pounder gun at the encampment with ammunition captured from the Australian troops when they were in retreat from the initial invasion by the Japanese.

At the planning session the boat skippers, the Commander, Billy Holmes and Peter sat around the mess table in the command boat and discussed the ways and means of attacking the headquarters encampment at the far end of the island. Scott Jackson, the lieutenant in command of the No 4 boat, suggested that a division of boats could attack from the sea whilst a land party took advantage of the diversion created and attacked from the landward side.

Billy made a drawing of the layout of the camp, suggesting the purpose of the individual buildings. Peter pointed out that the slave labor employed by the Japanese might be in the line of fire during the working day.

Billy pointed out that they normally left the compound at about 5.00 pm to their own quarters outside the fence. The gates were closed then until morning, unless there were men to be recovered.

The timetable for the attack was set for the next morning; the diversionary attack to be carried out by three boats under the command of Commander Henry whilst the land attack force under Peter's command would concentrate in infiltrating the compound and capturing the Commanding Officer, if possible.

Nine boats left the mooring, the three attack craft plus the six boats loaded with the landing party, cruising quietly through the darkness. The landing party was dropped off at the small inlet perhaps three miles from the compound. Sending the scouts to clear the way, Peter said a quiet farewell to Bob Henry, checking watches for the last time and went ashore to catch up with his land force. The six-man group accompanying him spread out on both sides of the line of march and the group travelled in line abreast, following the broad trail left by the main party ahead of them.

They neared the main party, hearing the sounds made as the large group made their way to the ambush point. It was the man on the right flank who gave the warning. A tug on the sleeve of his nearest neighbor was passed along the line to Peter. They stopped and the flank man reported that there were people following the main party.

Chapter Thirty

The man who had acted as scout for the party went off to check and see how many men were involved in the group following the main party.

Peter's party waited for ten long minutes until their scout returned with the news that there were five men tracking the main party. They were under the command of a Japanese NCO and they were being very careful and very quiet. Peter wondered how the men had found them, then the scout reckoned that they may have been with the search party sent out to the far end of the island. They had returned and found their Captain and the rest of their platoon gone, they had found the tracks of the Australian landing party and spotted the boats and the prisoners.

To be where they are, Peter guessed that they had been travelling all night to get this far.

"We need to stop them getting round the party in front and giving the game away." He looked around the men gathered round him. "We will have to take them out." The grim faces made replies unnecessary. "Well lead, on MacDuff," Peter said, drawing his knife from its scabbard and holding it up.

Nodding, the others all drew their knives and—securing the straps of their slung guns—they carefully followed their guide to the place where the Japanese party was resting.

The fight that followed was short and savage. While the attackers had the advantage of surprise, the reactions of the Japanese was swift and almost effective. The first of the men to reach the enemy selected his target with care, going for the man seated furthest away. He crept round behind him and when the others were in place he stepped in and stabbed his man in the neck. The effect of his strike was to paralyze his victim who collapsed immediately. Turning from his man he went to the aid of the youngest of the group who was struggling with his target. Peter was too busy with his own man to worry about the others, his opponent was struggling to stop the knife from going in further, it having broken the skin of his neck but not deeply enough to hinder him. Blood was spilling from the wound making the haft of the knife sticky. Peter was tiring fast and the man was young and fit. If he did not finish things quickly the man would get away. With a final effort he managed to wrench the man's hand causing the knife to slash across the windpipe of the unfortunate Japanese.

Peter stood back in relief as the man collapsed, clutching his throat, unable to breath.

Looking about he saw the last of the following party fall under the combined efforts of two of the men.

"Right" Peter surveyed the bloodstained men "I don't know what the enemy will think but just looking at you is enough to scare the shit out of me. Let's get on, time is wasting." He turned and led off once more in the direction of the main party.

They caught up with the main group within the next half hour, just before the assault party reach a viewpoint place above the enemy camp.

They set up the group in positions around the perimeter of the compound and settled down to await the arrival of Commander Holmes with his boats.

With the swift onset of dawn the low growl of the boats engines could be detected, the assault group tensed awaiting reaction from the base below them.

At first there was little to indicate that the noise had been heard. Then gradually the base awoke and men appeared. The guards on the seaward side all started to peer out to sea to try to identify where the noise was coming from. The sudden burst of fire came as the first of the boats surged into view, all guns firing at the guards and the HQ building on the shore above the beach. In the compound men rushed to one of the sheds and started to haul round the 25 pounder gun standing there. From the slopes above the scatter of fire was lost in the noise created by the gunnery from the three boats that were now in view.

The effect of the fire from the slopes was to stop the men pulling at the gun trail, those men who survived scattering looking about for the source of the attack.

By now the garrison was wide awake and the soldiers forming up still mainly unaware of the presence of the attacking party on the shore side.

A heavy machine gun opened fire from an emplacement at the top of the beach, the group manning it coming immediately under fire from the slopes. The lack of all round defences meant that the rear of the emplacement was open and vulnerable to the fire from the surrounding slopes.

The Japanese Sergeant Major, seeing the men at the gun emplacement running away from the fire from the attackers, ran out shouting and flailing about with his sword, driving the men back to their posts. The look of astonishment on his face when the hail of bullets hit him would have been amusing in a different situation. He died with the puzzled look on his face.

In his office the Commandant crouched beneath his desk, all too aware that things had gone badly wrong. The non-return of the search party had been causing him worry last night. He now realized that his other men must have been captured by this unknown force that was attacking the compound now.

He raised his head gingerly, the firing was slacking off. A swift count of the bodies lying in view made it clear that most of his remaining men were captive or killed.

Major Hari Asawa rose fully to his feet and for a moment contemplated the hilt of his sword. Then he straightened his shoulders put on his cap, looked in the mirror to see that his cap was straight. Stepping to the door he opened it and strode out into the clear area on front of the office. Looking around at the now silent ring of enemy seamen he identified the senior officer and marched over to him. He halted and saluted and in halting English said "Major Hari Asawa, Imperial Japanese Army. I formally surrender."

Peter looked slightly bemused at the little man standing in front of him, then he returned the salute and said "I accept your surrender, Major." He nodded to a nearby PO. "Disarm him and take him into No 1 boat, keep him under close guard."

The PO saluted and, calling for two of his men, he stepped over to the Major and accepted the unclipped sword and pistol holster containing the Major's gun.

At his shouted order the small party marched off down to the pier where the boats were now assembled. Commander Holmes was walking up to the compound, accompanied by a party of armed men. He spoke briefly to the PO before continuing up the slope to the compound where he joined Peter.

The labor force was put to work collecting the bodies of the dead Japanese soldiers. The wounded were gathered into the medical centre for attention alongside the several wounded from the attacking force.

Discussing the situation with Bob, Peter decided that the flotilla would return to Madang with the prisoners and casualties; the Japanese boat was usable as well, so there should be space for all the extra personnel.

The only difficulty was that there was no way anyone could predict the weather and the signs were not good. Billy was of the opinion that the weather was due to turn bad and time was against them so either the greoup moved off immediately or would be caught in the approaching storm.

Without any more delay they loaded the party onto the boats splitting the prisoners among the flotilla.

They set out on their way back to New Guinea following a course along the chain of islands on the north side of the Solomon Sea. The sky darkened from the north and the wind rose, nothing too heavy to start with anyway, but the ongoing situation was looking ominous.

Billy shook his head at Peter "This is going to be a bad one, Skipper. I think we should try for shelter if there is any. The real problem is that a lot of these islands are still occupied so we could have a serious problem finding moorings."

The sea was building up, creating problems for the boats as the length of the waves increased, causing the boats to pitch over the crests; this caused the engineers problems with the racing screws having to be slowed while out of the water. Not an easy task at any time and in a pitching and rolling state the conditions in the engine rooms was hellish.

The first casualty was the captured Japanese launch. It lost its screw in the open water gap between islands and was, with great difficulty, taken in tow by No 11 boat. Luckily the skipper of No. 11 was an experienced ocean racing yachtsman whose expertise was taxed by the daunting task he was faced with.

All the boats were forced to reduce speed and it was with anxious eyes that Peter found himself studying the charts for a bay that could offer the boats shelter until the storm eased.

There were several marked bays but what was needed was an area big enough for all thirteen boats to swing at anchor, preferably on an island known to be clear of the enemy.

They decided to thread the needle through the New Georgia Group, hoping the proximity of the small islands of the group would give sufficient shelter to make a difference. Signalling the alteration of course to the other boats, the No 1 boat headed for the gap between the islands as the other boats started to crab round to the new course.

Once between the islands the size of the waves reduced and it was possible to get shelter to the northwest end of the island in the lee of the big island of New Georgia itself .Peter was loath to use it without some reassurance that there were no enemy forces there.

The storm took two days to blow itself out and during that time they lost the captured boat. The tow parted during the first night and the helpless craft was driven ashore on one of the small outer islands before anything could be done. The three men still on board at the time were all drowned, their bodies swept up on the beach surrounded by the shattered pieces of the launch.

They resumed their passage on the third morning, passing between the islands of Kalambangara and Vella Lavella. The two Japanese destroyers appeared as they cleared the first of the small outer islands. The Japanese commenced the engagement from the shelter of the point of land at the north eastern end of Kalambangara.

The salvo of shells were short but sufficient to wake the flotilla up and respond to the order to increase speed. As the twelve boats swept round the headland, Peter had his first sight of the attacking destroyers. They were located on the other side of a shallow water area that cut them off from the open sea. They had apparently been sheltering form the storm and were now in process of getting out of the sheltered waters to the open sea once more.

The first reaction from Peter was that the two ships were protected from a torpedo attack by the underwater sandbank or reef that lay just below the surface in the waters between the enemy ships and the boats. His second was to notice that the water beyond the reef must be deep enough for the ships implying that the reef must drop off steeply on the far side.

"Torpedo attack boats, one two and three, set shallow settings." The order over the RT came crisply as the lead boat started to turn through the shell-shattered water to line up on the lead destroyer. Shrapnel from the latest shell strikes spattered the boat, and the starboard Oerlikon gunner jerked as he was hit by one of the pieces of metal that drew a red line across his back. Peter was encouraged by the sight of him being immediately helped from his post and another gunner taking his place. The reassuring chatter of the gun joined the overall racket created by the noise of all the guns that could bear in action against the growing target of the Japanese destroyer.

Peter looked through the bridge torpedo sight. "Fire torpedoes one, now two" He called. The separate firing anticipated the possibility of the first blowing a gap in the reef, the second passing through to the ship beyond.

The boat jerked in response to the firing of the two torpedoes, and Peter immediately altered course away from the action at full speed.

He watched the torpedoes run, anticipating the contact with the reef. To his surprise he saw a torpedo fly out of the water to hit the ship beyond the reef halfway between her waterline and the deck, amidship. The stricken destroyer suffered an explosion that took the entire bridge structure away in one devastating blast. The ship reeled over on to its starboard side, a great gap between the fore and after sections. As Peter watched the forward guns fired and the entire forwards section seemed to twist in response to the recoil of the gunfire causing the bow to rise twisting skywards, breaking the ship in two. The ruined ship disappeared within seconds beneath the water even as the shells from her final salvo landed in the empty sea area behind the racing boats.

The surviving destroyer was stopped, her stern having taken a hit from No 3 boat. Peter called the next section forward and No 4, 5, and 6 took up the task. While 5 and 6 created cover fire No 4 went in with her torpedoes, firing both at the stopped ship. There was no sign of submission from the Japanese ship and no suggestion of mercy from the Australian boat which managed to get too close to make sure of the shot, it suffered damage and was seen to start spouting smoke after firing her torpedoes. The RT burst in life with the message that there was no panic, just the cook had spilt the fat from the fryer. They would be back to full operation shortly. Both torpedoes hit their target and the second destroyer drifted aground in flames.

"It's like Guy Fawkes night in Brisbane." Commented Billy as the ammunition on the stricken destroyer was exploded by the rising flames.

Making no attempt to rescue the stranded Japanese survivors, Peter turned the flotilla back onto the course for Madang.

The flotilla never made it to Madang, they were refuelled by a tanker and redirected to Manaus in the Bismarck Archipelago; where they found the base in turmoil, caused by the speed of the advance being made by the US forces leapfrogging from island to island.

The flotilla was assigned to take part in the mopping up operations with the forces allocated to clearing the bypassed islands with the enemy still in possession.

For Peter, his operational tour was over. He handed the flotilla over formally to Commander Bobby Holmes with regret tinged with relief. The boys gave him a send off before he left Manaus and his recovery on the flight back to Sydney was a painful reminder that he was not as practiced at the party game as the Australian members of the flotilla.

The return to Sydney was low key and Peter was ordered to act as liaison to the US Carrier Group supporting
the landing on Okinawa. Whilst visiting the cruiser *USS William T Spruance* he was standing chatting on the bridge
wing of the cruiser when the carrier was attacked by a group
of Kamikaze-piloted aircraft. Martin Stewart, Captain of the
cruiser was looking in the direction of the action on the island when the air raid warning started to shriek from all the
ships including the *Spruance* The aircraft seemed to Peter to
be there before the warnings finished sounding. The guns of
the fleet opened up with an ear-shattering noise.

The main target was the carrier and the cluster of dots
rapidly developed into enemy aircraft. The rising sun clearly
showing on the wings of the attackers.

The first wave swept in and dived straight at the carrier
which started to manoeuvre as soon as the aircraft came into
sight. Several of the planes caught fire from the savage curtain of flak put up to screen the ship, but to Peter's horror he
saw that four had survived the hail of ack-ack and they were
plunging directly at the vulnerable wooden deck of the great
ship. The first plane missed the deck and crashed into one of
the gun sponsons on the starboard side of the carrier sending
a wave of flame down the side of the hull enveloping the
next gun position in the fuel fed fire.

The second attacker crashed onto the centre of the main
deck and slid over the port side of the ship. The third plane
landed square in the centre of the deck and blew up evi-
dently the bomb it was carrying enhanced the power of the
blast creating a big crater in the centre of the deck. Smoke
and flame rose immediately in a great column from the
wound in the ship and men appeared in fireproof gear playing hoses on the conflagration. The fourth plane faltered and
was caught by the close range weapon from the cruiser, and
it exploded alongside the bridge of the carrier sending a
wave of shrapnel and burning debris through the shattered

windows of the bridge and killing the entire complement stationed there.

"Oh my God," Captain Stewart said and swore under his breath. He turned as the signal rating came and reported with a message. He read the message swiftly, then read it again slowly. Without a word he passed the signal to Peter. The message was terse and dramatic. The Admiral and the Captain have been killed. As Senior Captain in the group, you are now in command. Please confirm immediately.

The Captain turned to the signal rating while Peter was reading the message. "Send reply immediate I assume command date and time." The signal rating ran off as Stewart hit the p/a button "Commander to the bridge."

"Helm; bring us alongside the carrier for personnel transfer. Messenger advise the Chief to rig the breeches buoy." The acknowledgements to his orders were immediate and things happened fast.

The Commander arrived out of breath from his position down aft in the cruiser.

"Commander Michelson I am assuming command of the group, you will take command here. Please ensure the log is entered accordingly. Do you accept command?"

Michelson stood to attention and saluted "I accept command, Sir."

With a return salute and a shrug and a wave to Peter, he was gone racing down to the main deck where his striker was already waiting.

The scream of a diving aircraft suddenly reminded Peter that there were still enemy aircraft attacking and they seemed to concentrating on the cruiser now that the Carrier was out of action

The ship was vulnerable, running alongside the Carrier whilst the transfer was being carried out, and the guns were in action continuously for the entire time. Commander Michelson received his near-fatal wound as the two ships separated once more. Standing on the bridge wing while the two ships parted company he was struck by the wingtip from a falling aircraft from the flight deck. The ship was in action and no one noticed at the time. It was only when no helm orders were given and the ship was in danger of cutting a destroyer escort in two that it was noticed that the Commander was down and judging from the blood was not in charge.

Peter—who was still on the bridge—realized there was a problem and called for a change of course. The surprised helmsman reacted to the command and the collision was avoided.

The concentration of the attacking aircraft was causing damage to the ship which was not actually under control of its officers, The Executive Officer was in the sickbay with a chest wound and the First Lieutenant had been blinded by an exploding flare. The most senior officer available was the engineer who was a Lieutenant Commander with no command experience.

The doctor called Peter over to the wounded Commander, "He needs to talk to you," the doctor looked anxious. "Quickly please!"

Peter bent down to the Commander who spoke weakly. "Take command please, Captain; there is no one else with the experience in the ship." He gripped Peter by the hand "Save my ship."

Peter nodded and shrugged "Right. I accept command; now let the Doctor do his thing."

He looked round the bridge at the crewmen. "I have been given temporary command by your Captain." He turned to the helmsman "Resume mean course. Signals inform the Admiral I have assumed command and await his orders."

Seeing Peter there, the Lieutenant. jg who had come rushing to the bridge, sighed with relief and saluted. "Captain Murray; Sir, I am Lieutenant. jg Robert Cornwell at your command, sir."

"Lieutenant Cornwall, you are now Executive Officer on this ship. I want a full report of damage and weapon status."

"Aye aye, sir. Bo'sun, follow me." The newly promoted Executive Officer turned and slid down the ladder to the operation centre one deck below the bridge closely followed by the Bo'sun.

The next few hours were hectic. The support group came into the area to assist the hard pressed Carrier group, the series of air raids continued into the late afternoon, and the *USS William T Spruance* was in the thick of it. Peter did not see the acceptance of his temporary appointment, sent many hours before until the evening brought relief from the continual stream of enemy aircraft.

The carrier was at last leaving the scene of her injury, the thin stream of smoke still indicating the location of her wound. The Kamikaze had not managed to get through to her again and her guns had added to the barrage protecting the entire group.

As night started to fall a barge approached the cruiser now resounding to the clatter and banging of the repair groups making good as much of the damage as they could, taking advantage of the lull in the attacks.

Peter was exhausted, sitting in the bridge chair, his white uniform stained and dirty where he had been flung to the deck by a close bomb blast.

The mug of coffee thrust into his hand cleared a path down his throat that had felt as if it was full of mud. The plate of sandwiches reminded him that he had not eaten for some time and he was eating, his mouth full of baloney sausage and bread when the American Captain arrived on the bridge. Peter rose wearily to his feet and returned the salute of the Captain.

"Captain Robert Peter, USN, sir; reporting to assume command. Sir." The hawk-like face was expressionless though his eyes were everywhere.

"You are welcome Sir, and may I commend the crew of this ship for their exceptional skill and devotion to duty, especially the Executive Officer, Lieutenant jg Robert Cornwell, who has risen to the challenges of the past seven hours, and the bridge team who have been tireless in fighting the ship."

The mess on the carrier had been cleaned up and the after deck was clear for the crew on parade as the great ship entered Manaus Harbor. The newly promoted admiral in command of the group, former Captain Martin Stewart USN, stood in front of the serried ranks of the officers and crew. Seventeen men were lined up in front of him two on crutches. Peter was standing to the right of the file, having been directed to fall in there.

One by one the men stepped forward to receive their medals and awards until finally all were dealt with.

The Admiral addressed the assembled ranks. Motioning for Peter who was still standing to come forward he said, "In all my service with the US Navy, I have never heard of nor dreamed that I would be in this position. I don't mean as an Admiral; I mean handing a commendation and a medal to a *Limey*, sorry British Officer, for services on an American ship." There was a shimmer of amusement at his comment. He allowed the murmur to die down and continued.

"When we speak of our Royal Navy allies, we tend to dismiss them here in the Pacific as a minor part of the war against the Japanese, regardless of their efforts in the Atlantic and elsewhere. The presence of Captain Murray here at this time was as an observer. For the US Navy it was clearly fortunate and it demonstrated clearly the dedication and the skill of our allies, by reacting to the situation in which he found himself Captain Murray acted in the best tradition of both our navies."

"By order of the President it gives me great pleasure to present the Navy Cross and a Presidential Commendation to Captain Peter Murray DSO and two Bars. RNVR. Having been on the bridge of the Cruiser *USS William T Spruance* when the Captain was seriously wounded and no other command officers available, he took over command and continued to fight the ship throughout the rest of the action in the defence of her Task Force Carrier, delivering her and her crew to fight another day."

Chapter Thirty-one

The boatyard was silent for once, the smell of wood and the dust in the air was still present stirred by the faint breeze. A half-finished hull on the stocks was surrounded by the tools put down by the workmen. The atmosphere was of suspension rather than stoppage, it would all carry on as before the moment the workmen returned, only it would never be the same, for the hub on which the boatyard turned would not be coming back, for Mike Murray was dead, the yard was closed for the funeral.

The graveyard at the local Church in Christchurch was packed. Mike Murray was a popular, well-known personality and the district mourned his passing.

Grace Murray stood by the open grave. Peter Murray stood beside her in full uniform with Claire, also in uniform, beside him. Paul Waterstone stood behind Claire and the workmen from the yard stood in rows behind Charlie Watts, Mike Murray's right hand man for the past 30 years.

The war with Japan was now over to all intents' the atom bombs had seen to that. Peter's part in the Pacific War had been reduced to watching from afar for the past few months as the Admiral's Aide.

The news had arrived whilst he was en route back to England, luckily by air courtesy of the US Military Air Transport Command. It meant that he was able to be here with his mother for the funeral, John his brother was still held up in transit from Singapore. He was due home soon but there was no way of knowing how soon.

Peter looked across at his mother, Grace was now quite grey haired but still upright and full of spirit, though she was looking unhappy today.

Mike's death had been expected, after years of unremitting toil his heart had finally given up the ghost and Mike had dropped dead suddenly with a chisel in one hand and a mallet in the other. Friends all nodded sagely and said, "It's the way he would have wanted to go."

Grace said something else; her attitude had been that the old fool knew he was overdoing it for years and despite warnings from his doctor had refused to slow down. If he had taken notice they would not all be standing here getting wet, waiting for the minister to stop droning on.

It was time for them all to get back to the house and start planning for the future. Grace was finding it difficult to hold back the tears. To herself she was thinking; *You silly old bugger, we could have had years together yet, but you had to finish this boat, then the next and the next until the next one couldn't be finished because you dropped dead. You left me to live on alone, the bloody war is over now and just when we should be enjoying a holiday perhaps or just looking forward to the boys getting married, you had to spoil everything.*

In truth Grace had been devastated, but the anger kept her able to handle things.

The Minister ended his sermon and called for a hymn, when the motorcycle drew up beside the cemetery gate. John Murray ran in to the graveside slapped Peter on the shoulder in passing and wrapped Grace in his arms and said "I'm so sorry, Mum."

It was the last straw for Grace. She burst into tears, having kept her composure for the entire time since Mike died. The Minister hurried the remainder of the ceremony and the family were able to return to the house where the friends and family were able to put Mike to rest properly.

Claire was-red eyed and exhausted when she saw the last guest away. Grace was lying down having been prescribed a sleeping pill by the family doctor. Peter and John were sitting together having a final drink before going to bed. She joined them settling down with a sigh in an empty chair. "The end of a chapter?" her words were almost a whisper.

It was John who answered her question. "The start of another for us all."

The End